ETHIC VI

BY

ASHLEY ANTOINETTE

Ashley Antoinette Inc.
P.O. Box 181048
Utica, MI 48318

ISBN: 978-1-7328313-6-0

Trade Paperback Printing July 2019
Printed in the United States of America

This is a work of fiction. Any references or similarities to actual events, real people, living, or dead, or to real locales are intended to give the novel a sense of realism. Any similarity in other names, characters, places, and incidents, is entirely coincidental.

Distributed by Ashley Antoinette Inc.
Submit Wholesale Orders to:
owl.aac@gmail.com

LETTER TO THE FANS

Dear Ash Army,

It's finally time to say goodbye and let this world go. It is with the heaviest heart that I present to you the final book to this series. I appreciate you for enduring the ride. I hope you've loved as hard as I have on these pages. Now flip to page one and go deep with me as I turn ink into love.

-xoxo-
Ashley Antoinette

To Ash Army...I fucking love you.

To my editor Mia Lynn, thank you for the beautiful work you've done on my babies during this entire series. You not only understand literature, but you understand the sensitivity of the artist. I appreciate you more than I can ever express.

To the ladies… never settle for less than an Ezra "Ethic" Okafor

DEDICATION

To my son, Quaye Jovan Coleman, everything I do great in this world is in tribute to you. I hope to always make you proud, Big Man.

Love Mom

WARNING

This series has been known to cause *The Ethic Effect*. If you experience shortness of breath, palpitations of the heart, day dreaming, overactive emotions, out of body episodes, lustful thinking, or inexplicable yearning for an imaginary man/woman...find your book bestie and discuss immediately!

Happy Reading!

ETHIC VI PLAYLIST

Call Out My Name, The Weeknd
Close, Ella Mai
Trust, Keyshia Cole ft. Monica
This Way, Khalid & H.E.R.
When It Hurts So Bad, Lauryn Hill
If I Ain't Got You, Alicia Keys
Hard Place, H.E.R.
Bad Habit, Destiny's Child
Softest Place on Earth, Xscape
Thug Style, Ciara
Every Kind of Way, H.E.R.
Big Ole Freak, Megan Thee Stallion
Like You'll Never See Me Again, Alicia Keys
Speechless, Dan + Shay
The Way That I Love You, Ashanti
Never Would Have Made It, Marvin Sapp
Love You Too Much, Lucky Daye
Neighbors Know My Name, Trey Songz
Take You Down, Chris Brown
Still, Mali Music
Heavy, Kiana Lede
Change Me, Justin Bieber
Rain on Me, Ashanti
Officially Missing You, Tamia
I Gotta Be, Jagged Edge
Run to You, Whitney Houston

You Are, Charlie Wilson
One Sweet Day, Mariah Carey
Eternal Sunshine, Jhene Aiko
Say Something, A Great Big World & Christina Aguilera
Greatest Love, Ciara
My Song, H.E.R.
If Only You Knew, KeKe Wyatt

CHAPTER 1

Messiah?"

Bleu's voice cut through the dark room. Messiah heard her, but he didn't respond. He sat on the bathroom floor, head leaned back against the wall, gun resting in his lap, defeated.

A soft rap at the door was only meant to be polite because Bleu pulled open the door without invitation.

"Messiahhh," she whispered, kneeling beside him.

"You didn't have to come, B," he said.

"I know," she answered. "Especially, since I took the bullets out of the gun before I brought you the bag." Messiah opened the chamber and scoffed, before she removed the gun from his hands and placed it inside her handbag. She sat on the floor beside him.

"You want to talk about it?" she asked.

"Nah, B. If you just sit here, that'll be dope. I need a minute. I'll be a'ight, though."

Bleu nodded and sat shoulder to shoulder with Messiah on the bathroom floor.

"You think you can love more than one person at a time, Bleu?" Messiah asked.

It was a question she had asked herself many times before.

Bleu wasn't a stranger to love. She had experienced two, really big ones in her life, and she had a feeling that she was entering a third. A different kind of connection. An odd one, but love, nonetheless.

"I think so," she whispered.

He turned his head to rest his chin on top of her head.

"Yeah, me too," he said.

They sat there for two hours, in silence, until the nurses came in with breakfast.

"Come on," she whispered, as she stood, dusting off her jeans. She reached down and helped him to his feet, allowing him to rest his weight around her shoulders, as they walked back into the room.

"Hey, Ms. Hollis," she greeted, smiling at the old woman.

"Good morning, Bleu," the woman greeted, as she lifted a bite of the Jell-O into her mouth. Bleu helped Messiah to the bed and then lifted the silver pan to reveal his meal. She frowned.

"I'm gonna get you some real food. Will you be okay while I leave? Just for a minute," she said.

Messiah leaned back on the pillow. "Nah, B. I don't care about the food. My taste buds are fucking messed up anyway. It all tastes the same. This is fine. I just kind of want you here. Somebody I know to be here."

Bleu's brow dipped in concern, as she pulled up the chair next to his bed. "Okay," she said. She picked up the fork from his plate, dipped it into the food and lifted it to his mouth.

"You've got a good girl. A beautiful, young lady. You two make a fine couple," the old woman said.

"Oh no," Bleu said. "We're no couple. He has a beautiful girl, but it isn't me. He's just too stubborn to call her."

"Well then, he has two beautiful girls. You might not be that girl, but you're his girl, that's for sure. It takes a life partner to go through cancer with you. Somebody that ain't gonna give up on you when it gets rough. That's you for him, little girl. Sometimes, the greatest loves of our lives are our friends."

"She's senile as fuck, B," Messiah snickered.

"Senile this," the woman said, sticking up her middle finger.

Messiah and Bleu laughed along with the old woman.

Messiah held up one hand, opening his palm, and Bleu hesitantly placed hers against his, letting their fingers form a joint knot.

"Thanks for coming, B," Messiah whispered. He brought her hand to his lips and kissed it. There were no butterflies for them, no anxiety, no nervousness, just purity, simply friendship...a love so strong that nothing would ever scare them from one another. Their foundation was solid. She wasn't abandoning him. She refused to, and he was undeserving...grateful.

Bleu pulled her hand away and took a seat in the chair, pulling out a bottle of nail polish, as she propped one foot on the side of his bed. He focused on the television screen. They didn't always talk. Sometimes, they said nothing at all for hours, but just her presence soothed him...distracted him from the feeling that had almost made him take his life just hours before.

"You have to find him, Ethic," Morgan shouted, as she took aim at the paper target in the distance.

BANG! BANG! BANG!

Bella covered her ears, as Morgan curled the trigger. Ethic stood back in awe, watching her put bullets through the center of a bullseye. Repeated shots. Repeated kill shots. She wasn't even trying. She emptied her clip and popped out the magazine, handing it over to him.

"He taught you that?" He asked, stunned at how comfortable and accurate Morgan was with a firearm.

Morgan looked out at her target.

"He wanted me to be able to protect myself. From him, I think." Morgan's eyes clouded. "I think he's in trouble, Ethic. He has to be. He loved me. At first, I thought he didn't, but I still feel him. It's like he's right here next to me... only I can't see him. If he just left me and he's done with me, I need to hear that from him. I need to hear him say it. I need to see him. I have no closure. He's just out there somewhere and it doesn't make sense that he... I need to..." Morgan stopped talking and sucked in a deep breath. "Please, just find him."

"I will, Mo," Ethic stated. He passed the unloaded gun to Bella and then stood beside her. "It's your turn, B. I avoided this for a long time because I didn't want any of you to grow up in a lifestyle that eradicates black people. I didn't want you a part of it; but sometimes, it finds us. So, if it ever comes knocking, I need you to know how to handle yourself." Ethic glanced at Mo. "Messiah was right. I'm glad he taught you."

Bella's hands trembled, as she pointed the gun at the target.

"Daddy, my heart," she whispered. Her shoulders rose and fell. She was hyperventilating. Panicking.

"Your heart is fine, B. As long as you're the one with the gun, you're the one with the steady heart. You're the one who holds the power; but with power comes responsibility. You don't pull a gun, unless you're prepared to pull the trigger, and you don't hesitate. We not gon' focus on the target right now. I just want you to get used to pulling the…"

BANG!

Bella's finger curled on the trigger, before Ethic could finish his sentence, and she breathed heavily as her arms shook.

"Bella, you have to follow my instr-"

"Ethic," Morgan called. He looked up at Mo and then followed her gaze out to the target ahead.

Bella's single shot had hit dead through the center of her paper target.

Ethic looked at Bella, in shock. He smirked, running a hand down the top of his head, overwhelmed.

He shook his head, as a reluctant smile lifted one side of his mouth.

"Okay."

The threesome stayed inside his gun range for hours. Ethic stood in the middle of Morgan and Bella, tattooed arms extended, finger curled, as they fired. Round after round. Ethic and his angels. His devils, apparently, because they were fucking shooters. Baby Bella, not even thirteen yet, was a fucking beast. Her ability to measure line of sight like the geometry angles she had perfected in school gave her an effortless kill shot. What had taken Ethic years to learn, Bella had done in one session with her father. Morgan had been taught by Messiah, and Ethic had taught him.

He hated to admit that he was proud. Instead, they lit up the targets, so he could be sure they knew every aspect of a firearm. How to clean it, how to load it, how to shoot it, how to control the emotions that came with using one.

Kendrick blared through the air, as Ethic annihilated his target.

I got loyalty, got royalty inside my DNA
I live a better life, fuck your life
This is my heritage, all I'm inheriting
Money and power, the making of marriages
Tell me something…
You motherfuckers can't tell me nothing…

They emptied clip after clip - therapy. A way to release all the *fuckedupness* of their world. When they were done, Ethic pulled in a deep breath and closed his eyes, placing balled fists against the ledge in front of him. He bowed his head because he didn't want this for them; but at any moment of any day, they could become victims to tyranny. Messiah had taught him that. No matter how much love and protection Ethic poured into his girls, some boy would eventually come along. Messiah had hurt Mo. She hadn't been equipped to handle a man like him. She hadn't stood a chance. The next nigga would receive a different Mo. The first nigga to even attempt with Bella would be at a disadvantage. The streets wouldn't swallow them whole. He couldn't let them. So, he had to chip away at their innocence a little to make sure they could handle the world around them. It hurt, but it was a necessary evil. He felt Mo's head hit his shoulder, as she snuggled beneath his left arm and Bella took her position under his right.

He had to protect them at all costs. It was his job. One he took seriously, but he couldn't be there every second of the day, so he had to make sure they knew how to protect themselves.

CHAPTER 2

The sight of Eazy standing in his white karate uniform made Alani smile. She sat on the sidelines with the other parents, snapping pictures because it was his first class. Eazy hadn't been formally diagnosed with ADHD. If it were up to Alani, he never would be. She would keep him in every physical activity she could think of, to exert some of that overflow of energy he possessed. She wished she could borrow some, in fact. It was always some old-ass, mad-ass, wrinkled-ass bitch complaining about the youthfulness of children. In Alani's opinion, Eazy was doing exactly what he should be doing…being a kid…her kid… and as long as she was around, she would go to war for him.

The smile he gave her, after he successfully completed every move, melted her. It was a welcome pick-me-up. Alani's mood had been altered. Her miscarriage was haunting her. She had been bleeding for some time and it made her mean. The misunderstanding of God's intentions for her life made Alani ill-tempered. It seemed that bad shit always happened to her. Hard times came more often and lasted longer than any good moment in her life. This was one of them, and she was having a hard time. She was distant, lost in heartbreak from the loss of another child. She didn't even count miscarriages as real babies anymore. She had been through it so many times that it was making her bitter and Ethic had no idea that she was dying a bit inside.

The sensei dismissed Eazy and the other students and he ran over to her.

"Did I do good? Did I do good?" He was so enthusiastic and excited that Alani had to smile brightly.

"You did good, kid," she confirmed. "How about ice cream?" she asked.

"I did that good?!" he shouted.

"You absolutely did that good," Alani answered.

Alani took Eazy's hand in hers and walked out of the building.

"You lost one of your heartbeats," Eazy said.

Alani frowned. "What do you mean, Big Man?"

"Well, a couple days ago when you held my hand, I felt two heartbeats. Now, I only feel one. You lost one," Eazy observed.

Alani stopped walking, looking at him, mesmerized by his ability to connect with her so naturally.

"Yeah, I lost one," she whispered. "But all I need is one to keep loving you. Right?"

Eazy nodded. "Yeah, that sounds right."

"Hey! Can we stop by to see my mom? You like to read, right? We read to her. Can you and I go? She hasn't even met you yet," Eazy stated. "She said she wants to, and we passed the cemetery on the way here."

His eyes lit up and Alani stiffened.

"I don't know, Big Man," Alani answered. She was hesitant. It felt a lot like she was about to overstep her boundaries. "That's something you do with your family, Eazy. Your dad and Bella. Don't you want to wait for them?"

"No, I always go with them. I want to go with you," he countered.

It sounded so simple to a seven-year-old boy, but to Alani, it felt like mental math. Her head was all twisted up, trying to resolve if this was okay…if it would be okay to Ezra… to Mo.

"Okay, Big Man," she conceded. She called Ethic so many times; and every time he didn't answer, her anxiety grew. Before she knew it, she was sitting in the car at the cemetery, holding a cup of frozen yogurt in her hands.

"Maybe we should come back with everyone, Eazy," she said. She didn't know why her voice shook.

"But she's right over there! Come on," Eazy said. He bounced out the car and Alani sent a text.

Alani
Please, call me back. It's important. We're fine, but it's important.

She climbed out the car and watched, as he ran across the grass to his mother's headstone. Alani's heart stalled a bit. It was so close to Kenzie's and Love's. Not even a hundred feet away.

"I can just sit with them while Eazy sits with his mom," she whispered.

11

Alani's chest was so tight, as she began to walk toward Eazy. He bounced around the grave, flipping, and talking, as if Raven was standing right beside him. The sight made Alani smile.

He has all that energy because she's living inside him. He's living for two people. He couldn't sit still if he wanted to, she thought.

"I'll be right over here, Big Man, okay?" she called out.

"Who do you know here?" he shouted.

"My kids are here, Big Man."

"The ones from my dream?!" he shouted, running toward her. "Kenzie and Love? I want to meet them!"

Alani's eyes betrayed her. She nodded, as he rushed to her, grabbing her hand as she pulled him to their graves.

She sat on the lawn, Indian-style, right between the two graves, and Eazy tucked himself right in the middle of her lap. Alani held him so tightly, as she cried silent tears. She kissed the back of Eazy's head and rocked side to side. God, this hurt so badly.

"Kenzie, Love, this is Eazy. Eazy, this is Kenzie and Love," she whispered.

"Your mom is really cool," Eazy said, aloud.

Alani laughed through the tears, as Eazy hopped from her lap. He was so carefree in this cemetery. Where most were reduced to tears, Eazy found joy. She sat there, watching him chase two butterflies around the graves. Alani fingered the grass growing over her babies. "I'm so sorry," she whispered. "If I could go with you, I would. I'm so sorry, my babies."

They sat out there for hours; and out of respect, Alani kept her distance from Raven's grave.

She didn't realize how much time had passed until the sun began to set. She pulled out her phone.

"Damn it," she hissed, climbing to her feet. She wiped her eyes and jumped to her feet. "Eazy, baby!" she shouted. "Your dad is probably worried. Let's go, Big Man."

"Wait! You have to meet my mom! You have to come say hi!"

Alani didn't want to say no. How could she tell him no?

Alani walked over to Eazy and stared at the headstone of Raven Atkins.

"Mom, this is Alani. She's taking care of me," Eazy said.

Alani couldn't breathe. She was so nervous. Like Raven was watching her every move.

"I'm really happy to share this with you, Eazy," Alani said. "So honored to meet your mom."

Eazy's arms around her waist, holding her tightly, just unearthed emotion inside her. It felt like she had so much to live up to. To love Ethic and his children, after Raven, was intimidating.

"We've got to head back, okay?"

"Okay," Eazy said. He leaned forward, putting lips to stone. "I love you, Mom."

Alani had to look away, she was so emotional. It was the only way he would ever kiss her. The only way she would ever kiss her babies. A damn shame. Alani bent and touched the engraved name. Raven Atkins.

"I don't know if this is okay, but I promise to love them.

I hope that's okay. That deal you wanted to make? The one from Eazy's dream. That's a bet. Please, love on mine," she whispered. Alani sniffed. She had a hard time controlling her tears and she lingered there for a little while, before gathering herself and standing. When she turned to head back to the car, she froze.

Ethic stood, leaned against his Range Rover, arms folded across his chest. She could read his disposition from twenty yards away.

"Dad!" Eazy shouted, as he took off.

Alani was slower, timid, in fact.

I shouldn't have brought him here.

Alani stopped walking, when she was at the edge of the road. Ethic didn't speak. Eazy had already climbed in the back seat of his car.

"He begged me to stop, Ethic. I tried to call to see if it was okay. I didn't want to say no, and I didn't spend much time with her. Just a moment at the end. I just kept an eye on him, while I sat with my kids. God, why did I come here? I should have told him no." Alani was rambling. Explaining, and Ethic was just standing there. She couldn't read him. Couldn't feel him. Silence was a bad thing, right? Alani was in knots, as he kept her trapped there, under his stare. "Can you say something?"

Ethic swiped a hand down his mouth, fisting his beard, as he ran his tongue along the inside of his jawline.

"It's a sensitive subject," he said. There was a hint of anger, but it was masked in something else. Sorrow. He was drowned in sorrow.

"Are you mad?" she asked.

"I feel something," he said. "It ain't anger. If I look at all angles of the board, there's no way I can really be angry, but I'm not comfortable with this, Lenika. I'm not ready to share this part yet. That has to be okay."

Alani swallowed the lump in her throat and nodded.

"Come."

Alani crossed that road so fast that she might as well have flown to him. She loved the way he hugged her. Every time. Encompassing. Protecting. He was her protector, but somehow, she knew that today she had inflicted pain. She hadn't protected him in return. She could feel his hurt, as he wrapped strong arms around her.

"I'm sorry," she whispered, as she buried herself under him, in the space between his neck and shoulder. It was the closest they had been in days because Alani didn't want to be touched. She couldn't be touched while there were pieces of him being flushed down the toilet daily. She was experiencing death, right now, in this moment, losing life and he was clueless.

"Will you ever open up that part of your heart? Or will I forever be on the outside looking in?" she asked.

He craned his neck back to look in her eyes. He didn't answer, and Alani knew better than to push. She wasn't looking for a fight, just an answer because it kind of felt like she was filling the shoes of a ghost. Like Ethic had a wife that he loved with his whole heart and she was the side chick. He turned her, placing her back against the car, and then hovered over her, staring right into her soul before forcing kisses that he knew she would resist. Her body was rigid, uncomfortable, but he kept kissing her, until her contention disappeared. She submitted, lifting delicate fingertips to his face, as she kissed him back.

HONK!

They looked into the car where Eazy pressed on the horn. "I think he's jealous," Ethic said, smirking. Alani smiled.

"He doesn't have to be jealous. He's my number one. He lets me all the way in," she said. She blew Eazy a kiss and he beamed, before settling back against the seat. She turned to leave but Ethic snatched her back. She came crashing into his chest, as he seized her chin.

"You're not on the outside," Ethic stated.

"If only I was naïve enough to believe that," she whispered. "You try, and I appreciate you for trying, Ezra." She fingered his lips, wiping away the color her lipstick had left behind. "But I'm very much an outsider. I'll follow you home."

Ethic caught her fingers, before she was out of reach, and she looked at him, frowning. "What is it?" she asked, noticing his disposition, his hesitation.

"I've got to handle something, I'm not headed home right now. Take Eazy and I'll meet you later. We'll talk when I get back," he said.

Alani didn't know why her heart stalled, but the handling of *something* scared her. He wasn't a normal man. He was a man in position; a man of power. *Something* could be

ASHLEY ANTOINETTE

anything. It could be dangerous. It could be life-changing. It could be murder. He could be going to murder someone.

"Big Man, get in the other car," Ethic called out. Eazy climbed out. Worry etched all over Alani's forehead, as wrinkles filled it.

He knew she had questions. Instead of providing answers, he simply kissed her lips, a quick peck that spoke volumes.

Don't worry. I'll be back.

Don't ask questions, just do as I said.

Alani's lip quivered, as she corralled Eazy. "Come on, Big Man, let's get home."

She opened the back seat of her car and he climbed in. She rounded the back of the Tesla, with a knot in her gut. *What the hell is he going to do? What does he have to handle?*

She opened her door.

"Ezra?" she called. He was about to get into the Range. He had one foot in and one on the pavement, as he peered above the door. When he saw her headed his way, he stepped out.

"What's wron-"

Her arms were around his neck and her tongue danced in his mouth, before he could pose the question.

"Dadddddyyy!" Eazy groaned, peeking out of the back seat.

Ethic held up one finger to Eazy, putting him on pause, without even breaking the kiss. Alani's face was wet, as her tongue sent shock waves from his mouth to his dick, and then bouncing from there straight to his heart. She was sending a ping pong of emotions through his entire body. Fuck, he loved this woman.

17

She pulled back, reluctantly, a bit breathless, as she hurriedly fingered the tears that fell.

"I didn't want the other kiss to be the last kiss, just in case it's the last kiss," she whispered.

He saw it. Her fear. She wasn't asking questions, but she wasn't taking any chances either. She wanted him to know exactly how she felt about him before she pulled away from him. Her intuition was going haywire, and she didn't like that it felt like he was about to dirty his soul a little.

"I love you," she said.

"You'll do me a favor?" he asked.

Her face lightened a bit, as confusion painted on her features. "Of course."

"Fry some chicken tonight and make some macaroni and cheese. Some greens. Homemade, not the shit in the can, and some biscuits from scratch. Oh, and that pound cake you think I don't know Nannie made the first time you fed me."

Alani smiled. "I made that!" she shouted, lying through her teeth.

"Nah, nigga. You made it again about a month ago and the shit tasted way different, so I know Ms. Pat made the first one," he said.

Alani giggled, crossing her arms. He had distracted her, effortlessly. Eased her worries. Switched her focus and she didn't even realize it. He knew it would take her hours to prepare the meal. She would have to go buy the stuff because his refrigerator wasn't stocked with soul food ingredients, and then she would have to cook. It would leave her no time to worry over him. She took the bait.

"You don't even eat soul food like that," she answered.

"I'm saying, though, a nigga in the mood for it, so I need you to whip that up for me. You got me?" he asked. He ordered up the full-course meal like he knew she wouldn't say no. So damn cocky.

Alani nodded. "Okay," she answered. "But you've got to walk through the door tonight to eat it."

"I'ma always walk back through the door to you and my babies," he said. "You know what it would take to stop that from happening?"

He nudged her with his nose. A challenge. "Only real nigga ever came close to stopping that from happening is this little live wire named Nika from Susan Street."

She nudged him back, smiling, heavy breathing, gulping him in. His nose caressing the side of her face. Breathing her in. Just a little oxygen. A little saving. CPR, for a gangster's soul. A little glue for a damaged woman's broken heart. His aura. This man. Her affection. This woman. The way they loved one another. The way they expressed it. The way they stood there, his pinky locked around hers, unknowingly, pinky swearing to return. A promise he wouldn't break. Nothing else needed to be said.

Alani walked to her car, got in and pulled off.

CHAPTER 3

Ahmeek took the plastic-wrapped stacks of money and stuffed them into the couch cushions of the brand-new furniture. He looked around his mother's business. The business he'd purchased her. He washed every single dollar he trapped through the successful, neighborhood business, and the warehouse was the perfect place to hide cash that hadn't yet gone to the cleaners.

He zipped up the cushions and then took the plastic to the entire couch, wrapping it until every inch of the fabric was secure.

He snatched up the empty duffle bag and pulled up his hoodie, as he headed out the back door.

"Ahmeek Harris, 25 years old, mother is Marilyn Harris, 1224 Avenue B; daddy is detained by the Michigan Department of Corrections at Jackson Prison. Inmate #7913420841."

Meek reached for his pistol, without hesitating.

"You pull it, you better kill me, nigga," Ethic stated, calmly, as he sat on the hood of Meek's car.

Meek gripped the handle of his gun, staring Ethic down, a game of wills, as he bit into his bottom lip in frustration. Ethic's hands were empty - for now. Didn't mean they would stay empty, but he clearly hadn't come to kill. Ahmeek knew if that had been the case, he would have never seen the bullet coming. He left his pistol holstered and then used his thumb to finesse his lip. One swipe. Then, two. He swung his hands in front of his body, clasping his hands, before finally resting one hand locked around the opposite wrist.

"Ezra Okafor, 36 years old, 3330 Maywood Street, Grand Blanc, MI."

Ahmeek spit the information back at Ethic, without hesitation.

"Is that a threat?" Ethic asked.

"I just thought we were fact-checking, O.G. No threats given." Ahmeek stated, holding up hands in surrender. "It's all respect until one of us get disrespectful."

Ethic scoffed. "You niggas. You niggas with nothing to lose. You think it makes you untouchable."

"I never thought that," Ahmeek stated. "Just if I got to go, I got to go. I'ma do it like a man. I'm chasing this paper full speed. I know the risks. You have always been the biggest fucking risk."

"And you took the risk anyway," Ethic stated. "I know Messiah's reasons. What's yours?"

"Because he my mans and I'ma ride through the mud with him, right or wrong. I don't apologize for that. It was never personal."

Ethic drew on Ahmeek, in the blink of an eye.

BANG.

"Neither was that," Ethic stated.

The bullet sent Meek staggering backwards, as he gritted his teeth, placing one hand over the hole in his shirt. Ahmeek's legs loss strength, as he reached for his pistol.

"I'ma put the next one between your eyes, if you fucking pull that gun," Ethic stated. "You ain't dying. Hurts like a mu'fucka, but you'll live," Ethic stated. "If you get to the hospital in time."

Meek backpedaled until his back hit the brick wall of the building, and then allowed his weight to stumble to the ground.

He blew hot air out of his mouth, puffing his cheeks with every breath, trying to control the burn that seared him.

"You tell me what I want to know, and you can be on your way. You ain't got forever. Shit's gonna bleed out," he stated.

"Fuck you, nigga," Ahmeek stated, spitting blood out of his mouth, as he took labored breaths. He leaned his head back against the brick wall and chuckled. "Fuck," he whispered.

"The crew the three of you built. Young, hungry," Ethic stated. "I saw it. I respected it. Carving your names in the concrete. This wasn't a part of the game. You niggas should have stayed out the way. You could have been getting pussy and money; but now, you're here, under a nigga gun. You miscalculated your moves, young."

Meek rolled over to the side, pulling away a bloody hand, as he groaned in pain. He reached into his pocket and Ethic kneeled in front of him, putting the gun under his chin. Meek pulled out his phone and Ethic pulled it out of his weak hand.

"See, I know Messiah. I know he's a hothead and the other lanky, little mu'fucka, Isa. He is too. You thought this shit out, didn't you? What? Messiah was supposed to get close to Mo? Then what?"

Meek gritted his teeth, as Ethic pressed his gun harder into the soft skin beneath Meek's chin. "Mo was never involved. She wasn't a part of the plan. Having her around was…" Meek groaned, as he closed his eyes, absorbing a deep breath and more pain.

"Was what?" Ethic sneered.

"Was the sun, man. We been thuggin' since we were kids. Shit got dark. Can't feel shit. Don't give a fuck about shit. Shit's like winter, hustling these blocks, man. The block is cold, and Mo was the sun," Ahmeek stated. "These blocks turned us into men. Mo gave us a chance to reverse the clock and be boys. We got to be young around her and her people. It wasn't about the play when he brought her around."

Ethic burned a hole through Ahmeek, as the realization that Morgan had become a queen of her very own kingdom hit him. Ethic was a man and he knew infatuation when he saw it. She had turned whole gangsters to putty. Two of 'em. They were wrapped around her finger. The wars a girl like Morgan Atkins could spark. She wasn't a baby anymore. He could see her entire future playing out before his eyes. She had unknowingly earned the allegiance of not just one man, but two; and if Ethic had to bet money on it, he was pretty sure Isa would be a third. She had shooters. She had a three-man army. Killers. Ethic knew because he had taught one of them, and undoubtedly, Messiah ran with men of equal pedigree because Ethic had taught him that too. To make sure his team was thorough. The fearlessness he saw in Meek told him that he was built for this, he was prepared to die for this. He was certified. Morgan was no longer his and he didn't realize it until that very moment. Messiah had made her a woman.

"Where's Messiah?" Ethic asked, through gritted teeth. "Huh?"

"Even if I knew that shit, I wouldn't have a motherfucking thing to say. You might as well pull that trigger."

Ethic retracted his gun and tossed the phone at Meek's chest, before heading back to his car and driving off into the night.

Bella stood in the middle of the football field with the other middle school girls. Spring had finally arrived, and after running two miles on the high school track, Bella was exhausted. She leaned over, hands on her knees, as she looked up at the cheerleading coach. Some of the other girls were already acquainted. It was clear that some of the girls had been on the team last year, cliques were already forming, and the team wasn't even chosen yet. The incoming 7th grade girls were silent, and Bella didn't rush to make new friends. She stood straight up and folded her arms across her Nike cropped hoodie.

"Okay, we're going to learn three cheers and one dance routine, over the course of two days. You'll each perform them solo on Friday...I'm going to give you ladies ten minutes to grab a drink and we'll go right into the cheers... but..." Bella's ears went deaf, as she saw Hendrix and three other boys come strolling onto the field. They walked by the girls and took a seat at the top of the bleachers.

"Is that Li'l Henny and them?" one of the girls behind her whispered, getting excited, as she let off an uncontainable squeal. "He's going to Central next year. What he doing back at the middle school?"

A caramel-colored girl, with long feed-ins and what Bella was almost sure was a stuffed bra, piped up. "He's here for me. That's my man."

Bella didn't even realize she was staring, until the girl snapped, "Damn, your eyes stuck? What you looking at?"

"A liar," Bella scoffed.

"Who you talking to?" The girl asked. "I swear these little dusty-ass kids, straight out of the crib, still got milk on they breath. I'll smack somebody out here. This one got staring problems and that one shouldn't even be here. Look at her shoes. Them boys talking." Bella bit her tongue, but she felt a bit of sympathy for the other girl.

"Yo, Pretty Girl!"

All the laughter and chatter stopped, and the group of girls looked at Ms. Loudmouth, assuming he was talking to her.

Bella flipped her hoodie up around her long hair and made her way over to the fence that separated the field from the bleachers.

"What are you doing here, Hendrix? What if my daddy had been here?"

"Then, I would have stayed low-key," Hendrix answered. "How long are tryouts?" he asked.

"Four hours," she answered.

"You want to spend four hours doing this or four hours doing something else?" he asked.

Bella looked back at the group of girls who were all standing there gawking at them.

"Hey, Henny!" Loudmouth shouted, adding an extra sweet tone to her voice for him.

"She's so thirsty," Bella muttered, rolling her eyes.

"Yeah, well, I ain't got no drip for these hoes," Hendrix said.

Bella's eyes widened.

"I call 'em how I see 'em. How you think you got the name Pretty Girl? We out," he said.

Bella looked back at the group of girls, reluctantly. Ethic was at Mo's apartment, an hour away. Alani was sick. Lily wouldn't be back until the end of tryouts. "I need to be back here in three hours, way before my ride gets back."

"I'll have you back in two."

Bella snatched up her duffel bag and walked next to Hendrix. His friends lifted from the bleachers.

"These my niggas, Kyrie and Emil," Hendrix introduced. "Fat nigga up there is Lynch."

Hendrix pointed to the top of the staircase. The field sat low in the valley, next to the school, and the hefty kid at the top had opted not to climb down the steps it took to get to the bottom.

Bella walked up the stairs where three motorcycles and a four wheeler were parked.

Hendrix climbed onto the four wheeler and revved the throttle, as he waited for Bella to hop on. She glanced back at the field of girls and then climbed on.

"Hold on tight, Pretty Girl," he said.

Bella reached around his waist and placed her face flat against his back. "Tighter," he said. Bella locked one of her hands around the opposite wrist.

"Agh!" she shouted, as he took off. He lifted on the rear wheels and steered with one hand, flexing the other behind him to secure Bella, as he maxed out the speed.

He rode a quarter mile, popping a wheelie, before putting the dirt bike on all four wheels.

Bella's heart pounded, and she laughed in his ear, as the wind whipped through her hair.

"That was crazy!" she shouted. "I thought I was gonna fall off."

"As long as I'm on, you ain't never got to worry about falling off."

CHAPTER 4

I thought about slitting my wrists," Morgan admitted, as she laid in her bed, phone to her ear.

"But you didn't," Nyair answered. "You're fighting, Mo. That's dope. That's progress."

Morgan yawned.

"That baby kicking your ass over there," Nyair said, chuckling.

"Butt, Pastor," Morgan answered. He amused her every time he let his gangster show. "You're probably going to hell; you know that, right?"

"You'll sneak me into heaven through the back door," he said.

She laughed. "It's late. I'm gonna try to get some sleep."

"A'ight, Mo. Close your eyes."

"Our Heavenly Father, we come to You humbly, asking for covering. Cover Mo in Your love. May she feel it so strongly that she never doubts the plans You have prepared for her life, despite that she can't quite understand the design. Order her steps, dear Lord. Make her legs sturdy, so that she may bear the load. Bless the life growing within her and fill her with faith, so that she will never doubt the beautiful outcome that is ahead. We ask these things in the name of

the Father, the Son, and the Holy Spirit. In Your son Jesus'
name, we pray…"

"Amen," Morgan finished.

"Goodnight, Mo."

"Night, Ny."

Nyair was a godsend. Therapy with him kept her breathing
on days she just wanted to give up. He was a confidant. She
was learning that even without the cloth of God, he was
just a solid dude who wouldn't spill her fears to anyone
else. Nothing she said ever got back to Ethic, and he never
judged her, not even a little bit. It gave her an outlet. One she
needed, because after the phone call with Messiah, she was
barely making it.

Morgan tossed and turned. Another night of restlessness
kept her up and the damn morning sickness was killing
her. She was pulled from the bed by nausea. She rushed
to the bathroom and her knees hit the hard tile full force,
as she heaved up her soul. Morgan collapsed her back
against the wall, her knees pulled close to her body,
her elbows on her knees, her hands clasped together
desperately, acting as a resting place for her bowed head.
She cried. This was so hard. Being pregnant. Being lonely.
It felt like she was dying slowly, like every day that ticked
by, her baby grew but she shrank. She had dreamed of
this time in her life so many times, but the reality was
nothing like the fantasy. It was harder. It was miserable.
She had asked for a baby and God had given her one,
but he had snatched the man she thought she loved in

exchange. If she had known she couldn't have both, she would have never asked for this at all. Messiah was supposed to be bringing her ice cream and Coney dogs, because Morgan had an overwhelming urge for a fucking Coney dog with cheese and relish on top or lamb chops. It was close to midnight and that's what she wanted, and he wasn't around to fulfill her need. She managed to her feet, flushed the toilet and brushed her teeth. She gagged the entire time. Even the toothbrush in her mouth was too much. It activated her gag reflex so badly that Morgan threw up again.

She splashed water on her face, brushed her hair up into a ponytail, and slipped a pair of leggings beneath the jersey. She grabbed her keys and her handbag.

Can't have Messiah, but I can have my fucking food, she thought, as she stormed out her apartment with an attitude. He used to make runs like these. Messiah would drive from an hour away to bring her what she desired. Those days were over. Darkness swallowed Morgan, as she hustled to her car. She drove the two miles to the nightclub she performed at sometimes. They had the best food, and Morgan could devour the entire menu in her current state.

She bypassed the line to the club, uncaring that she wasn't dressed for the occasion.

"Mo' Money, what's good, baby? Didn't know Stiletto Gang was performing tonight," the bouncer said.

"Hey, Dee. They're not. I'm just here to grab food," she said. He lifted the rope and she walked right in. The people in line groaned in protest.

Morgan made her way to the bar.

"Hey, Mo!" the bartender greeted.

"Hi, Carla. Can I get the lamb chops with mac and cheese and a Coney with relish and cheese, no onions?" Morgan ordered.

"What kind of combination is that?" the bartender asked.

"An amazing one," Mo replied, with laughter.

"I'll get it right out for you."

Morgan took a seat at the bar and planted her nose in her phone, as she scrolled through her social media.

She felt the presence next to her but didn't look up. "Yo, baby, for real, it's a lot of women in here in heels and all types of sexy shit to grab a nigga attention, but the J's and the jersey got me blinded…you just wake-up like this, huh?"

Morgan rolled her eyes and placed her phone face down on the bar top.

"Hey, Carla, how much longer on that food?" she asked, ignoring the man beside her.

"About a good twenty, Mo. Kitchen's backed up."

"Great," she mumbled.

"Yeah, that mean shit is perfect. My bitch can't be too friendly, anyway. Spin niggas just like this when I'm not around, and I'll give you the world. Fuck around and marry you."

"Nigga," Mo stated, finally placing eyes on the flirtatious man beside her. He was easy on the eyes. That part would be hard not to notice. He had a little paper in his pocket too, based on the watch he sported, but he could be a billionaire and it would do nothing for her. He wasn't Messiah, so he wasn't for her. "I'm so uninterested it's not even funny."

"A nigga like me can change your life," he said.

"And a bitch like me can get you hurt, so walk the fuck away," she snapped. She was so used to having that card to pull...her Messiah...her ace when she got into a tight spot. He was her muscle and he would come blazing on her behalf, all she had to do was let him off his leash, clench her teeth, and say, *Psk, psk.* That nigga would bite. She had forgotten that he was no longer available for moments like this.

"Get hurt? Watch that pretty-ass mouth before I put something in it."

"Nigga. Get. The. Fuck. Out. Of. My. Face. With your lame-ass," she said. Morgan placed her hand in her crossbody bag and went to stand, but he blocked her. He gripped her elbow and frowned as he stood, towering over her.

"Bitch, I'll..."

Morgan stuck the gun in his side, before he could even get the words off his lips. Messiah had taught her well. She clicked that safety off so fast it wasn't even a thought. *Red means dead.*

"Bitch, what? What was that?" she asked.

He lifted his hand from her elbow.

"Now, leave me the fuck alone," she stated.

She saw the challenge in his eyes and her heart fluttered nervously.

"Oh, you a shooter? Somehow, I don't think you're a shooter. Pull that shit, bitch..."

He had called her bluff, but before Morgan had a chance to test her own gangster, the man was picking his jaw up off the ground.

"Meek!"

"Fuck you talking to, nigga?" Meek asked, as he leaned over the guy, gripping his shirt, as he delivered a heavy fist across the man's face. His wheat Timberlands straddled the man while he beat the life out of him. Meek felt every stitch that the doctors had used to sew him up, threatening to tear, but he had already pressed go. He couldn't stop himself if he wanted to. He was a calm-ass nigga until he wasn't. Once he became aggressive, he had to get it out of his system.

He hit the man, again and again, again and again. The whole damn crew had aggression problems... because Meek didn't stop. Just like Messiah. It was on sight, without thought, full speed, no brakes. Meek snatched him up, like he was weightless, and pressed his bloodied face into the bar top. The gun was pulled so swiftly that Morgan didn't even see it coming. Meek pressed it to the man's temple so hard that Morgan could see the man's head denting. Skulls weren't supposed to dent that way.

"You talking to her?" he asked, delivering the man before Morgan. "You think shorty won't curl a trigger. How about me, huh?"

"Ahmeek, stop," Morgan pleaded.

"Niggas real slick with they tongue. Better know who the fuck you addressing, homie," Meek gritted, as the man struggled beneath his grasp. "Fuck you think this is? She affiliated, nigga."

"I ain't know!" the man yelped. "My bad, Meek. I was just fucking with her. I ain't mean no disrespect. I apologize, my dude."

"That apology ain't owed to me, nigga," Meek stated, as he sent the butt of his gun crashing into the man's temple.

"I'm sorry! I'm sorry!"

Meek pushed him so hard the man fell. "Take that nigga for a walk," Meek barked. Two workers made the man disappear. Morgan didn't have to wonder if she would see him again. She knew she wouldn't. Nobody would. He was already a memory.

"What you doing in here, Mo?" he asked, holstering his burner behind his back, hiding it in his waistline, and pulling his jacket down over it. He winced, as he felt the bullet wound in his middle throbbing. His entire abdomen was on fire. He wasn't even supposed to be moving around yet, but there was money on the floor; and when there was paper at play, Meek got in the game. He rubbed his hand over his head, frowning so hard wrinkles filled his forehead.

"What are you doing here?" she shot back. "Ain't you supposed to be playing disappearing acts with your boy?"

"We got money up here, Mo. Money don't stop. I'm in and out, though," he said.

"Then be out then. I don't need your help," she snapped. She was so glad that she was carrying so small. Morgan's morning sickness was so bad that she was actually losing weight instead of gaining, and her belly was barely visible.

He chuckled, as he finessed his beard. "I see." He took her in, head to toe. "It's normal to shake. It's normal to be afraid to pull the trigger. Especially, the first time. It's different than shooting paper targets. Next time, you shoot first, ask questions later."

Morgan didn't respond. She turned her head in the opposite direction. Ahmeek's presence made her so emotional. It made her miss Messiah more. He knocked on the bar twice. "You be easy, love." He turned to leave, and Morgan finally spoke.

"Thank you," she said, giving in, as a sigh escaped her. "For getting rid of him."

"You the queen, Mo. Niggas got to play they part," he stated.

Morgan's eyes watered, as she looked at Meek. "Does he even think of me?" She couldn't help but ask. She had been ex-communicated. Meek was her only line to Messiah. She wanted to be stubborn and pretend she was okay, but she couldn't.

"I'm sure he does, Mo," Meek stated. "He was never going to hurt you. You weren't a part of it. It wasn't about you."

Morgan looked down and closed her eyes, and then batted sad eyes back up at Meek. "The things he said…he just left me, Ahmeek. He left. He's not coming back, is he?"

Meek sighed and looked off, grabbing the edge of his hat, before letting his arms swing.

"I don't know, Mo. Messiah's off the grid. It's necessary. After everything that went down, he's…I don't know. He didn't just leave you, Mo. He left everything. Dropped everything. I don't even know where he is. We talk about the money and then he gets off the phone. He's pulled away from everybody, it's not personal."

"I'm not everybody. He was my everything. It doesn't get more personal than that," Morgan answered. "I've seen him be cold and cruel to everyone else. How could he do me like this? Like I'm one of them...like I'm not a part of him..." She let a tear fall and Meek looked away, frowning, as he blew out a sharp breath.

"Come on, Mo. A nigga not trying to see you cry. One time was too much."

She nodded, but the tears continued, flowing so heavy that she had to lower her head because she couldn't stop, and it was humiliating.

"Morgan..."

Ahmeek ran a hand down his wavy head and blew out a sharp breath. Her tears made him uncomfortable. Morgan swiped at her cheeks, clearing them, but more came to her. She was so overwhelmed. How was Meek this close but Messiah was so far away?

"I'm sorry, Mo," Meek stated. Morgan couldn't control herself. She sobbed, turning toward the bar and reaching for napkins, and then resting both elbows on top, as she planted her face in her hands.

"Mo, I don't really feel comfortable just leaving you out here like this. You got to let me know you're straight out here, before I walk away," Meek said. "It's late as fuck and you out here dolo like shit is sweet."

"I'm straight," she answered, lifting her head, only to lower it again.

"Okay, fuck it. Ways to cheer women up," he said, as he pulled out his phone and typed the words onto the screen.

Morgan frowned and then snatched his phone.

"Nigga, are you Googling it?" she said, a laugh breaking through her somber. "Not Ahmeek Harris. Not Meek with all the hoes. You don't know how to stop a girl from crying? I know you know how to make them cry; so, you don't know how to stop the tears you cause?"

He smirked at her sarcasm and snatched his phone back. "It ain't like that. I don't be on no shit like that."

"So, you're not a hoe?" she asked. His silence pulled another laugh from her.

"I give women what they want, they give me what I want. Love ain't never what they ask for. If somebody came along and asked for that, I'd do that."

She nodded and looked at him curiously. "You know what will make me feel better? Besides these slow-ass lamb chops!" She said the last part to Carla.

"I'm on it, Mo," the bartender shot back.

"What's that? What makes Morgan Atkins smile?" Meek asked.

"Dancing," she said, as she hopped up from the bar stool. She pulled his hand. "Come on."

"I don't dance, Mo. Hell nah," he protested.

"Today, you dance," she said.

Ella Mai crooned from the speakers.

I don't know what's living in my body
'Cause I don't recognize a thing about it
That don't even matter, I'm just glad I got into the party

Morgan smiled, as a group of people on the floor fell into a popular ballroom step. A Detroit groove that she knew well, and she joined in, as he stood in front of her, dreading it. The original Hustle put new-school vibes like the Wobble to shame. It was smooth. It was a dance she had seen her mother do with her father back in the day. A groove. Ballrooming was a groove that just made people feel good. The light footwork and easy, old-school steps were impossible for anyone to mess up. It reminded her of the old-school barbecues that her father used to host when she was a kid. They would hustle and flow all night, as the fireflies lit up the night sky. She remembered, and instantly, with the rhythm of the music, Morgan felt her chest lighten. "I know you know this. You can't be from Flint and not know this," she said, as she Hustled. "Come on, Meek. I won't tell nobody," she teased. She danced around him, snapping her fingers to the beat.

She raised her eyebrows, impressed and furthermore surprised, as Meek matched her movements in a cool way that didn't make him look corny at all. In a subtle way that made him look like the coolest kid in the room.

"Oh, so you dance?" she asked. "You a whole gangster in these streets. I thought hood niggas didn't dance. Like you had bricks tied to your feet that stopped you from having rhythm." She laughed, as she snapped her fingers, and then clapped her hands, as she kept the rhythm.

"Funny shit, Mo. You Mike Epps out this bitch," he said.

She laughed.

"See, no more tears," she said.

Ella Mai was an entire vibe, as he took her hand, partnering with her, as she spun and hit footwork and stuck her tongue out, trapping it between her teeth, arrogantly, as she smiled.

She laughed. The first, genuine laugh she'd experienced in a while. He wasn't fancy with it, but he hit a cool two-step. Enough to attract a random girl on the dance floor who came up trying to intercept. He leaned down and whispered in the girl's ear and she shot Morgan a dirty look before dancing off.

"See! Hoe shit! You're a hoe," she teased. "You're smooth on your feet, though, boy!" she exclaimed.

Meek blushed, beneath all that chocolate skin, and Morgan laughed some more. The song ended, and she shook her head, looking at him in mystery. He was a hard one to figure out. Quiet. Silent. Deadly, but clearly there was something deeper beneath the surface… a soft spot that he didn't expose for the world.

"What, nigga?" Meek asked, brow bent. Back to being hard.

"Nothing," she said, lifting hands of surrender.

She shook her head, as she looked toward the bar where Carla was beckoning her. "I'm gonna head out," she said. "Food's ready."

"You good? To get home? And after everything that happened. Are you good?" Meek asked.

Her eyes misted, but she nodded and offered a weak smile as consolation. Then, a heavy shrug. Then, a shake of her head and the sob that was choking her escaped.

Meek stared down at her, forehead full of wrinkles. He could never understand why Messiah and Morgan had even chosen to expose themselves to heartbreak. People couldn't break something they never held, and as much as he knew Messiah had broken Mo, he didn't think she realized that she had broken him too. It was a fucked-up equation of love where $1+1=3$. It made no sense to him. It wasn't worth the risk. It wasn't worth the pain he was staring at right now. She rolled hurt-filled eyes up to him, then away, because he was staring too hard, looking much too deeply. If he looked hard enough, he'd figure out her secret. That the emotions and the weight gain was evidence of what was growing inside of her. Thank God she was carrying this baby small. She was all hips. Her stomach barely showed.

"I'll be fine," she whispered.

"You ever need anything…you ever need a nigga to pull up on you because corny niggas got too much bass in they voice… You can put in that order. Isa and I will ride down on a nigga if there is ever a problem…"

"Everybody except Messiah," Morgan scoffed. She shook her head. It was absolutely absurd. "I can call you but not the nigga I fucked every day for months…" She shook her head in disgust. Protected by his crew but not him. In contact with his friends but not him. She could never make sense of that.

"Yo, Mo, that mouth of yours …chill," Meek said, swiping a hand over his distressed face.

"I'm just saying. It's ridiculous. He's a coward. He fucked me over and then left me on stuck. How could you know that, Meek? How could you know what he had planned and just smile in my face? You were around me almost every day," she said, suddenly feeling an unbelievable burn in her chest. She was mad as hell at him too. He held blame in all this too. Not just Messiah. Messiah. Isa. And Ahmeek. They all had made a fool of her. Bleu had been the only one to try to warn her. In so many words, Bleu had told her to let Messiah go. Morgan was mad at the world, these days. Fuck all three of these niggas. She wanted to throw away the whole damn crew. "He was going to put a bullet in the only family I have left, and then console me at the funeral? Is that how that was supposed to go? Or would I even be here? A bullet for me too? Bella? Eazy?" Morgan pushed him. "Why would he do this to me? How could he? Ethic was good to him! I was good to him!"

"There's not a bullet out there with your name on it. The nigga loading the gun would be erased before he could even get close. You ain't got one set of eyes on you. There were always three. Three shooters, covering you from all angles. That was the order Messiah put down, when it came to you. Even Aria. Once you're on the inside, that's just how we move. We did a lot of wrong. A lot of fuck shit that we can't take back now, but you were always safe; even still, you're safe. All it takes is a call. The streets will run red on your say so. All you got to do is say so. You be good, Mo. I'm out of here. I've already been here too long." A quick ten-minute money grab had turned into a distraction.

"Ahmeek, you're bleeding," she whispered, as she looked down at his shirt. A small circle of blood was spreading through the fabric of his shirt. "Are you hurt? Is Messiah?

ASHLEY ANTOINETTE

Is he hurt, Ahmeek? Is that why he hasn't called? Where is he?!" He followed her eyes and realized his wound was open. It was excruciating, but he couldn't sit down to heal. He and the crew had money and product in the streets. Order to maintain. Blocks to secure. Zip codes to keep under control, stretches of highway to keep on lock. With Messiah MIA, all the weight was on he and Isa. So, even through the pain of being shot, Ahmeek had to get to the money. Bake the cake, and then cut the slices into three portions.

"I don't know, Mo. I don't think he's hurt. He don't say much when we're on the line," Meek said, as he zipped his jacket, grimacing, as he cleared his throat and locked his jaw, trying to absorb the pain. "He's just keeping shit low for a while. It's necessary. Your people find him and that's a problem. This hole in me came from your pops."

"Ethic? He shot you?" Morgan asked. She couldn't say she was shocked. She knew how Ethic got down. She knew he was king. There was only one way to handle an uprising... Kill the opps. Ahmeek was the opps. Isa too. Her poor Messiah too.

"Put a hole in a nigga like it was nothing," Ahmeek stated.

"You kind of deserve it," she said, looking away from him.

"Yeah, I do," he stated. "I can admit when I've fucked up."

"That's more than some people," she whispered. "Come on."

She went to the bar. "Hey, Carla. Can you hand me the first aid kit?" she called.

43

Carla reached below the bar and handed Morgan a large, red box. "You can use the bathroom in the office."

"Thanks," Mo answered. She led the way to the back, as the loud music faded with every step she took. Meek followed, in silence.

"Lift your shirt," Morgan sighed.

"I'm good, Mo," he said.

"You're bleeding all over the place. It's gross. Lift your shirt." Her tone was full of exasperation. Full of sorrow. Impatience. A part of her wanted his ass to bleed to death for what he had contributed to, but still, she held some compassion. Mo wouldn't be Mo if she didn't have a little empathy for him. This man used to be her friend. At least she had thought so. She had spent countless nights with him, playing cards and kicking shit over crazy topics, while Messiah sat nearby, silent, normally smoking, sometimes drinking, always watching her. Hawking her. She wondered now if he was plotting. Had he not been able to enjoy the easy times because he was busy planning for murder in his head? Had he felt guilty for watching her parlay with his team, watching her smile and laugh, while the threat of destruction lingered over her head?

Meek lifted his shirt, holding it up with one hand, exposing the gun resting on his waistline and defined abs wrapped in bloody gauze. Morgan removed the old dressing and then opened the first aid kit, placing new gauze against the wound. He stared down at her. The silence ate up the space in the room.

"Morgan…"

Morgan looked up from his stomach where she was soaking up the overflow of blood and applying peroxide.

"I'm sorry."

She stared up at him, eyes prickling, and lip quivering for a moment longer, and then rolled tormented eyes back down to his wound. She didn't respond.

She re-wrapped his torso and then tossed the dirty bandages in the trash.

Meek readjusted his shirt and then zipped his jacket.

"I'll tell Ethic to fall back. I don't want anyone else hurt. I'm hurt enough for everybody," she whispered.

Ahmeek's brow pinched, as he stared at her. Morgan cleared her throat and moved away from him. "When you see him… When you talk to him. Tell him…" Morgan paused.

"Tell him what?" Ahmeek asked.

She thought hard. She had so much to say to him, but if she could only say one thing to him, she had to pick the right words.

"That I love him," she whispered. "Still. Tell him I still love him. Nobody ever has, but I did. I do. I just want him to know that."

Ahmeek nodded. "I will," he answered. He walked out, and Morgan followed him, her eyes capturing him, as he headed for the door.

It hurt to let him walk away because Meek was the closest connection to Messiah she had experienced in months. The aura, the aggression, the protection. She missed it. It was so reminiscent of Messiah that it almost felt identical. If she had closed her eyes with Meek standing in front of her, she could have pretended it was Messiah. That's how familiar it felt. She turned and watched Meek walk out the door, noticing how every man and woman he passed took notice, acknowledging him in some form, as he made his way to the exit. She shook her head. They all had the same effect. They all exuded power. Some men you just didn't miss. They garnered effortless attention and Meek was no different. Bossed up, dripping in money, and layered in aggression, he was just a god amongst mortals. He was just that nigga. Not *her* nigga, but definitely that nigga, and he was a reminder of what she had lost, of the deeply-rooted betrayal. It was time to go home because the night had been ruined.

CHAPTER 5

Morning brought clarity to Morgan. She had cried so hard that she feared what it could be doing to the baby growing inside her. She had already done enough self-inflicting, self-loathing, self-destruction behind Messiah. When she awoke, she promised herself she would do better. She couldn't take any more damage. She had looked to Messiah to repair all her broken pieces and he had; but when he left, he took all her confidence with him. It was time for some self-care, some self-love; and when Morgan put feet to the pavement the next morning, she promised herself she would never not love herself again. A phase of her life had ended. The crawling stage...the caterpillar stage. Messiah had wrapped her in a cocoon and she had transformed inside it. She wanted to fly. She had to fly. She had a baby on the way and would be raising it alone. She couldn't afford to slip up. Morgan woke up, for the first time in weeks, without conflict on her heart. Messiah was gone. Messiah had lied. Messiah had wanted to hurt her. She couldn't change any of that. She couldn't control any of it; what she could control is how she let it affect her. She climbed out of bed and walked over to her closet, grabbing the box filled with cosmetics from the top of it. She dumped the contents on the floor and then went to Messiah's side of her dresser. She pulled open each drawer, packing away Messiah's things. Everything had to go. She couldn't keep one thing because seeing even something as simple as the coconut oil she used to re-twist his locs would make her fall into the empty hole inside of her. That hole was dark. That hole had almost swallowed her. That place had made her want to die. She couldn't live there, so she packed it all away. She came up on a picture of the two of them and her hands froze. It was a little strip of photos that she had forced him to take one day in the mall. Morgan's eyes closed to stop the dew of emotion from clinging to her lashes. They looked so happy. They had once been so extremely happy. She would never understand how things had turned out to be so fraudulent. She shook her head and placed the picture inside the box.

A knock at the door pulled her toward it.

"One second!" she yelled out. She hightailed it to the door, and when she looked through the peephole, she frowned. She pulled open the door.

"Bash? What are you doing here?" she asked.

Bash stood at her door. In his hands, he held up a pair of Louis Vuitton sunglasses.

"You left these in my car yesterday," he said.

She took them and looked down at the ground, before looking up at him. "Thanks, Bash."

"Not a problem, Mo. Take care," he said. He was halfway to the elevator when Morgan stopped him.

"Bash!" she shouted. He turned. "I owe you an apology. I've been going through a lot and..."

A bolt of pain jabbed her, and Morgan recoiled, as she placed one hand on her stomach, the other gripping the doorframe for balance. The wind had been knocked out of her.

"Morgan?" Bash called, frowning, as he doubled back to her. She sucked in air. "What's happening right now? Are you okay?"

Morgan waited, bracing herself, because somehow, she knew that whatever had just hit her was coming back for a second punch.

"Agh!" she shouted. She reached for Bash, almost doubling over into his arms. "There's something wrong. Bash, I'm pregnant. There's something wrong." She cried. He picked her up, scooping her into his arms.

"Okay, Mo, I got you. We're going to get you to the hospital," Bash said.

Morgan felt a wetness fill her panties and stain through the fabric of her leggings.

"Bash, something's wrong. Something's wrong, something's wrong. Oh my god," she whispered, her eyes filling with tears, as she clung to his neck. He rushed to his Jeep.

"You're going to be fine, Mo. You're okay. You're okay," he repeated, as he placed her in the passenger side. When he pulled back his hand, he noticed blood on his palm. He rushed to the driver's side and pulled off recklessly, causing cars behind him to come screeching to a stop, as Morgan sat beside him, panicking.

"Bash, please hurry," Morgan whispered, as she gripped the dashboard. It felt like lightning was flashing through her body. Her skin felt like it was on fire, like someone had turned up the temperature in the car and there was so much blood. Her heart pumped a million miles an hour.

Bash didn't even park his car. He pulled directly in front of the door to the student medical center, leaving his car door hanging open, as he rushed to Morgan's side and carried her into the facility.

"Help! Somebody, help!" he shouted. A team of nurses approached him, one wheeling a chair in their direction. "She's pregnant and there's blood!"

He placed Morgan in the wheelchair and she was immediately whisked away.

"Bash!" Morgan shouted, as a nurse continued wheeling her away. "Please, let him come. I don't want to be alone… agh!"

"What's happening to her?" Bash shouted. "Morgan…Mo!"

Bash's voice faded, as Morgan felt a burst of pain erupt in her womb and then nothing…nothing, as a white light overcame her.

Morgan felt a chill in her bones, as she lifted heavy lids.

Her first blink revealed Alani. She heard the steady beep of a heart monitor and felt her teeth chattering so hard that they felt like they would chip.

"It's col...lld," she murmured.

"That's the anesthesia," Alani whispered. "You're okay, Morgan." Alani's voice was small, shaking, as she stood over Morgan's bed, rubbing her hair out of her face. She reached down to the foot of the bed and pulled up the blankets at the bottom.

"The baby," Morgan whispered. "There was blo..." She cleared her throat and tried to swallow the lump in her throat.

"Shh," Alani whispered. She reached to the stand beside the bed and grabbed the Styrofoam cup. "Drink some water." Alani held the straw and placed it to Morgan's lips. She drank from the cup and then rested her head against her pillow, pinching her eyes closed.

"You were pregnant with twins," Alani said.

Morgan's eyes glistened. "They're gone, aren't they?" she whispered. A tear rolled down the side of her face and landed in her ear.

"One of the embryos implanted itself in your left fallopian tube, sweetheart. There was nothing the doctors could do. It burst. That's where the pain and the bleeding came from. You didn't feel pain, Mo? The doctor's said there would have been a lot of it..."

"Nothing hurts as much as my heart. I can't feel anything else except that, the pain, in the center of my chest..." Morgan said. "What about the other baby? You said it was twins..."

"The other baby is fine. He's strong, Morgan, but they're worried. Your heartbeat is irregular, beating too fast they said. This baby is really taking a toll on you. You have to take better care of yourself, Mo."

"It's a boy?" Morgan asked. She was both crushed and fulfilled at the same time. One baby lost, another saved. A piece of the love of her life...a mini Messiah. It felt a bit like punishment. She'd have to look into the eyes of a little boy that looked like Messiah for the rest of her life, and she knew it would hurt. She was already dreading it; but somewhere deep down, she felt relief that at least one of her babies was okay.

Alani nodded. "You're 20 weeks. Halfway through your pregnancy and barely showing," Alani said. Alani placed her hand on Morgan's belly. "But he's in there and he's baking. You've just got to be strong for him."

Morgan gasped, when she felt the jolt in her stomach.

"Did you feel that?" she asked Alani, in astonishment. Her eyes widened, and she placed a hand over the spot where she had felt it. Alani laughed, as tears clung to her lashes.

"I did," Alani cried, through the joyful tears, hurriedly swiping them away. "He's kicking. He's letting you know he's doing his job in there. All you have to do is do your job out here and you'll be meeting him soon."

Morgan nodded, and Alani removed her hand. "Ethic will be here soon. He went to grab the kids from school. We didn't expect you to wake-up for a while. Your friend, Sebastian, is here too. I'm sorry I'm the face you woke up to. I'll leave and give you some privacy until they get back."

Alani went to leave, but Morgan grabbed her hand. "Could you just sit with me for a while?" she whispered. "I know I

have a baby boy, but the one I lost..." Her lip trembled. "...
that's all I feel right now."

Alani nodded, and tears came to her eyes. "I know, Mo. I
know." She knew the pain Morgan was experiencing. Seeing
her like this, sitting in this hospital, brought Alani's turmoil to
the surface. She gripped Morgan's hands, and then climbed
right up in the bed with her and held on tight, hugging her
shoulders. "God, I know."

Morgan sobbed into Alani. She hated that she needed her,
hated that she wanted her in this moment. No other shoulder
would do because she knew that Alani knew what this felt
like. She knew it from every aspect...loving a man who had
deceived you, losing a baby you hadn't thought you wanted,
but deep down in your soul knew that you needed because it
was all you had left of the person you loved most.

A knock at the door was the only thing that caused them to
part. Alani stood, as Bash peeked his head through the door.

"I just wanted to make sure you were okay. I know your
family is here. It just didn't feel right leaving without you
seeing me," Bash said. Morgan nodded.

Alani walked toward the door and placed a hand on
Bash's shoulder. "Give her the flowers, boy," she said,
smiling, because she could see how much Bash liked
Morgan. Morgan was a pregnant, teenaged girl with a
thug for a baby's father and Bash was stuck on her. He
had been more nervous than them all, when Morgan was
in surgery. There was just something about them Atkins
girls. Alani pitied this college boy. He didn't stand a
chance against Morgan.

"Oh, yeah," Bash said. He walked closer to Morgan and handed her the flowers. She gave a light smile, one that didn't reach her heart, and accepted them.

"Thank you." There was an awkward silence, as Bash placed his hands in his pockets and rocked on his heels.

"I'm really sorry, Morgan," he offered.

"No, I'm sorry. I owe you an apology. I've been so rude to you. I'm really sorry for the way I treated you," Morgan whispered.

"Like a punching bag? No worries, I'm tough, I can take it. Pretty girls are normally the mean ones, right?" he joked.

Another weak smile.

"You can sit," Morgan said.

Bash sat in the chair beside the bed. "How do you feel?" Bash asked.

"Like I was hit by a bus," Morgan answered. "Bet you don't want the pregnant girl to be your future wife now? Pretty girl, college dropout, kid out of wedlock. Won't look too good on paper to those ritzy parents of yours, huh?"

"I still see it. You're definitely my future wife. Besides, I like kids. Who said I didn't like kids? I think I could get the stepdad thing down," Bash said, with a chuckle. "You know, do that Russell Wilson thing."

Morgan laughed and then grimaced because it hurt to laugh.

"Who says you have to drop out of school, Mo? That doesn't have to be your story. You know that, right?"

Ethic popped his head in the door and Bash stood. "I'ma head out. Let you get some rest. If you need anything,

54

Morgan, hit my line, a'ight? Don't even think twice about it. If you need a light bulb changed, you don't have to lift a finger. Just hit me."

Morgan nodded, and Bash turned to leave. "It's nice to meet you, sir. Bad circumstances, but still a privilege," Bash said, as he extended his hand to Ethic.

Ethic stared at the hand for half a beat before shaking Bash's hand. "Thanks for calling and for being there," Ethic said.

Bash left, and Ethic went to Morgan's bedside. "We've seen the inside of a lot of hospitals lately, huh, kid?" Ethic said, as he leaned down to kiss her forehead. "How are you feeling?"

"I don't know, honestly," she whispered.

"I want you home, Mo," Ethic stated. "For the summer, at least."

She shook her head. "I think I want to take summer classes in Europe. I love you, but you're smothering me. You try to love the pain away and it's not going anywhere. It's stuck inside me. Everything reminds me of him. When I pull up to the house, I think about the first time I said his name, or I picture him sitting on the porch, the night Nish was killed. I see him and feel him everywhere. My apartment. My car. I just want to get away from every place he's ever been. I think London will be good for me, or this tour with Aria. I can't dance on stage, but I can choreograph. The promoters will pay me. I don't know. I just want to get away from here. Figure things out on my own. Messiah is trapped in my head…"

"And this Bash nigga? Who's he? I don't even know him, Mo," Ethic said, slightly perturbed at the idea of another man in Morgan's life, especially at the moment. Morgan was vulnerable. "You want me to send you around the world with a man I don't know, while you're carrying a baby in your stomach? I can't reach you over there. I can't just hop in a car and come step to a nigga if something goes wrong. That's too far, Morgan, no."

"I'm not really asking," Morgan whispered, placing one hand on Ethic's cheek. "I love you and I know you want to heal this for me, but you can't. I have to leave. Bash is harmless. He's a nice guy. A really good friend. I'm not going to Europe because I'm chasing behind him. It's not about him. I'm running from Messiah and chasing myself. I'm trying to figure out what life can be without him in it. Bash is safe. He's…" Morgan paused, as her mind traveled to the past, to a time when Justine Atkins was living and breathing. "…boring," she finished.

"Be careful, Mo. Boring or not, you don't play with a man's emotions. Don't use him to get over what you lost. It never ends well, and I don't want to have to put hands on every, little nigga you encounter," Ethic stated. He kissed her head. "I'm going to stay with you for a few days, while you're healing. If you're more comfortable at your apartment, that's fine, but you can't be alone. I know you're grown, Mo. I know you think you're grown, but I worry. I'm going to worry about you as long as I'm breathing. I just want you to be okay."

"I will be, when I'm away from here…far away from here."

CHAPTER 7

One Month Later

M o, this is some real bullshit," Aria protested, as she folded a pair of jeans and placed it in the suitcase. "Why won't you just come on tour with us? It's not even Stiletto Gang without youuuu." Aria pouted, as she flopped down on Morgan's bed.

"This is why," Morgan said, lifting her shirt and revealing her belly. "I'm six months pregnant. Nobody wants to see a pregnant girl on stage."

"You're so small. We can hide that shit. I can barely tell, when you're in hoodies. It just looks like you gained weight 'cause you're def thicker than a Snicker," Aria said, trying her hardest to convince Morgan. "You can choreo...you don't even have to come on stage."

"I need to be in one place. I have doctor's appointments every week. After losing one of the twins, I can't skip even one. I'm high risk."

"But London with Bash is okay? That's the highest risk, Mo. You don't even really know Bash. He could get you over there, away from your family, and start whooping your ass or something. What your fine-ass daddy got to say about that?" Aria asked.

"You gross me out every time you say that," Morgan said, with a laugh. "Ethic doesn't like that I'll be so far away, but I promised to come back way before my due date, and Alani found me a great doctor over there. I'm doubling up on classes, and it's a good opportunity, so he's trying to let me make my own decisions. I'm really trying to make the right ones this time. Lord knows, I've made a lot of bad ones to last a lifetime."

"And Messiah?" Aria whispered.

Morgan shook her head and ignored the burning threatening her eyes. She could barely see, they prickled so badly.

Aria knew better than to press the issue. It was a sensitive subject, one that would send Morgan seeking death if she pondered too long.

"I'm going to miss you. I don't like them other bitches like that, and Nick works my nervessss," Aria whined, dramatically.

Morgan laughed. "Listen, when I drop this baby and I'm all healed, I promise to do the last show with you," she said.

"Fine, and I want to see your face sometimes, heffa, so you better FaceTime me," Aria said. "And you know I'm going to need some help with choreo, so don't think I'm going to let you get rusty." Aria got eye level with Morgan's belly. "And you be nice to your mommy. Keep baking and growing. Auntie Ari can't wait to meet you."

Mo shook her head, smiling, and Aria stood with tears in her eyes. "I'm really going to miss you, Mo," Aria said.

"Me too," Morgan answered, as they embraced. Morgan dabbed at her tears with one finger and then sniffed them away. "You better get out of here. Tour bus leaves in a couple hours and I know you're not packed."

Morgan walked Aria to the door and she held her composure all the way until she closed it. Morgan rested both hands on the wooded door and her head hung in grief, as she cried. She had to force herself to calm down. She didn't want to harm her baby. She knew she had to be careful with the way she handled her emotions but hearing Messiah's name just made her emotional. This was *his* baby. She was here, making the family he had never had. She was fulfilling her end of things. She had the makings of a home right inside of her, and he was nowhere to be found. It was cruel, and the longer he stayed away, the more she came to terms with the fact that he was Mizan's brother. Messiah might not have physically abused Morgan, but emotionally, she was black and blue. Morgan grabbed her phone and dialed ten numbers. She had erased his contact in an effort to stop herself from communicating with him, but there was no erasing her memory. She knew everything about him by heart. Morgan didn't know why she was even attempting contact. What he had done, who he had turned out to be, it was all so unforgivable. Still, she wanted him to fix it. She wanted him to tell her that she wasn't hurting alone, and that if he could, he would be at her side. She wanted him to ask for her forgiveness. Even if she didn't extend it, she wanted him to want her. Messiah had deserted her, as if he had never even cared, and it was killing her. The lack of remorse was eating her alive. If he would just answer the phone…if he could just hear the injury in her voice…all she had to say was his name…he would know in the way that she called out for him that she needed him, and he would come home. He would come to her, because she was home, and even dogs who were dangerous, dogs that had bitten, dogs that were disloyal found their way back home. The sound of the voicemail picking up only frustrated her. He hadn't answered in months. She knew Messiah was cold with the rest of the world, but he was supposed to be different with her…he had been different with her. Had disarming her been all a part of his plan? Was he able to disconnect so easily because he was never truly connected to her at all? If that was the case, she was carrying the child of a man that she didn't know, and that was terrifying. Morgan grabbed her keys and rushed to the door. When she opened it, Bash stood there, fist in midair.

"Oh!" Morgan exclaimed, stopping dead in her tracks.

"You ready?" Bash asked, as he stepped inside her apartment, bypassing her. "I thought we would leave a bit early, avoid the traffic on the way to the airport. Grab some food or something on our way…"

He turned to her and stopped speaking when he saw her distress.

"Mo, what's wrong? Is it the baby? Is everything okay?" he asked.

"I… umm…" Morgan backpedaled toward the door. "I'm fine. I just forgot to take care of something. I have to go, I'll be back. You can go ahead of me. I'll meet you at the airport. I just have to…I have to go."

She was rambling, as she rushed out.

"Morgan!" he shouted. "The flight leaves in three hours! Whatever it is...it's too late!"

Morgan prayed to God that it wasn't...too late.

She pulled up to Bleu's house, hoping, praying, that Messiah's white BMW would be parked curbside when she arrived. She was aching for just a piece of him to show up in her life somewhere. She climbed out the car and walked up to Bleu's door. She rang the bell, as desperation filled her.

"Baby boy, don't spill that juice all over the kitchen floor..." Bleu was unfocused and yelling, her neck swiveled to the back of the house, as she pulled open the door all at once. When she turned to face the porch, she froze, her words halting instantly when she saw Morgan.

"Where is he, Bleu? I know you know, and I need you to tell me. I need you to get him here because I need him. I need him to explain this shit to me. I need him to tell me how he could lie so easily, Bleu. It's been so long since I've seen him and so long since I've heard him say my name. He won't answer my calls and my entire life has fallen apart. I just need to talk to him," Morgan rambled, crying, hysterical, melting down, right there on Bleu's porch. Morgan wanted to pull the baby card so badly that she had to bite down on the inside of her jaw to stop herself from revealing it all. She didn't want his love by default. She didn't want him to only come back because she was pregnant. She didn't want a baby daddy. She wanted her man. She wanted an endless love, a flawless love, like the one she had thought they shared. She wanted to be M&M again. She wanted sleepless nights filled with love making. Morgan couldn't even remember what Messiah smelled like. She wanted to be enough for Messiah. She didn't want him to come back because of a pregnancy. She wanted him to crave her. That's all she had ever wanted, ever since she was the girl who couldn't hear and the one he didn't see. She wanted him to notice her. She wanted to be worth the work it would take to repair what he had broken. Why wasn't he here trying to gain her forgiveness? Where was the groveling? The *'I'm sorry'* gifts, the extreme gestures. He had told her he didn't say *I love you* because he was busy showing it, but he was doing neither now. He had abandoned her.

Where is he?

"Oh, Mo," Bleu said, sympathy lacing her tone.

"Bleu, please, he's my man and I need him," she whispered, as she held onto the railing and then lowered her head in shame. "I need him, Bleu. He's mine and I want him. I don't care what he did. He belongs to me. He promised. Messiah's my whole life. I have a whole life waiting for him. I need my man to come home." She was embarrassed to be out here like this, pleading to contact a man that hadn't thought of her in months.

Every, single part of Bleu wanted to tell Morgan where Messiah was. Instant guilt filled Bleu because she had been sitting in the seat that belonged to Morgan. She had been a substitute to ease Messiah's suffering when it was Mo who should have had the privilege to walk him to his grave. It wasn't right. The night at the beach flashed in Bleu's mind and her lip quivered. Suddenly, sex with Messiah felt like betrayal.

They hadn't thought of Morgan, they hadn't considered her at all, and Bleu felt low because Morgan deserved the utmost respect from them both. Bleu could hold Messiah's hands for a thousand hours, but she could never give him the peace that Morgan could with just one glance. Bleu wanted to fill her in on his sickness and then hop in the car to drive the three hours to go see him, but she couldn't. Bleu had made Messiah a promise, and no matter how much she liked Morgan, no matter how sorry she felt, Bleu couldn't break it. Her loyalty was to Messiah and his word was law. He had a right to die the way he saw fit. She wouldn't bring Morgan to him without permission. He had decided, regarding Morgan, and Bleu was forced to respect it.

"I don't know where he is," Bleu lied. Her voice cracked, and tears filled her eyes at the mess that had become Morgan Atkins. She knew what this felt like. The heartbreak that came with loving a man like Messiah. Someone older, more mature, someone who was doing 90 MPH in the fast lane of life, while Morgan was trying to pace her college years. Bleu knew the hard shoes Morgan walked in because she had trekked those miles as well. It had destroyed Bleu and she was now watching it erode Morgan. "He calls, sometimes. The next time I speak to him, I can give him a message for you. I'll try to convince him to call you, Mo."

Morgan nodded. "He calls you but can't pick up the phone to call me?" The realization of that was like a slap in the face. "Are you fucking him, Bleu?"

"What? Morgan, no! God, never!" Bleu denied it vehemently because what she and Messiah had done hadn't

63

been about sex. Yes, they had been intimate, once…
once, under unbelievable circumstances, and never had
they thought about it before. Bleu couldn't admit to that,
though. Not to Morgan. Had anyone else asked her, Bleu
would have told the truth without shame; but if Morgan
ever found out, it would break her, and Bleu had no ill will
or intention toward Mo. Mo was such a lovely girl and onus
pressed down on Bleu heavily. Morgan searched Bleu's
eyes for deception and found none. She was sorry for
even accusing such a thing, but her thoughts were not her
own…grief had taken over. She no longer knew what to
think. Everything she had thought was solid had crumbled
beneath her. Morgan needed something solid to steady
her…she needed him.

"He has no idea what I've been through…what he's
putting me through," Morgan cried. Morgan shook her head,
ugly crying, trying her hardest to stop to no avail. "Bleu, you
don't understand. It's been 24 weeks," Morgan whispered.
Her tears just kept rolling. "Bleu, I need him…."

Bleu knew Messiah would kill her for what she was about
to do, but she pulled out her cell phone and dialed his
number. "Just wait, one second, Mo. I'm going to call him,
okay? Come in."

Morgan wiped her tears and stepped inside the house, but
there was no settling her sadness. She had tucked her lips and
folded her arms across her chest to muffle her sobs, but they
still attacked her, one after the other. Iman and Saviour sat in
the living room. Iman glanced her way and Morgan turned to
the door, not wanting more witnesses to her sorrow.

"You can have a seat, Mo. Make yourself comfortable," Bleu offered. "I'll be right back, okay?" Bleu said.

Bleu stepped into the next room and placed the call, putting it on speaker phone. Messiah answered the phone on the first ring,

"What up, B?"

No Shorty Doo-Wops were extended. He hadn't called her that since the beach because she knew it reminded him of Morgan.

"Mo's here, Messiah," she said. "She needs you. She's here and she's crying. She is a wreck. The way you're doing this is devastating her. Can I just bring her to come see you? We can be there in a few hours. She needs you, Messiah. This is wrong. You're making *me* wrong, Messiah. I don't want to do this to her. I can't even look her in the eyes."

Messiah was silent on the other line of the phone and she knew he was fighting a war with himself, convincing himself that dying without Morgan by his side was the punishment he deserved for lying to her about who he was.

"No," he finally answered. "Stop fucking asking me the same shit, B! I said I don't want her here!" He yelled the words. Barked them.

He hung up and Bleu turned to find Morgan standing there, lip trembling, eyes glistening with a pool of sadness. Sick Messiah was a mean Messiah and he had yelled it so loudly that Morgan had heard him through the phone. He had denied her. *He doesn't want me. He doesn't give one fuck about me.*

"Morgan, he really does love you. He doesn't love anyone more than you. He's just…"

Morgan put her hand up, silencing Bleu, as her face melted in agony and abandonment.

"I'm letting this go," she whispered, sobbing so badly that her nose ran. "When he realizes what he gave up, tell him don't come back. He is a fucked-up person. He's the worse kind of man and I wish I had never met him. I'm done, Bleu. Since he talks to you every day, make sure you tell him that. It's fucking over."

Morgan's dejection swallowed her, as she walked out, flipping the hood to her jacket up over her head to hide her shame. She got into her car and promised herself she wouldn't look back. He had made his choice, repeatedly, and she had to be woman enough to walk away.

"I kind of want to tell you that you can't go, Mo," Ethic stated, as he sat in the Range, gripping the steering wheel with one hand. He looked over at her and his eyes burned. He cleared his throat. "I just want to shrink you and do the past twelve years all over again. You're my baby."

"I'm going to always be that little girl," she whispered. "But I can't stay here."

"I'm still looking for him, Mo. I've got people on it, but I taught Messiah exactly how to disappear if he ever needed to. It's taking me a bit of time," Ethic stated.

"You can stop," she answered. "I don't want to find him anymore. I just want to move on. Isa and Ahmeek too. You can stop that too. They were moving on his command. Just let them be. You shot Meek, he gets the point. I've never known you to shoot and not kill."

"He said something that bought him a ticket to breathe," Ethic answered.

"What did he say?" Morgan asked.

"I'm sure he'll tell you, some day," he answered.

Morgan frowned. She shook her head in confusion, as she looked at Ethic.

"My heart," he said. "This shit hits different. Sending you to college was one thing. Sending you to another country with a baby in your stomach…" Ethic shook his head in disbelief and then scrunched his nose, as he looked out the driver's side window. Morgan was unearthing all types of emotions in him. He pushed open the door. "You're going to miss your flight," he said, clearing his throat, masking devastation.

He walked behind the car, opening the back and pulled out her luggage. He squeezed the bridge of his nose.

"I'll be fine," Morgan whispered. "It's just for the summer. I'll be back before I have the baby."

Ethic nodded and pulled Morgan in for a hug. He kissed her cheek, before handing her rolling luggage off to her.

Bash stepped out of the sliding glass doors. Bash threw up a hand, in greeting. Ethic glowered, sticking both hands in his pockets. Morgan smiled and shook her head.

"I love you, Ethic," she said. "Go be happy with Alani. I

need to find myself. I'm lost right now, but I know the way home. When I need you, I'll come running back."

"Fuck up the world, Mo, and remember you're the..."

"Sun," she finished. "Everything revolves around me."

It was what he had told her since she was a little girl. A similar sentiment out of Ahmeek's mouth had convinced Ethic to let him live.

"Make sure you shine bright, Mo," he said. Ethic stood there, watching her as she walked into the airport with Bash. A group of other students greeted her inside and Ethic's heart wrenched. It was hard to watch her leave, but he knew that she had to in order to grow. Morgan had been sucked into the world of hood politics, simply because she had fallen for the wrong man. He hoped this new path would line up a world of opportunity for her and help her discover the girl he knew was waiting to burst free on the inside. The brave girl, the confident girl, the young woman he had raised her to be.

"What the hell is wrong with you?!"

Bleu came bursting through Messiah's door fussing as she tossed her hand bag into the chair beside the bed and then folded her arms across her chest. "She came looking for you, Messiah. She's not mad, she's not holding grudges. She wants you to come back for her! You are just determined to die alone. You're robbing that girl of time with you, Messiah.

Do you know how cruel that is? Why are you punishing her?"

"Because she made me feel all this shit, B. She ain't the only one hurting, B. You think I want to think about the niggas she gone fuck with after me, or the babies she gone have, or the nigga Ethic gone walk her down the aisle to? That's supposed to be me, B. Mo was so hard headed man," Messiah said, shaking his head as he leaned against the pillow and lifted eyes of dismay to the ceiling. "I told her no. I tried to stay away from her because I felt myself breaking code with her. Mo makes a nigga want to break every rule just for a little bit of time with her. She made me wish I had more time, but I don't. Time's up and she don't need to see me go and I don't need to see her cry about it. Half the time we would spend together anyway would be me explaining. Me apologizing for all the shit I put her through. Rehashing her fucking sister and Mizan and none of that is about us. None of that helps anything. It'll just be more tears and more fucking guilt. I don't give a fuck if you think it's cold. She'll get over it one day."

Bleu's chest was heavy. "The way you love on people is fucked up Messiah."

"Yeah well you ain't got to like it. That's all I got for shorty. It is what it is," Messiah snapped back. "I've already ruined her life, B. I ruined that girl. I want her so bad. I want her so bad I might ask her to come with me, B and Mo loves me so much she would give up her last sip of air to follow me. Shorty would die with me, B, and I'm selfish and I'm fucking terrified, so I'd let her. I would hold her hand and ask that girl to die for me. I lose my mind around Mo. It's better for everybody if I do it like this. Alone."

"But you were going to go back Messiah! When she called, you wanted to get to her. You're torturing yourself for nothing! You deserve to see her," Bleu argued. The love story of Messiah and Morgan was one of the saddest she had ever seen. She wanted to change the ending that Messiah was determined to write but he was putting it down in ink. She couldn't erase it.

"I was being pussy. I heard her voice and she pulled me back. I just can't hear her voice. If I don't hear her voice, I can go through with this. I can do it on my own if I just don't hear her say my name," Messiah whispered.

Bleu's eyes went wet and she had to close them to stop tears from falling down her cheeks. Her chin trembled and Bleu gritted her teeth so hard to try to gain some composure. Messiah was dying. He was her best-damn-friend and he was slipping away in the most painful way. The shit hurt. It crushed her but seeing the self-imposed pain he was forcing himself to go through made it ten times worse. Bleu's nostrils flared as she sucked in air. She blew out a sharp breath. She couldn't stand here and cry. Her hurt didn't matter. Not when he was going through much more.

"Messiah what can I do? I'm running out of ways to make you fight. You're giving up on me and its tearing me up inside," she said. "She can make you fight Messiah. It's just me and you don't fight hard enough for me. Mo and Ethic and the crew…you need everybody Messiah. You need your village."

"Nah, seeing her is the thing that's going to kill me. You

keep me alive a little longer, B. Just keep me alive, man," Messiah said.

Bleu nodded, blinking through a vision full of pain; tears blinded her. She reached for the wheel chair near the door.

"Okay," she whispered. "Come on, you asshole."

Bleu stood in front of the bed and Messiah swung weak legs over the side. He was so thin. Tattoos against his skin seemed smaller with the weight loss. He was less menacing. Just a man. Not a goon. Not a thug. Just her friend. He was her best fucking friend. Stripped of all his emotional walls, all of his aggression. Stripped of all his will. Messiah was beautiful.

He reached up to cup her face in his hands.

"Keep me alive, B." It was a plea and Bleu wasn't strong enough to chase down the sob that left her throat.

She reached down wrapping her arms around his back and lifted him. She turned and put him in the wheel chair.

She bent in front of him to pick his legs up and put them in place then she hung her head, placing her hands on his knees. Another sob. And then her head in his lap. His hand on the back of her head. She sobbed.

Messiah leaned over onto her and held her as she cried.

"Shh," he consoled. She looked up at him and he pressed his forehead to hers. "I'm gon' die, B. When I do, I want you to remember this right here. I ain't gave this to nobody, B. Nobody has seen me like this. Weak and shit. Fucked up. Scared. I gave you this. You've been an angel in my life Bleu so when you need me, I'ma be there. I'ma be the devil in you. When you need to boss up on a nigga, when you scared and you need to reach in your chest and pull out a little bit of strength, I'm there. You gave me heaven and I'ma give you hell so you can give the world hell, B, cuz' you're the fucking best, man," Messiah said. "You're my best friend."

Bleu plunged into him, hugging Messiah tightly and crying hysterically. She couldn't even breathe. Messiah was weak but still the strongest person she knew. His arms were a fortress that no danger could penetrate. She sucked in air, trying to calm herself and he was patient. She let it all out before standing. She wiped her eyes and sniffed away the sorrow before releasing the brake on the chair. "Let's get some fresh air."

Bleu pushed Messiah out of the walls of the hospital and into the visitors' garden.

She stopped him in front of the fountain.

She took a seat on the edge of the concrete and reached her hand down into the water.

Messiah lifted, using all his strength to sit next to her.

"How do you feel? You feel okay? Anything hurt?" Bleu asked.

"Nothing hurts, B. Right now, I feel pretty damn good," Messiah said.

"You sure?" Bleu pushed, forehead knitted in absolute concern.

Messiah chuckled. "Nigga, I'm good."

"Cool," Bleu said. "I don't have to feel bad than."

"Bad about what?" Messiah asked.

"This," she said. Bleu pushed Messiah backward into the fountain but not before he grabbed her wrist, pulling her in after him.

She screamed in surprise as her entire body submerged, soaking her everywhere. He laughed from his gut as he splashed water in her face.

"Messiah!" she shouted.

"Nah, nigga catch all this smoke," he teased. She laughed as she stood only for him to snatch her back into the water. The bottom of the fountain was so slippery she fell all over the place, submerging again.

Messiah held his stomach he laughed so hard.

"You work my nerves," Bleu complained as she smiled wide and shook her head.

Messiah threw his arms over the edge of the fountain and Bleu rested under one arm as the fountain sprayed around them. "This definitely should be added to the fuck it list."

"Top of the list," Bleu agreed. She wrapped her arm around his midsection and squeezed him tight. "Number 1 on my list, Messiah."

CHAPTER 8

"C an we go to Nannie's today after church?" Bella asked, as she walked into the kitchen, eyes glued to her phone as earbuds plugged her ears.

Alani stood over the stove, scrambling eggs. Her hair was tied in a scarf and one of Ethic's shirts covered her body; bare, peach-painted toes graced the tile floor.

"Summer just started, and you want to spend it at Nannie's? I thought we'd hit the bookstore after church to get some books about Michigan. I was thinking a week's road trip to the Upper Peninsula. We can use the books to look up places we want to hit on the way up. Then, maybe, stop at the farm on the way back down to ride the horses," Alani said.

"That sounds cool, but can we do that next week? Nannie said I could come stay a few days when school was out," Bella stated.

Alani glanced at Bella, curiously. "Umm… well, I guess I can push the road trip back by a few days. Did you ask Daddy?"

Alani bit her tongue because the question flew out her

mouth so fluently that she didn't get a chance to remove herself from the sentiment. She was trying to maintain an appropriate relationship with Bella and Eazy...working extra hard to not feel like she was attempting to be their mother. Ethic was their father, their daddy, not the daddy that she had chosen to make them with...*I should have said your dad. Did you ask your dad...*Alani in no way wanted to overstep.

"Ask Daddy what?" Ethic asked, as he entered the kitchen, only catching the tail end of the conversation.

He walked up to Bella and gave her a quick hug. "Good morning, baby girl," he said, then went over to Alani, trapping her with his frame against the counter. He took his time greeting her, feeding her his entire tongue, and then pecking her cheek and whispering, "I like that daddy shit. Keep calling me that," he said.

Alani blushed and turned to get his plate. He read her disposition, as soon as he entered the room, noticing her gears turning, saw her mind overthinking. He calmed every worry with one sentence. Damn, she loved this man.

He took the plate to the kitchen table and scooped a bite of eggs into his mouth. "You made these with olive oil?" Ethic asked, surprised, because Alani was the pork-cooking, butter-using queen.

"I mean, you got me doing yoga every night, sir. That butter slows me down," she said, with a smirk.

He licked his lips and she wondered if he had washed her off of them yet. Ethic pointed his fork at Bella. "Off the phone, B," he said. "You know the rules at the table. We eat as a family."

Bella sighed, smacking her lips, before planting her bottom into the chair and tucking her phone.

"Now, ask me what?" Ethic said.

"She wants to spend time at Nannie's," Alani said.

"That's fine with me," Ethic answered, without a second thought.

"Eazy! Breakfast!" Alani shouted. Ethic lifted eyebrows to Alani and shook his head. There was nothing she could do that he didn't like. Anyone else, yelling in his home, would have unsettled him. Having her here, leading the ship he had built, was a dream manifested. Alani heard Eazy's feet flying down the hallway upstairs and then down the steps. Every thud and bump was audible, as he barreled into the kitchen and plowed into a chair.

"Morning, Big Man," Alani greeted, as she kissed the top of his head.

"Good morning," he said.

She pointed toward the hallway. "Now, go all the way back to your room and walk," she instructed.

"Aww, man," Eazy said, looking to his father for help. Ethic chuckled and shrugged.

"You heard her, homie," Ethic said.

Alani knew it was torture for Eazy to retrace his steps and he sulked back into the kitchen right into her arms. It was the little things that Ethic's children had missed out on over the years. Ethic had done a phenomenal job of parenting alone. She had never met better kids their age, but the spoiling, the overcompensating, the lack of rules. He hadn't wanted to play bad cop because there was no good cop on the other end to balance it out…the strict part of parenting is what had been missed.

"Are you happy?" Eazy asked, pouting.

"Very," she said, laughing. "You're a gentleman. You walk indoors. It's bad manners to run. Save all the energy for outside."

She handed him a plate of food and then served Bella. When she reached for another plate out of the cabinet, Ethic came up behind her. "Have a seat, baby, I got it," he said.

She froze, in stun. Alani was used to taking care of everything. Like every other black woman, she came last on her own list of priorities. Ethic wouldn't let her. He would never allow that. If she didn't take care of herself, he would, and even this small gesture proved that.

It was the small tokens of appreciation that Alani loved about this man. The large home and cars were nice, but she didn't need any of that. None of that was required. She would live out of a cardboard box with Ethic, as long as he treated her with such regard. His love was so intense. It blazed so strongly that it could burn down anything and everything that stood in their way. It had burned down the things that stood in their way. She still couldn't believe that she had almost given him up, given them up.

He fixed her plate and they sat together, eating, laughing, like this was always the way things had been and they didn't know anything else. Alani did know something else, however. She desperately wished she had met Ethic at a different time in her life…in a different way. If she had, Kenzie would be sitting in the chair next to Eazy. *She would have loved him.*

She turned her head to the space at the edge of the table next to Bella. The space where she could have placed a high chair for Love.

Alani didn't realize her eyes were watering, or even that a tear had escaped her, until she felt Ethic's thumb on her skin. She jumped, snapping out of her reverie. "You okay?" he asked.

She sniffed and forced a smile, nodding.

Ethic's back stiffened. He reached for her hand and stood from the table. "We're leaving in fifteen minutes," he told his children, as he led her into his office and closed the door. He pulled her into his chest, holding her by the back of her head. "Just cry."

And she did. She wrapped her arms around his strong waist and sobbed.

"If you need space. From me...from my kids..."

She shook her head. "No space. I don't want space. It's just a bad morning. I just want this...I just need this hug. Love it away, Ethic. Like you always do," she cried, as she pinched her eyes tight.

He held her until she stopped crying, and then said, "If Ny has time, we'll meet with him after church. The kids can go home with Nannie. We need him."

Alani's heart fluttered. He recognized a need for God's word...a need for God's guidance. That was growth for a man that hadn't believed in God at all, and she felt pride because he was becoming her spiritual anchor. She nodded, tucked away her turmoil, and walked out of the room, gathering Eazy and Bella, so that she could head to Sunday morning service with her family.

Ethic stepped out into the aisle of the church, extending his hand for his family to exit first. It had been a long program. First Sunday and communion. Something he wasn't used to. The body and the blood of it all had drained him and it would take some adjusting to have to sit through time and time again. He still didn't believe he had to follow religion to be spiritual; but he couldn't lie, something about being under this roof with a whole familial unit felt right. He was sure he was the biggest sinner in the building, but he was trying…for her…he was giving his all. She enjoyed everything about this place. He could see it in her eyes. From the announcements, to the altar call, to the sermon, to the hymns that she knew by heart but sang off key…Alani's eyes sparkled, when in the presence of the Lord. So, for her…yes, he would try.

"Ezra!"

His head turned to the sound of the voice. Alani's did as well. Alicia, the church hoe, came rushing up the aisle to him. "It's so good to see you!" she said. She leaned into him and gave him a hug. Ethic's entire body stiffened. He wasn't big on allowing strangers into his space; especially, to lay hands on him so intimately, while the woman he was truly intimate with watched, but he didn't pull away. He didn't want to appear rude.

"You as well," he said.

"I know you haven't formally joined yet, but I would love to treat you to dinner sometime, tell you all the perks of belonging to our little, church family. I promise to be a great date," she said.

Alani's eyebrows lifted at the audacity.

"Ezra won't be needing that, love. I've got it taken care of. Every night I'm taking care of that," Alani said, with a flat-lipped smile and challenge burning in her eyes.

"Oh! You two are together?" Alicia asked, feigning innocence. "I had no idea."

"That I was fucking him? Or that we were together, because I kind of doubt that there was any question about either." Alani said, losing all patience. She had no time for niceties. Any bitch who was brazen enough to step to Ethic in front of her needed to be prepared to be checked in front of him. The cross hanging on the wall didn't change one thing. Alani called it like she saw it. She would pray about it later.

Alicia held up hands of surrender and took a step back. "I didn't mean any disrespect," she said.

Alani looked up at Ethic. "Why are we still standing here?" she asked.

Ethic finessed his beard and guided her up the aisle where Eazy and Bella were standing with Nannie and Mr. Larry.

"Yo, since you into sinning in church and all, I'm tryna see something, because you in that dress is doing something to me," he whispered in her ear, walking behind her and placing a hand around her waist. A titter of amusement fell off her lips and he kissed the nape of her neck. Hugs were exchanged, as they said goodbye to the kids and headed toward Nyair's office.

"Ezra, what up, G?" Nyair greeted, as soon as they walked in. Nyair slapped hands with Ethic and they embraced briefly before Nyair extended a kiss to Alani's cheek.

"So, we still not refraining I see," Nyair said, with a smirk, as he closed his office door.

Alani blushed and cleared her throat. She felt like she had a scarlet letter burned into her forehead.

"We have been," Ethic, simply, answered. "Lately. She has been."

Nyair lifted a brow, in stun, as he shot eyes to Alani. "Saying no?"

"She hasn't really wanted to be touched for a couple weeks," Ethic stated. "She's emotional. Crying. Grieving," Ethic answered. "When she looks at me, she sees my actions, not my intentions, and I don't blame her for that. I've done some things in my past, some unforgivable things." He glanced at her and she reached for his hand. Their fingers intertwined. Alani couldn't tell him that her mood wasn't a mood at all. She hadn't touched him because she couldn't. The miscarriage had caused her to bleed for two weeks straight. She had been mending a wound he didn't even know existed, excusing it as an abnormal period. Lying. Alani had been looking him in the eyes and hiding the loss of another baby. Their baby, and it ached to even think about. She hated that he thought she was upset with him.

"I'm fine, Ethic," she whispered. "I don't see that. When I

look at you, that's not what I see. I just had a rough couple of weeks. I'm fine now."

Ethic stared into her eyes, forehead full of wrinkles, as he tried to decode her. Alani was an abyss that terrified him. Discovering the darkness of the depths of her heart was a challenge because she had mastered hiding her pain.

"Sometimes, when she looks at me, I just see the hurt in her…" he said the words to Nyair, but he never took his eyes off his queen. Alani felt see-through, as guilt ripped through her.

I can't tell him. I can't tell him there's another life lost between us.

"You can't erase who you were, Ethic. Who you were and what you did brought you here. That remorse planted you right here. Look at your hands. They're knotted. She can't even sit two feet away from you without touching you, G. She's tied herself to you, adhering herself to you, soul to soul. Contact is important. Connection is vital, but sex clouds judgement. She's refrained for a few weeks and now she's seeing you with 20/20 vision, and look at her, G. She still clings to you. Still so overwhelmed with standing next to you that she's holding her breath."

Alani let out an audible sigh, because she had been. Holding her breath. Anxiety and her lie was eating her up.

"Yeah, she remembers the old you. She won't forget that part of you. There is a lot of that part. This man sitting in God's house with different intentions is moving differently. Your choices are different. There's very little history built up on this side; so, yeah, her memories are painful. You got to love that away. You've got to earn that away. Day by day, on this side of things, on God's side of it, you'll earn a little more of her faith in you as a man...with every good action, every prayer, every time you take in a little more God, the part the devil had a hold of gets erased. It's not a sprint, bruh, it's a marathon and you running the race every day. There's road blocks on the road, bullshit in the game..."

"Ny!" Alani exclaimed.

Nyair chuckled. "See, we all got a little bad in us. No matter how holy a nigga claim to be, it's in there. I lose that battle, at times. We all do," he said. "Point is... You got to run up the points on God's side to combat the MVP you became in the streets. I'm aware of what it took to command the city in the way you did. That's a lot of years in the dark. Let her lead you to the light, and when you see your shadow start to cover her, and you see that emotion, that fear in her eyes, because she's weary of your dark. Tell her...tell her you see she's afraid, but you want to drown in her light."

A knock on the door interrupted them and Bella peeked her head inside. "Excuse me. I'm sorry. We forgot our bags in the trunk."

"Oh, here. I'll come help you guys. I think we're almost done here anyway, right, Ny?" Alani asked.

Nyair nodded.

"I'll be right out," Ethic said. He leaned forward onto his knees and waited for the door to close.

"I want to marry her," Ethic stated. "I want to find her father, her mother too, if possible. Let them know I've got it from here and that there's value in what they discounted.

Let them know that what they made is the best thing to ever happen to me. I need to do that. It's important."

"I can ask around. Cecil was always in and out, you know? He never really stuck. He was a smooth dude, when he was around, but it never lasted long. He had that rolling stone thing going on," Nyair said.

"That bitch nigga thing going too, eh?" Ethic grumbled. He held animosity toward anyone who had ever hurt her. He didn't need to hear the other side. "Let me know what you find. Her mother too. I'd like to meet her parents." He stood and the two shook hands before Ethic headed to the door.

"And your parents?" Nyair asked. "You don't think she should meet yours?"

Ethic's feet stalled. He turned back to Nyair, brows lifted, half from curiosity of where Nyair was going with this, the other half in challenge at the audacity. Most men didn't test Ethic. They let him speak and they listened to his logic. Nyair was always a man, always standing on his own two, in his own power. He was Ethic's equal. Man to man, he was presenting a question without an ounce of apology for being intrusive, and Ethic wanted to choke him out. Fire burned in Ethic's eyes because his father was a subject he didn't broach with anyone. It wasn't a fond memory.

"Focus on her people. All the people I need are in my possession at the moment," Ethic said.

Nyair nodded, but the look he gave Ethic was a knowing one. This walk of faith, this journey to becoming a better man, wasn't always an easy road. It hurt. Today was one of those days. Nyair had picked at an old scab and Ethic could feel himself bleeding out. He only hoped he could keep the turmoil hidden inside because his relationship with his father was where he would draw the line. There was no fixing that.

CHAPTER 9

E thic looked at the address that was scribbled on the sticky note on his dash board and then up at the motel in front of him. It was run-down, old. He knew the area well. It was a gold mine to young niggas. He had trapped out of these rooms years ago, and as he watched the young hustlers parlay in the parking lot, he knew not much had changed. It was the address Nyair had given him. The location of Alani's mother. He sat there for a long time. Almost an hour. Contemplating. Weighing his options. To pursue this or to leave it alone. He had taken so much from this woman. Her child. He couldn't imagine what it took for Alani to love him. He knew that she struggled with her choices to stay, and yet she was holding on tightly. It had to be lonely. It had to be terrifying. He just wanted to replenish. He knew he could never replace, but he could replenish, he could attempt to repair. He hoped to begin to piece together the puzzle of her life that had been destroyed…by dysfunction, by disease, by disarray. She had been destroyed by abandonment, long before he had met her. He just wanted to restore what had been lost, or at least attempt to do so. He wanted to design a family so beautiful and strong that on her darkest day she could always find the light. Her parents were necessary. He needed to see where she had come from. He needed to see what was generational inside her and what had been developed through the nature of her circumstances. Ethic climbed out of the Range, locking his truck, before flipping his hood up over his head, as he swaggered to the door. Room 7.

He lifted a heavy fist to the door.

He saw the curtain on the glass window rustle and the face that frowned at him from behind it took his breath away. Alani. This woman was Alani. It was who she would mature into. Her mother. They shared the same face. This woman's was weathered a bit. By age. By life. The sight of her still made his heart skip beats. It was like getting a glimpse into the future. The curtain was snatched closed and a few seconds later the door was pulled open, slightly, the security chain catching it.

"Who the fuck are you?"

Damn. Even her voice. His mind was blown.

"My name's Ethic. Are you Joy?" Ethic asked.

"Not if Joy owes you money," she shot back.

"I'm here about your daughter, Leni…"

"You know Nika?" she asked.

Ethic's brow creased. Her mother shouldn't call her that. Her mother should call her Alani. The woman was telling him a story of discord, without even knowing it. His heart ached for Alani. Was she so distant from the woman who birthed her that not even she could call her Alani?

"I'm taking care of her. She's my lady. Can we talk for a minute? Preferably, inside, so I don't have to blow one of these li'l niggas' heads off out here?" Ethic asked, as he looked over his shoulder, paranoia eating him alive, as the young block huggers looked at him in awe.

The door slammed closed and Ethic heard the chain come off before she pulled it open again.

"Come on in," she invited.

Ethic's eyes bounced around the room, as he assessed the situation in seconds. The bottle of half empty gin that sat on the nightstand stood out. Everything inside the motel was worn, dusty, and filth-covered.

"You can sit," she stated.

Not wanting to offend her, he took a seat on the old couch.

"How Nika land a big money bag like you?" she asked, as she took a seat at the table. She reached for the pack of cigarettes that sat on the table that separated them and tapped the bottom of the pack against her palm, before pulling one out. "Pulling up on me in your fancy truck with your fancy clothes. You smell like money. You fine too. Nika finally learned that she ain't no better than the rest of us. I see she fucked her way to the top. I hope she fucking you good. She better be fucking you *real* good, like I taught her. She don' lucked up."

Ethic cleared his throat, slightly unnerved at her frankness. *Fuck that mean?*

"Nah, I'm the one that lucked up," Ethic corrected. "She's a beautiful girl."

"You be careful with that girl. She's selfish. All that pretty and she don't ever want to share it. Her mean-ass."

"Who is she obligated to share it with?" Ethic asked. His defenses over Alani reared effortlessly.

Joy looked at him, scoffing, as she balanced her cigarette between two fingers. She shook those fingers at him, smiling. "Yeah, she's fucking you real good."

"I want to marry your daughter," he said.

Joy's smile faded.

"You gon' marry Nika?" She scoffed. "Good luck with that."

"She needs family. You're her mother. She doesn't talk about you much, but we only get one mother. You're still breathing, still able to repair whatever's broken here."

"I'm not interested." Joy said the words so casually, you would think she was saying no thank you to something as worthless as a piece of gum.

"She's not particularly interested either," Ethic stated. "But you don't get to choose where you come from. You can choose where you're going, though."

"I'm not going nowhere near that girl," Joy stated.

Joy lifted the sleeve to her shirt, scratching her arm, and Ethic saw the tracks.

Damn.

Heroin. She was addicted to heroin.

"You need some help with that?" he asked.

Joy pulled her sleeve down.

"You need some help with that?" She asked, lowering her gaze to his manhood. "You leave a couple dollars, I'll show you where Lenika learned her shit from."

Ethic frowned and stood.

90

"I just wanted you to know your daughter's safe with me," he stated.

Joy moved over to him, gripping his forearm with one hand and running her hand to his crotch with the other.

He gripped her wrists so tightly Joy cringed.

"Never touch me," he stated. He wasn't aggressive, wasn't callous, but he meant what he said. "You should really count your blessings. She's one. You ever wanna get right with her... The child you birthed... The child I'm feeling like you might have done some foul shit to, and it's taking everything in me not to press it to you about it," Ethic stated, flicking his nose. "You ever want to make that right. You call me. I'll get you off this shit and help you reconnect with your child. She's your child. I don't know if you think about her or worry about her...but you don't have to. She's mine and I'm going to take care of her; but for what it's worth, I think she needs you. She'll never ask for you, never seek you, but that's not her job. She's the child, you're the parent. Get yourself together and come see about your daughter. I think there's a void in her life. A few voids. Some I've caused. I'd like to fill this one."

Ethic headed to the door, stopping to pick up the ink pen that sat on the table near the exit. He wrote down his number and then glanced back once more. Joy was already leaning.

He shook his head, as he pulled open the door. He was glad he hadn't told Alani about this visit. It had proved to be pointless. It seemed he was all she had. He would work hard to make sure she felt like he was enough. He pulled off, headed home. They had plans tonight. An invitation to

91

dinner at Nyair's home; but as he drove, Joy's demeanor scratched at the intuition in him. Her disregard for Alani. Her words. The animosity. He felt something…something he didn't even want to consider, but damn he was considering it and it made him want to go home and hold his woman.

She better be fucking you real good, like I taught her.
All that pretty and she don't ever want to share it.

He would never ask Alani, but he had a feeling she had endured more than she would ever reveal. His poor Alani. If what he suspected was true, it explained so much about her. Her walls. Her distinction between Alani and Lenika. Why she didn't let anyone, not even him, call her Alani - unless she was sure they meant her no harm. His kids. His kids called her Alani. Nyair and Nannie were the only other exceptions he had ever heard utter the sacred name. They were the only ones she allowed to tap into the most innocent parts of her. His beautiful, damaged Alani. He knew he would have to hold this discovery of her history. He would have to pretend like he hadn't uncovered it, unless she wanted to invite him into that piece of her past. Until she wanted to expose that confidential hurt. She might not ever, and he would be okay with that, because he would love her extra, protect her more, to compensate for the people in her life who hadn't done it enough. He sped through the city streets to get to her. Rushed and Ethic wasn't a man who rushed to do much. He had an address for her father, but after the heaviness he felt from visiting her mother, her father would have to wait.

He hit the button to let him into his estate and pulled in, leaving the angst he felt in the Range, as he climbed out. Ethic entered his home.

R&B and sage. Alani was in a good mood. Alicia Keys was singing so powerfully throughout his home he could have sworn it was a live rendition.

Some people want it all, but I don't want nothing at allllll
If it ain't you, baby
If I ain't got you, ba-bay

Ethic didn't even take off his shoes. He knew she would bitch a fit about those shoes on her carpet, despite the fact that it was his carpet, but she said what the fuck she said.

She was in the mirror, wearing her robe, freshly washed, hair wet and clipped in a pile on top of her head.

Alani was an entire vibe. The steam from her shower smelled like coconut and shea butter.

"Some people want diamond rangs!" she sang, into the mirror, off tune.

She saw him in the mirror and turned to him, still singing, as she opened her arms.

"BUT EVERYTHING MEANS NOTHING! IF I AIN'T GOT YOUUU!"

Alani smiled, and he wondered how she could smile after what she'd been through. She looked down at his feet.

"Ethic, your shoes!" she fussed, but he didn't care. He crossed the space of the room and put a strong hand to her neck, pushing her against the mirror. The energy behind his kiss made her gasp. It wasn't even a sexual kiss, but it was deep, and she felt it. He pulled back to look at her for three second, before wrapping her in his embrace, holding the back of her neck tightly. She submitted. Wrapping her arms around his shoulders. She didn't know if she needed this hug or if it was him who required it, but it felt good.

He pulled back and pinched her chin, lifting it so that she looked in his eyes.

"Get real pretty for me tonight, baby." A quick peck and he turned to let her return to her routine, leaving her reeling.

"I'll be ready in five minutes," Alani shouted. Ethic took a seat, finessing his beard and wincing because there was no way she was walking down those stairs in the next five minutes. He reached for the remote and turned on the game, extending one leg and gripping his dick with his free hand, getting comfortable. He didn't mind waiting. If she required time, he'd extend it. He was on her time, all the time, because it was her castle…her world. Ethic was just grateful to be living in it. The normalcy of waiting on a woman to walk down the stairs, of growing agitated because although she had showered first she still wasn't ready, felt like a gift to him. Even the things about her that drove him mad were lovely. Alani made him feel normal…the amount of love and forgiveness she was filled with made him feel worthy. After years of trying to find his value in the streets, of building reputation and clout and legacy in the mud, he didn't find fulfillment until he found himself submerged in her. Women before her had coveted his power, loved him because of that, wanted him because he was the king. Alani loved him because of his weakness. Without exploitation. He could strip himself of the crown he had earned as Ethic, and Alani would still love Ezra...probably more. He rested one hand on top of his head, as he slouched lazily.

"Get off my pillows, Ethic."

She hadn't picked out a single thing in this house, but she claimed it all as her own, and he let her because all that he was, every, single thing he had, was hers now.

"It's a couch, baby. It's meant to be sat on," he said. He leaned forward, because although he was talking shit, he knew better than to keep smushing them. When he turned to her, words evaded him. Alani would always be new to him. Every time she entered his space, she just enamored him. He remembered the first time she had wandered into his shop. Ethic had felt just like this, then. Like someone had carved out a canyon in the pit of his stomach. Dizzy, a bit. Speechless.

Alani was oblivious. She had no idea what she did to him. If she did, an insecure thought would never fill her pretty, little head about how much he loved her. She stood in the mirror that hung on his wall, head tilted to the side, lips parted slightly, as she put earrings in her ears. She saw him staring in the reflection.

"Ethic?" She turned to him. Black dress and stilettos. His woman. One he was still so grateful for. One that he wouldn't ever take for granted because he knew the commitment it took for her to stay. He couldn't form words.

She frowned and stepped toward him. "Baby, what?"

When she was in arm's reach, his hand looped her waist and pulled her into him. He buried his face into the crook of her neck, gripping her by the back of her head, fisting her hair, and sliding his other hand from her waist to her ass. He pulled her body into his, like he wanted to absorb her. Like they weren't even meant to be two, separate people. He inhaled the scent of her hair and Alani melted, soft hands reaching around his neck. She lived for him. This connection. Such a gentle beast of a man. God, how she loved him. God, *how* could she love him? Fuck it, how could she not?

He didn't even speak. He just kissed her cheek, pulled back, grabbing her hand to lead her out of the house. They were halfway to his car when he heard her voice behind him.

"Ethic," she said, planting her feet to get him to stop moving. He glanced back, double taking, because Alani held her silk panties up with one finger before balling them in her hand. "I mean. We can be late."

"Agh!" she screamed, in laughter, as he doubled back for her, picking her up and pressing her back against the side of the house. Cloaked in the shadows of the trees that lined his driveway, they kissed. Alani undid the buckle to his belt and then tackled the Ferragamo pants. She freed him, and her eyes closed. Such strength. A whole man in the palm of her hands. She bit her lip, as he pushed into her. Alani tensed because she expected it to hurt. Her body was healed but her heart and her mind had taken a beating. Alani was just a woman who anticipated pain. Ethic noticed, and he went still.

"Breathe," he whispered. He gave her air, lips so close to hers that she inhaled every word he spoke. He kissed her. He groaned, as he tensed into her. "Damn." He loved how it soaked for him. Every time. Anytime. She was always ready.

"Go slow," she whispered, timidly.

"I ain't got a choice, baby, this shit got a nigga weak. Fuckkk, you can't keep me out of this. Don't do a nigga like that. What I do, baby? Whatever a nigga did, I'm sorry. You know I need to feel this. Don't punish me like that," his voice was pained, as he stroked her slowly, sliding all of him into her until he hit bottom. He anchored that pussy, fucking her up the wall. Every time the base of his dick met her clit, he stroked her in circles, playing with it, letting the pressure of his body knead pleasure from her nub.

"I won't, baby, I won't," she cried out. "Unnnnnh. Ezra, wait, baby, wait."

Her cries urged him further. He gripped beneath her ass, spreading her open, fucking her deeper.

The flood light over the driveway came on and Ethic looked down at the mess he was making. She was dripping all over his designer pants and he loved the visual... His dick sliding into her wetness. Her swollen clit, peeking through her glossed lips. He had a taste for her. Watching the way her body worked was like watching a chef moving about a kitchen, preparing a dish he couldn't wait to indulge in. Ethic wanted to put his mouth on her. He wanted to run his tongue through each fold of her flesh, and then suck on her clit until his stomach ached because she was the sweetest thing he'd ever tasted.

"It's sooo hard. God, how is it this good?" she gasped.

Ethic wasn't an ego man. He didn't need his fed or boosted, but her calling his name… The way she whined it. The way her face was destroyed with ecstasy. He liked that shit. He was hitting that pussy GOOD, ass tight, fingers digging into her skin, teeth biting into his bottom lip. The most mannish grunts of pleasure escaped his throat with every stroke. "I'ma nut, baby, if you keep calling my name like that," he admitted, as he squeezed his eyes shut as her soft hands clung to his neck. He pressed his forehead to hers, slowing, damn near stopping, but Alani kept going. Legs wrapped around him like vines to an old tree, she snaked her middle. Ethic closed the space between them, because Alani was working him, and he wasn't ready to blow. He needed her to stop. Just for a second; because after the way she had put him on freeze for two weeks, he wouldn't last.

"Fuck, Lenika, you got to stop, baby."

"Daddy, nooooo," she cried.

He gripped her ass tighter, keeping her locked on his dick, pressing her into the side of the house.

"That daddy shit is gon' take me out, baby," he whispered, panting, then kissing her, swallowing her entire tongue.

"But that's who you are," she gasped, as he lifted her, sliding her on and off his dick, like he was deciding if he should keep hitting it or pull out with every stroke. "God, you're my whole damn world, boy."

Normally, Alani was his victim. When he got his hands on her, she submitted, because Ethic ran circles around her sexually. He knew ways to pull pleasure from her soul that she never even knew existed; but tonight, he was swimming in her deep and her tide was drowning him. The way he throbbed inside of her felt like someone was holding her hostage with a vibrator. He was at her mercy, as she threw it at him. It was like she couldn't get close enough. He couldn't get deep enough. They were struggling for connection, because they hadn't connected at all since her miscarriage, and he didn't know why. She wanted to fuck the worry from his mind, reassure him, because she knew he had been consumed with silent fears of her fleeing. She wasn't going anywhere. She had promised him she wouldn't, and she'd meant it. Alani wrapped her arms around his neck as he turned and placed her on her feet in front of the Tesla.

Without words, he turned her, without warning, he folded her, with wanting, he split her. Alani's dress pooled around her waist and so much ass sat on her back that Ethic couldn't help himself.

SMACK!

He made it hurt a little. Punishment. Resentment for being stingy, for not sharing. Rough hands gripped the top of her ass, as he pulled her back on it. She was so wet he couldn't even stroke yet because the head of his dick was pulsing, cum sat at the tip.

"This pussy too good," he groaned. "Ohhhhh, shit."

His dick was so thick and long that her other hole pulsed every time he slid in.

"Ethic, baby, I'm cumming," she whispered.

"Mmmmm," he appreciated. He could see it. She didn't even have to tell him. His dick coated with her love, as he kept stroking. There was no doubt in his mind that he was next. He licked his thumb and played with her ass.

"Agh! Zaddddyyyy!" she said, thighs spreading wider, pussy stretching around him like it was made to wrap his flesh.

SMACK!

He'd told her not to say that shit. He'd never liked it, never found it sexy - until now. Lenika screamed that shit like he was her ruler, like she would lay down and have a football team worth of kids for this nigga, and she would...if her body would cooperate, she would do that and more, anything he wanted, she would give. Ethic had to slow down, again, because the way her lips were kissing his dick was playing tricks with his mind. His neighbors weren't close, but he was sure they could hear what was going down. He didn't care. The music they were making, the pitches she was hitting, was symphony of love and lust. He could only keep the tip in, it was so good. He was trying to talk himself into going deeper; but damn, the way that her pussy bit back at a nigga, he wouldn't make it back out. He wanted to fall in and die because it was heaven.

"Fuck!" he shouted. Five strokes. Long. Hard. Fast. Rest. He had to go after it in rounds. Interval training with her wet ass.

SMACK!

He wouldn't be nutting this fast, if she hadn't made him wait so long.

He opened his fingers wide and moved his palm across the horizon of her behind, before gripping the other cheek as he pulled back out to the tip.

"My god, baby."

All Alani could do was moan. She was hoisted up on the hood of the car, spread wide, ass high, one hand held onto the windshield wipers, while the other reached behind her to try to control his pace.

"Ethicccccc, baby, waiittttt," she screamed.

He couldn't wait. He couldn't stop. Alani came for the third time. A quickie in the driveway had produced nothing but pleasure. Ethic had knocked out three orgasms for her, like it was nothing. Where some men were clueless about the ways to use a woman's body, Ethic was a surgeon with the dick, and he took great care of her whenever she laid her body in front of him.

"I swear to God that mu'fucka gon' be the death of me," he said, as she stood, pulling down her dress. He adjusted himself and she leaned into his strong chest, blushing, and a bit embarrassed, as he nipped at her ear before burying himself in the crook of her neck. She reached up to hug him, and the way he closed her in, wrapping his arms around her, made her want to cry.

"I'm so in love with you." She whispered it like it was a flaw. "I'll kill you, Ethic. Like, seriously, murder you dead, if you ever leave me, if you ever cheat on me, if you ever hurt me. I'ma spazz, because I'm all in. You've taken all my logic. I'm operating off raw emotion. I'm not all the way right in the head when it comes to you."

He snickered, tilting her chin and then stealing quick kisses. He was so exquisite. A beautiful couple with a deadly past.

"Yeah, well, me neither, Lenika. You've fucked me all up. I'm not leaving." Another kiss made her believe him.

"Let's go clean up and get out of here," he whispered. "I'ma shower in the guest room, cuz I'ma get that if we do it together, and then it's fuck Nyair's dinner altogether."

Alani laughed, as he grabbed her hand and pulled her into the house.

"We're so late," Alani said, as she stood on the porch to Nyair's home. The beautiful, two-story, six-bedroom home was tucked away in the affluent hills of the city of Rochester. It had taken them an hour to get there and another hour to re-dress because Ethic had lied. Using the guest bathroom didn't stop him from sliding in the shower behind her when he was done. Round 2 had been even better. Phenomenal head under the rainfall shower, and it had left Alani's body humming. Her clit throbbed right now, just thinking about it, and she discreetly placed her hand on the seat of Ethic's pants, rubbing, as she stood in front of him.

"I swear I will fuck you in Ny's bathroom. Stop playing with me," Ethic said, kissing the back of her hair and nudging his pelvis forward, pressing dick into her backside. Alani was so tickled, she turned red, as she laughed. Ethic wrapped an arm around her body and pulled her back into him.

"You gon' have to do something about that," he whispered, seducing her ear and her neck with soft, wet kisses. He was up her skirt and inside her panties before she could protest, and when the door swung open, he was back to normal, only he was licking her off his fingers.

"Ny! Hey!" Alani yelped. "Sorry we're so late."

Ethic rubbed those fingers together and then put his tainted hand in his pocket, as he extended the other one to Nyair. A gangster's embrace.

"Y'all good. We're just getting started. I've got some people here I'd like for you two to meet. Niggas with big money who came from the hood and they're willing to put money back into the hood. That gun thing you did on the block the other day. Man, we could turn that influence you got into something real special, if you with it. Get some of these kids off the street. Send 'em to college. Turn them into men. I think you have a really bright future in politics, Ethic. Flint needs someone that they respect and that they understand. You ever thought about doing more than just buying up the block? Maybe be the one to lead it?"

"I love that idea, Ethic," Alani whispered.

Ethic tensed, and Alani saw his jawline chisel.

"There's a lot of people here that I want to connect you with, G. Just get a feel for 'em. If you not with it, then I understand; but if you are, we can really get some things done in the community. You got a beautiful lady, beautiful kids. Your story is incredible. Let's really wear these crowns, G."

"Can we have a minute, Ny?" Alani asked. She could feel Ethic's discomfort. He had practically turned to stone next to her.

Nyair nodded and pinched his chin, biting his lip, as he backpedaled.

Alani turned to Ethic.

"Were you not expecting all this?" she asked.

"It's a lot," he said, swiping one hand down his wavy head. "He doesn't know what he thinks he know about me. What I've done. Who I am. I've stayed free because I've stayed low-key," Ethic whispered. "Politicians have no privacy. Every, single thing I've ever done in my past will be dug up. Everything, Lenika," he stated. His stare was saying something his lips couldn't convey and she knew instantly. Her stomach tightened. Kenzie. Any type of political aspirations would unearth the murder he regretted, perhaps even the ones he didn't. He couldn't ever allow that to happen. As much as he hated the thought of being caged like an animal, he hated the idea of anyone bringing that sin crashing back into Alani's heart even more. "This isn't how I move. All these people I don't know? I was trying to be respectful, so I didn't walk in here strapped, but I need a burner on me around all these people. I'm nobody's leader."

Alani cupped his face. "You're mine. You're *my* leader because I'ma follow you anywhere. You just have to decide where to go, and I'ma have your back, sometimes your side, sometimes your front. Your past doesn't dictate your future. Nobody knows about what you've done, but me, and I'm not telling anybody. If you want to do this, you can. If you don't, I'm okay with that too. At least stay and shake some hands. I got all dressed up and I want to stay for a while. I want to be the couple people look at and say, 'wow, they're in love'. Can we do that?"

When she spoke to Ethic, he got tunnel vision. He placed his hand on the small of her back. "Yeah, we can do that."

Ethic tucked the part he showed Alani. The part he had begun to show Nyair too and returned to the reserved and guarded man he presented to the world. Shoulders squared, eyes brooding, temple throbbing; as he gritted his teeth, he walked around the room with Alani's hand in his. She smiled and spoke to the people she knew. To his surprise, she knew a lot.

"La La!"

Ethic raised a brow, as a young woman approached them with open arms.

"Hey, Zo!" Alani returned, beaming brighter than he had ever seen her glow before.

"You look so good! I haven't seen you in forever, it feels like," the woman said. She was beautiful. Brown-skinned, dark-eyed, raven-haired, and with sharp curves that Ethic was positive were deadly.

"You're off running the world, working with the stars, leaving us little people behind," Alani answered. "Just like your brother."

"Never, La," she answered. Ethic knew they were close because she was just *La* to this girl.

"And who is this?" the girl asked, turning a flirtatious gaze on Ethic.

"Remove that look out your eyes. I beat bitches over this one right here. Even ones I love," Alani said, chuckling. "This is my..." Alani paused and looked up at Ethic. She didn't always know how to answer that question. Who was she? Where did she fit in his life? What should she call herself? "Everything," she whispered. "He's my everything." They shared a moment. A split second of acknowledgement. Yeah. He was going to fuck her real good in one of these rooms.

"Ethic, this is Nyair's sister, Zora. Zo, this is Ethic," she introduced.

"So, I can stop hoping you and Ny will eventually work things out, huh?" Zora said, jokingly, as she sipped the glass of champagne she held daintily in her hands.

Alani had one hand wrapped behind Ethic's back, and she was tucked beneath him with her other hand on his chest. She felt it turn to steel. Alani's heart sank, but she put on a concealing smile and shook her head. Ethic removed his hand from around her shoulder, as Nyair walked up with another man.

"Yo, E, let me introduce you to a friend of mine. Merci, this is Ethic. Ethic, Merci," Nyair introduced. Ethic was on fire. He burned a hole through Alani who looked up at him, eyes prickling, apology living in her stare. Ethic's nostrils flared. He may as well have been breathing fire. He ran his tongue along his jawline and pulled in a breath, before extending his hand to Merci.

"Nice to meet you, my man," he said.

"I've heard good things from Nyair," Merci stated. "Heard good things that other way too."

"I don't even really have them types of conversations with niggas I don't know," Ethic stated.

"Ethic," Alani whispered.

"Respect. There's a time and place. We got time for that. My people is your people. Zya sends her love," Merci stated.

"I don't know who that is either," Ethic stated, not even looking Merci in the eyes, as he swept a hand down his head.

Merci smirked. "Yeah, she said you'd say that too," he chuckled.

Ethic kept a straight face. He didn't know Merci and he wasn't confirming shit, but if he was connected to Zya, he was official. If he knew Ny, he was seeking an exit from the game. Ethic didn't have time to figure it out. His heart was aching. Alani was ripping the shit out of his chest with this new truth he had just uncovered; and as much as he wanted to address it, he didn't want to embarrass her. It took everything in him to grab her hand to let her know that he was still on her team. To reassure her that despite his anger he was still hers.

"Ethic, I can explain," she turned to him, standing directly in front of him, not caring that she was boxing out the rest of the small circle that had formed. She needed to take him back to their world. Ethic and Alani Land. She just needed to talk to him.

"I'm good," he said, gritting those teeth so hard she was sure he was wearing them down. His temple throbbed. His stare was cold.

"Alani?"

Alani turned and blinked away emotion, as stun froze her. She died a little inside. What the fuck had Nyair done? Assembled a party of all the people who housed her skeletons in their closet?

"Everyone, my wife, Noni," Merci said. "Noni, this is Ny, Zora, Ethic, and..."

"Alani!" Noni finished, her eyes batting quickly in surprise. "I haven't seen you in a long time. I must have called you a thousand times. Baby, this is the woman. The one who was going to let us adopt," Noni said, breathless, in disbelief. "What happened? You just disappeared on us."

Ethic released her hand.

"Umm...I..." Her voice was trembling. "I lost him." Alani couldn't breathe, and her eyes were clouds now. Clouds of emotion that she couldn't see through, and Ethic had let go of her hand. He was walking out of the room and Alani was dying. "A still birth," she whispered. "Excuse me for a second..."

She went after him. "Ethic," she called out. He didn't answer her, as he made his way through the crowd of people. "Ethic," Alani called, again, walking around servers, and in between groups of guests to catch up to him. "Ethic!" she was crying now, despite her best efforts to hold it in. It was too much to contain, however. She couldn't imagine what he was feeling. Actually, yes, she could. Betrayal. He pushed open the front door so hard that the people in the front room stopped chattering, surprised at the outburst.

"I'm sorry," she apologized, as she followed him out.

"Ethic!" She was louder now that they were outside, but still he ignored her.

He swiped both hands down his face and turned toward her, suddenly, causing Alani to back up a bit in surprise. He pointed toward the huge home.

"Go back in the house, Lenika," he said.

"Ethic, please!" she reached for him and he slapped her hands off the lapel of his jacket.

"I need a minute, Lenika."

He turned away from her and pinched the bridge of his nose, pulling in a deep breath.

"It was a long time ago," she whispered. "Ny and I are just friends."

"And you making the choice to give up my fucking kid without me even knowing he existed? What about that?" Ethic didn't yell, but his tone was lethal. Suddenly, she was grateful he wasn't carrying a weapon. "I need a minute," he said, as he shook his head.

"Fuck your minute, Ezra, I'm not going back inside without you!" she shouted.

"I've fucked up with you, Lenika. I gave you a lifetime worth of pain, so I don't have a right to be pissed off at you, but you're fucking trying me. Got me in this nigga house talking about politics and bullshit that ain't meant for me. That's for him! You got me baring my fucking soul to a nigga that you used to fuck."

"We were kids, Ethic! Nyair and I have nothing now!" she shouted. "I just caught you sending money to a bitch for a baby you pretend isn't yours! Settle that shit first, before you throw stones! Do you really think you have room to be mad about a relationship I had over ten years ago?!"

"I don't give a fuck how long ago it was. The nigga know what you fucking taste like and you got me in his face! Got me inviting that nigga to my home!" Ethic barked. "You want him? That's what this is about? The fucking church bullshit, the praying, the being a man of God? You trying to turn me into the nigga you lost?"

"Ethic, no!" she cried. "I just wanted you to give this a chance. To give God a chance. If you knew about Ny, you wouldn't have trusted him. I just wanted you to try!"

"You gon' make me light all this shit up!" Ethic stated, waving his hand at the house. "Air that nigga out over you. You playing with me. I been real easy with you, real passive, for you!" he couldn't even stop the venom he was spitting. His face went from anger to devastation.

"Then, you hid my son from me. You were gon' give him away like he wasn't a part of me. You were gon' send my boy out in the world without me," he said, taking a seat on the bottom step. "I would have murdered you, Lenika. I would have put a bullet in your head over my son. I wanted my son." Elbows to knees, he hung his head and rubbed all over it, like he couldn't grasp how he had gotten here. How had they gotten here?

It was the first time he had allowed himself to feel Love's loss since the funeral and it ached.

Alani recoiled at the harshness of his words.

"I know. I know you would have, Ethic, because that's who you are, right? A killer. That's what I was protecting myself from. That's who I'm trying to change."

"Might as well walk the fuck away then, because I'ma always be that," he said.

The door to the home opened, and Nyair eased out, with Zora peeking out the cracked door. She came out as well.

"Yo, La, you good out here?" Nyair asked.

Alani closed her eyes because she knew that a simple question of consideration would be taken out of context. *Ny, mind your business.*

"Anybody that belong to me gon' always be good, G. That's what you call yourself, right? G? I'm your G. You're my G? We all gods out here doing God's will and such," Ethic stated. "I'm real curious, Nyair. What you gon' do if she ain't good out here?" Ethic asked. He was past the point of civil.

"Ny, I'm fine, go back inside," Alani said. "Your parents are in there. We don't mean to cause a scene. We're going to go. I'm really sorry."

Nyair swaggered down the stairs.

"This ain't your business, Nyair. You keep coming down the steps and I'ma think it's a problem, homie. Nobody wants that," Ethic stated. "Cuz I only solve my problems one way."

Nyair held out his hands. "I know your heart, Ethic. You ain't gon' kill me. I'm with the fade, if that's what it comes to. I done rocked a few niggas jaws in my day, so it's whatever you want to do, G," He was calm, as he rolled up his sleeves, but challenge lived in his cocky stare. His nostrils flared, as he descended. Alani meant the world to him. He loved her. They had been everything to one another at a point in their lives; and although they weren't romantically linked anymore, he would always love her. He would always defend her.

"Nyair!" Zora shouted.

Alani watched, as her present met her past. Alani reached out for Zora's arm because she was sure her legs would give out. She had seen Nyair fight before. He had dogged out plenty niggas on the block, coming up, and had a reputation for fighting on the field. He had a temper problem that often ended in lawsuits. It was one of the things that had ended his football career. He was a beast, but she was almost certain that against Ethic, Nyair had no wins. Ethic sidestepped Nyair's punch and delivered a bone-crushing body shot to Ny, folding him, before slamming his head onto the roof of someone's car.

"You ever touch me, and I'll burn you, nigga. Send ya ass up outta here," Ethic whispered in his ear, before shoving him away.

"Ezra!" Alani shouted, as she and Zora rushed over to them. She grabbed Ethic's arm, as Zora pushed Nyair back.

"Burn me, nigga?!" Nyair shouted over Zora. "You supposed to be my brother! I been praying for you every night and you gon' shoot me? I'm trying to put you onto some new shit, but you worried about old shit! Tighten up, G! Your slip showing!" Nyair was livid. "She deserve better!"

A crowd had spilled out onto the porch and Alani was mortified.

"Son!"

Nyair spit blood from his mouth and snatched away from Zora, as he walked toward the man that had called him. Ethic stood frozen, as he watched the man wrap an arm around Nyair's shoulder and give him a pat of encouragement. The hair stood up on the back of his neck.

"Ethic, baby, let's just go. Let's go home." Alani was tugging on his arm, pleading with him, but her voice was warped. Ethic couldn't hear shit, as he took in the scene in front of him. He didn't even realize he was moving, until his fist collided into the man's jaw. The entire world around him went dark.

"Ezra!" Alani yelled.

Ethic's eyes burned into the man's in front of him, incinerating him with contempt, with resentment, with rage.

"Where the FUCK you been?!" Ethic growled, as he hemmed the man up against the wall, as if he was lifting a child. He looked into the eyes of his father. Ezra Ezekiel Okafor, Sr. He hadn't seen him in thirty years; but as soon as he'd heard the stern tone of his voice, Ethic's skin had crawled. He had come to Flint searching for his father years ago. It was what had brought him to town in the first place. Meeting Benny Atkins had been a plus...Benny had been like a substitute, an upgrade, to the biological man that had been impossible to find. The man's feet didn't even touch the floor, as Ethic choked him out. He was sick. The image of this same man, these same eyes staring down at him that day in the hospital all those years ago, played in his mind like a horror film. This man had abandoned him, abandoned his mother. The day he left might as well be inscribed on his mother's headstone, because that was the day her heart had stopped working. It was the beginning of the end of a normal childhood for Ethic. He felt hands pulling at him. He heard Alani, Nyair, and Zora screaming for him to stop. He saw the other guests spilling out of the house. A hard shove from Nyair threw him off balance, causing him to release his father, who bent over, coughing uncontrollably. Nyair punched him and Ethic quickly countered, hitting him so hard he was sure either his hand or Nyair's jaw was broken. Perhaps, both.

"Ethic, stop it!" Alani cried. She stood in front of him, both hands pressed into his chest.

"Where the fuck you been, man? You left me to die! Left my mama to die!"

He slapped Alani's hands from his body so hard that her forearms stung.

"You knew this shit?!" he asked, accusing her first, because her betrayal hurt the most. Alani's eyes held pure fear, as she braced herself. She just knew he was going to hit her. She almost felt the blow before he even made one move. He frowned, looking at her through wounded eyes, like the lens he had been viewing her through had cracked.

"You think I'ma hit you?" he asked. "That's the picture you painting of me? You in your fancy dress in front of these fancy people and that's the role you playing? Like I'ma hurt you?" He scoffed, shaking his head, as he took steps away from her. She knew him. She knew him and somewhere deep down she still feared him. Ethic's stomach hollowed. He had taken a lot of L's. He had been hit with a lot of unexpected hardships, but this one touched him differently. This one connected with the little boy inside him. His mother's face flashed in his mind and made him want to fold. His stomach ached so badly that he wanted to double over, but he didn't. He couldn't. Not in front of these people who were his clear adversaries...adversaries that had been plotting with one another against him. His sweet Alani, and Nyair, had made a fool of him.

He looked to Ny in disgust, as he backpedaled, rubbing the top of his head, as his face contorted in pain. "You knew this shit?"

"Knew what?! Ethic! Knew what?! Baby, please stop!" Alani was a mess. Snot everywhere. Tears everywhere because she could see his torment.

"Don't touch me," Ethic stated, chin quivering.

"That's my fucking father and you knew that shit," Ethic accused.

Alani looked to Nyair, stunned. She saw the revelation hit him too, and then Zora. The only person who wasn't surprised was the man she had come to know and love as Ezekiel. Big Zeke, for those whom he considered a friend.

"Ezra," Ezekiel spoke, as he staggered forward. "Son..."

"It's true?" Zora asked, shouting, in disbelief. "Daddy!"

Ethic removed the car key from his pocket, scoffing.

"Ethic, baby, let's go. I didn't know...I'm sorry I brought you here. I'm sorry I didn't tell you about me and Ny, and about Love, but I didn't know this. I didn't know about your father."

Ethic walked right by her, stopping at her side, as she reached for his hand.

"You don't want me, *La*," Ethic stated, harshly. He had never spoken to her with anything less than his whole heart, but there was no love in this tone.

"Ethic, don't do this," she whispered. She felt him pulling away.

"Fuck you, Lenika," he said, calmly. She saw him build a wall around his heart and leave her on the outside and it crushed her. He snatched his arm away from her, and then swaggered to his car. He climbed in without her and pulled off into the night.

CHAPTER 10

The view of the Canadian skyline twinkled outside the windows, as Ethic overlooked Downtown Detroit from the top floor of his favorite hotel. He had come here many times. The last time was with Alani. He had bared his soul to her in this room. The walls held secrets he would never tell anyone else. It was a bad place to come to clear his mind, because remembering what he had done to her in this room before was only torturing him more. His phone buzzed, as he sipped the cognac-filled glass in his hands. He hated to drink, but it was needed. He needed something to numb what he was feeling.

He pulled his iPhone from his pocket and Alani's face was on the screen. Her name didn't appear. The words 'God is Real' popped up. It was what he had her saved under because she was proof, and he needed the reminder. Her presence in his life was evidence that the God he was seeking forgiveness from actually existed. He declined the call.

KNOCK! KNOCK!

He turned to the door and then heard the release of the lock. He had left a key at the front desk.

YaYa floated into the room, carrying a jumbo, vintage, Chanel bag and wearing a blush pant suit that he was sure had put every woman she had encountered all day to shame. His heart skipped a beat. She lifted the large sunglasses up over her messy-on-purpose bob. The tousled waves swept off her face, as the glasses sat on top of her head like a crown. She was stunning. Flawless. Concern lived in her eyes.

She held her plane ticket up.

"Only the sound of your voice could have me catching commercial flights without notice, Ethic. Next time, send a jet," she said, blowing out a flustered breath. She dropped the ticket on the stand next to the door and let her purse hit the floor, as she walked over to him. He received her with appreciation, wrapping strong arms around her, as she rushed into his embrace.

She pulled back and then stood on her tip-toes to kiss his lips. Ethic turned his head.

"You're not here for that," he stated.

"Then, what the hell am I here for?" she asked, attitude surfacing, brow bending in confusion.

"Ya, I need you to stop playing with me and let me know what's real. You causing a lot of trouble for me," Ethic stated.

"I am trouble for you," she said, smiling devilishly.

"That, you fucking are," he agreed, rubbing one hand through his beard, as he massaged the side of his face. "I got into a fucking screaming match with someone I love today, and she mentioned you. Alani mentioned the fact that I have a kid out here. One that I'm not involved with. One who doesn't know me. We screamed so many things at one another tonight and that shit is sticking with me. It's all fucking with me, but that one thing is digging into me, YaYa. I need to know the truth."

YaYa's long lashes lifted, as her eyes widened in shock. She took a step back.

"We can play a game. Truth or dare. If you win, I'll take the DNA test. If I win, I leave, and you take my word for it. You trust me, like you would have before you met this damn girl," YaYa stated.

"You know I'm not the game playing type, Disaya," he answered.

"And you know I'm not the explaining type. Especially, since I know you're here because another bitch wants the answers," YaYa stated, brow raised in challenge.

"Watch ya mouth," he said, temper flaring slightly.

"How about you watch it for me? You like to watch it, when I wrap it around your…"

"Disaya…" he interrupted.

"The game, then?" she proposed. "Truth or dare."

"Truth," he answered, leaning against the door, one foot propped up against the wall, as he stared down at her. She was so damn striking. He knew she knew it. His type. She was a made woman, but Ethic hadn't made her. She had bossed up before him. Ethic had crowned her, though. He had upgraded those jewels in her crown and they were flawless now. YaYa was exactly his type; and somehow, they hadn't ended up together. The universe had a way of mixing things up like that, and for a long time, he had questioned why she had evaded him. It wasn't until he met Alani that he realized there was a reason for everything. He couldn't keep YaYa if he wanted to have Alani. Alani was a win. She was a win that made up for all the losses, and suddenly, his taste had changed and what used to be his type no longer was.

"Is it true that you want to fuck me right now?" she asked.

Ethic snickered and shook his head. "Fucking trouble," he muttered.

"Is it true that the question made your dick hard?" she pressed. YaYa stood and walked over to him, reaching down until she felt like thanking God. He had that type of dick. The kind you appreciated. The kind that felt like a blessing.

"Ethic, let's just do what we do best. We love one another. We make love to one another. When we can, we do. We never miss the chance to. Why start now? I know you want to," YaYa whispered.

"You know I can't," he whispered.

"I don't know that at all. I know what you can do. I know what you have done. Nobody makes me feel what you do. I don't ever ask for anything. I'm asking for this because I need it, because I need you," YaYa whispered, as she stroked him.

Ethic's anger toward Alani was what allowed YaYa to do this much. He knew he was riding a fine line, maybe even crossing it. The way Alani had crossed it when she had him taking advice from a man she had fucked. The secrets Alani kept were tearing him up inside. Testing him, making him feel like he didn't know her at all. YaYa was temptation. YaYa was someone who had never lied to him. Who wouldn't lie to him. Even when he didn't like her truth, she still laid her cards on the table for him. She allowed him to decide if he wanted to put up with her bullshit or not. She didn't try to cover it up. He respected her for that. It was the reason why he never second-guessed if her son belonged to him or not.

"I can't keep dipping in that like it's mine, YaYa," Ethic stated.

YaYa pulled back a bit to look him in his eyes. She was risking everything and didn't even care. She would put it all on the Pass Line for him. Every roll, anteing up on that seven or eleven for Mr. Okafor, parlaying the bet until she crapped out.

"It's been yours since our very first time," YaYa whispered.

"Yeah, well, a lot of shit has changed," Ethic answered.

"What did she do?" YaYa whispered. "Last time you were hollering how she was the one. There's a reason you called me."

"My son," Ethic groaned. "Ya, your hands. I'ma need you to stop doing what you doing."

YaYa stroked him through the fabric of his pants, rubbing, grabbing, gripping, as he grew for her.

"He's not your son, Ethic. Why else did you call?" she asked. "She must have messed up. How bad? Cuz I got ways to fix whatever's broken, Ethic. I can hop on her head or hop on this dick. Choice is yours. Which way would you like me to play it?"

Everything about YaYa was seductive. She was turned on, always turned on for him; but since Alani was now center stage, YaYa was willing to remind Ethic why she should be the one, even if he could only be number two in her life. From the tone of her voice, down to the scent of her perfume. She was screaming to be fucked but Ethic wasn't a man whose loyalty was flexible. When he was with someone, he endured all things. YaYa was a beautiful woman, and he was a man who appreciated beautiful things, so his body was betraying him, but his mind was stuck at Nyair's house. He could practically recite the argument with Alani word for word. It was on a loop in his head. He lifted a finger under YaYa's chin. Those sparkling pools of emerald that she called eyes pleaded with him. YaYa was so damn beautiful. If Alani had been any other woman, Ethic wouldn't take pause, because he didn't really want to press stop. He wanted to bury himself in YaYa because he knew she gave enough pleasure to stop the pain he was feeling. Alani wasn't any other woman, however. She was the one woman he had searched for. She was the one that had taken years to find and months to convince that he was worthy of forgiveness. Yes, she had fucked up, but he couldn't afford anymore fuck ups when it came to her. So, YaYa wasn't worth it. One more night with Disaya wasn't worth the lifetime he would be giving up with Alani. The exchange wasn't worth the loss that would result. YaYa was near his ear now, hands unbuckling his Hermes belt, as her soft lips kissed his neck.

"I miss you, Ethic. I'm so in love with you," she whispered.

"Hey." YaYa pulled back, as her eyes met his. "Hands off. Last time I'ma say it."

YaYa rolled her eyes and removed her hands because he wasn't asking. He was serious. He adjusted his clothes, gripping his dick, because YaYa had put him in a mood that only pussy would relieve him of, but it couldn't be her. He wouldn't do that. A man who had no restraint was a boy, and Ethic hadn't been boyish in many years.

"I shouldn't have called you. Fuck am I doing?" he asked, rhetorically. "You shouldn't even be here. I'm fucking up right now." He bypassed her and took a seat on the bed. Just months ago, he and Alani had been in this very suite, making love on this same bed.

"You really love this girl, don't you?" she asked.

"I fucking do," he answered. He shook his head because life would be so much simpler if he just let Alani go. If... he had the willpower to stay away from her. If they just admitted that the problems between them were big enough to crush them. He couldn't. He didn't care if she hated him for the rest of his life, as long as she stayed...as long as she blessed him every once in a while... with that smile. As long as she sprinkled a bit of love in there to interrupt the bad times. One good day with Alani was worth all the bad ones because her love was magnificent. It outshined all the animosity. It made him whole and he was risking it all just by being in YaYa's vicinity.

"I don't like this at all," YaYa answered, stubbornly, as she retreated to the couch.

Ethic scoffed, "I know."

His stress was evident. It wore him down, weighing, pressing and YaYa could see it forcing his elbows to his knees and his head to hang in despair. Ethic's strong hands moved in a circle over his head.

"You want to tell me what all this is about?" YaYa asked.

"She lied to me, Ya," Ethic stated. He knew Alani wasn't a liar at heart. He knew what it was like to hold information for the sake of someone else's emotions. He had done it to her when he allowed her to love him without divulging his role in her daughter's death. He was still doing it to this very day with Morgan. He hadn't told her that he was responsible for Raven's death either. The information would kill Mo. He knew the revelation would kill Alani. The truth. The painful secrets that were vaulted inside him were never hidden in malice. He just wanted to love and cherish the people in his life. He silenced himself to protect the ones around him. He had been right about Alani's fragility. He hadn't thought she'd be able to handle the truth and he had been right. Mo couldn't handle the truths he hid either. He knew this. So, he omitted. He was guilty of the exact same crime he was punishing Alani for. Her omission of truth, and he was angry at her for it. He knew it was a double standard, but it was an emotion he couldn't hide.

"Ethic, you killed that girl's baby," YaYa said, bluntly.

Ethic's head snapped up, eyes burning her, forehead wrinkled, shoulders locked.

"Negro, don't look at me like that. You called me here. I made up a whole lie just to come see you and I ain't getting no dick. I'm on her side. You killed her kid and she's still with you, still loving on Eazy and Bella like she birthed them. You better get the hell over whatever lie it is that she told. She could tell a thousand lies and you would have to eat every single one," YaYa stated. "You did the ultimate, Ethic…the ultimate hurt. If she stays, she's going to give a little back to you over the years. You don't call up the next bitch just because she hurt you a little bit. You niggas are so damn finicky and hypocritical. You want her to accept the worst. Well, can you accept her worst? She tells one lie and you on the phone calling me."

Ethic groaned because he knew she was right.

"What did she lie about?" YaYa asked.

Ethic couldn't tell YaYa about his past. Recanting it once to Alani had been hard enough. His lips wouldn't even move to begin to recall it again. Instead, he gave her half the story.

"She was pregnant. We're supposed to have a son. She lost him, but before that, she was going to give him up. She was going to give my son up for adoption, without telling me," Ethic whispered. "Then, she throws you in my face. The fucking letter you sent. The once a year thing. The pictures. She pulled the shit out the mailbox, Ya, and it's fucking with her. She thinks he's mine. So, I just need to know, if he's mine. I can't have a kid out here and not be involved. I can't let another nigga raise him, and I can't not know."

"Well, I'm not taking another test for her. I told you, I took care of it. Paternity has been established and he's not yours. If my word isn't good enough for her…"

"For me, Ya. Your word isn't good enough for me," Ethic stated. "So, cut the bullshit. Is he mine? I need papers, Disaya. Or I'ma come straight to the source about mine." Ethic thought about all the years he needed his father. All the things that might have turned out differently if his dad had just been around, not even for his mother, but for him. If he had just shown up. No way could Ethic repeat that cycle. He couldn't continue with the uncertainty. He didn't know what would happen if the baby was his. Alani would probably leave, and he wouldn't blame her, but his children were his children. If there was one out there that belonged to him, he wanted to be there.

"So, you're going to blowup my household because *she* has doubts in me. Do you? Have you ever? Have I ever given you a reason to doubt me?" she asked.

YaYa was pissed. He could hear it in her tone. He was stuck between knowing a concrete truth or believing the one YaYa created for him. A convenient one that allowed them to live separate lives but have an excuse to keep in touch.

"I get that you've found someone, Ethic. I get that you love her, but you know me. You know, right? You know why I can't answer these questions and the man I know wouldn't make me. It's not fair for you to have her and leave me with nothing, Ethic. If he's yours, are you going to forget her? Are you going to leave her and be mine?"

"When I offered you that, you didn't want that. You're selfish, Ya. You only want it now because she has it."

"I've never not wanted you. You sent me back to him!" YaYa shouted.

"I ain't see you putting up no protests either," Ethic said.

"I just couldn't leave him. I would have, if you had pushed a little harder, but you didn't and so I went back to familiar. I just can't leave him. It's not easy. I can't explain why, I just love him. Doesn't mean I don't love you. You might have to answer to her, but I don't. Tell that bitch to mind her business."

Ethic stood and crossed the room in frustration, yoking YaYa up from the couch. Her face was in the U of his hand, as he pushed her against the wall. "Is he my fucking son?" he asked, a chastising finger pointing in her face. He was right on top of her, so close that she tasted the liquor on his breath.

"Get your hands off me, Ethic, because this angry shit makes me wet," YaYa whispered. He was such a grown-ass man and YaYa knew better than to play with grown-ass men, but she loved this frustration, this rage, this reaction. Her entire body was on fire by the rough way he handled her. She would throw pussy at this man for the rest of her life. Ho shit. Ethic had her on some hoe shit and she didn't even care. The husband and two kids at home didn't even matter, when she was in his presence. "The bitch wants you to have a baby with me so bad. She better take this favor I'm extending. I said, he's not yours. She better stop digging before I fuck you, again, and give her a stepchild that will ruin her life. She loves Eazy and B, because they don't come attached to anyone else. How do you think she's going to feel with me around? You think she's going to stay through that? I don't think so, because pretty, plain Jane was shook when I came through for Eazy's birthday. I'ma be like a noose around that bitch neck over mine, so she might want to think twice before she asks you to ask me this again. He's not yours. Next time you call me, let it be because *you're* summoning me. I'm here anytime you need me because I for damn sure need you, but don't call me because your new queen is insecure. I'm not particularly interested in making her feel better. Simple-ass bitch."

YaYa pushed Ethic off her and then grabbed her twenty-thousand-dollar handbag and walked towards the door, as Ethic stood, watching her leave. She opened it.

"Disaya," he stated.

YaYa paused, turning to him.

"What, Ethic?" She was angry, her ego a little bruised. She hated how much he loved Alani.

"The checks…" he said.

"I know," YaYa answered. "She wants you to put a stop to them. It's exactly what I would do if I was in her shoes. The thing is, you're not sending them for fun, Ethic. You're sending them as insurance. Just in case. You take care of the people who belong to you and you know that I do, and you know why. I don't care if she signs the checks or if you do, but I expect them once a month. In fact… You can double them. Tell sis I said nice move but checkmate."

Ethic was all over her ass, pulling the door closed and pressing her into it. His level of frustration could be exhausted one of two ways. To kill somebody or fuck somebody.

"You're everything to me," YaYa whispered, as she clasped his hands that were around her neck. She knew he wanted to choke her, he wanted to kill her. Her slick mouth, her ultimatums, her disrespect for the woman he loved. She knew, but he wouldn't. He couldn't, because just because he had found someone new, it didn't unbind the ways she had tied his soul.

"Don't do that. With the disrespect. Not with the letters, not with the sideways comments, none of that. You keep it respectful when it comes to her. The money will be put in an account. No one will touch it. When you're ready to give me a test to show that he's mine, everything in that account will be yours. A separate account for him will be set up that he alone can access at eighteen, for college, regardless if he's mine or not. Until you're ready to clear the smoke you're causing, this got to be it, Ya. I'm done. I can't keep her and keep you."

"And you're choosing her?"

"If I was a better man, I would let her go," Ethic stated, releasing her. "But I'm selfish, and what she's given me…" Ethic paused, shaking his head, as he turned from YaYa. "Yeah, this between us is a wrap. In every way. Unless you can tell me a reason why it shouldn't be. When you're ready to take the test, you holla at me, but us, this," he said, pointing between them, and then rubbing the top of his head in distress. "It's over. I'm choosing her, YaYa."

She recoiled, and he knew why. She gasped, like he had struck her, and he understood because it felt like a blow. His stomach hollowed at the thought of never seeing her again.

Of the letters stopping. The random texts, the phone calls. He did love Disaya. There was a time in his life where he thought she was the one, but that time had passed. She had been a season in his journey. Like summer. She had come to thaw his cold heart so that he could love again. She wasn't supposed to stay forever.

"I'm so angry with you," she whispered.

"I know," he said. "But let's be real, Ya. You're not really a woman that men get to keep. Once you get what serves you, you seek something else. It's in you. The chase. The constant need for more. What do you call it?"

"My Prada plan," she whispered. "It's a fucked-up way to be. I wish I could be different for you. I wanted to be. I would have tried for you, but you sent me back to him..."

"You were going back anyway, Disaya. Maybe not that day, but one day you would have gone back to the nigga who raised you. Timing has always been our problem," he said. "And now I've met..."

"Your healing," YaYa finished. She stepped to Ethic and placed a hand on the side of his face, the imperfect side, her absolute favorite side. She kissed his scars and he felt the wetness from her tears. "Goodbye, Ethic."

YaYa walked out, leaving Ethic even more confused than before she had arrived. Her presence flustered him, left him discombobulated. YaYa was like good dope. She kept a nigga coming back for more. Just a small hit of her, even something as brief as the moment they had just shared, left him reeling. The answers he sought were evasive and YaYa had left devastation in her wake. She always left him craving her presence, wondering what could have been between them. With Alani showing him colors in her that he didn't know existed, a part of him wondered if they would make it at all, or if he was simply wasting his time, holding onto a love that could never truly grow.

CHAPTER 11

The standoff that Alani was engaged in was torture. Her versus the clock. The red numbers ticked away, taunting her, torturing her, because hours had passed, and Ethic wasn't home. She tried sleeping. She willed herself to close her eyes and just deal with the argument in the morning. Surely, he would be home by then. Surely, he hadn't meant what he had said. The more time passed, the more foolish she felt. The sun slipped through the blinds and Alani's heart ached. Dawn was unacceptable. Sunrise was disrespectful.

Where is he?

Her devastation from last night's events were transforming. She had felt sadness, initially. The look on Ethic's face had cut her deeply, making her want to remove all that ailed him. Guilt accompanied that. For keeping things from the man she loved... but Ethic's absence was turning it into anger mixed with nausea. She was sick. Her mind raced. She knew he wasn't the type of man to cheat, but where else could he be, then with another woman?

He knew the kids were at Nannie's. *He had to know I would come home. He has to know I'm waiting. He's making me wait on purpose. I'm on his time. Passive-*

aggressive-ass, Alani thought. The home had never seemed so big until this very moment. No laughter filled the halls. No sound of Eazy's running feet or Bella's voice bouncing off the walls. She even missed the sound of slamming doors from Morgan. Alani wanted to call Morgan, to see how she was doing, but she knew it would seem fake, like she was looking for Ethic, so she didn't. She reached for her phone, hoping there was a missed call awaiting her. There was nothing.

Motherfucking Ezra!

How could he go this many hours without talking to her, after finding out something so devastating? How could he make her worry? He had to feel her pain. No matter where he was, she knew he felt it because she felt his…it was pulling at her, destroying every bit of peace she had inside. No way could he not feel this energy they shared. He was cutting her off on purpose, depriving her of him because he knew that it would hurt her to not know where he was. Her heart was stitched in agony. Every, little thread he had used to sew it up, as he pieced it back together, was being unraveled. She knew he wasn't the same as men in her past. He wouldn't cheat just because he was mad. He wouldn't lie. He was just taking some time, cooling off. That's what Alani told herself, but those insecurities she had buried were surfacing, driving her crazy. Alani was in the wrong. She knew she was to blame for the night's events, but it didn't stop her from wanting to fuck him up. Every damn second that ticked by had her ready to tear shit up.

Alani kicked off the covers. She was going crazy, thinking of what he must be assuming of her. At the time she had been making the decisions about adoption for their unborn child, it had felt like the right thing to consider. Even her choice to refrain from telling him about Nyair had felt worth the risk. She wasn't interested in Nyair anymore. They had sustained a friendship for years after dating, so the precursor didn't seem necessary to divulge. She hadn't known they would become close outside of the counseling sessions. By the time she felt the need to tell Ethic about Nyair, she didn't quite know how. She knew that Nyair would never volunteer the information.

Zora's big mouth. God, Zo is his sister. Nyair is his brother. How the hell did this happen? I don' been dicked down by brotherrrrsss. Ho shit. I'ma goddamn hoe by default.

Alani had no idea where he could be. That hurt settled in her soul different, when Ethic was unaccounted for. He was dangerous when he was in this state of mind, but she knew he wouldn't fly off the handle because the only person he could punish for this was her. Alani hated fighting with him. They had spent so much of their relationship at odds. This didn't feel good. Going back to animosity was unbearable. Alani wondered where he could be. He wasn't the type of man to keep friends, so he wasn't blowing off steam with the fellas or making it rain on dancers at a strip joint. He wasn't a typical man, so he wasn't doing typical 'mad nigga' shit. Her mind traveled back to the ball, back to the suite he had taken her to when he had sought respite, when he needed peace to allow himself to feel something…when he had allowed himself to let her all the way in. He had gone there, without thinking twice, without making a reservation. Ethic was a man of habit.

Maybe he's there. Maybe he just needed a little space to clear his mind. Alani opened the browser on her phone and typed in the name of the hotel. She was calling before she could stop herself. If he was there, she knew she would seem crazy for tracking him down, but at this point she didn't care. She just needed to be near him. She needed a little relief from what her mind was speculating.

The phone rang in her ear and she held her breath.

"Thank you for calling the Marriott at the Renaissance Center. How can I direct your call?"

Alani cleared the lump from her throat, as she responded, "Could you connect me to Ezra Okafor's room please?"

"Sure, one second."

Her heart thundered in her chest. It beat so hard that she could hear it. It felt like she was having a heart attack.

Why the fuck is he at a hotel? Who is he there with? Why isn't he answering the phone? God, he's with someone. Please, don't let him be with someone.

Alani hung up the phone and hopped up. She threw on a t-shirt and jeans, stepping into Converse sneakers and tossing on a Nike hat, before rushing out. She was so afraid of what she might find that she was trembling. Nannie had always told her not to go looking for trouble, but she couldn't help it. Ethic wasn't home. He had stayed out all night and wasn't answering her calls. She knew where he was. She had to go see for herself. She had to find out what had kept him out all night.

Alani drove the hour distance with a heavy heart, parking valet, before rushing into the lobby. She had learned a long time ago to just act like she belonged. Pretending like she was a guest at the hotel and was entitled access to his suite would surely get her a key. She knew he was in the penthouse. It was just his way of living. She waltzed over to the desk.

"Hi. My husband left a key for me at the front desk. He's already checked into the penthouse. His name is Ezra Okafor," Alani said.

"Oh, I'm sorry, I thought the key was already picked up. Of course, I can get that for you right away," the man behind the desk said.

Alani felt like someone had hands wrapped around her neck. *Who picked up a key?*

Alani took the key and rushed to the elevator. The entire way to the top, she had to force her tears down. She knew what she was about to find. She felt it in her gut that she was rushing toward heartbreak. She almost turned back but Alani was a glutton for punishment. If he was with a woman, she needed to see it with her own eyes. She needed to feel the cut, the burn, the excruciation of betrayal, so that she could stay away from him. She closed her eyes, as she placed the key card in the door.

The suite was dark and silent, but there was a light under the closed bathroom door and the sound of the shower running. She looked at the crumpled sheets on the bed, but before she could take one step toward the bathroom, the water stopped. Alani froze. She braced herself, because if Ethic stepped out of that bathroom with another woman, she was going to kill him. She was going to kill him and then kill whatever mystery tramp he had sought comfort in. Her chest tightened and then he slid the barnyard-style door to the right.

He froze when he saw her. Alani's chin quivered at the sight of him. He was naked, baring all. A delicious, chocolate man with a body so disciplined he didn't look real. He wasn't too strong. No body builder physique on this god of a man, but lean and solid, every, single inch of him was defined and Alani lost air just looking at him. He made no move to cover up. A king, walking through the suite, drying his body, like he was born to stomp around the earth naked. His dick was so heavy, it slapped his strong thighs as he walked.

"What you doing here?" he asked. He didn't even need to ask how she'd found him. He knew she had some crazy in her. Normally, he liked it. Today, he just wanted time apart, a few more hours of distance because he had never been so pissed with her and he didn't want to take it out on her the wrong way. He knew he'd gone a bit too far the night before. He had spoken words with the intent to hurt her and that wasn't his style. It wasn't who he was as a man, but more damaging words were at the tip of his tongue. So angry. She was the love of his life and he was livid with her. Alani went into her handbag and removed the shea butter she kept inside. She wasn't sure why her hands were shaking and her heart was racing. She dipped one finger into the homemade concoction and avoided his gaze, as she rubbed her hands together, before placing a delicate touch to his chest. The butter melted over his skin, but he didn't move. He looked down at her. Hawking her. Alani was so intimidated under his scrutiny. She dipped her finger in the small canister, again, and rubbed her hands together first and then over his abs.

"You didn't come home," she whispered, her voice breaking because she was so insecure, so nervous, about the way this conversation would go.

Shea. Rub. Ethic.

Still, he said nothing, as her fingers pirouetted across his dark skin. Alani was moisturizing him like his skin was a fine leather that needed conditioning. Her dainty hands didn't miss a spot. "Tonight, I saw you broken, Ezra," she whispered. "I never want you to think I'd ever contribute to breaking you. You're my king."

The V cuts in his groin were next, and still he didn't respond. Not with words. His dick jumped, as she moved to his sturdy thighs.

"I waited up for you," she gasped, as she lowered to her knees, as her fingers dipped into the canister again.

Shea. Rub. Ethic.

Alani grabbed his dick and he groaned when she took the tip of him between her lips. Her hands worked him over, like she was grinding pepper. She sucked him in, inch by inch.

Ethic grew, thick and long. Alani was mesmerized by every inch of him. His body, his mind, his heart. He was so damn regal, as he reached down, cupping her face. She had a mouthful of him, as she lifted sorrow-filled eyes to his. Their stare connected for a beat and then she fluttered those long lashes down, focuses on his strength. She needed to milk him. Wanted to swallow his power, so that she could be strong like him, so she could be royal like him, because Ethic was a king. Her king, and he felt betrayed by her. The fact that he was angry at her for something she would never do caused her great injury. He weakened a bit, she felt his stance compromise, as she focused on his lifeline, the vein on the underbelly of his length. The vein that snaked up those glorious inches, like the Nile river snaked through Africa. Alani dipped her finger in the jar, again.

Shea. Rub. Ethic.

"Fuck," he groaned.

She was doing her job. Rubbing oil into him, taking care of the place he held her future babies, massaging first with her hands and then allowing her tongue to follow, before pulling back to taste the pre-cum he was forming. His knees went weak and he reached for the couch with one hand and wrapped four fingers of the other hand around the back of her neck. He damn near took her head off when he tensed into her mouth, but Alani relaxed her throat, as he pumped into her again.

"Mmmm," she moaned. She felt him pulsing. Then, she got her reward. His orgasm. His seeds. The taste of him on her tongue. She closed her eyes, savoring it on her palette like he was a delicacy. He had earned this head. A night full of secrecy and hurt had destroyed him. A little head was needed. It was necessary. She knew she wasn't shit for keeping such monumental details from him, and she was on her knees with the apology because her pride wasn't too great not to build him back up after tearing him down.

"Lenika, damn," he whispered. She planted a kiss on the tip of him, before rolling back on her legs, sitting, as he retreated to the edge of the couch, legs wide, elbows to knees, dick limp. His head was bowed, as he scratched circles all over his scalp.

She came up on her knees in front of him, placing one hand on top of his head, and then running it down the back of his neck. He lifted his head and Alani saw brokenness in him. It was like his eyes were a shattered mirror. He was fragmented, and she had contributed to it.

"I don't like sleeping without you." Alani's voice was tiny. "I can't sleep without you, at this point. It's like I don't even know how. My body doesn't rest when you're not beside me."

Her hands were so gentle on the side of his face. He was so mad with her. She knew it. She felt it. He had no response, so he offered none. "I was worried. Afraid." He pulled back and his body steeled.

"Yeah, cuz you're afraid of me, right? You flinched last night. Like I would lay hands on you. Like I've been hurting you? Fuck you here for now? If you that scared, we don't need to do this at all. I'm not that man and I won't let you paint me as that man," he said.

He was still furious, but even more so - insulted. He'd seen men break women one too many times. Seen bruises on delicate skin, black rings around the prettiest eyes. He watered two graves behind bitch-ass niggas who had abused women he cared for. Raven Atkins was a victim. He could never be a perpetrator of that. Not even Alani had him wrapped around her finger tight enough to let people think he was abusive.

"I didn't mean to make it seem like that, Ethic. You were just..." she paused. "So angry. You went dark, like someone had turned off your heart. I don't think that you'd hurt me. I know you would never..." She stopped speaking and closed her eyes because she didn't want to cry. Didn't want to turn herself into the victim, when she knew it was him who needed the rescuing this time. "I'm so sorry for lying to you," she said. "I should have told you about Nyair and I should have been honest about what I planned to do once Love was born. I'm sorry, Ezra."

Ethic walked over to the closet and pulled out the bag of dry cleaning. The hotel had cleaned and pressed yesterday's outfit. He wished it was as easy to re-do the entire day. Wash it and iron it out, start over and try it again...just like the clothes. Time didn't work that way, however. He was silent, and it ate Alani up inside.

"Please, say something."

"You don't want me to speak right now, Lenika," he stated. "I didn't come home because I didn't want to say some shit to you I can't take back."

"I couldn't sleep, Ethic. All night. I tossed and turned. I spent months away from you. I don't want to spend nights apart. I don't care if we fight. I don't care if it gets bad, but you're supposed to be with me, fighting for us *with* me, next to me. You told me to pick a room and be mad in it. Practically, held me hostage in the house, so I wouldn't leave, but you just left. I can't be the only one fighting. I lied to you.

I was wrong, but we stay. We aren't kids. We don't leave, Ezra. You don't leave me."

Ethic began to dress, sliding into boxer briefs, and then yesterday's clothes.

"A nigga get tired of fighting," he said. "I been fighting, and you been lying."

Alani was crushed. "I don't know what that means." Tears clung to her lashes.

"It means give me some space, Lenika, damn!"

Yeah. He was in a mood. He was big mad. Alani had fucked up.

"I'm not leaving. I'll be home. I'll be at your house because it's mine now too. It's our house, Ethic, and I'll be there. In *our* bed. With *our* kids. Waiting to work it out. I'm waiting for you, Ethic," she whispered. "When you're ready to talk."

Alani turned and stopped at the door. She didn't want to pull it open. She didn't want to walk out of this room without him, but he was still so furious, so brooding.

"I didn't know about your father. I wouldn't ever keep something like that from you."

"Oh, there's a limit to the lies? Lying about having my kid and giving him away to strangers is equivalent, no?" Ethic asked.

Alani took it. She took the verbal blows and pulled open the door. Her eyes fell onto the plane ticket on the stand by the door. Her blood froze in her veins. The entire room spun, as she picked up the piece of paper.

"Lying about canceling bitches with green eyes and having babies you don't acknowledge. Equivalent, no?" Alani wasn't strong enough to yell the words, so she whispered them. Her tears fell, silently, as two invisible forces brutally ripped at the curves of her heart, stretching, tearing, pulling it apart...she was in pieces. Ethic looked at the plane ticket in her hands and his stomach hollowed.

"It ain't that, Lenika. Whatever you're thinking," he stated. Just that fast the ball had been stolen. It was back in her court, and if he knew Alani well enough, he knew she was going to slam dunk that bitch. "She..."

"Doesn't even matter, Ethic. I'm a liar. You're a fucking liar." She shook her head, as he crossed the room. She caught the lone sob that exposed her hurt. She was choking on it, as he took her face in his hands. "We did it. We almost healed one another," she whispered, tears falling. She was drowning. It felt like the night at the debutante pageant. Like he was about to drop her into the sea of emotions that killed her every time. "It felt like..."

"It's not what you think. She was here for..."

"I don't give a fuck why she was here. She shouldn't have been here at all. In your suite, in the middle of the night." She hit his chest with balled fists and gripped the collar of his shirt, resting her forehead on his chest.

"You gon' let me talk or you want to keep assuming?" Ethic asked. He was so damn arrogant. Alani scoffed and let go of him. She stared up at his face. He was so damn fine, so charming, so gangster, and official, but in this moment, he seemed so typical. "I don't want to hear shit. She can have you, Ethic." She tossed the crumpled plane ticket at his face, before storming out.

Ethic was on her ass before the door could close behind her. He pulled the security bar out so that he didn't lock himself out of the room and then stormed after her. She was pressing the elevator call button repeatedly, praying that the doors opened. He grabbed her arm, spinning her toward him, and then he trapped her body against the wall in the hallway.

"That's not what we're doing. Don't ever threaten my life, Lenika." His forehead was pressed to hers, her face was squished between the tight grasp of his hand, as he held it hostage in one hand.

"I didn't threaten your life. I threatened my presence in your life," she said.

"Same fucking thing," he barked at her. "It's the same thing. You're life. You make the shit worth it. The pain. You make it make sense. I had to feel that to love you right. So, don't threaten my life. Don't ever fucking come out your mouth with that shit," he said. He was so passionate, she almost believed him. She was falling apart under his grasp. His words were agonizing, like a plea, like he was begging. Like he was on death row appealing for clemency. Vulnerable. Ethic was strong with everyone else, but with this woman, this one enigma of a woman, he was weak. He didn't know why they couldn't get it together. They tried so hard. Gave so much effort. There was always something, always a factor, threatening to destroy them. He loved her. He didn't particularly like her, in this moment, but he couldn't deny that he loved the fuck out of Alani.

He buried his face in her neck and Alani lifted eyes to the ceiling.

"I can't do this, Ethic. I don't want to anymore. You called her here, didn't you?"

His silence was confirmation and Alani's legs weakened. "Why would you call her? Of all people? Her!?" Alani melted right in his arms. It shocked him how affected she was. How badly it hurt her... She clung to him, as she sobbed.

"I had questions. I just needed answers about her son... about the little boy you think is my son," Ethic stated.

"And you called her, after we fought? You called her and put her on a flight, after saying fuck me. She jumped for you. So you could talk about your son? Or so you could fuck her to spite me?"

"If I wanted to fuck her, I'd just do it," Ethic spat. "I wouldn't need to use an argument with you as an excuse."

Alani's neck jerked back, in stun.

"Wow," she whispered. "I hope whatever you did with her was worth it." She turned, and he grabbed her arm.

"Don't touch me. Go touch her. Go be her man. Go play daddy to a son that may not even be yours. Or is he yours? Just tell me what I'm up against!" she asked.

"Lenika, it's complicated. She says no. Says she's not taking a test. Nothing happened. That's my word. On Love..."

"Don't put that bullshit on my baby's name! Don't put him and that bitch in the same sentence ever," Alani said, pointing a warning finger at him.

"Nothing fucking happened," Ethic stated.

Alani scoffed, shaking her head in disgust. "So much happened. You fucked your baby mama tonight. I fucked Nyair *real* good ten years ago. How I'm the one being villainized is fucking astounding."

Ethic's nostrils flared. He flicked the tip of her nose, causing Alani to jump in surprise, as he chastised her. Her entire face throbbed, as her eyes watered from the light blow. *Did this nigga just thump me?!*

"You fucking trying me, Lenika. All night you been trying me. Stop while you're ahead, before I dig that nigga grave," he stated. "Don't bait me. I'm soft with you. I'm the realest nigga living to everybody else. I will murder your little boyfriend."

"Fuck you, Ethic," Alani shouted.

"Exactly that. Do that. Sit on this dick, instead of talking shit," Ethic answered. "Your ass ain't gon' do shit but cry and then come back home. Stop fucking playing with me. No more playing. No more games, because every time I let you slide, you risk another nigga life."

Alani's clit pulsed. The warning had been issued. She was playing with a king. Goddddd she loved this nigga. She would fight with him every damn day just to fucking make up. That gangster shit. That mean shit. Even the flick to her nose made her panties wet. Still. He had trespassed. She would never call another man after fighting with him. She would never seek comfort with someone else. No one else could even supply comfort to her. Ethic had crossed a line and it was teetering on disrespect. That, she didn't tolerate.

"We might as well wrap this up, Ezra. We're pretending. You have a-whole-nother bitch that jumps when you say come. I have a problem with that. I was gonna give Love away and not tell you. You have a problem with that. You found your father and then you ran to another woman. You found solace in another woman when it should have been me. I'm done. I'm out. You have me in a rat race with this bitch. It's a competition and I forfeit. I'm not competing for a man. You have me so fucked up. I quit. She wins," she yelled. She pushed him off and the elevator doors opened. Ethic looked at her, in despair, as they closed. He didn't know what lie in store for them. He was so angry at her that he was almost glad that she'd discovered the plane ticket. She'd hurt him, and he'd given a little back to her. It shouldn't have felt like fair play, but it did, and that fact scared Ethic. He loved her, but maybe they were forcing this. Maybe, just maybe, they wouldn't make it after all.

CHAPTER 12

"D addy, where is Alani?" Eazy asked.

Ethic steeled, pausing, as he tucked the .9mm pistol in the back holster he wore beneath the black with white stripes, old-school, Adidas track suit.

"She's at Nannie's, Big Man," Ethic answered. He sported three diamond chains on his neck, a Rolex on his wrist and matching sneakers fresh out the box.

"But she's been there every day. What did you do? Why won't she come home?" Eazy asked.

A fucking jab to the heart. His son missed her. He could tell by the forlorn look on Eazy's face that Alani's absence was a weight on his little heart.

"She's just taking some time for herself, Big Man. Women need that, sometimes. Daddy messed up and she just needs to think about some things."

"Well, you should stop messing up. I like it when she's here. When she wakes up here. You should bring her home today, Dad. After Bella's party, we should all come home together." Eazy turned and walked out, but he had no idea how closely related their emotions were.

Ethic felt his son's turmoil. Too many days had passed without him hearing her voice. She was a woman of her word, so Eazy and Bella saw her often. Nannie picked them up, faithfully, but Ethic kept his distance. He wanted her, wanted to see her, to love her, but the lies, the revelation of his father's presence, and his own stubbornness kept him away. Her self-worth kept her away. Today, they were forced to face one another. It was too special of a day to avoid. Bella's 13th birthday. Ethic's stomach was missing its bottom, in anticipation of colliding with Alani. A man who had never been intimidated by anyone, couldn't stop the sick feeling that invaded him. He knew he owed her an apology, but one was owed to him too, and he wasn't quite ready to let things go. Ethic had thought of Ezekiel for days. The idea of the man that had made him, taking care of two other children while leaving him to fend for himself, wrecked things inside Ethic that he wasn't aware even existed. Nyair had called him several times, but ego stopped Ethic from answering. His children stopped him from murdering Ny because he wanted nothing more than to end him. He knew his thoughts were irrational, but emotions and jealousy over the bond Ny shared with Alani wouldn't allow him to let it go. He wanted to put a bullet in Nyair. If he was honest, he'd admit he wanted to put a bullet in Alani's ass too. The level of anger and resentment he held toward her is what made him let her be. Still, through all the ill feelings packed in his heart, he longed for her. The thought of losing her made him feel like he was dying. He didn't want to love her in vain. He wanted to love her intentionally, masterfully. He just didn't know how to calm the storm of emotions inside him. A man who was normally so controlled felt everything but.

He pulled a Cardinals baseball cap over his head, as his phone rang in his pocket.

His heart fluttered. Morgan Atkins. Seeing her face would surely lift his spirits.

Her face appeared on his screen. Eyes red, because he knew she'd been crying, but smile shining because she was trying to fight through all that Messiah had left on her heart.

"Hey, old man," Morgan greeted. She was so damn pretty that Ethic released a smile.

"What up, Mo' Money?" he returned.

She laughed. "I misssssss
you guys," she cried out, dramatically.

"We miss you more, Mo. How you feeling?" he asked.

"Fat. Super fat," she answered, laughing.

"I got a call that you missed your first appointment. Lenika worked real hard to get you in with that doctor, Mo. He's the best in London. If you don't want me on the next flight, I need you to make every appointment," Ethic scolded.

"I'm sorry. I was just so tired. The time difference took some getting used to. I slept for days, after landing. I promise, I'll make the next one."

"Tell him I'll make sure of it," Bash interjected. Morgan tilted the phone to show his face. They were walking down a busy street.

"That nigga's on the inside of you? Fuck is you doing, homie? Move my daughter to the inside of the sidewalk, before I make that trip," Ethic stated, shaking his head.

"Ethic, I'm fine," Morgan stated, removing Bash from view.

"Did he switch?" Ethic asked.

Morgan giggled. "He did," she confirmed.

"Ain't he a square? He should know shit like that. You sure about this nigga, Mo?"

Morgan inserted headphones and Ethic smirked.

"Don't want him to hear me doubting his manhood, I see," Ethic snickered.

Morgan stopped moving. "You can get us a table. I'll catch up," she said, looking away from the phone. Ethic waited, and when Morgan was alone, she re-focused on him.

"Be easy with him, Ethic. He's treating me really well. He's a good guy," Morgan answered.

"So, that's your boyfriend now?" Ethic asked. He'd never get used to the idea of Morgan having men in her life. She was still his baby girl. Still the snaggletoothed little girl who captured his soul all those years ago.

"My friend boy," Morgan said. She laughed, and Ethic swiped a hand down his face, while shaking his head. Morgan was a handful. He would worry about her every day for the rest of his life.

"Where's B? I called to tell her Happy Birthday but she's not answering," Morgan added.

"She's at Lenika's. We're headed over there now. Block party starts in an hour."

"Alani isn't there with you?" Morgan asked.

"It's complicated. We're taking some time," Ethic answered.

Morgan went silent and chose her next words carefully. "Maybe that's for the best." Her voice was soft because she knew he didn't think so.

"Maybe," he stated. "We're about to get out of here, Mo. When I get to Bella, I'll have her call you. Put the phone to your belly."

Morgan giggled and lowered the screen to her stomach.

"You're loved, little one. Hold on tight in there," Ethic stated. He had called to remind Morgan and her unborn child of that every day. Morgan's eyes misted, as she brought the phone back to her face.

"I love you, Ethic," she whispered.

"I love you most, Morgan," Ethic stated. "Call me if you need anything."

"K. Bye," Mo said. She ended the FaceTime and Ethic put the phone away.

"Big Man, let's go!"

With that, he headed out the door.

Bella sat in the chair in the middle of Nannie's living room, as Margo finished her hair and makeup. Eight, feed-in braids to the back, baby hair resting perfectly, and a light, natural beat that made Bella smile as she looked in the mirror.

"Yeah, we can take that red lip off," Alani said, as she mixed the seafood salad with a huge, wooden spoon.

"It's pink, La, relax," Margo said, laughing. "If I remember right, I gave you this same pink lip on your 13th birthday."

"And I was popping it in the back seat of a car later that night," she said. She put the spoon down, washed her hands and walked over to Bella. She picked up a makeup wipe and removed the lipstick from Bella's lips and then sifted through the array of shades on the table. She placed a pretty nude on Bella and covered it with gloss.

"That's better," she said. She stepped back and took Bella in. She couldn't believe how her heart swelled. It was like she had known the little girl for years. "You're beautiful, B. Happy birthday." Bella sat before her in distressed jeans, with a white, tulle skirt over it. Her tank top showed a sliver of belly button that Alani hated but she didn't push. The Valentino, rock stud, flip flops she wore accented her pretty, polished toes.

"Thanks, Alani," Bella beamed. I'm going outside! Lyric and nem are waiting on me!" Bella bounced out of the house, as Alani smiled. She froze when she heard Bella shout, "Daddy's here!"

Alani's stomach knotted.

"Don't be looking dumb now. Avoiding that good man," Margo said, laughing at Alani's discomfort.

"Nobody asked you," Alani said, smiling, as she hugged Margo and then pulled out three hundred-dollar bills. She handed them to Margo.

"Now you know I'm not taking that," Margo said. "Consider it her birthday gift."

Margo turned to gather her items and Alani slid the money in Margo's smock for her to find later. Eazy came running full speed through the front door and barreled into her.

"My favorite guy in the whole world is here!" Alani said, as she hugged him, picking up all 75lbs of him, as he held her just as tightly.

"Is the dunk tank here?" Eazy asked.

"It's in the back. You bring your swim shorts? If you're gonna be the one people dunk, you got to put them on."

"Yup! They're in Daddy's truck," Eazy answered, as Alani placed him down.

"Why don't you go grab them, Big Man? Get changed."

Alani lifted eyes to Ethic and then looked away quickly. Her entire heart gave out. She had to turn her back to him and re-focus on the food to stop herself from running to him.

"Hey. How you doing?" Ethic said, speaking to Margo.

"Good; and you?" Margo asked.

"I'm well. Thanks for showing up. Bella looks pleased, although I'm not too thrilled about the makeup," he said, chuckling. He went into his pocket and removed a knot of money. He peeled off ten hundred-dollar bills. He extended it to Margo.

"Oh, not necessary," she said.

"Very necessary. You've been taking care of my girls for a long time," Ethic stated. "I remember you."

Margo smiled. Ethic just had a way with women. He made them feel like the center of his world, if only for a moment. Margo accepted the money.

"I always will. Including this one here," Margo answered. "See you later, La!"

Alani didn't answer. She just kept cooking, back facing Ethic, heart pounding. She was nervous. She felt like she turned to stone when she felt his hand on her hip, his dick pressing into her, and the chill of his wet tongue on the nape of her neck, as he placed a kiss there. She stopped stirring and her lip quivered, as he lingered there for seven seconds. Breathing her in, nose buried in her messy curls. She closed her eyes, and just as quickly as he had come, he was gone, releasing her as he made his way through the house toward the living room.

"My favorite girl. You looking good, Ms. Pat." Alani shook her head at the compliment.

"Well, come take an old gal on a stroll down the block then," Nannie countered. Alani heard the front screen door open and then close, as Ethic and Nannie walked out of the house.

Alani felt like crying. She missed him so much. Every second. Every day. She sniffed away her emotions because today wasn't about her. It was about Bella, and she would stay focused on that to get her through the birthday celebration.

CHAPTER 13

Bust Down Thotiana
I wanna see you bust down
Pick it up
Now break that shit down
Speed it up
Now slow that shit down

Bella stood in the middle of the street with her friends, as the DJ spun a hot record. Bella, Bianca, and Lyric formed a circle and did the popular dance challenge. The entire neighborhood was out to show love to Ethic's princess, and Bella was the center of attention. Hendrix stood across the street, curbside, as he and his crew bantered while watching all the girls on the block walk by. The entire street was sectioned off and the crowd was so thick that Bella could barely see him, even though she was only a few feet away from him.

"Bust it! Bust it! Bust it down!" Lyric yelled, as she danced, turning up her lips while breaking it down.

"What you doing, little girl? If you gon' fuck it up, you got to fuck it all the way up!"

Bella turned toward the voice and smiled wide, as Aria broke through the crowd.

"Aria!" Bella shouted, hugging her tightly.

"Happy birthday, Bella! You know Morgan wouldn't let me miss your birthday party. "Your presents are on the gift table already. One from me, one from Mo. She says to call her later."

Bella smiled. "I can't believe you're here! Come dance with us!"

"Yeah, shake a little ass for a nigga, Ali."

Aria turned around so fast that she stumbled a bit. Her heart sank, as she stared into Isa's pretty, light brown eyes. He didn't say another word. He grabbed her hand and Aria let her fingers slide through his, as he pulled her down the block swiftly. His motorcycle sat parked at the cross streets and she pulled back. She hadn't seen him since that fated day. Since the day Messiah had broken Mo beyond anything Aria could comprehend. Aria was the friend that was always ready to go to war. She had fought battles for Mo that she didn't even realize, taking a bat to Messiah's windshield, before Morgan had ever thought about busting windows. If Mo was mad, she was going to be mad. When Messiah made it right, that's when Aria would drop it; until then, she wasn't crossing the picket line.

Fuck this nigga, Aria thought.

"Where the fuck have you been?! Is Messiah here? Why would you just..."

Isa interrupted her, gripping her neck and pulling her toward him, as he bullied his tongue into her mouth. He tasted like a pink Starburst, taking her by surprise, as he reached around her body and pulled her into him, gripping her ass and making her moan. Aria's panties were ruined with lust. He pulled back. "Shut that ass up and get on the bike. Ethic see me around this bitch and it's fucking curtains."

Aria hesitated, as Isa climbed on and started the engine, gripping the throttle. She looked back at the block and then threw caution to the wind, as she hopped on the back of the motorcycle. Isa took off.

Aria held on tightly, as Isa took her outside the city limits to a small apartment community. Three buildings with five apartments each.

Isa pulled up his hood and kept his head down, as he practically dragged her behind him. As soon as they were inside one of the units, he trapped her against the door and stole her mouth. Aria groaned but used both hands to push him off her. Isa pushed her ass back and gripped her chin so tightly it felt like he would leave dents in her cheeks. He kissed her, again. Aria swung. Her little fists connecting with his jaw.

"You want me to beat yo' ass, Ali," he said, snickering, as he finessed his chin. Aria pushed him, again, enraged.

"Where have you been? Where is Messiah?! Do you have any idea what the fuck has happened since you bitch-ass niggas went ghost?" she shouted. She pushed him, again, and he picked her up, hands under armpits as he lifted her and hooked her on the coatrack on the back of the door. Aria was so short that her feet dangled, as she kicked against the wooden door. Isa cracked up, lifting a balled fist to his mouth, hollering in laughter.

"Little-ass ain't tough now, huh, Ali?" he taunted.

"Isa, let me down! I promise you I'm fighting you when I get down! You got me fucked up!"

"Got to get your violent-ass down first," Isa said, walking away from her and sitting on the couch. He pulled a bag of weed out his pocket and started rolling up. He clicked on the Bluetooth system, as Aria reached behind her, trying to free herself.

"Isa!" she shouted. He was taunting her. He didn't even look her way, as he turned up the volume on the Bluetooth. Aria folded her arms across her chest and stopped struggling, as music filled the air.

Aye, big ole freak
Big booty, big ole treat
I'ma make him wait for the pussy
Hit it 'til you big ol' skeet

"I swear I hate you," Aria said.

"You gon' quit showing yo' ass?" he asked.

"Yeah, man. Let me down, Isa." It took everything in her to surrender.

He lit the blunt, took a long pull and then took his time blowing the smoke in the air. He stood, pulling up his pants, as he walked over to her. He hawked her, looking in her eyes and then holding the blunt to her lips. Aria hit the weed, held it like a G, and then blew it out slowly. He hoisted her up against the door, leaving her hooked at the top. She was at his mercy, or so he thought. She wrapped her legs around him and rolled her hips to the beat. Only Aria could twerk while hanging from the back of a door.

Nobody know, I fuck with him on the low
We never show up together, but I text him when I'm ready to go

"You want me to fuck you, Ali? I'ma tear this little pussy up, you keep playing with me," Isa said, as he tilted his head to the back and hit the blunt again. He blew the smoke in her face. Aria worked Isa so well, he lifted her off the hook and balanced the blunt between his lips, as he held her weight up against the door. His gangster came alive, as she took the blunt from his lips and hit it while riding him through clothes. Aria took a deep pull and closed her eyes as she blew out the smoke.

"That pussy wet ain't it, Ali?" he asked. "Let me taste that?"

Her clit ached, it was so swollen. The pressure from practically dry fucking Isa had her soaked. She knew what her fingers would be doing later because she was so bothered. His face was in the side of her neck, tongue everywhere, hands exploring.

"You so fucking dope, Ali. A nigga missed the fuck out of you," he whispered. "I ain't even supposed to be around this bitch, but a nigga head gone off you. I ain't even hit this shit yet and I know it's good. I wanna fold yo' little-ass."

Aria didn't even know why she liked this rude-ass boy. He was mannish, and mean and violent and…

So damn fine, she thought.

Her mouth opened to welcome his tongue, again. She didn't even want to kiss him, but her body had a mind of its own. He had her in a lust-filled bubble. Then, Morgan flashed in her mind. She hopped out of his arms and pushed him away.

"No, Isa. I can't," she whispered, panting.

He snickered and bit his bottom lip, before adjusting his dick because it was hard and tempting her. He held it, rubbed it. Mannish-ass nigga. "Know when I hit that, I'm knocking all that shit in there over for making a nigga wait," he said. He walked up on her so aggressively that she backpedaled until the door trapped her. He licked her entire face, starting at her chin and going to the top of her forehead. She tasted just like her skin tone. Chocolate as fuck.

Aria frowned and closed her eyes, as he showed her the most erotic and disgusting form of affection that anyone ever had.

"I swear I hate you," she said.

"I hate yo' ass too," he answered. "Can't lick that pussy, might as well lick the second prettiest thing on your body," he said. He took the blunt from her hands and walked over to the couch, sitting down, legs wide, as he resumed his smoke session.

Aria wiped the spit from her face, smirking, flattered, as she joined him. She snatched his phone from the Bluetooth and plugged hers up. The song changed.

BOOM BOOM
Come here, let me take you down
We ain't got no time to wait around
Just let me know if you gon' play around
Cuz I got options they stay around

"You gon' tell me what you're doing here?" she asked.

"I missed the visual," he said, winking at her.

Aria's entire body warmed.

"I need you to call Messiah," she whispered. "Morgan's…" she paused. She had promised to keep Mo's secret. "She needs him, Isa. He has to come back for her."

"Bruh is off the map. He ain't taking no calls. Mo and Messiah ain't my business," he said.

"She's hurt, Isa. She's made a lot of bad choices since he's been gone. I just need five minutes on the phone with him."

"I just need five minutes with you," Isa answered. "You worried about the wrong thing."

Aria picked up her phone and sent Morgan a text.

Aria
Isa's back, Mo. He's sitting in front of me, right now, Morgan. I know you said not to say anything, but…

Before she could even finish typing, Morgan answered.

Mo' Money aka Main Thang aka My Bitch
You promised, Aria. Don't say shit. Fuck Messiah.
I don't want to ever talk to him again.
Keep Isa out of my business.

Aria's phone was confiscated, as Isa pulled it out of her hands. She had such a heavy heart, as she looked up into his eyes. She wanted to blurt the words…tell Isa that Morgan was pregnant, in hopes that it would bring Messiah back for her friend, but it wasn't her decision to make.

"Why are you back? If Messiah is in the wind... If Meek is gone. Why aren't you?" she asked.

"I'ma pull up wherever you are, whenever the fuck I feel like it," Isa stated.

"I'm not your girl, Isa," Aria stated.

"And that's why I came the fuck back. Cuz you don't want to be. Cuz you ain't phased by a nigga. Shit's sexy, Ali. I dig that," Isa stated.

"And you're leaving again?" she asked.

"I ain't far. When you need me, I'ma pull up," he said.

"What does that mean?" she pressed. "I'm not interested in what you're interested in, Isa. You want to hit and put me on a shelf with the rest of your trophies. I'm not feeling that at all."

"I get it, Ali. I wouldn't do you like that, but I get why you think I would. I just want to take up a little bit of your time every once in a while. So, when you got a bit to share, call me. I'm about an hour away."

"Don't invest too much into me, Isa. I'm never fucking you. I'm never going to be your girl, so if that's what you want, you might want to go about your business. I don't even like you. In fact, I kind of hate you."

"You play with that pussy at night while you think about a nigga, though," Isa stated, matter-of-factly.

"Arrogant much?" Aria asked.

"I don' got a lot of pussy, Ali. I know when a bitch want me to fuck," Isa stated.

Aria's brow lifted.

"And I know when a nigga ain't shit," she shot back. "Call me out my name again and I'll burn this whole damn building to the ground."

"It's insured," Isa stated. "I ain't worried. We own all this shit. Building next door is Messiah's, this my shit we in, Ahmeek shit to the left, baby. Burn away and we'll take the insurance and blow a bag on some shit.

"You're so damn cocky," she said, shaking her head. "I bet that pussy you getting is trash, just like this trash, Bobby-Brown-ass weed you got me smoking." He smiled, turning red.

"You funny, Ali. That mouth so damn reckless," he said. "Show me what you do when you think of me at night."

Aria's clit screamed.

"I don't think of you at all," she answered, keeping her cool.

"Yeah, you do," he stated. "Cuz a nigga wrap his hand around his dick with you in his head every day."

Aria's nipples hardened. "You have no home training," she whispered, crossing her legs. She felt the wetness between her thighs. His words, alone, were making a mess of her. He leaned over and unbuttoned her jeans, sliding the zipper down, as he leaned to kiss her stomach. The tongue he dipped inside her navel made her suck in air.

Go Boom Boom
wait a minute, wait a minute, wait a minute, wait a minute
Ooh, ohhh
Can you make the bed go…

"Touch it, Ali," he whispered.

Aria slid her hand inside her panties and gave her clit the attention it was craving, and then pushed two fingers inside her before pulling them back out. They were clear and soaking wet. She rubbed those two fingers under his nose, all in his mustache.

"It taste good, don't it?" she whispered, challenge dancing in her eyes, as she rubbed it all over his lips. He pulled her two fingers into his mouth and cleaned them.

"Mmm... hell yeah," he groaned.

"Now, you don't have to imagine what it tastes like when you beating your dick at night," she whispered, bringing her lips so close to his that they almost kissed. Aria stood and pet the top of his head, like he was her dog. "You be good, and I'll feed you for real one day. With your dog-ass."

Isa barked at her. Startling her, as he wrapped his arms around her waist, tackling her to the couch cushions as he buried his face between her legs.

"RUFF! RUFF!"

Aria hollered, as she squirmed beneath him, as he tickled her. She laughed so hard she couldn't breathe. "Isaaaa! Stopppp!" He bit her stomach and then stood, pulling her to her feet.

"Sweet-ass," he muttered, smacking her ass, as she walked by, toward the door.

He pulled a key off his key ring and slid it in her back pocket. "When I call you and tell you I'm coming to town, you meet me here. You can come whenever you want; but when I call, you better bring your ass, you understand?"

Aria rolled her eyes and walked out the door in front of him.

"You gon' fuck shit up for every bitch that ain't you," he stated.

"Good," she replied. "Now, take me back to my car."

CHAPTER 14

There were so many people on the block that Bella's mind was blown. The amount of love was overwhelming, as people she didn't even know, grown-ups, walked up to her - and mostly Ethic - to hand her gifts and cash. The DJ was spinning non-stop and Bella and her friends stood around doing a pretty girl two-step, while laughing and filling the air with gossip. The little kids on the block ran wild, yelling and screaming, as Eazy ran around starting water gun fights. Alani was busy, running in and out of the house, making sure the food was always replenished and piping hot. She hadn't even bothered to dress up. She wore yoga pants and an old t-shirt because time had gotten away from her and she didn't have time to get cute before the guests started pouring in. Even her hair was undone, hidden in a ponytail through a black, Nike hat, but this was her show. The block party was running smoothly, thanks to her planning, and Bella couldn't be more pleased. Ethic sat on the porch with Nannie, overseeing every angle of the block. It was a perfect day in the hood.

Bella walked into the house to catch a quick break from the commotion.

"Is everything okay?" Alani asked, as Bella entered the kitchen. It was empty. Only the two of them were inside. Bella nodded.

"Thank you for choosing us, Alani," Bella said. "I know it was hard and I'm sorry that it's hard, but you choose to be here with us. I don't know why you've been sleeping here instead of at home, but I'm not going back home until you do. I kind of love my room, though, sooooo can you hurry and decide to make up with Daddy? You can't leave him, because that means you're leaving all of us, and we really love you."

Alani's eyes misted, and Bella's shone pure emotion, as she walked into Alani's arms.

"I really love you guys too, Bella. Like, with my entire heart, little girl," Alani admitted. "Your daddy and I have made it through worst. We'll get through this too, but it's your birthday. You shouldn't be worried about that. Go have fun. I hope you're enjoying your party."

"It's everything," Bella said, laughing, as she pulled back and wiped the stray tears that had fallen.

"Today is a happy day. No tears," Alani said, using her thumbs to clear Bella's emotions and then wiping her own. "I'm going to run to the bakery and pick up your cake."

"Oooh... did you get it from..."

"Devereaux Catering, yes, ma'am! Just like you requested," Alani interrupted.

"I get my cake there every year. They're the best! Thank you!" Bella beamed.

Alani grabbed her tote bag and her car keys and tossed on

a jean jacket. "If anyone asks, tell them I'll be right back. All the food is filled, so everyone should be good for the fifteen minutes it's going to take me to run this errand. Let your daddy know."

"Okay," Bella said.

Alani headed for the door and shouted, "Oh yeah, B! Get some more napkins from the basement and put them out please!"

"Okay!" Bella shouted back. She headed downstairs and pulled the string at the bottom of the stairs to illuminate the space. She located the napkins. The sound of heavy footsteps descending the stairs caused her to look up.

"Happy birthday, Pretty Girl."

Bella smiled. Hendrix stood in front of her.

"Sing me a song, Henny," she said.

"Happy birthdayyyyy to you-oooo," Hendrix sang. He exaggerated every note, as he walked up on her and pushed her further into the basement. He was trying to keep his voice low. The house was empty upstairs, but he wanted to be careful. Bella's birthday could easily become the day he died, if he moved wrong.

"Your voice makes the hair stand up on the back of my neck," Bella whispered.

"That bad, huh?" he asked.

"That good," she corrected.

"Happy birthhhhdayyyy, to you-oooo-ohhhhh-ohh."

Bella smiled.

"Happy birthday, pretty girl youuuu, happy birthdayyyy to youuuu-ooo."

Bella's lips were on his before he could finish the last note, and when she felt his tongue part her lips, her eyes popped open in stun. She pushed him away.

"My bad, that's too much," Hendrix stated. "I forgot you're a good girl."

"It's just…I don't know…it felt…it made me feel…" Bella couldn't find the right words, as he heart galloped in her chest. She was jittery and feeling things she had never felt before.

"Did you not like it?" Hendrix asked.

"I just wasn't expecting it," she answered.

"You want me to stop?" Hendrix asked.

Bella couldn't even look at him. She didn't want him to think she was childish. *Maybe I should just do what he wants me to do.* "If I say no, will you still like me?" she asked.

Hendrix's forehead tensed, as he jerked his neck back. "Hell yeah, Pretty Girl. If you say no, I'ma like you more," he said. "You wasn't supposed to tell me you were thinking about it, though, you just tell a nigga to stop. Because you said so is enough. No is law. You say no, I hit the brakes."

"Well then, yes, please stop," Bella whispered, embarrassed. Her body was tingling in places that she had yet to explore. It was both the most terrifying and exhilarating thing she had ever felt. The traveling heartbeat that started in her chest, yet somehow ended up between her thighs. Her panties felt sticky and cold. She shivered. She knew about sex. The technicalities of it, but she had no idea kisses felt like this. "Maybe just a normal kiss."

"You're the prettiest chick I've ever seen, Bella. I don't think there's a such thing as a normal kiss," Hendrix said. He leaned into her, gripping her chin, and planted a soft kiss to her lips. No tongue this time, and Bella's legs trembled. She placed her hands on his shoulders and lowered her head.

"So, I kind of want to be something other than a pretty girl to you," she whispered.

"Like what?" he answered. "Whatever spot you want, you can have."

"Like the smartest girl you know, the bravest girl you know, the most loyal girl you know. I don't know," Bella shrugged. "Pretty just doesn't seem that important when you compare it to the rest of that stuff."

"One day when I'm older and you're older, I'm going to hear you tell my daughter that."

Bella giggled. "What are you talking about?" she blushed and was so grateful for the dim light because he would have seen her fluster.

"I'ma hustle real hard for you, Bella. I think life is going to take you to some crazy-ass places and I'm going to have to let it go for a while, but when you come back, I'ma be here and I'ma make sure I'm ready and I'ma make you my girl. Then, one-night, I'ma hear you tell our daughter to be smart, and brave and loyal. You're dope."

"That's a long way away," Bella whispered. She was heaving and breathless and so damn nervous that she felt like she had to throw up. "I don't want to really go anywhere if you're not coming, so I need you to come too. To my high school when I get there, to the college I choose, I want you to come with me to see the world wonders, to Africa to volunteer for a year after that, wherever I go, you have to come too, because I don't want to come back and find out you're gone. If you stay in Flint long enough, you won't make it out."

"Bella! Daddy wants you!" Eazy called down the stairs.

"I've got to get back to the party, but today was perfect. The kiss was perfect," she said, smiling coyly. He pulled out a small, gold necklace. A small, gold, letter H hung from it.

"Hold out your hand," Hendrix said. Bella extended her open palm and he dropped it inside. "I know you can't wear it around your pops, but maybe at school or something or around the way."

She nodded.

"Bella!"

"I'm coming, Eazy!" she shouted back.

"I'll sneak out after you're outside. I'ma hit you later, a'ight?"

Bella nodded. "Okay."

Going back to the other guests at her party was torturous. She just wanted to stay in the basement with him forever. If she could do that, it would be a perfect day. If she could live her entire life in the shadows of that basement, what a perfect life it would be.

Alani rushed into the bakery, flustered and hot. Pulling off Bella's block party had worn her out. She had been cooking all night and hadn't slept a wink to make sure everything was ready for the celebration. She was running on fumes and she couldn't wait for the festivities to end.

"How can I help you?" the worker behind the counter asked.

"I'm here to pick up a cake. Last name Okafor," she said.

"Oh, for baby girl Bella! We always look forward to her order. That cake was already picked up. About twenty minutes ago," the man informed.

Alani frowned.

"By who?" she asked. "I'm the one who ordered it. No one else should have picked it up."

"Let me check the receipt and see who signed for it," the man said. He went into the register and pulled out a book with handwritten receipts. "A Dolce Martinez picked it up."

"Come again?" Alani's chest ignited. "She has no business picking up anything. Why would you give my order to her? She doesn't even know where the party is. She's not even invited."

The man stood wide-eyed. "I'm sorry. We recognized her from previous events. Mr. Okafor has sent her before. The address to the party was on the invoice we gave her. She should be arriving any moment now. I'm sure it's just a miscommunication. Everything will be fine."

Alani pushed out of the bakery and headed toward the car. She picked up her phone and dialed Ethic, only for voicemail to pick up. She didn't know what the hell was going on, but she was furious. *If he called her... If he asked that girl to pick up this cake...* Alani couldn't even think straight. She knew one thing. If Dolce pulled up to her house without invitation, it was going to be a problem.

"Dad, you throw like a bi..."

DUNK!

Before Eazy could even finish the sentence, Ethic hit the center of the target, sending Eazy plunging into the tank full of water.

"Haaa! Little Eazy gon' get that ass whooped talking big dawg shit to the king," a neighborhood boy bantered, as the crowd laughed. Eazy popped out of the water.

"Dad! I was gonna say big loser! You throw like a big loser!" Eazy defended.

Ethic chuckled, tossing the ball into the air. "Ain't no bitch in my blood boi," Ethic stated, smiling wide, feeling nothing but love, for the first time since his fight with Alani. Eazy shook water out of his ears and climbed back up on the platform.

"Birthday girl, your turn," Ethic called out, summoning Bella from the group of neighborhood girls.

Bella stepped up to the line.

"Now, Bella, she throws like a bi..."

BONK!

Bella hit Eazy in the face with the ball, knocking him off the platform and sending him splashing into the water.

"Hey!" Eazy cried, coming up coughing. Bella and Ethic laughed with the crowd, as Eazy spit out a mouth full of water.

The sound of a horn honking caused Ethic to turn toward the driveway.

"Daddy, what is she doing here?" Bella asked.

Tension built in Ethic, as he watched Dolce climb from the C-class Benz, the car he had purchased her.

Ethic placed a hand behind his neck and blew out a sharp breath, as he swaggered down the driveway toward her. His forehead was bent in irritation.

"Hey, babe. Can you come grab Bella's cake?" Dolce asked.

"Daddy, Alani's gonna kill youuuu," Bella whispered under her breath, as she walked beside him.

"Happy birthday, B!" Dolce sang. She pulled out a huge Louis Vuitton bag that had a blue bow on it. She handed it over to Bella who reluctantly took it. "Ethic, can you grab the cake out of the back seat? Dolce pulled out all the stops. She was stunning, in nude leggings and a nude, baby t-shirt, with nude, strappy heels. A floral print duster barely covered her sharp curves, and her hair was pulled back in a long, sleek, ponytail, no weave required. Every young nigga on the block was tuned in, as she walked up to Ethic and placed hands around his neck.

"Oh, now I know this hussy done lost her mind," Nannie said, using a cane to stand up from her chair on the porch.

Ethic seized her hands, removing them from his body, and burned her with his stare. "The fuck you doing right now?" he asked. His jaw locked, a pure sign of rage in Ezra Okafor, and his temple pulsed, as he gritted his teeth. He hadn't heard from her in months. Her pulling up, out the blue, was unacceptable.

"It's time to stop playing, Ethic. It's in your best interest to stop playing with me," she said, in a low tone. Nobody heard her but him. Everyone else only saw the smile and dreamy eyes she was giving him.

"Get in your car and drive away before I fucking lose my patience out here," Ethic stated. He was trying hard not to embarrass her because he wasn't into public humiliation, but she was testing him.

Things went from bad to worse, when he saw the Tesla pull up behind Dolce's car, blocking it in. Alani climbed out the car.

"Bella, get Eazy and your friends and take the party to the basement for a minute," Alani stated.

"Alani…"

"Bella, right now," Alani barked.

Bella disappeared, without another word.

"You called this bitch to pick up Bella's cake?" Alani asked. "You're that mad at me?! You wanna hurt me back that much?" Ethic could see the hurt on her face. He could feel it in the air.

Before Ethic could offer a response, Dolce stood on her tip-toes and whispered in Ethic's ear. "You remember the bloody shirt? I put two and two together, Ethic. You killed that boy and that little girl that night and I've got the proof. Now, end this shit. Stop this little pity party relationship you got going on, before I end you."

Alani didn't even realize she was running until she was swinging on Dolce. That ponytail was around her fist before she could stop herself.

The crowd erupted, as she cocked her fist back, time and time again, tagging Dolce.

"Lenika!" Ethic shouted, as he grabbed her.

"Get the fuck off me!" she screamed. She had lost all decorum.

"Get her ass, Nika!" Connie shouted. "Disrespectful-ass bitch. We don't play that around here!"

"She lose that fight, she gon' fight me next," Nannie said, pointing her cane from the porch. "Alani don' beat a lot of asses for less. Let her ass go, Ethic!"

Dolce squared up with Alani, as Ethic tried to diffuse them, standing in the middle. When Dolce swung at Alani, Ethic lost his composure. He shoved her so hard she hit the Mercedes with a loud thud, bouncing off the frame of the car and falling to the ground. She struggled to stand, as she pointed at Ethic in hysteria.

"Fuck you, Ethic! I put years into you! I'll see yo' ass locked up before I see you with this bitch! What kind of mother are you?! You want to tell everybody how you're still fucking him after he killed yo'..."

Ethic was on Dolce before she could finish, hand covering her entire face, damn near suffocating her, as he jerked her hard. "Get in the car," he threatened. "You gon' make me snap your fucking neck out here," he whispered. "Stop talking and get in the car. This my daughter's party and you showing your ass? Why would I want that?" Only she heard him. This wasn't for the crowd, it was for her. "You know me. You know what I'll do to you. What I'll do to everybody you love. Act like a fucking lady and leave. This ain't the place or the time for this conversation. I'ma call you and we gon' talk. Leave, and wait for my fucking call." He could see her eyes bulging because she couldn't breathe. His hand covered her mouth and nose. He wanted to put her ass to sleep, but instead, he released her. He pointed to Connie. "Move the fucking Tesla so she can leave." Connie sprang into action.

He turned to Alani and he could see her defeat. He could feel the questioning stares from the crowd. It was silenced by Dolce's half accusation. Alani placed a hand over her mouth and another over her stomach. Her entire chin quivered and then she attacked the car.

BOOM! BOOM!

"Bitch, get yo' ass out the car!" She was kicking size eight dents in the body of Dolce's Benz. Ethic grabbed her, and Alani swung on him too.

"You told her?! You pillow talking with this hoe?!" Alani was nowhere in sight. Nor Lenika. Not even Nika. Nik Nik was acting the fuck up. She hadn't been in a fight in years, and she would probably have to ice every part of her body tomorrow, but she was determined to fuck shit up today.

178

She beat his ass all the way to the house, swinging blows for not only Dolce, but Green Eyes too, as he forced her inside. He was grateful that Bella had listened and gone into the basement. He carried Alani, kicking and screaming, all the way upstairs, forcing her into the bathroom, before letting her go.

He swiped a hand down his face, feeling scratches from where she had tagged him.

Alani gripped the sink and sobbed, as images of her daughter ran through her mind. Dolce had spat the words at her, in disgust. They were like acid hitting her skin, burning her. "How does she know?" Alani asked.

"She was at my house the night it happened," he admitted.

"Are you still fucking her?" Alani asked, unable to look at him.

"No, only person I'm fucking is you. Only woman I'm loving is you," he answered it so matter-of-factly that she ran into his arms.

"My baby, Ethic. God, my baby," Alani sobbed.

Ethic gripped the back of Alani's head, pressing her into him, holding her. "I know."

"She has the shirt, Lenika. There's blood all over the shirt. My DNA is on the shirt. I've got to go handle that," he stated.

"Please, just stay. Stay here with me," Alani pleaded.

"She's irrational right now. I need to go see about her," he stated.

He saw the fear in her eyes. The doubt in him. The mistrust. He saw the questions forming in her mind. What lengths would he go to in order to stop her from talking?

179

Would he fuck her? Would he kill her? Would he keep her on the side to keep her in pocket? Alani was filled with angst. It ate away at her, like a disease. She didn't know how to fix this for him or herself.

"I'ma need to do something you won't like, baby," he whispered, pressing his forehead to hers and closing his eyes. Alani cupped his face.

"There are just so many things in our way. If this was in any of God's plans, it wouldn't be this hard, Ezra," she whispered. "Doing what you're talking about doing pushes you further away from God. Just be with her Ethic. She doesn't want to lock you up. She wants me gone. She wants her spot back. Just do that. If that keeps you free, without staining your hands with more blood, just give her what she wants. Otherwise, you're back at square one. You're back to ending lives and deciding judgements when you're so much more than that. You're not a killer. You're not some monster. You're a king. You're my king. I was never on your level, Ethic. I'm the poor girl with the sad story, looking up at the handsome king from the crowd. All this fighting and forcing we're doing. Now, her. The threat to your freedom. Just give her what she wants. Be with her. You were with her before, shouldn't be that hard."

"Shit is fucking impossible after you. You hear me? It's unbearable after us," he stated. He kissed her forehead. "I'ma fix it."

Alani pulled away from him.

"Lenika," he called after her. She didn't look back, as she closed the bathroom door. She heard him hit the wood with a balled fist and she touched the place where she knew his head rested. She closed her eyes. They had been here before. On opposite sides. Last time, she hadn't opened the door. Last time, she had left him in the cold. Alani's heart split in half, right down the middle, as she reached down for the doorknob. She pulled open the door and Ethic was there, standing there, where she knew he would be, exactly where she felt he was. Shock shone in his eyes because Alani was a runner. Alani was a woman who shut people out. She had shut him out before. Blocked him from her heart, like they had never even existed. She rushed into his arms and he stumbled backwards, knocking shit over as he held her. He held her so tightly that it hurt.

"I love you, Ezra," she whispered, sniffing, and crying into his chest.

"Free ain't free if it ain't with you, baby," he whispered the words in her ear, kissing her messy hair, holding her. "I don't want it if you ain't a part of it. You're in me, baby. I'ma fix it, but sometimes I just need you to sit down and hold my babies. I need you to hold our babies. All of them. Living in front of us and in here," he said, as he touched her chest. "You do that and don't ask no questions, and I'ma fix everything else. Just wait for me with love at home...at the home I've built and waited for you to fill. You hold us down there and I'll hold us down everywhere else. That's on Love. You don't got to worry about nobody else outside those walls. Wait there for me and trust me. Can you do that?"

Alani looked up at him. She had never loved him more. "I can do that forever."

CHAPTER 15

Alani's eyes hawked the clock on the nightstand beside her bed.

11:30 p.m.

He had left three hours ago, and she hadn't heard a word since. She was a ball of nerves because she knew what he was going to do. Commit murder. She was sick to her stomach, just thinking about it. She sat up in bed and reached for the cardigan that rested at the foot of the bed. She slid it over her shoulders and stepped into Chanel espadrilles, a gift from Ethic, before grabbing her keys. She knew Ethic wouldn't return to Nannie's after he did what he had to do, but she didn't want him to go home to an empty house. She felt like a hypocrite, because when he had murdered her family, Alani had judged him. She had thought he was a monster. Now, she was on the flip side of the coin. She was under his arm, a part of his tribe, and she understood that protection was necessary. Ethic wasn't a terrorist going around inflicting harm at random. He was calculated and only dangerous if provoked. Dolce had provoked him. She had goaded him by threatening his freedom and by disrespecting his queen.

Dolce's words had cut so deeply that Alani still felt them. Her soul was open tonight and she could feel it leaving traces of evidence, pools of her hurt behind her, like footprints.

"Where are you going?"

Alani was surprised to see Eazy awake in the living room.

"Hey, Big Man, I'm just going to the house. I want you to get some rest, okay? It's way past your bedtime. Lights out. I'll come back for you guys in the morning," she said.

"That means you're coming home for good?" he asked, excited.

Alani nodded. "Yes. I'm coming home, baby boy."

"Yes!" he said, pumping a fist and hopping up to rush her. Alani gave a half-hearted laugh and hugged him tightly, before rubbing the top of his head.

"Now, upstairs," she said. "And turn off that game. No sneaking to play under the covers."

"I won't! I promise!" he called out. He was already halfway up the staircase, as Alani slid out the door.

She slid into the Tesla and drove the twenty miles to Ethic's house. *My house,* she thought. She pressed the button inside the car that opened the gate and drove through it. The headlights behind her took her by surprise, blinding her, as she pulled up the driveway. The person behind the wheel of the car switched on their high beams and Alani's brow dipped. "What the hell?" She threw her car in park, and when she climbed out, her blood boiled.

Alani stood face to face with Dolce. Both women sized

one another up, in seconds. Alani saw a stunning woman. Perfection. She looked like she was ripped from the pages of Elle magazine or something. Her clothes were fancy, her body flawless, and her face exotic and beautiful. Alani shrank in front of women like this. Her insecurities began to gnaw away at her, until there was nothing left, when in the presence of women like Dolce.

"He thinks I'm playing," Dolce whispered, shaking her head.

"What do you want?" Alani asked.

"No, bitch, what do you want?" Dolce asked. "I've been here. You just got here."

"I'm not anywhere I'm not wanted. I don't do that. I don't force shit that's not meant to be," Alani stated.

"Meant to be!" Dolce laughed. "That nigga murdered your daughter and your brother. He came home to me and we popped a bottle of champagne and fucked in the shower afterwards, like nothing had even happened. There was no regret. No conflict. He shot your kid in cold blood and you sucked his dick afterwards? You think he loves you? He's with you to control what you say and what you don't say to the police. He'd rather not kill you, so he's fucking you into submission. What kind of mother falls for that?" Dolce shook her head. "What kind of woman lays next to their child's killer? You're a desperate-ass bitch and your time is up."

The gun seemed to come from nowhere. Dolce pulled it so fast that Alani was stunned. Her life flashed before her eyes. She always thought it was a cliché, but here her shit was, playing like an old-school movie in her head.

"You're going to shoot me? Because I beat yo' ass for pulling up to my house unannounced? Or over a man who doesn't want you? Which reason is good enough to commit murder?"

Alani shook her head, as she reached for her handbag and turned for the door. She half expected Dolce to put a bullet in her back. Her hands shook, as she fished her phone out of the side pocket. She texted him.

Alani
Home. She has a gun.

She knew Ethic was headed to Dolce's place. She needed him to know that Dolce was here. She needed him to bring his ass home, because she was sure that Dolce wasn't wrapped too tight and that at any moment she just may pull the trigger. She wanted to slap fire from this girl, but she couldn't. She needed to keep her calm until she got in touch with Ethic. If she incited Dolce, things could end badly. Ethic's freedom was no longer the only thing on the line. Alani's life was in Dolce's hands.

"Look, I'm too grown for this. You don't know me. You have no idea who I am. Ethic isn't here. He's on his way home. Whatever you need to work out, it doesn't have anything to do with me. The gun isn't necessary. You can wait for him inside, and when he gets here, you two can talk," Alani said. "I don't want to die over a man. You can have him. He's on his way, okay? I told him to come."

Her words took Dolce by surprise. Alani walked into the house and Dolce followed her inside, all the way to the kitchen. Alani's heart raced because Dolce hadn't put down the gun. It was still pointed at her. Still ready.

Alani opened the pantry door.

"Aht, aht!" Dolce said. "Sit down."

Alani pulled out a bottle of red wine. "I'm just looking for something to take the edge off," Alani said. "If I'm going to die tonight, a glass of red is needed beforehand." She felt Dolce's eyes on her, as she opened the drawer and removed a wine opener. Alani stuck it into the bottle and twisted, removing the cork from the twisted metal piece. She placed it on the countertop.

Alani pulled down two glasses, filling both, before she slid one across the island to the other side where Dolce sat.

Alani grabbed a knife, a cutting board, and three blocks of assorted cheeses from the refrigerator.

"So, tell me exactly how this is supposed to work? You kill me, and then Ethic ends up with you?" Alani asked, sitting on the stool and cutting the cheese. She appeared much cooler than she felt. She was terrified.

"We were fine before that night. Before you. I've been here for years. Doing things I would never do for any other man. He took all my good years. My entire twenties, and then he just starts dating different women. The bitch from New York was first, now you. I'm not having it. I'm not going for it. That nigga owes me. So, yeah, he can go to jail or I can put you in a ditch. Either way, he's not riding off into some sunset without me. If I can't be happy, he can't be happy. Niggas love to fuck you good then call you crazy. I'm not crazy. He did this to me."

"I don't think you're crazy," Alani whispered. She would agree with every single word Dolce said, in order to finesse the gun out of her hand, but somewhere deep in her heart she empathized with this woman. "You did the most and he gave the minimum, but you allowed it. Ethic's not a liar, so he probably told you that he wasn't serious, but you thought you could change him. Why we think we can change grown men is beyond me. I'm doing the same thing. Hoping to change his heart, hoping to turn it into something that's unnatural to him. Godly, like he's just going to start praising God overnight. I'm being a fool for him and I don't care. It happens to the best of us. Your heart was in it, and I get how your heart could be in it, because when he looks at you…" Alani stopped and closed her eyes, as her heart ached. *Ethic, where the fuck are you?* "When he looks at you, you feel it everywhere. He makes you feel like you're the only one in the room."

"And he talked to me like he cared. He told me I was smart and that I could do things, you know? Like, start a business or design clothes, come out with my own cosmetics line. He tried to help me find what I was good at, you know?"

"Why didn't you ever do anything? Why not do those things? You feel like all you have is him, but why not do things for yourself? Accumulate something for yourself that no woman can take?" Alani asked, as she sipped the wine. She cut a square of cheese and ate it off the tip of the knife.

"I didn't need to do that stuff. I had the boss, so why would I go to work? I was spending his money just fine, I didn't need my own. I had a king. I just needed to convince him that I could be a queen."

Alani knew what that felt like. Ethic had a way of making the most common woman feel extraordinary.

Dolce sat there, talking like she was zoned out. Like she was in some far away land where she and Ethic existed as a pair. Alani watched the gun in her hand like a hawk, and when Dolce pulled back the hammer, Alani froze.

"You're beautiful," Alani said, honestly. "Why would you allow a man to measure your worth? You could be with anyone. Another man would marry you, would prioritize you…why would you stay around this long for a man who tells you he isn't interested?"

"Because I don't want just any man. I want that man. I want my man. He's not yours! He's mine! He just keeps forgetting! You bitches just keep getting in the way! Nobody makes him feel like I make him feel when we're in bed. I've mastered that dick. I've made him cum so hard that he calls out to God. I do that. Not you. I take it however he wants to give it. I tried to just get him to give me a baby. If he had done that, we wouldn't be here. He would be mine. I'm so sick of you bitches! That bitch, Raven, then the other one, and you!"

Alani's lip quivered, as she blew out a deep breath.

"Not me. I'm not like the others. I will get out of your way. I'll leave him alone. You're right. I've already lost too much. He's using me. He's finessing me, so I will stay quiet. I'm quiet. I'm out of it. I really just want to walk out of here."

"You're not walking out of here. I saw how he looked at you today. He loves you. He's giving you everything he's supposed to give to me!" Dolce chuckled, as tears slid down her face. She tilted the wine glass to her lips and then tossed it at Alani's head. Alani dodged left, causing the wine glass to explode against the cabinets behind her.

"You can't want this. You're losing it. Pull yourself together. Stop letting this man ruin your whole damn life. So, you've wasted ten years. I get it. Niggas lie every day. You gonna shoot me and then go to jail and let him be the reason you lose the rest of your life? The dick ain't that good, sis. Fuck that nigga."

Dolce's hand shook.

"I just want him," Dolce cried. She lowered the gun, placing it on top of the island. "I just want him so bad." Her shoulders shook, as she placed her hands over her eyes and then flipped her hair backward. Alani lunged over the island to the gun but Dolce was quicker. It went flying across the island and to the ground. They scrambled toward it. Dolce reached it first but Alani gripped Dolce's wrists, forcing her aim to the ceiling, as Dolce pulled the trigger.

BANG! BANG!

"Stop!" Alani shouted, as she used all her strength to prevent Dolce from aiming at her face. Dolce was pulling the trigger without remorse, and Alani knew if she let go of Dolce's wrists she was a dead woman.

"Arghh!" Alani shouted, as she pushed Dolce toward the counter. She backed her into it hard, causing Dolce's back to crash into the edge.

BANG! BANG! BANG!

Alani's eyes fell onto the knife and cheese block on the counter. *God, please.*
Alani let Dolce's hands go and ducked.

BANG!

Dolce fired where Alani's head had just been. By the time she re-centered her aim, Alani came up with the knife in one hand and rammed it in the side of Dolce's neck. The gun clanged to the floor and Dolce's body weight fell into Alani, as she opened her mouth in agony. Alani's eyes misted, as she fell to the floor, unable to balance Dolce in her arms.

"Oh my god, oh my god," she whispered, as she scrambled away from Dolce. She scrambled to her phone, placing bloody fingertips to screen.

Ethic, help. Help me.

9-1-

Before she dialed the third number, she paused. Dolce was gurgling blood. She couldn't call the police. If they saved her, Dolce would undoubtedly tell what she knew. She still had the bloody shirt. Alani was at an impasse. Her morality or Ethic's freedom. Her lip quivered, as she erased the 1, then erased the 9. She leaned her head back against the wall and closed her eyes, as she listened for 38 seconds, before she heard Dolce take her last breath.

Alani bawled until the sound of his voice filled the house. "Lenika!" he shouted. She heard the terror in his voice, but she couldn't move.

"Ethic!" she cried. She, finally, scrambled to her feet and ran into his arms. "I killed herrrrr!"

He held her tightly to his body, as his eyes bounced around the room, counting the gunshots in the walls and trying to paint a picture of what had gone down.

"Shhh!" he whispered.

She was limp in his arms, but he held her up, as she sobbed. Ethic picked her up and carried her to the second floor. "I need you to listen to me," he said. Her head was on his shoulder and her arms around his neck, like she was a toddler. She cried so many tears that his shirt was wet.

"Lenika, I need you to hear me," he whispered.

He felt her trembling. Fear. Catching her first body was pulling pure fear from her bones. He leaned back and placed her on her feet. Her eyes were closed. Tears wet her cheeks. He gripped her face. "Look at me."

Alani's eyes popped open.

"Take off your clothes, put them in a plastic bag. Get in the shower. Wash your body until the water runs cold. Do you hear me? Someone is going to knock on the door in about four hours. Her name is Aries. I need you to answer for her. Don't open the door for anyone else. She'll take care of the rest. Okay?"

Alani nodded, frantically.

"Run it back to me, Lenika."

"S-sshower, hot water, put my clothes in a bag and wait for Aries."

"Good girl," he whispered. He kissed her nose, and then her forehead, and then her nose, again, and then the space above her lips, and her chin. "You're okay, baby. You're okay."

"I'm not," she whispered.

The admission tore him apart because he knew what murder felt like. He knew what that first one did to a person's soul. How it tarnished it.

"I'll be back. After Aries leaves, you get under the covers and you wait for your man to come home to you. Okay?"

"Ethic..."

"I've got to get rid of the body, baby," he whispered. "I have to be thorough."

She sobbed so hard the cries were inaudible. He pulled her head to his lips and kissed her forehead, before pulling away and disappearing down the stairs.

Alani's eyes burned. She didn't know if it was from the bleach and chemicals Aries had used to clean up the blood, or if it was from the crying. The tears wouldn't stop. Her pillow was soaked. The hours passed by so slowly that Alani felt like time had frozen. She heard him come in, as the sun rose. He showered first, thinking that her turned back and closed eyes meant she was asleep. She wasn't. She heard every bead of water as it hit the tiled floor in the en suite.

She wanted to scream to him. Call out to him. *Boy, fuck that shower*, but she couldn't find her voice.

It took him half an hour to emerge, and he brought the scent of Tom Ford body wash with him, as he lifted the covers and slid into bed. He came up behind her and pulled her close. Her back to his chest.

"It's over," he whispered, kissing the back of her head. "I'm so sorry, baby."

He laced his fingers in hers, as she held on for dear life. It was the first time she found no comfort in his arms. Normally, she was attempting to right his wrongs, remove his sins, but this one was hers.

"What if someone finds her?" she asked.

"They won't," he promised.

"I'm going to jail," she whispered.

"That'll never happen," he answered. "I would never let it. I took care of it. It never happened, you hear me? You had a fucked-up dream, baby, that's all."

She nodded and turned to him, burying herself into his body.

Neither slept, they just held one another for hours and her tears never eased. Even after he left the bed to go get his children, she stayed there, unable to tear herself from the grief of the bed.

She was afraid to even step foot in the kitchen, after what had happened there. She was afraid to step foot out of the bed, in fact. It was like, as soon as she lowered her feet, she expected someone to grab her ankles and pull her under the bed into the pits of hell.

Even when Ethic returned with the kids, Alani couldn't pull herself out of bed. He walked into the room and Alani just laid there.

"I smell her blood, Ethic," she whispered.

"It'll go away."

"I can't live in this house. I can't cook in that kitchen," she said.

"Okay. I'll buy you a new one. I'll build you one with my own hands, if I have to, Lenika. I just need you to be strong. She put bullets in the wall, baby. It was you or her and you got to walk out of that equation every time," he said. "I'm sorry you had to do that. I'm sorry. I'm sorry."

He laid with her all day because Alani wouldn't let him go. When they heard the knock at the door, Ethic said, "I'll send them away."

"No," Alani whispered. "I need them."

Ethic climbed from the bed and opened the door.

"Come here, Big Man," Ethic stated. "Bella!"

She popped her head out of her room.

"Come."

His children looked up at him.

"Am I in trouble?" Bella asked, fearing the worst. She had been keeping secrets, so his beckoning could mean anything.

"No, baby girl. We just want you guys in here for a while."

Bella peered past Ethic and saw Alani balled up in bed.

"Is she okay?" she asked.

"She's not feeling well. Nothing a little love can't fix."

"Well, I got LOTS of love!" Eazy shouted, as he pushed by Ethic and rushed over to Alani.

He nestled right in front of Alani, turning his back to her, and she caressed his head, planting a kiss on the top of it, as Bella climbed in behind Alani. Bella placed one arm over Alani's body. Ethic watched Alani close her eyes for the first time in hours. Wrapped in the love of his children, she felt safe, she felt a purity that he didn't possess.

"Don't leave," she said, as he turned to the door.

Ethic pulled out his phone. He didn't want to call on the person he was about to contact, but he had no choice. Alani needed more than Ethic was equipped to give. He would have to swallow his pride for her. He would have to mend a bridge for her.

Ethic
Need u to come to the house ASAP. It's Alani. She needs u.

Ethic wondered if he would come. The last time they had saw each other, they had come to blows. A man didn't easily forget that type of confrontation. Ethic's brow lifted, when his phone buzzed in his hand.

Nyair
On my way.

When Ethic opened the door thirty minutes later, he was forced to tuck his ego. Nyair, his brother, stood in front of him.

"She's upstairs," he said. "Something happened, and before I speak on it, I need to know that it stays here."

"I'm your pastor, but beyond that, I'm your blood. What's spoken ain't repeated, G, no matter how many times we come to blows," Nyair stated.

Ethic sniffed, flicking his nose, before stepping back and allowing Nyair into his home. He steepled his hands in front of him and shook them, as his temple throbbed. He was struggling with this, fighting the acceptance of a brother that he associated with the moment his life had been ruined.

"I didn't know about you. Me or Zora," Nyair stated. "Pops never spoke about you or his life before moving to Michigan. Until the other night, I didn't even know his real name. He changed it. Ezekiel Hawthorne. I don't even know who he is right now, G. Spent my entire life idolizing a lie."

"I overreacted at your party. I know you and Alani have history. I'm not a man that worries about what happened before me...it just-"

"I loved her, but I fucked that up," Nyair interrupted. "It was a long time ago. I was young, dumb. I was chasing something outside this city and she represented everything that is this city," Ny stated. "So, I abandoned her. I took my opportunity to get out and I never looked back. Never came back for her. It took me a long time to make amends for that, to even be her friend, G. She's one of my best friends. A lot of people turned their backs on me, when I got let go from the league, but Alani was the same. She was waiting at home with the same smile, same hugs. She never judged me for my mistakes. I'm not waiting for a second shot with her, man. I'm not lurking or playing the friend zone, G. She's just a valuable piece of my life and I want her happy. She's happy with you. I don't know how you feel about the whole bloodline thing, but I want to know you, G. Not as the nigga I heard about coming up in the streets either. I want to know my brother. Real shit."

"That preacher talk goes out the window real easy," Ethic stated, smirking.

"I do more praising than sinning, these days. Big Homie know my heart," Nyair answered, snickering.

"She's upstairs," Ethic stated.

Nyair nodded and turned to the staircase. When he got halfway up the landing, he heard,

"Yo, Nyair," Ethic called. "That brother thing? It'll take some time for me. Some work. Got to come to terms with the fact that my brother fucked my girl."

Amusement lived in Nyair, as he rubbed the back of his neck. "Yeah, G, that's a tough one," he stated. "If it's worth anything, it was my first time up at bat. I struck out more than I hit home runs. I'm sure she has a few embarrassing stories of me."

Ethic scoffed, as he finessed his beard. "Nah, nigga, that don't help at all. Go take care of my lady, man."

Nyair nodded and Ethic shook his head, as Nyair disappeared up the steps.

Alani laid behind Eazy, with Bella resting her head on her back, as they watched the old movie on the television screen.

Alani saw the picture playing in front of her, but she wasn't focused, couldn't focus. All she heard was gunshots ringing in her ears.

Knock. Knock.

Alani sat up in bed, as she and the kids looked towards the door. Nyair leaned against the frame, hands in his jeans pockets.

"What up, La?"

Alani's eyes burned into Nyair's and prickled, as her lip quivered.

"Bella, take your brother downstairs. We'll finish the movie later, okay?"

Bella and Eazy arose from the bed. "Hey, Pastor Ny," Bella greeted.

"What's up, Bella? Eazy E?" He greeted, giving them both a nod, as they bypassed him.

"Close the door," she whispered.

Nyair looked at the door. "I don't know if that's the best…"

"Nyair, close the goddamn door." The words rushed out of her so urgently that he complied.

Alani collapsed, when that door closed. Head to the bed, she brought praying hands above her head, as she sobbed. "I killed her, Ny!"

Her body was wrecked with sobs. She felt his hands on her back and the next thing she knew she was in his arms, like a baby, balled in a fetal position, head on his lap, bawling. They had done this before. He had consoled her, just like this, when they were kids, when her parents used to break her heart.

"What happened, La?"

"His ex. She tried to kill me, Nyair. The gun. She kept pulling the trigger. She kept…she…I stabbed her, Ny." The truth felt like infection being purged from her soul. She had felt trapped in this house, in this room, by worry, by fear… by the fact that she would have to move on and pretend like this hadn't happened. "He got rid of the body, Nyair. What do I do now?"

Alani whispered that last part and Nyair lifted her face.

"It's so heavy, Ny," she muttered. "Loving him. It's heavy. He…"

"He what, La?" Nyair asked, frowning because she was falling apart.

"He killed Kenzie," she whispered. "It was him, Ny. He killed my babyyyy." The shit hurt so bad. It was excruciating to say the words aloud to someone who could judge her. To admit that, then love him anyway, was a shame. "And I know Lucas did wrong. I know he was there because Lucas raped Morgan, but it still hurts, you know? He was my brother and I haven't really admitted to anyone that it hurts that he's gone. I didn't know him as a rapist. He was my baby brother and I've felt ashamed to mourn him. Now, this. Now, me, taking that girl's life, Nyair. It's like I've become him; because even before she came here with a gun, I wanted her dead. I wanted her dead because she threatened him, and I love him. I get how he came to my house that night looking for Lucas, but my baby was there, and now she's gone, and I still love him. Nyair, this hurts so bad."

Nyair leaned over on both knees and blew out a sharp breath. His heart ached, and he could hear every beat drumming in his ears. "Ethic isn't a bad man. He's done some horrible things, La. A lot of things that he thinks he has good reasons for, but it's all fueled by hate. I've heard the rumors. I know the stories. He's chosen you to expose the man beneath all that to. If you had told me this when you first met him, I would've told you to run away from this, La. I would be helping you pack your shit right now; but if I force you out of here, you're going to come right back. He's a part of you now. His DNA is in you. You carried a baby for him and he's put his heart in your hands. I know you love him. I can see it all over you. You've got to pray for him, La. You've got to pray for you. He's got demons. Heavy shit. His demons can infect this entire household. Blood on his hands, blood on your hands. You've got to search your spirit and get down on your knees and ask God to deliver him from the edge because he's one step from darkness. He can pull you over with him or you can pull him back. You have a right to protect yourself, La. If she was going to hurt you, you did what you had to do. It doesn't justify the sin. Sin is sin, but forgiveness is the Lord's to give. Pray for forgiveness. You've been filling up on Ethic, you need to fill up on God's love. You need to refuel; because right now, Ethic is ordering your steps. You've got to let God lead.

You've got to give control back to God and your love can be cleansed. You can forgive him, and I mean... really forgive him, not just suffer in silence. There is no right or wrong answer here, La. You can't let love lead you to the devil, though. That's not love. If love has you selling your soul, that's the enemy disguised in something that feels good. You know this, though, La. You know better than I know that the devil comes in the form of something good. You say Ethic's a gift. Well, who sent him? Who is the gift from? Is he coming from the Most High? Or from somewhere else?"

"A godly woman wouldn't be here. A godly woman wouldn't kill someone and not say anything. I have to tell someone, Ny. The police," Alani whispered.

"Let me ask you this, La. If you go to the police to confess, are you telling it all? You telling about Kenzie too? Or just your part? Just what you've done?"

"I'd never put him in jail, Nyair. He doesn't deserve that," she said. "Every, single action after that night has been made with the intention to love me back to life. He's fucked up, but he's not...he just doesn't deserve to be locked up like an animal, Ny." Alani stopped speaking because her logic wasn't quite logical. It was wrapped in love that caused her to justify his misdeeds. She didn't care. She could never do that to him. She could never do that to Bella, Eazy, and Morgan.

"And you do?" Nyair countered.

"You know I'm covered in this cloth, La, but a nigga cut from a whole different cloth too. You behind bars don't make a whole lot of sense to me, and telling half-truths to get justice for some bird that came at your head won't exonerate your sins. You'll just be a sinner that's not free. You have told someone. You're telling me, and I'm going to take this confession and carry it for you. You don't have to carry it anymore. I got you. You're already forgiven, but you have to re-align your faith and your devotion to the Lord, La. When I was in the streets, it was girls I knew I couldn't even approach, La. Cuz I wasn't on their level. I had to get my weight up before I even fixed my tongue to shoot my shot. That's you. That's how you have to be with God. Get your spirit up. Ethic ain't ready, and you're lowering your spiritual gate, so he can hop over it and play in your yard. You got to speak God's language, Alani. It's foreign to Ethic, but if he loves you enough, he'll learn it just to be able to reach you. He'll have to in order to connect to you."

"Her birthday is coming up, Ny, and I have this knot in my stomach. It's like I'm afraid of my own daughter's birthdate. I'm so lost, Ny. Can you just pray with me, Ny?" Alani whispered. She was so overwhelmed. She heard everything and felt everything Nyair was saying. She just didn't know if she was good enough to overpower all of Ethic's bad. It felt like she was becoming bad too.

Nyair and Alani clasped hands and he sat in that room with her for hours, praying and talking, praying and sorting through her thoughts, praying and wiping her tears. When he emerged, he saw Ethic sitting on the hallway floor, back to the wall, elbows propped on his bent knees. He looked so defeated.

"She's leaving," he said, voice full of burden…full of expectation that their time was coming to an end.

Nyair had never seen a more haunted couple. It was beautiful and horrifying all at the same time.

Nyair closed the bedroom door and looked down at Ethic.

"Nah, she's not doing that. I don't know what kind of love you over here serving, but I don't think she will ever leave, even if she knows she should. She'll just die here, trying to love you. If you care about her, you either got to let her go or you got to implement change, G. You ever put her in a position like this again, you'll have to kill me, bro, because I'ma try to kill you. Alani's been my family for a long time. I care about this girl and you're going to be the death of her. You can't protect her soul, if you're living through hell. Shake them devils, G."

Alani emerged from the room. "Ny. Wait," she whispered. "Can you drop me off at home?" she asked.

Ethic steeled. His heart stopped. Breathing stopped. He was going to lose her. He felt it.

"Yeah. I'll wait in the car," Nyair said.

Alani couldn't even look at Ethic.

He didn't speak. He didn't want to force her to stay.

"I just need some time," she whispered. "I can't sleep here. Can't be here."

Alani took five steps away from him, and every, single time she placed one foot in front of the other, her heart felt like it was being ripped in half.

"Ethic?"

"Yeah, baby?" he answered. He sounded so dejected,

and she closed her eyes because she knew he was feeling desertion.

"Is love enough?" she whispered.

"I don't know," he answered, honestly.

Alani walked out, and Ethic took a seat on that top step because she had taken all his strength with her.

CHAPTER 16

I thought you wanted to go to Nannie's?" Nyair asked. Alani looked out of the passenger side window at the cement head stones that were lined up in the lawn. It was a perfect day. The sun shined down over the greenest grass Alani had ever seen. It reminded her of the color her daughter used to choose when she drew pictures on construction paper.

"The kids are there," she whispered. "They will think something's wrong."

"Isn't it?" Nyair's skepticism was written all over his face.

Alani sighed. "I don't know. I just couldn't stay there. I just..." she paused. Her heart was weighted. She was burdened by the fact that she had run out on Ethic yet again, filled with remorse from killing Dolce, sickened by fear of the consequences that may follow both actions. "I just need to think."

Alani pressed her head against the head rest and shook it in disbelief.

"He killed my daughter Ny," Alani whispered. "This is crazy. This has to be some type of depression. A psychotic break. He killed my daughter and I sleep next to him every night."

"La if you want out. If you want me to go grab your shit…"

"Stuff Nyair. I swear your mouth," Alani scoffed. "You're the most devilish man of God in the world."

"I'm serious La," Nyair said, staying focused. "If you want me to give you an out. To tell Ethic you're done. I will."

"If only it was that simple," Alani answered. "He's a stain on my heart. I can't get him out."

"I don't think he can get you out either," Nyair admitted.

"I don't know how I love him, but I do. So much."

"And that's okay," Nyair said. "I'm here if you ever need me. You know that, right?"

Alani nodded. "I know." She sighed and her eyes took in the empty cemetery.

"You need to be near Kenzie?" he asked.

"I'm here to see Lucas," Alani said. "I haven't been here. I was so mad, so confused by what he did that I haven't even been back. I didn't even bury him near Kenzie. Something just didn't feel right about burying them side by side."

"Let me ask you something La," Nyair said. "What was Kenzie doing sleeping that closely to Lucas?"

Alani's heart stopped beating. Why was her eyes watering? Instant anguish. Immediate turmoil. Her gut flipped. Why was her body going haywire? A mother's intuition was a motherfucker. She knew what was going to come out of Nyair's mouth before he even said it.

"Did he sleep like that with her when you were home? Ever?" Nyair asked.

Alani went through her mind in a flash.

Did he? He didn't. Never while I was there. I've never ever seen her in his room. Why was she under him? Her thoughts jumped her in, initiating her into a gang called truth that was so deadly that Alani's soul screamed for mercy, screamed for it to stop.

"Baby girl didn't talk much. She was timid. Fearful around me almost. Around men."

"What are you saying?" Alani asked.

"I'm just asking," Nyair said.

"But what are you saying?" she shouted. Her stomach. God her stomach. She closed her eyes and pulled in air.

"Lucas was a predator Alani. He brutally raped Mo. You worked so much…"

"I had to work! I had to feed her and clothe her Ny. I had to pay for health care and Nannie's medicine and…"

"I know, La. I know you did. You were the best mother to her. She would light up when she saw your face. You're the best mother I've ever seen, but I'm just asking-

"I would have noticed, Nyair! I know what that feels like! My mama never protected me! I would have noticed, Ny. Right?" Alani couldn't see. Memories and tears flooded her.

"He was her uncle," Alani whispered.

"If everything happens for a reason, La, what's the reason for this? For Ethic to kill a child? I don't know if I'm reaching La, but Lucas was no saint. If he was hurting Kenz. If she was afraid to tell you or maybe couldn't tell you. She was just a baby, maybe she didn't even know it was wrong. If he was terrorizing her. If your home was hell, maybe God sent an angel He lost a long time ago.

Maybe He lost Ethic and He put all this in motion to save two souls that belonged to Him. Maybe Ethic was sent into your house that night to bring Kenzie back to God and that single sin pushed him into your life and is reeling him in, right back to God too. Maybe Ethic ended Kenzie's pain and gave her back to God where He could keep her safe. Now she's okay and Ethic's okay and his children have you, a beautiful woman, a mother. Kenzie won't miss time with you, La. This earthly time we go by feels like a long time to you, but when you return to the kingdom, she won't have missed a moment. A lifetime to us is like a minute where Kenz is. She's not suffering. God comes like a thief in the night, La. You know that. Ethic came and stole Kenzie away from the devil like a thief in the middle of the night. He didn't leave her. He stayed. He held her, until God brought her home."

Alani placed both hands over her mouth. "God, he hurt my baby."

Everything came out of her. She pushed open the door and couldn't contain the vomit that erupted from her. He was at her side and she reached up, gripping his forearm as she sobbed. Alani wiped her mouth with the back of her hand and glanced up through her tears. Lucas' gravesite was only twenty yards away. The freshly dug grave beside his was so new that shovels still lied in the dirt. Alani stood to her feet, determined, conflicted, torn the fuck to pieces on the inside. Alani picked up the shovel from the grass and gripped it tightly in one hand as she stalked over to Lucas' head stone.

The scream that erupted from her as she swung on her brother echoed through the air, causing birds to flee from the tree tops.

She took that shovel to Lucas' headstone so many times that it was barely legible. The words 'brother' and 'uncle' were completely damaged. Alani was exhausted and her chest heaved as grief snatched her to her knees, right in the grass.

Nyair picked Alani up from where she fell, and she wrapped her arms around his neck. She couldn't even speak.

"I'm so sorry La," he said, kissing the side of her head as he gripped her with love. He was strength wrapped in the word of God. A friend when Alani needed one most. "I'ma take you home. I wouldn't give you to a man that I thought would hurt you. He won't," Nyair promised. He carried her back to the car and tucked her inside the passenger side before pulling off.

Alani was silent the entire ride back to Ethic's. So many things ran through her mind. So much regret. Sorrow. A woman had never been more haunted. The passageways to a woman's heart were infinite. With every experience a woman built new walls, sometimes they twisted and turned, creating a maze of emotions that caused her to lose herself. If she made one wrong turn, she could spend years misdirected from happiness. Alani had built a castle of sadness in her heart and she was the wicked queen that sat on the throne. She was filled with torment. Alani believed whole heartedly in the puzzle Nyair had put together and while it made her look at Ethic in a new way, she also judged herself. She was responsible. She was a mother. She had worked hard to provide a safe home for her daughter all the while the greatest threat was living under her roof. She had failed her child and that failure lived in her bones. When they arrived, Alani saw Ethic in the garage, bent over the open hood of an old school car. These cars. This hobby. Fixing shit. Rebuilding shit. His heart was the only thing he didn't know how to repair. A tangible metaphor of him as a man. He looked up at her in surprise as she emerged from Nyair's vehicle. She stood in the middle of the driveway and he remained rooted in the garage, but the energy that filled the space between their gaze was magnetic. Her chin trembled.

"It was a really bad day," she said.

He nodded and bit down on his bottom lip. "Yeah, baby. It was," he agreed. He was emotional. Anyone else wouldn't have been able to tell, but the way his shoulders rounded forward slightly, the deepest lines etched in his forehead, and the way he was squeezing the red mechanic's rag in his strong hands. She knew he had been through hell every minute she had been away. She had left, but she had come back. Words evaded him.

"I want to talk, but I just need a minute," she said.

Ethic looked to Nyair who stood behind Alani, hanging out of the car, one hand on the roof. Nyair gave him a nod, one that Ethic returned before diverting his attention back to the old school because well...he had to fix this shit. They both needed some time to think. Some time to process all that had happened. Nyair got in the car and pulled off as Alani walked in the front door. As she looked around Ethic's massive home, she released another sob. Everything had happened for a reason and Alani let out a deep breath as she walked upstairs to retreat to the master bedroom to rest her weary heart.

Alani entered the garage. She pulled at the hem of the t-shirt, his t-shirt, her nightgown as she saw half of him. His face was hidden behind the lifted car hood, the sound of the tools he used echoed in the air.

She stepped closer into view and he paused, looking up in alarm. She hadn't been able to get out of bed all week. She was such a godly woman that murder had taken the strength out of her legs. She had drowned herself in the Bible. He found her up at all hours of the night, listening to Sarah Jakes sermons and praying. Her tears seemed endless. Alani's soul had been disturbed, again, because of him, and she would never be the same.

"Come."

Alani's gold-painted toes crossed the concrete floor, instantly. He opened his arms wide, as she wrapped her hands around his body. He was covered in sweat and grease.

"I'm filthy, baby..." He didn't close his arms around her body because she was clean. She was brilliant, and he was dirty. She was cleansed, and he was soiled. The pure versus impure. Alani felt that. She knew he felt it. The baptized and the wild. There was a difference between them. A line drawn in the sand between them and he didn't want to taint her.

She decoded the hidden message, instantly. The mind of this man was so complex that it was easy to miss his intent. It was easy to misinterpret, but Alani was so aligned with his spirit that she spoke his love language effortlessly. There was shame hanging from him. Like he was insecure about the tar that covered his soul and he couldn't even touch her for fear of staining her.

Alani looked down at the pan of oil that sat under the hood. She dipped both hands inside it and then closed her eyes, as she ran those dirty hands down her face and around her neck. He was stoic, as he watched her dip them, again, and then she reached up to touch his face.

She took hold of his beard, gripping it, as she stood on tip-toes to bring her face close to his. Alani's eyes closed, and her breath hitched, because this man…God, this man just did things to her…things she had never felt with anyone else before…shit she couldn't even explain. It was like her body malfunctioned around him. This love had to be the most potent ever known to man. "I want to be covered in whatever covers you, until we figure out how to clean it all off - together…how to get it all out… we'll just have to be filthy together. I don't care, Ezra."

He closed his arms around her, planting his chin in the top of her hair and kissing her scalp in appreciation. Her hands slid south, trailing grease down his wife beater, and then gripped the bottom to pull it over his head. She trailed one finger around the waistband of his sweatpants and the dick print expanded. One touch and his desire grew. Alani jumped up and Ethic's hands caught her beneath her ass, as he moved her against the tool rack. Her back hit something hard and she didn't even flinch because she felt the heat of his flesh more as he invaded her.

"Shhh," she laughed, as all types of tools fell to the floor, clanging loudly. "Ezra! They're going to wake-up."

Ethic ignored her, as he lifted both her legs over his shoulders.

"Mmmm," he groaned, as he pushed into her depths. Alani's back rested on the tool rack and she felt all types of shit stabbing into her, but she didn't care. The pleasure was more than worth the discomfort, as he took her on a ride.

"Ethic, baby," she whispered.

There was so much aggression in him, as he pulled her hips into him as he hit her with deep strokes.

Dirty as fuck.

Ethic wasn't a quick fuck type of man. He took his time, he pulled pleasure out of every inch of a woman, but the way he was busting her open in this garage felt like he was desperate for this nut, like he was racing to feel anything other than what he felt…like he was fucking the guilt from his soul. These strokes were deadly. He took no pause to consider the size of him. He put a pounding on her pussy.

"Mmmm, Ethiccc," she moaned. He lifted her back up until they were chest to chest and Alani wrapped her arms around his neck, as he moved her to a wall. She kissed him, biting his bottom lip, as he gripped the back of her neck with one hand and the bottom of her ass with the other. "I'm done, baby, I'm fucking doneeeeee," she cried out, her pussy convulsing.

It was the quickest orgasm she'd ever had and the fucking best. He placed one hand on the wall behind her and buried his face in the crease of her neck.

"Fuck," he groaned. She felt him. Every seed he left inside her felt like healing, they felt like repeated apologies, as their heavy breathing filled the space between their lips when he pulled back. He placed her on her feet and adjusted himself, but he kept her there, trapped between his body and the wall. He placed his palms to the wall around her and kissed her, long and deep. He was a whole gangster, so cold, so stern, but with her he was soft. He was vulnerable in a way that no one else got to witness.

"I'm sorry. For everything, Lenika. With all of me, I am sorry," he said. "What you had to do..."

"Was what needed to be done. I understand so many things. I get how a good person can end up with blood on their hands. I get how a person can be pushed to do the unthinkable to protect someone they love. I get how you never really look at yourself the same, how you wash your hands a hundred times a day, trying to clean them, how you feel heavy all day afterwards. You've been walking around like that since I met you... probably longer. I didn't know how heavy it was, baby. I get it now, Ethic. I get every part of you and I'm so sorry for judging you before. That wasn't my place," she whispered. "You're the most beautiful man I've ever met. Nyair gave me a lot to think about, and when I get to the end of every, single thought...every, single plan of what I'm supposed to do next, you're there...every notion of how I move on from this leads me back to you. I would do it all over again to protect you."

"I'm not fucking worthy, man," he scoffed, shaking his head. "How the fuck did I even end up with you? I had the nerve to be mad at you over some fuck shit, some dumb shit. Over a father that I don't even know. Over a nigga you were with before me. Over Love, when I was the one who put you in the position to give birth by someone you feared. I was out of line, Lenika, and you still stepped over a nigga, you still..."

Tears clung to her lashes.

"Ethic, you had every right to be upset with me. I owe you so many explanations," she whispered, as his eyes bore into hers.

"You don't-"

"You said I was trying to turn you into him," she interrupted. "I would never try to turn you into someone else. You're perfection. There's no need to change you. Niggas need to study you, be more Ethical about their shit, be you, do everything like you. Walk like you, talk like you, fuck like you, everything. I wouldn't ever want anything else. This was about your soul. About your turmoil. About finding someone I thought you could connect to that could help you work those things out. I just wanted to help."

"You have. In ways you can't even comprehend," he stated. "I'ma show you. I'ma be the man you deserve. Every chance I get, I'ma show you because you've shown me that love is evidence that God is real; and if God is real, that means a nigga can be saved. That all the shit I've done can be forgiven. Thank you for teaching me, for saving me..."

Alani was ruined. She rested her head on his chest, as she sobbed. She cried from her soul and he held her because it was his job. It was a job he didn't take lightly, and she knew that no matter what storm they encountered, he would make sure she was always okay.

Ethic watched the oil rinse down the drain, as he stood in the shower, hands to the wall, head bowed. He wondered if it was truly that easy. To cleanse a man. Just to dip him in a little water and erase all he had done before. Meeting Alani was an introduction to so much more than a woman. She had introduced him to God; and while he was still figuring it out, he couldn't deny that he believed in Him. Her love had to be from God. Any earthly connection would have been destroyed by the things he had done. No, Lenika's love was being supplied from somewhere else. He felt her step in behind him. Her hands on his back. Her lips on the back of his shoulder. Then, her hands wrapping around him.

He turned to face her.

"We'll go to second service on Sunday," Ethic stated. "So, get some rest." He kissed her forehead, and then her lips, before stepping out. She reached for his hand.

"Hey," she whispered.

He paused, looking at her, witnessing her anxiety as it danced in her troubled eyes.

"What is it?" he asked.

"I'm fine with church Sunday. I need it, but I'd like to spend some time at home this week…"

"You are home," he interrupted.

"Nannie's. I need to leave. My daughter's birthday is this week. I can't be here with you on that day," she whispered.

Remorse lived in him and his stomach went missing. He hated that there were days that she wouldn't be able to stand the sight of him. On those days, there would be nothing he could do to make it better.

"Okay," he answered.

He turned and walked out of the bathroom. His spirit was unnerved because he wasn't sure if Alani could endure days like that. Honestly, he didn't know if he could withstand them either. The pain and resentment was heavy between them. Even Ethic could feel the burden.

CHAPTER 17

Alani sat on the porch, nose tilted, as she got lost in the words on the page in front of her. Writing out the pain that this day had brought was necessary. It felt like she was bleeding onto the journal she had in her hands. Like the ink from the pen was leaking from her veins. It was Kenzie's birthday, and it just hurt so damn bad.

"Yo! Hold up, hold up! That's big homie pulling up!"

Alani heard the group of young boys across the street announce his presence, but it wasn't necessary. She felt him before she even heard the words. Alani looked up, in stun, as he stepped out of the Range Rover. It never failed. Her heart skipped beats every time she was in his presence. She wondered if she'd ever get used to him being hers, if he even was still hers. She hadn't seen him in a few days. She hadn't even heard his voice. This visit was unexpected.

He was casual, in Nike joggers, grey, hoe attire and Alani felt her temper flare as her eyes zeroed in on the print that had made her call his name nights before. She quivered, as he took long steps in her direction, wrapping her in his embrace.

"Hey," she greeted, as he lifted her chin and kissed her deeply…always deeply, always drowning her, making that print jump in wanting. He wanted to fuck her. It was a constant mood. Heightened sexuality between the two of them that they never resisted. "Hmm," she groaned. "Why do you do this to me?" she whispered, in the milli-second that he released her lips, before pulling the bottom one back into his mouth. He didn't care that they were outside, in broad daylight, neighbors coming and going, kids jumping through the fire hydrant that had been cracked open in front of the house next door, Nannie sitting on the porch, sipping coffee, while Mr. Larry gassed up the lawn mower. Ethic accosted her like he owned her… like he didn't need permission…because he didn't. Alani would drop that thang like it was hot wherever he wanted her to, whenever he wanted her to, and from the feeling of his need pressed against her…he wanted her to…right here, right now.

"I fucking miss you," he groaned.

"I missed you too," she replied. His hands were in her hair, pulling, controlling her gaze, her neck easing backward, so she was staring up at him. The pads of his fingers massaged her scalp and she wondered if he meant to do stuff like that…massage her worries away as she drowned in his gaze. He couldn't be that in tune with her needs, couldn't be that thoughtful, it had to be just coincidence.

"You look stressed, like somebody's pulling the Lenika out of you," he whispered. Those words let her know that the scalp massage was intentional…everything he did to her was intentional, no guessing. He was in tune with her mind, body, and soul.

"Everybody gets Lenika, Ethic. Except you. You're the only one I give Alani too," she said, eyes glistening, always so emotional around this man. "You make me sound crazy, talking about myself in third person."

"You got a little crazy in you, baby. A little nut to you," he said, tapping her temple, before kissing her lips, feeding her his tongue, while sucking out her soul. She cupped his face with her hands. "The nut is my favorite flavor."

The pulse that filled her body traveled to her clit. "Ethic, stop, you know it doesn't take much to make me..."

"Nut," he finished. "I know. I'm tryna do that... ASAP," he returned.

"I thought I asked for space? It's a hard day for me, Ethic. I went to the cemetery today. It's her birthday and I have to visit a grave to see her. It's fucking with me. I didn't want you to feel the energy I'm giving off today," she explained. "It's not good. I'm angry today. Sad."

"I know. Ms. Pat told me," Ethic said. "I can leave, if you want. We can spend today apart, but I'd rather spend it with you. Even through the bad days and the shitty mood. I'd still rather be here."

"Ethic..." she whispered.

He pinched her chin and pulled her forehead to his. "I really want to eat your pussy, baby. Like, I can taste that shit on my lips. Let me suck the pain away," he whispered. Alani's eyes fluttered, and her panties soaked. He pecked her lips.

"Go throw on some clothes," he said. They both knew that she couldn't say no.

Alani pulled away, reluctant to even leave his embrace; and although she was walking, it felt like she was floating. She had to look down to make sure her feet were even touching the ground. Alani climbed the wet porch steps and Nannie snickered.

"What, old woman?" Alani asked, smiling.

"I knew you wanted him around today. Fake mad behind," Nannie said.

Alani glanced back at Ethic who was relieving Mr. Larry of the lawn mower and giving a friendly pat on the shoulder. *Such a gentleman.*

"I'm not fake mad. I'm not even mad. It just hurts," she whispered.

"When a man is sorry, you let him show you he's sorry. Loving him doesn't mean you love Kenzie any less. It was a mistake. He's yours. You better act like it before someone comes along that knows exactly how to show him he's appreciated," Nannie schooled.

Alani sighed, a heavy sigh, the kind that came from a woman's soul, before leaning to kiss her great aunt on the cheek. Skin so soft graced her lips and Alani wrapped both hands around Nannie's neck. "Thanks, old lady. I love you."

"Mmm hmm. Love you too," Nannie replied.

Alani rushed inside. She took the stairs two at a time, rushing, like she was preparing for her very first date…like Ethic would pull away if she made him wait…like there was a carriage that would turn into a pumpkin if she took too long.

Her hair was a mess. If this was a date, she should be sleek, dressed in a fancy dress with a beat face. Put on for her man a little to remind him that she could match his effortless fly. Hers took some effort, however, and today all she could scrape up was a sleeveless sweater dress with a cowl neck and big, bouncy curls from the flexi rod set she had done the night before. A pair of open-toed, open-heeled, thigh-high boots dressed it up a bit. Eyeliner, Ruby Woo, and six swipes of mascara. She was ready.

Laughter flowed from the living room, and when she rounded the corner, she found Ethic laughing while embracing Nannie.

In her hand was a slender, burgundy box. The word *Cartier* was pressed in gold on the top. Nannie pulled back and patted his cheek and said, "You're a good man. Thank you, baby."

He stepped toward Alani. "You ready?"

"Uh huh," she answered.

She looked over her shoulder and watched Nannie remove a beautiful, pearl necklace, before allowing him to lead her out the door. He held her hand, lacing their fingers, and then opened the passenger door. The gentle pat to the ass as she slid between his body and the car set Alani on fire. She turned to him slightly, eyeing him, completely intoxicated with his aura. She was overdosed on Ethic, high...drunk...but she knew that couldn't be true, because if she was 'Ethical' about her shit, then these bad notions wouldn't be filling her mind...wild thoughts ran rampant inside Alani's pretty, little head before he closed the car door.

A burst of heat hit her, as soon as he opened the passenger door to the Range. It was scorching outside, and the inside was like an oven. Her hair swelled, instantly, and she feathered it, as Ethic quickly rolled down the window until his air conditioning adjusted. "To preserve your edges," he said. She looked at him in shock. How the hell did he know her so fucking well? It was like he could read her thoughts. She had complained about sweating her edges out enough times, sure enough, but damn, did men even pay attention to things like that?

"I'm not in the best mood, Ethic," she said.

"I know," he said. He leaned into her and maneuvered her chin toward him. He kissed her lips, the gloss she wore making their skin stick slightly, before he pulled back. "I know."

He pulled away from the curb and Alani crossed her arms, remaining silent, as they drove away.

"A bottle of wine would be great right now," she uttered, as she looked out the window. She saw the dots on her window. One. Then, two. Then, four.

"Is it raining?" she asked, leaning forward, nose curled up as she pushed her eyes up, her brow crinkling, as she looked at the sky. A streak of lightning cut across the sky. The sky was crying. Out of nowhere, the sunny, summer day had clouded, and rain was falling. It reminded her of her tears because all day she would explode in a downpour of emotion without warning. The rain gave her pleasure, for some reason, because now the sky matched her mood. A gloomy and sad day. God was crying, and Alani's eyes prickled, because she knew He had her daughter with Him. It was a day of mourning and it took everything in her not to let the tears fall down her face. She pressed a finger to the corners of her eyes and sniffed, before looking out the window. Ethic's hand reached for hers and she felt his warmth as he laced his fingers through hers. His skin was hot, always warmer than hers, always burning when in her presence, and she didn't deny him. She squeezed his hand tightly, but didn't look his way, because she couldn't without crying. She loved him, but on her daughter's birthday, she hated him. It was something he would just have to accept. Three days out the year, her emotions would change. She would go dark, because he had mistakenly taken her daughter away. Mistake or not, the shit still hurt, and Alani wore her pain on her sleeve today. "We might as well go back. Nobody wants to be out here in all this," she said. Lenika was out in full effect today.

"We won't be out long," he said, pulling their joined fists to his lips and kissing her hand. Even his lips there left a tingle behind. He was love. He exuded love. A whole-ass gangster with a weakness for her and he had come into her life like a storm…much like the one developing outside her window…unexpected and unforgiving. The rain picked up and the sound of the tires racing through puddles of water created a soundtrack of turmoil, as they rode in absolute silence.

"Where are we going?" she asked.

"Somewhere I think you'll like. Somewhere that will make you feel purpose," he said. "I miss my girl."

"I saw you a few days ago, Ezra," she said.

"Nah, baby. I saw Lenika a few days ago. It's been awhile since I've seen Alani. I miss her," he said.

Alani went silent, feeling guilt, because she knew she'd been carrying him with resentment. Ever since Dolce's murder, and the days leading up to this day, Alani had been distant, spending more time at Nannie's than at home with him. She had dreaded this day, this month, it was like an old scab had been peeled back and she was bleeding all over again.

"I love her too. She ride it real good," he said, pulling that bottom lip into his mouth and sucking on it…savoring it, because… hey, she glossed that bitch almost every night.

Alani turned red and her entire body warmed. "Ezra," she whispered. "Your mouth is filthy."

"I put everything in it, it should be," he shot back.

Alani quivered, and when she blinked, images of him feasting on her, from front to back, leaving no part of her untouched, as she gripped her ankles in the center of their bed, filled her mind. He did. He ate everything. Every time. Like he was starving.

He smirked at her modesty, and then maneuvered the car into the parking lot at their destination.

"Ethic, are the kids hurt?" she asked, panicking, as they arrived at the local hospital.

"Everyone's fine. This is for you," he said. He exited the car and Alani's confused gaze followed him around the car, as he made his way to her door. He opened the door and she sat there, hesitant and staring up at him. Her eyes rolled to the hospital.

"You trying to commit me, Mr. Okafor?" she asked.

He smirked, a half leer that pulled at the corner of his mouth. "Can you just trust me?" he asked.

A sigh. A stubborn one, because if she could trust no one else, she could trust him. Her mood just didn't allow her to follow behind him without protest.

"Have you cried? Have you allowed yourself to cry?" he asked.

Such consideration. Such selflessness. She nodded.

"But you're crying alone. You're trying to hide that you're hurting," he said.

She nodded, again.

"Don't hide from me, Lenika," he said. Her eyes prickled. "If you cry, you do it in my arms, baby. No other place. No other way. You cry to me. It's because of me, so let me collect the tears."

It never failed. He stunned her to silence. Loved her into submission. A tear slid down her face and he caught it with his thumb, swiping it away, and then brought his thumb to his lips, kissing it. Her tears to his lips. She lowered her head into the center of his chest and wrapped her arms around his waist, as he pulled her into his embrace. He was her security, her protection, her connection. He kept her safe, even from her own thoughts that crippled her. He kept her more secure more than any outside force ever could. He protected her from himself, because today of all days, her anger, her sadness, was a product of his actions.

"Come on," he whispered, grabbing her hand and leading her into the hospital.

Alani followed him into the building and up to the seventh floor.

"Who's here, Ethic?" she asked, as he pushed through the doors of the pediatric wing.

"Mr. Okafor, so nice to see you again. I have to say. You chose the perfect day to do this. We're short-staffed today. Your arms are needed today," the woman said. "You must be Lenika." The nurse extended her hand and Alani paused for a beat before extending her own, nodding.

"I've heard so much about you. It's a pleasure to meet you," the lady said.

Alani rolled confused eyes to Ethic and then back down to the woman. "Nice to meet you as well."

"Right this way."

Hesitant feet allowed Ethic to lead her down the hall and she paused when she stood in front of the nursery.

So many beautiful babies were lined up in bassinets on the other side of the window. Alani's stomach churned. Angst filled her. She'd had one of those before...a gift...the ultimate gift from her creator...a baby to call her own, and now she didn't. Because of him...the man she loved...she didn't. She rolled eyes of discontent over to him. She tried to control the resentment. She was usually quite good at keeping it concealed, hiding it from him; but today, on her late daughter's birthday, it was impossible.

"Come."

The command she always followed.

She held his hand tightly, as they entered a room, a sterile space with metal sinks.

"Wash your hands and forearms and then put these hospital gowns over your clothes. These babies are susceptible to illness because they were born so prematurely but they're fighters. They don't have mothers and we don't have enough hands to go around. So, you two coming here is a blessing. The renaming of this wing. The Love Kenzie wing, in honor of your donation and the program you've put in place to help these babies and their mothers. Wow. It's going to do a lot of good."

Alani darted misted eyes to Ethic. "What wing? What is she talking about, Ezra?"

"I was going to wait until tonight to tell you about your gift, but I guess now will do," he said. "I've partnered with the pediatrics board here and donated to help update this entire floor. They've agreed to name it in Love and Kenzie's honor and pair it with an initiative to help mothers dealing with the loss of a child. It will pair grieving mothers with babies whose mothers have died during childbirth. They'll donate time to come in and hold the babies on this wing and receive therapy to help deal with their grief. Each mother who commits to an 8-week program will be backed by a benefactor who will donate $50,000. Half of which will go into a scholarship fund for the child to access in the future. The other half will go to the mother, to help subsidize during her time of grief. You're standing in the Love Kenzie wing of this hospital. The program is for Kenzie. A birthday gift for her. To honor her memory, and it's a cause for you to lead, in honor of all you've lost."

Alani was speechless. Who the fuck thought of shit like this? What man? Ethic raised all standards. The expectation with him was always heightened, always unreachable by any other man behind him. A motherfucking whole floor of a hospital named after the children she had lost. This nigga here. Alani blinked away emotion, pressing a delicate finger to the corners of her eyes, and turning away from him to hide the tears. It had to have taken him months to plan. He had thought of this day in advance. Premeditated to ensure that everything would be ready to present to her. She hadn't even known he was aware of her daughter's birthday.

"Can we have a minute?" he asked. The question was only a nicety because Ethic was a nigga with decorum. It was really an order. An indication to leave immediately and the woman nodded with a flat-lipped smile.

"Come inside when you're ready," she said.

"I'm going to fuck you so good tonight, boy, it's not even funny," she whispered.

The laugh that erupted from him caused her to turn around. Her cheeks were wet, but her eyes sparkled. "Ezra, this is incredible. It's..." she shook her head because words were elusive.

"I know that this day will be hard for the rest of our lives, but I'm here. I'm here when you don't want me here. When you're fucking mad as hell. When you're drowning, I'm here, Lenika. I'ma jump in after you every time."

His thumbs swept over her face, clearing her tears. "You want to go inside? Meet some of them? If it's too much, you don't have to hold them. You don't have to do anything you're not comfortable with."

"I'm comfortable. They need someone," she whispered. It came out urgent, like she was afraid the gift was refundable. She turned to the sink and washed her hands and arms, as Ethic did the same. He slipped a hospital gown over her clothes and then put one on himself, before taking her hand. Alani's throat tightened, and it felt like she was sipping air through a straw, barely getting enough to stay alive, barely enough to function. She gripped his hand so tightly that her knuckles hurt.

"Do you see one that you'd like to meet?" the woman asked.

"All of them," she whispered. "I want to hold them all."

Ethic and Alani sat in the two rocking chairs, side by side, as a nurse brought over one of the babies.

Alani's chest locked, as a baby boy was placed in her arms. He was so small that she felt like she may break him. Tubes ran through his tiny, button nose and his eyes were closed. The tiny rise and fall of his chest brought her to tears. What she wouldn't have given to see her son take just one breath. He'd never gotten the chance.

"So precious," she whispered. She placed the receiving blanket over her shoulder and lifted him to her breasts, and then lifted on her tip-toes and rocked the chair backwards. A gentle sway, as her eyes closed, sealed shut with tears. "He's so small, Ezra." Her voice was a notch above a whisper, like she was afraid if she spoke too loudly his little ears might break. "He's all alone." Her eyes were still closed, and she rocked. "My heart has been aching all day, just unbelievable pain...until right now..."

She popped her eyes open. "How do you love like this?"

The coarse skin of the back of one dark finger swept across her skin, clearing tears. It was flint to stone, just that simple contact, igniting a fire in her heart. Had any other man committed the crime that Ethic had against her, Alani would have hated him. She would have killed him, but she had no wins against Ethic. A man like him was designed to love. It was a travesty to waste any other emotion on him besides love.

"It ain't for everybody, Lenika. I love you like this. Only you," he stated. "Everyone else gets a much different version of me."

The nurse brought another baby to Ethic. He shook his head. "I'm just here for her," he said. There was a tone. A somber that lived in his voice, and Alani blinked misted eyes to him.

"You can hold him, Ethic," she whispered. She knew why he wouldn't touch another baby. She knew, and it broke her.

"No, I can't," he stated. The finality in that. It hurt her in the deepest parts of her soul. Holding babies reminded him of Love and he didn't need a reminder of their stillborn son. He didn't want to betray that memory. The feeling of his son in his arms. Even holding YaYa's son had diluted the memory of the feeling of Love in his arms a bit. He had been filled with guilt ever since. If he couldn't hold Love, he didn't want to hold any other baby. It just didn't feel right.

Alani didn't push him. She knew what it felt like to be forced to heal before you were ready. They stayed in the nursery for hours, like they were there to work a shift. Alani held all eight babies, for an hour each; and when it was time to go, she couldn't will herself to leave the room.

"Ethic, I can't just leave them here," she whispered.

"You can come back, baby. Whenever you want," he said, cupping her face.

"Tomorrow?" she asked.

"Every day, if you want," he promised. He pulled her to his chest and she rested a cheek against him, as his fingers massaged the nape of her neck.

"I made a reservation with your body tonight, baby, and I can't cancel that," he whispered. Alani's heart stopped, and her fingers curled on his sweatshirt, gripping, like she needed to hold on tightly because he was about to take her on a ride.

"You're going to kill me, Ezra. The shit you say. The things you do...my heart can't take it," she whispered.

"I can ease up. If you're overwhelmed. I don't want to. I want to press you, Ms. Hill. I want to put full-court fucking pressure on you until the day I die, because the shit I feel for you I got to get out...it's so damn strong... but if I'm doing too much... If you're not ready..."

"I'm ready," she interrupted. "I just have to get used to a man doing what he says he's going to do. That's all. I keep waiting for the other shoe to drop."

"You don't have to wait for that. It ain't happening," he assured. He kissed her forehead and a sigh of relief left her lips. He clasped her hand, kissing her knuckles, before leading her out.

The car ride to Detroit was silent. Not even music filled the space between them. Just her thoughts and his love. They pulled into the five-star hotel, an hour later.

"Have you eaten?" "Are you hungry?" he asked.

"Not for food," she answered.

Ethic made a heartbeat fill her clit. The licking of lips and such always made her remember what he lubricated them with. Her. She came all over those lips almost every morning and he licked them just like that. Like she was the best thing he'd ever tasted. *Nasty-ass.*

The valet opened the door for her and she exited, waiting until Ethic was at her side before walking with him into the hotel.

She stood to the side, as he retrieved the key, and they headed to the top. Penthouse. She was used to the luxury, at this point. They walked inside, and the lights of the city skyline drew her to the window.

"This view is incredible," she gasped.

He wasn't at her side. He was near the door, back leaned against the wood.

"It's a fucking sight," he said.

She turned. He wasn't talking about the skyline. His eyes were on her. Alani made her way across the room and jumped into his arms, forcing him to hold her, as she wrapped her legs around his waist. Her lips on his. Her pussy pressing against hard dick. He walked. Headed for the bedroom. When he entered the room, Alani saw candles flickering everywhere.

At least a hundred, burning, casting a glow over the room. A massage table sat in the center.

He bypassed the room and headed for the bathroom. Champagne, on ice, sat on the floor beside the clawfoot tub. Bubbles filled the tub.

"Relax for a while," he said, kissing her cheek, a quick peck, before he turned. Alani caught his arm, pulling him back.

"Stay," she whispered.

"Not yet," he said. His hands rounded her waist and then rode the curves of her hips, cuffing her ass, as he pulled her into him. She groaned because even when Ethic wasn't ready, he hung so well that he made her want to ride him. He lifted the dress, pulling it up and over her head. Expert hands unhooked her bra, and as he bent, he took the time to acknowledge her breasts. His tongue antagonized her nipples, a quick swirl around each areola, as he pushed them together. They tightened. She could feel them, prickling, as they pruned against his tongue.

"Goddamn," he groaned.

He kneeled and then slid her panties down. She stepped out of them and placed her hands on top of his head, as he squared off with her femininity. Ethic versus freshly-waxed pussy; because who was she kidding, she knew he would partake in it today...she was sure Ethic would win. He leaned forward and kissed her there, sliding his tongue between her lips. He found her clit, disrobed it and sucked so long and so hard that Alani's legs gave out. She sat on the edge of the tub, thighs wide open, and his head between them. He kissed it one more time. Gentle. Quick, and then swiped his hand down his mouth, before standing to his feet. "Relax. Enjoy your bath. Take your time and then come to me."

Her chest heaved and all she could do was nod. Alani stepped into the tub and submerged in its depths. The champagne had her buzzing and the water erased every bit of tension that rested in her shoulders. She let the water soothe her for an hour before climbing out.

"Ethic, baby, are you hungry? This Dom has my head spinning a little," she called out, as she wrapped her wet body in a towel. She stepped into the room and Ethic sat on the bed, a white, hotel robe donned his body. He sat leaned over, elbows to knees, a tumbler of cognac rested in his hands. He swirled it and then lifted it to his lips. The music crooning in the room put her heart at ease. It was one of her favorite songs.

"I love H.E.R."

I wanna love you, in every kind of way
I wanna please you no matter how long it takes

"You're drinking?" she asked, a bit stunned, because Ethic didn't indulge much. Normally, he only did so when there was something on his mind. "Is everything okay?" she asked.

"I want to do something to you, baby. I want to do something with you," he said.

She walked to him, maneuvering between his legs and forcing him to sit up straight. He rested his head on her stomach, while wrapping one hand around her waist. He downed the rest of his glass. She frowned because she felt apprehension in the air. She pinched his chin and lifted his face. She stared him in the eyes.

Give you all
Give you all of meee
When you need it, cuz I need it

"Anything," she whispered. "You can do anything to me."
A knock at the door pulled Alani's attention and he stood, turning her chin back to him.
"You trust me?" he asked.
"With my life," she whispered.
He walked to the door. He pulled it open and a woman stood on the outside. Tan trench coat, six-inch heels and black-painted lips.
"Hello, Ezra," she greeted.
"Come in," he returned.
Alani stood, baffled, as the woman walked into the room carrying a canvas tote.
"Who is she?" Alani asked.
"I'm Syria," the woman introduced. Her tone was so soft, Alani felt like she had been kissed. The kindness in the woman's eyes and the peace in her smile caused a conflict in Alani's heart, because her intuition was telling her that this woman was comfortable with her man. "I'm a massage therapist."
Alani's brows lifted in confusion. She was taking her in. The heels and the trench and the huge, springy curls that framed her head like a lion's mane. "You work here?" Alani asked. Eyes to Ethic, question aimed at Syria.

"No, but I'm quite good at what I do. I'd like to show you, if that's okay," Syria said. "I do a lot of partner work, teaching him where to touch, how to touch, to remove tension naturally. It's very intimate. Very beautiful, when a man knows where a woman carries stress."

Alani's brow lifted. "And you've done this with him before?" Alani asked. She was so territorial when it came to him.

"No, just yoga," Syria said.

"Yoga?" Alani rolled eyes of disdain to Ethic. Every, single session of yoga he had ever done with her had ended up with his dick inside her.

He stepped in front of her, placing a hand to the side of her face, wrapping four fingers around her neck, while his thumb caressed her cheek.

"You know how my temper is set up, Ethic," she whispered. "You know me." Even the thought of him with someone else set her on fire. She was shaking, she was so angry.

"This ain't that, baby. Trust me," he said. "I just want to please you. This is about you. Let me."

Alani was at a disadvantage. His control over her emotions, the way he spoke to her, the baritone in his voice…she was no match for any of it.

I wanna love you in every kind of way
I wanna please you no matter how long it takes

She nodded.

Syria removed her coat, revealing a silk, black robe beneath. She was beautiful. Skin the color of milk chocolate and legs for days. Lean and perfect, with supple breasts that peeked out the top of a lace bra that lie beneath. She walked over to Alani and placed a hand to the back of her neck. She pinched the indentations at the nape of Alani's neck, and like magic, Alani's eyes closed.

"Women carry stress in their neck and shoulders," Syria said, as she moved those two fingers in circles. Her hands felt like feathers and goosebumps formed on Alani's body. Her brow pinched. "Please, get comfortable. I won't do anything you aren't comfortable with."

Alani opened her eyes and Ethic lifted her chin with one finger. A kiss. Just one, but the way he sucked her bottom lip into his mouth made Alani cream.

"Okay," she whispered.

"Lie on your back, please," Syria said. "The oil I use is all natural. It's almond oil, so it's healthy for your skin. You'll feel my hands first, as I show him the technique, and then you'll feel his."

Alani was so tense that she was holding her breath. Syria bent down to whisper in her ear. "Relax. This is about release. Breathe, beautiful." She smelled like coconut and Alani drew in a deep breath before blowing it out through her mouth and closing her eyes.

Warm oil was brushed over her chest, neck, and shoulders, with what felt like a paint brush; then, the softest fingertips she had ever felt gripped her shoulders. She held her breath, as she felt those fingers dance against her skin as they traveled across her chest, right where the towel was tucked.

Out of nowhere, the texture of the touch changed, and she relaxed as Ethic's rough hands took over. His touch was harder, more aggressive and she moaned.

"You can touch places I can't," Syria said. Her voice was like a melody. Soft. Gentle. Safe. "Your every touch should connect with her inner being. It's about intimacy. Trust."

If the world should end tomorrow and we only have todayyy
I'm gonna love you in every kind of wayyyy-ayye-ayyyee-yeah

Alani felt cool air, as the towel was undone, and her stomach tensed as his oily hands traveled over the mountains of her flesh, causing her nipples to react.

"Breathe," Syria whispered, her lips so close to Alani's ear that they felt like a kiss.

Alani was panicking, breathing too fast, as nerves took over her entire body.

"Your touch is too weighted," Syria said. "Use strokes."

Alani gasped, as those feather fingers replaced Ethic's. There was just a gentleness in the way Syria approached intimacy. A woman knew exactly where to touch another woman to elicit pleasure. Two hands, fingertips tapping, as Syria traveled down the center of her chest, sweeping outward over her breasts, tapping on her nipples, like they were punching bags and her fingers were the gloves of a world champ. "In and out breathing, goddess," Syria whispered. Down further to her stomach and then back up the same route. "Now, you try. Connect to her." The difference between his hands and hers made Alani's body shudder. It was a mixture of pleasure, both amazing, but uniquely different and she felt her pussy clench in wanting.

She opened her eyes and Ethic was right there, eyes boring into hers, with a look of love she had never seen. He stared at her, as his hands mimicked the exact movements that Syria had just done moments before - except he added a kiss. His entire tongue filled her mouth and Alani's back arched off the massage table. Like a metal to magnet, she was drawn to him. It was like someone had put a string through her belly button and was pulling her toward the ceiling…a puppet, and Ethic was her Geppetto.

"Mmm," she moaned.

"Hands stay on the table," Syria whispered, as Alani went to touch Ethic's face. Syria pressed her hands against Alani's arms, capturing her there, making her a victim to touch. Two sets of hands now. Coarse hands up top, soft hands at the bottom, causing two, different sensations that made Alani's lids squeeze tightly.

Alani felt Syria's hands, as they traced the outline of her womanhood, a triangle. Alani tensed.

I wanna love you
I gotta love youuu
I wanna love you

"Hey," Ethic's voice pulled her eyes open, and to her surprise, a tear slid out of the corner of her eye, pooling in her ear. "I love you. So fucking much, Lenika. Every day, baby. Every second."

Fingers, tracing her triangle, massaging the face of her delicacy. Alani's eyes closed.

"Look at me, baby," he groaned.

Her eyes fluttered open. "Can she taste it? I want to see you cum."

Alani's body had a mind of her own.

Why am I nodding? What the entire fuck?

"Agh!" Syria's mouth on her body, on her pussy, made Alani buck. Alani had experienced the best head of her life with Ethic. This was better. Syria's tongue felt like dick. It was amazing. Her back arched so far off the table that only her ass and shoulders remained on the leather.

"Sexiest shit I've ever seen," Ethic whispered. Alani reached for him, untying the hotel robe he wore. His dick was brick and she didn't hesitate to grab it. She pulled him into her mouth, as Syria drowned in her depths.

Alani's mind was gone, as she indulged in him, sucking like she had something to prove, licking and teasing, focusing on the head, her favorite part, as her wrist went to work. Thick-ass. Long-ass. He was perfection. Like a sculptor had chosen a warrior straight from the motherland and had chiseled every inch of his body as motivation.

"Fuckkk," he groaned. He gripped her hair, but she didn't need guidance. Alani sucked his dick like a porn star. An act that had once disgusted her, was her favorite pastime with him. She felt like she was in control when he was in her mouth, at her mercy, calling her name, because he did every time. She took his soul. Owned it. She held the title to that dick because she had paid the ultimate price to get it.

Syria was a silent investor. She didn't need the limelight. She was just there to make sure the pussy flipped right, so she said nothing, her tongue spoke a language all its own.

"It's about delaying the release," Syria whispered, as she used those fucking soft-ass fingers and pressed them to Alani's clit, rubbing in circles. "Don't rush to orgasm. It's so easy to get off track, with a woman like this." The compliment came with a kiss to her southern lips.

"Shit," Ethic groaned. He stepped back, gripping his erection and Syria stopped. Alani's stomach sank, as she panted, trying to catch her breath because her head was spinning. She didn't know if it was the champagne or the near orgasm, or the disbelief that she was in this position in the first place.

"Come."

An order. Alani lifted. He sat on the edge of the bed and turned her around so her back was facing him. He guided her down onto him, filling her. Reverse. He pulled her hair, as she rode him. Eyes to the ceiling, hands gripping his thighs, she rolled her body. Her neck jerked forward when she felt Syria between her legs.

"Goooodddddd," Alani moaned, as Syria pulled her clit into her mouth. "No! Wait...no, no, ssssss. ETHIC!"

Hands made of silk roamed up and over the flesh of her breasts, tweaking tender nipples, as Syria lifted, kissing her way up Alani's body, as Alani rode Ethic slow...hard...He kissed the back of her neck. They had made a sandwich of her.

Him in the back, her in the middle, Syria in the front, rubbing her clit. Syria touched her in a way she'd never thought to touch it before. Gripping her swollen sex between the slits of her fingers and squeezing, as she rotated a balled fist.

Syria's face was a breath away, her lips a fantasy away, and just as Syria went to kiss her lips, Ethic pulled her hair harder, forcing her chin up. Syria had already borrowed one set of lips, this one was for him, reserved only for him. Her kisses were his and his alone, because she let him take pieces of her soul and he gave her his in return - each time they shared a kiss. Syria's lips landed on her neck instead and she didn't seem to mind.

"You taste amazing," she whispered, her tongue tasting Alani's flesh.

"Turn around for me, baby," Ethic whispered in her ear.

Boy, it don't get no better than you
For youuuu
I wanna take my timmmmee
All nigghht

The song was on a loop and Alani couldn't keep up with how many times it had started over. She lifted and faced him. When she lowered on top of him, he groaned. "You're art, Lenika," he whispered, staring her in her eyes. "A fucking masterpiece." Alani forgot there was someone else in the room, as she worked him. Chest to chest, they fucked, slow, deep, and hard. No need to rush...no need to beat it...because rough sex was about punishment... it was a power struggle...between the two of them, those dynamics didn't exist. Those struggles didn't even matter. She submitted to him, willingly; and when she didn't, he knew that there was no shame in submitting to his woman when she was insistent on taking the lead. It was just the two of them in this moment. Face to face, his dick, in her flood, the connection too potent to acknowledge anyone else. If Syria was still touching her, Alani could no longer feel it. All she felt was him, traveling the route from her sex to her heart. Again, and a-fucking-gain.

So much energy had built up in her body that she could feel the orgasm coming. It traveled up her toes, her calves, her thighs that were shaking violently, and then he picked her up from his lap.

"I was so close, why would you stop?" she whined, heaving.

"He's building the orgasm, beautiful. Keeping you on the very edge until you can't hold it anymore. If you didn't reach orgasm, it isn't time to reach orgasm. Trust him. Lie down."

Alani looked to him and then followed directions. She was already halfway into the marathon. Might as well finish the race.

Her body was so oily that she was afraid to lie on the sheets, but she got out of her head. She shut off logic and acted off desire and she laid down on the bed.

"Your body on top of her body without penetration," Syria whispered. Ethic put a knee to the bed and hovered over her. Alani couldn't breathe.

"I'm going to love you forever," she whispered, gripping the sides of his face.

"That's more than I deserve," he answered. He reached for his dick and rubbed it against her wetness. "So fucking wet, baby, damn."

"Press your life source against her life source," Syria said.

Alani felt Ethic press the underside of his dick between her lips, and he was so hard that she died a bit on the inside. The pressure on her clit in this position made her groan. Two forearms made a prison around her head, as he stroked. He stroked without penetration and Alani screamed out in amazement.

"My fucking god! Boy!"

"What the fuck?" he whispered, surprised at how good sex without penetration could be. His dick was pressed so tightly between her labia. She was so wet that he slid all over the place, creating a sweet friction so pleasurable that it felt like he would bust with every stroke. The weight from his body pressing into her made her lips grip him like a good hand job, and every time he stroked her, he mashed her clit until she was delirious. She looked down, face twisted, confused on how this felt so good. It felt better than anything she had ever felt before, and the head of his dick played peekaboo as he stroked forward, then back.

"I'm about to nut, baby. Fuck," he groaned.

"To the edge, Ethic," Syria said, playing coach.

"Bitch, shut the fuck up!" Alani shouted, in ecstasy. Ethic snickered and then filled her mouth, tongue bullying her, as he pumped her harder, stroked faster until...

"I'm cummiinnnggg," she gasped.

"Me too, baby, damn… me too," he grunted. "Ohhh, shit…the fuck…" Alani felt his seeds spill on her belly, warming her skin, as he dug his head in the groove of her neck. Alani fisted her hair, looking up at the ceiling, in utter disbelief. She didn't even know what to call what they'd just done, but she wanted to do it again and again. He shuddered on top of her, kissing her neck, and then lifting to look her in the eyes.

"This shit is fucking gold. I swear to God I'll do whatever to keep this shit just like this forever, baby. Forever."

Syria didn't even speak, as she made her way to the door, grabbing her bag and coat on the way.

When she heard the click of the door, Alani placed her hands on Ethic's face. He was so handsome. Just fine. Exquisite, and he was hers. Her eyes prickled. Her heart filled. It was overflowing with love for him. She had prayed for him. Prayed for bliss. Prayed for a man that could take away all the pain. Much like tonight, he went above and beyond for her, every time. He was perfection. They were imperfect perfection. He kissed her nose, once, twice, and then a kiss to her shoulder, and then her lips. He placed a hand to the side of her face. The way he cared for her was incredible. It was other worldly. She saw tenderness in a man so hard that she felt blessed to be one of few exceptions. "Forever," she whispered. "I'ma be with you in this life and the next."

CHAPTER 18

Sunday Morning

Alani kept a gentle hand on Eazy's shoulders, as they made their way into the church.

She smiled and waved, as she led the way through the corridors toward the sanctuary. She was so happy to be present. She had been feeling empty, lately, and she knew the word of God would re-fill her. It would give her the fuel to keep fighting. It had taken the four-some some time to get out the front door, but they were here, and they looked like family. A good-looking one at that.

"Can I go to the kids' program?" Eazy asked.

"No, Big Man, not this morning. I want us all together today, okay?" she said.

"Aww, man," Eazy protested.

"And run me that video game in your pocket," Alani said, smiling, as she held out her hand. He gave it up, with dismay, as they eased into a pew halfway down the aisle. Alani went in first and put Eazy next to her, Bella sat beside him, and Ethic took the end. He was unusually stoic this morning. Alani had learned to let him be, when he was this way, so conversation had been at a minimum. The dip in his brow told her he was brooding, most likely thinking. A lot of darkness had clouded them, lately. They needed this sermon. Nyair was preaching, which was always a plus. His cool delivery of God's word made him relatable, it made it easy to understand and apply to one's life, and Alani was so glad that he had decided to switch today. He normally didn't preach on first Sundays, so when she saw his name on the marquee, she was filled with relief. God knew exactly when to fulfill a need.

Alani studied Ethic.

Is he nervous?

They sat in all black. They made a stunning family; and as Eazy leaned into her, already dozing off, Alani felt lucky to have them.

First Sunday service was always long. It was communion and Alani and Ethic normally skipped it, but he had insisted today. She wondered why he would demand they come if he would be so moody about it, but she was grateful for his attendance at all. She needed this, so she let him stay in his zone, as she enjoyed the service. Altar call pulled Alani to the front of the church, praying so hard that she had to grip the edge of the first pew to keep standing. Dolce's murder. Alani's sins. She had to keep reminding herself that if she hadn't killed Dolce, Dolce might have killed her. Bella joined her, intertwining her hand with Alani's and Alani's heart fluttered. Bella was such an intuitive girl. She could feel when Alani was weak, and somehow, she always made it better. They stood side by side, holding hands and praying together. They didn't return to their seats. They stayed in the front row where Nannie sat, holding hands, until Nyair concluded his sermon.

"Now, normally, we would wait until after communion and wait until next month to do this, but we've got special circumstances at play," Nyair said. "You see, I recently discovered that I have a brother. A brother that I've always respected but had no idea that I was of his tribe. That we were of the same bloodline. G through and through. Y'all know I'm talking about God, right? All G. All God. Not that other kind of G; although, I got a little bit of that in me too. I'm working on it."

"Work on it, Pastor!" a young, pretty woman shouted from the crowd. Nyair snickered, finessing his chin, as he blushed, smiling wide as those dimples deepened. "He called me late last night and said, 'Bro, I want to love my woman right. I want to love my kids correctly. I want to love them, but I got to love me first. I got to let God fill me first. I want them to love a man that's filled with love, not hate. A man filled with God, not the devil. I need you to put me under that tap, G.' We're baptizing a disciple today, family. Brother Ezra, come stand with me, G."

Alani's neck snapped backwards, as Ethic stood from his seat with Eazy in tow.

"Now, we're going to take care of our baby girl, Bella. Folks around here already know about her walk. We'll baptize her and little Eazy at the next communion, but my bro couldn't wait."

Alani's eyes filled with a river of tears, as he came down the aisle. He had always been so beautiful to her, but the way he swaggered down the aisle made her heart flutter. He was walking to God, shoulders squared, jaw locked, eyes full of determination.

"Praise God," Nannie said, clapping, as applause rang out in the sanctuary.

"Come to God, bro. Come home."

Alani felt the wetness on her face, as she stood. Nannie stood too and grabbed Alani's hand.

"You let him take this walk by himself. He has to go to God. You can't push him, baby," Nannie whispered. The choir director started playing the organ, slowly, and the choir started humming softly.

Never would have madddeeee ittt
Never could have madeee ittt without youuuu

Alani placed one hand over her mouth, losing control of her emotions, as she ugly cried. There was no hesitation in her man. No fear. He was so fucking regal. Shoulders squared. Suit fitting to perfection. His fists balling then releasing, as he made the journey to Nyair.

The choir amped it up a bit.

I'm strongerrr
I'm wiserrrr
I'm betterrrr
So much better

Eazy joined her side and Bella turned to her in excitement. "Did you know he was joining the church?"

Alani shook her head. "No. I didn't know, B."

Bella walked up to Ethic.

"I'm not letting him do it by himself," Bella said. "I know he's afraid of this, but I'm not, so I'm doing it with him."

"Me too!" Eazy shouted, running to stand next to Ethic. Ethic stood at the front of the church with his children beside him. A lion and his cubs had found their way.

"I guess we're baptizing three Okafors today," Nyair submitted, smiling, dimples deep, as he shook Bella's hand and then Eazy's. "Anybody that knows them knows they call the shots."

"Amennnnn!" The church members shouted, one after another.

"Amen!" Nannie chimed. "Bless them, Pastor!"

"My G, you're taking a leap of faith. All you need is a little bit, G. A mustard seed. God will flip what little you have into the whole thing, bro, just trust him," Nyair stated to Ethic, pulling him in for a gangster's shake.

Alani was bawling.

Never could have maddeee it!

"Nannie. We need you up here. I suspect that only you will do. We've got to get them changed, as we prepare the basin," Nyair said.

Nannie stood, and Alani's heart galloped.

"I'll take care of them," Nannie said. "I know you want to, but you can't. I got them. We gonna wash them clean.

Nyair is going to clean them up and give them back to you, baby. Your family is getting saved today. You just sit here and watch what God has restored." Alani nodded, as she watched Nannie disappear with them out the side door. She wanted to go with them. She ached to go. She needed to talk to him. She needed to kiss him, to hug him, but she couldn't. She had to let him do this for him.

Nyair approached her.

"Ny, is he doing this for me?" Alani whispered. "How is this happening? He's a gangster, Ny. I fell in love with a gangster. Is he really trusting God?"

"He's giving his life to God, La. He's ready. He doesn't know it all but he's faithful. He trusts Him, and he trusts you. You changed his heart, Alani. You didn't just pull anybody off the street, you brought the biggest gangster in this city to God. You have no idea who he is to niggas on these streets. The ways the devil have used him. You're a hell of a woman, La. He's a lucky man."

"Nooo, Ny. It's me who's lucky. I'm so grateful for him, Nyair. I know he's scared. He doesn't look scared, because strong is all he knows, but I know he is. I know him. I feel his heart racing right now, Nyair. Take care of him," Alani said, slightly panicking.

Nyair nodded. "Damn, La. I've never seen you like this with anyone before. Not even when you were with me."

"I've never been like this before. I've never loved like this before. He's my altar, Nyair. I know it's bad, and I know God is so jealous, but I would get on my knees in front of this man to soak up his essence. He has no idea how much of God is in him. I love him. I'm so in love with him."

"This act. This baptism is proof he loves you more, La. I got him. All you got to do is watch," Nyair said. He leaned to kiss her cheek. Alani couldn't bring herself to sit. She just stood, swaying to the choir, who was in full-blown praise.

Now I see, how you were there for me
Iii NEVERRRR

Never could have made it

Ethic, Bella, and Eazy re-entered the room. They stepped up to the baptismal pool with Ethic, holding out his arm to help Nannie up the platform. The huge cross illuminated above their heads, as Ethic stepped into the pool of water. Alani was breathless. He was such a beautiful man.

"My brother. Do you accept Christ as your Saviour, and will you demonstrate your faith by baptismal?" Nyair asked.

Ethic bit his bottom lip and nodded, becoming emotional, but quickly clearing his throat and regaining composure. "I accept Him."

"I now baptize you, my brother. Upon profession of your faith and of the Lord Jesus Christ, I know baptize you in the name of the Father, and of the Son, and of the Holy Spirit," Nyair said. Ethic closed his eyes and Nyair dipped him. The cold rush of water shocked his system and then, surprisingly, calmed him. His heart slowed.

Alani felt her feet moving but she couldn't see through her tears. She heard praises being sung. She rushed past the altar and up the steps and didn't even care that she was getting half her body wet, as she waded through the water to get to him.

"I love you so much!" She cried, as he wrapped her in his arms. Everyone disappeared. She didn't see anyone but him, as he placed a hand on the back of her head, keeping her so close to his body that he could feel her racing heart. It was the tightest cocoon of protection she'd ever been wrapped in. "I'm so proud of you. Oh my god, I'm so proud of you."

"Let's be clear, church family," Ny stated. "This is God's love we're witnessing. This is forgiveness and love and the work of two people allowing God to lead them; despite all sins, despite all hardships, they've trusted."

"I love you," Ethic whispered. The microphone above the water picked up every word and the entire congregation swooned. It was clear that they were witnessing something special.

"It's my turn! I'm next!" Eazy shouted. Alani laughed and turned to watch Eazy and Bella's baptism. As the kids made their way out of the water to Nannie and another church mother who was waiting nearby with towels, Ethic and Alani stood there, waist deep in water, under the hanging cross. She didn't need anything more. If she closed her eyes and the sun didn't rise tomorrow, this moment was enough.

"No more dirt, baby," he said, as he held her in place with one hand to her cheek, four fingers wrapped around her neck, as his thumb caressed her cheek.

"No more dirt."

CHAPTER 19

The house was still, and Alani was grateful, as she followed Ethic inside. Church had exhausted her. The overflow of emotions made her want to throw on a pair of sweatpants, take off her bra, and lay under her man while scrolling through Netflix for hours, because they could never decide what to watch anyway.

"You want food?" Ethic asked.

Alani didn't respond, as her brow dipped, and she scrolled down her screen.

"Ayo," he called. Alani's eyes lifted.

"I'm sorry. I was just reading this email; apparently, Alex has good news," Alani said, as she stared at her phone screen, while following Ethic into his home. Ethic groaned, as he stepped out of his Ferragamo shoes and then bent to relieve her of her Aldo heels. He slipped them off and put them in a neat line next to his. He stayed on his knees, lifting one of her legs to his shoulder. He kissed the inside of her ankle and then went north, until his lips were at her center. Sliding her panties to the side, he placed a soul-stirring kiss to her clit. Alani gripped his head, as hers fell back.

"I just wanted a taste, baby, I'ma warm that up later," he said, smacking her ass lightly, before returning her panties to their rightful place and then standing. He moved around her, licking his lips and returning to normal, like nothing had happened at all.

"Run it by me again. Who's Alex?" Ethic asked.

Flustered and wet, Alani couldn't even focus. Her forehead pinched. "He's...umm." There was a heartbeat in her pussy, pounding, making her head cloudy because now she wanted to fuck. "Umm... My professor. The one you threatened," she said, as she followed him up the stairs. She returned her attention to her phone, her finger scrolling down, as she read more details of the email.

"And he's Alex to you now?" Ethic asked. Ethic had dismissed the man from his mind because nothing about him was memorable.

"If he's going to be my book agent, 'Professor', in a group of publishing professionals sounds kind of weird, don't you think?" Alani asked.

"And what's the news?" Ethic asked.

"He says the contracts are in. I gave him your address to mail hard copies over. I hope that's okay?"

"It's your address too. You don't have to ask shit like that," Ethic answered. Something as small as her having mail sent to his home made it feel like her home. He had no qualms about that.

"They offered me fifty thousand dollars for the first book. Wow...that's insane," she said, in disbelief.

"It's not insane. You worked for that," Ethic said, as he removed the tie from his neck. He walked up behind Alani and unzipped her dress, sliding it off her shoulders and letting it fall to the floor. She never looked up from her phone, as Ethic grabbed one of his t-shirts, since it was her favorite thing to make pajamas of, and then slipped it over her head. Strong hands massaged tense shoulders. He was there to knead away the worries of a trouble-filled day…a trouble-filled life.

"Wait, he sent a mockup of the cover," Alani said. She placed a hand over her mouth. She held up her phone, so that Ethic could see over her shoulder. "My name is on a book."

"You should be proud. I'm proud of you," Ethic said.

He swept her hair off her shoulders and planted a kiss to the back of her neck.

"They're setting up a promotional reading. Magazines and media will be there. Wow, what am I going to wear to a reading? What will the kids wear? Do kids even come to book readings? Why do they have me doing an event for a book that won't be available until next year? Do you think Morgan would come back for it? I'd really like her there. Wait…have you spoken to Morgan lately? To make sure she's adjusting okay?" Alani asked. "Maybe I should remind her about her next doctor's appointment. She's already missed one and I had to get a million referrals to even get her in. I don't want her to…"

"Mo's fine," he said, planting a kiss to the back of her neck. "I called. Stop. You're going at a million miles per hour. One thing at a time."

Alani's head fell forward, and she sighed, while closing her eyes, as that kiss sent tingles down her spine. Her anxiety was on a trillion. She got that way, sometimes...most times... overwhelmed...she sucked in air to still her racing heart. "But the appointment..." she groaned.

"I..." He kissed her neck. "...reminded her. How'd we get on Mo, anyway? We should be talking about your book... about you and the remarkable thing you've done with your grief. Tell me why we ain't on that?"

"I don't want all this, Ethic. I'm not ready to stand up in front of anyone and read those words. Who puts a first-time author on the spot like that, anyway?"

"Don't talk yourself out of this opportunity. Don't question it. Just let the universe give you everything you deserve." Alani knew he was right. She was panicking. She was letting her anxiety convince her that this wasn't meant for her...making excuses for why she wouldn't be able to go through with it. It was too soon. She didn't have enough time to prepare. She'd prefer to wait for the actual release before she began to promote it. She could come up with a thousand reasons to back out. It was self-sabotage. It was fear telling her she wasn't worthy...the same fear that had told her she didn't deserve Ethic. She couldn't let fear win. "Stop overthinking." He reached for her hips and pulled her into his hardness.

It was all the motivation Alani needed to turn off her brain and focus on him. She faced him, pecked his lips, and then lowered to her knees. He never had to ask...never beg...if she felt the need, she obliged, every time, anytime, anywhere because he deserved a woman that would submit to him without reservation. Ethic was the type of man who earned his head, handling his role as a man so well that a woman just felt like she wasn't shit if she didn't keep him topped off as tribute for his effort. Appreciating...she was showing how much she appreciated him for uplifting her, for reassuring her, for supporting her...she would show him how much it meant, how much she needed him... right here on her knees, in her mouth, pumping him dry, as he groaned in satisfaction.

The taste of him, the notes of his flavor on her tongue, down her throat, was a delicacy. Alani had never, would never, could never, be this sexually free with anyone else. He pulled everything out of her. He made her want to express her love for him in every way. There were no limits in his bed or in her heart. She would go all the way with him every time.

She stood, biting her bottom lip and smiling so wide that he snickered. "Oh, you think you did something?" he asked.

She nodded, proudly, and amusement danced in his eyes.

"Nah, baby, you ain't did shit," he said, as he scooped her, throwing her over his shoulder so suddenly that she yelped in surprise. She laughed, giddily, as he carried her up the stairs, slapping her ass, as she protested all the way to the bedroom.

He tossed her on the bed, coming out of his clothes, as she leaned back on her elbows.

"I just gave stellar head, Mr. Okafor. I swallowed and everything," she said, jokingly. "Nothing you can pull from your bag of tricks is going to one-up that."

He grabbed her ankle and pulled her to the edge of the bed. "Stop talking," he groaned, as he began to undress her. So much woman lay in his bed and he pulled back, shaking his head, appreciating the fucking sight, before placing one knee to the mattress. He pressed her breasts together, wrapping full lips around firm nipples and electricity shot through her entire body.

"Boy, how the fuck do you do this to me?" she gasped, as she watched his head disappear down her body. He seized her clit through those full lips and Alani bucked.

"Niggas eat pussy for them," he whispered between French kisses of her southern lips. Ethic ate pussy like he was trying to lick honey off a plate. Like he was trying to suck the Kool-Aid stains off fingers, with ferocity, with intensity. "To get it wet. I get it wet before I even get down here. Before I even think about hitting this shit, it's wet for me; ain't it, baby?" he asked.

"All the time," she moaned. *Cocky-ass,* she thought, smiling a bit, but there was no point in lying. All day was foreplay with him. His every interaction with her made her want to fuck him. Made her want to throw him a little pussy because he did everything so damn well and he deserved it at the end of a long day.

"I'm eating this shit for *you,* baby. Hmm... damn," he moaned, as he pulled her swollen womanhood into his mouth and sucked. He released it with a 'pop' and then flicked his tongue over it with precision. Taking shots, busting that thang up, jabbing it, as he gripped under her ass, pulling her into his face.

"Ezraaaaa," Alani moaned. She was this man's buffet. He ate everything and went back for seconds. He was gluttonous for her. Even when he was full, he kept going. Insatiable. Ezra Okafor was voracious for Alani Hill. She tried to close her thighs because she couldn't take this much pleasure. Too much of anything was hazardous to one's health. Even head. Too much head made a bitch weak. He pried them back open. "Be a big girl, baby," he whispered. "Open these legs for me." He was making a slave out of her. She followed orders under this tongue. He was master, and she obeyed, butterflying her brown thighs wide open, as she dripped everywhere. Fucking messy. Goddamn nasty. This man was a beast in bed and Alani was his victim, his prey. He was going to swallow her whole. He pulled her orgasm from her soul and dared her to tap out before he released her. "Baby, okayyyyyyyyyyyy," she cried. She was conceding. Fucking giving up because she was dead. He had murdered it and he hadn't even entered her yet. He moved on, having mercy on her, as he kissed her inner thigh. He was so gentle with her that his touch tickled her. Alani put both hands over her face, giggling. "That tickles, Ethic," she whispered.

He added a different sensation, as he bit into the meat of her thigh. God, he had her body so confused. Pleasure. Different levels of ecstasy, and he was riding the elevator to the top floor.

"Turn around."

Yup. She was a slave. He said jump and she asked how high. She turned. All fours. He entered. She flattened. Defeated, again, and he hadn't even stroked her yet. Her stomach was to the bed, as he brought one leg up in the crease of his arm.

Alani's fingers curled on the sheets, pulling it from the mattress. A heap of 1000 thread count pooled around her, as he tensed into her.

"This pussy is fucking it, baby. Just you. That's it. That's all I want," he moaned.

"Boyyyyy!"

He hit her. Black eye for that pussy.

He pulled back, but Alani knew relief was only temporary because he split her in half with his next stroke.

"Aghh!"

It was like he sat back in the cut, plotting on the pussy before every move he made. Alani had never been with a man who was so well versed with a woman's body.

Ethic came down on his elbows, closing his fists, as he stretched her, riding that pussy so close that Alani couldn't do anything but tremble. There was no throwing it back at dick like this. She wasn't in control. This was his game. Alani wanted to take her damn ball and go home because this nigga wasn't playing fair. Another deep stroke gave her a busted lip to go along with that black eye. He was fucking her up. Beating it. A motherfucking bully. Where was Eazy? Bella? Why did they have to leave with Nannie? She needed them to come interrupt this. She needed them to stop this because she was losing this fight.

"Mmmmmmmm... Ethic, I'm cumming. Soooo harddd, boyyyyy, fuck you!" she shouted. She hated to lose. He knew it, but she always lost. To him. Every time.

The growl of laughter in her ear made her smile and she laughed too, then bit her lip, as her eyes closed. Satisfaction had never felt this good.

"Babyyyyy, I love you," she panted. "Righttt there. EZRA!" She knew the neighbors heard that.

"Oh, shit," Ethic groaned.

She came first. He followed. Letting her take the lead. She turned over, groaning, as she breathed deeply. His weight rested on top of her and she feathered the back of his neck, as she enjoyed the feeling of his heart racing. Chest to chest, the connection was so raw that the rhythm calmed her.

"It's something so strange about the way I feel for you," she whispered.

"How's that?" he asked.

"I'm giving you more love than I possess. Like, I'm in the negative with this shit, Ethic. I'm in debt because of you," she whispered. "If I ever had to. If it ever came down to it, I would die for you because there is only one of you. No other man like you. There are plenty of me's. Other women like me, but the world deserves to have you for as long as possible."

Every time she spoke her sentiments it put a weight on Ethic's chest. She recognized beauty in his brokenness but couldn't see that he was equally enthralled by hers. She had enchanted him from the very first time she had said hello, and Ethic wasn't the type of man who was easily impressed. Women worked hard to even pull his gaze. Alani had done so effortlessly, and he never grew bored of her. She never got old.

"If you believe that, I feel sorry for you. Nothing about you is replaceable," he said. "And there won't be any sacrificing of lives on my behalf, Lenika. You and my kids... I'm hopping in the grave over y'all every day of the week until my time is up. There is no tolerance in me for anybody that disrespects you."

He hovered over her, lifting some of the weight from her body.

"No, don't move," she whispered.

"I'm crushing you, baby" he answered.

"Un uh, you're comfort," she answered, closing her eyes. "People who go through trauma, they sleep with these weighted blankets..." she paused, as she fingered his beard, tangling her fingers in his forest, as her eyes searched his. "It's supposed to calm the anxiety. Stop them from panicking. You on top of me... The way you cover me. It stops me from panicking. I feel safe underneath you. It's all I want to do. The only place I want to be."

Ethic discovered devotion in her eyes and his widened in shock. The way she trusted him. The way she believed he could love her better than anyone else in the world...she had so much faith in him. It floored him.

"You know I'ma love you for a long time, right? Like even if you leave one day..."

"I'm never leaving," she whispered.

"But if you do. If the day comes where you have to leave, I'ma love you far beyond that. I'ma love you past the limit. Past this body, baby. Past my time here. When I'm right here, looking in your eyes, and when the day comes where my stare is just a memory to you, I'ma still be loving you. This type of energy don't go nowhere. Even when my heart stops beating, it'll still be yours. Even when I'm old, if I get to grow old, and when it's not new. When it grows routine. I'ma love you. I love you endlessly, Lenika."

She was speechless. Her eyes glistened, and her lips were parted to speak but nothing came out. She pulled his beard, reigning him in until her tongue was in his mouth. It was the most potent thing she had ever felt. She was convinced that this was the most a woman could ever receive from a man. Besides God, no one could love her greater. This nigga was a fucking king. Her king. Alani was drenched from him. He just did shit to her. Even after he had sucked her bone dry, he put in the work to arouse her, again, without even knowing it. Ethic fed her emotion all day. That was foreplay. It made her want him. The way he worked for her, the way he let her know how treasured she was every second. By the end of the night, she could hardly stand distance between them. She anticipated the moment when they were skin to skin. He fucked her all day, mentally first, and then he made her rain. She never told him no because he never made her want to. As she shifted, forcing him on his back, Alani mounted him, back facing him, reverse. Her mouth fell open, as she slid onto his strength and her flower blossomed, making room for him.

"Aghh," she moaned.

She rode him. Sis rode him like she was trying to tame him. Like she was trying to claim him. Like he hadn't just professed his love and she was trying to make him. Her hair was his reigns and he pulled it, arching her neck backward. His fingers opened, dragging across her scalp and then curled, pulling harder. She went faster.

"Look at you, baby," he whispered. Alani opened her eyes and stared into the mirror ahead. His black body beneath hers was like the darkest pigments of an artist's palette. She had never felt sexier. Alani rolled her hips in an "S" and she held her breasts, rolling her nipples between her fingertips. Her face collapsed. Her body came alive when she was in bed with him. She felt every touch, even her own. The slap to her ass stung.

"Damn, baby. That shit move so good," he said.

SLAP.

He palmed it, gripping what she considered fat, but he appreciated every dimple, every fucking stretch mark, especially the ones on her ass. He loved that shit. Again.

SLAP.

"Get lost, baby. Ride that shit like you mad at a nigga," he whispered.

She rocked him harder, lifting to her tip-toes just to accommodate his size and ride it to the top of the hill, before rushing to the bottom. She bounced on him and smirked when his toes curled. He didn't speak but those damn feet balled up so tight because she was squeezing him, she was pulsing on him, thanking God she did Kegels daily. She could milk the orgasm from his flesh. No hands. Her legs trembled but she didn't stop, as he bucked back. She knew he was close because that hand balled in her hair, pulling from the root, and one hand tightened on her waist. His fingers dug into her side. Alani reached down to hold onto his thighs. They were like boulders, solid, and she leaned forward, scooting, 'cause her thighs were fucking tired, but she wasn't stopping because it felt amazing.

Alani was spent, as she leaned forward and put her chest to the bed. Her whole ass spread over him and she felt him shudder beneath her, as he palmed it. "Ohhh shitt," he groaned. He filled her. Alani was done, but when she felt him sit up and pull her ass up into his face, she cried out, "Ethic, I can'tttt."

The nigga had no table manners, as he ate her from the back. Pussy first, ass last.

This man is fucking filthy. Alani just laid there, face destroyed in pleasure, arms extended over her head, as he made her cum for a third time. She couldn't even move, when they were done.

She felt his weight lift from the bed, felt a sheet cover her body, and felt his lips on hers, before her eyes closed. He had put her to sleep. K.O. She had lost this round and she didn't even care because, damn, it felt so fucking good.

The sound of the doorbell pulled Alani from the bed. She lifted from the deep slumber and slid into her robe as she made her way through the house and down the stairs.

"Coming!" she shouted. She knew Ethic must have been in the basement. If he had let the door go unanswered it was because he had zoned out. Alani pulled open the door without looking.

"Zeke!" she shouted in surprise.

"Alani? I uh," Zeke paused and looked over Alani's shoulder, eyes wandering the interior of the foyer nervously. "I wasn't expecting to see you."

"I live here," she informed. "I wasn't expecting to see you either." She didn't know if she should let him in or not. She knew that this was an uninvited guest.

"Is he home?"

"How did you get through the gate?" Alani asked.

"The code is his birthday."

Alani's neck whipped as she turned to face Ethic. He came up the basement stairs, shirtless, Nike tights, and a towel wrapped around his neck. His face held no emotion but the tension that filled his body made every muscle tight with rage. The veins in his forehead stuck out and his nostrils flared.

"Go upstairs, baby," Ethic said.

"But…"

The look Ethic gave her left no room for negotiation. Alani reached for his cheek, but he caught her wrist. He planted a kiss to the soft skin on the underside of her hand and then looked her in the eyes. "Now."

Alani took her ass upstairs.

Ethic positioned himself in the doorway and although his body language was unmoved on the outside, the inside of him erupted. He was at war, face to face with the man who had made him only to desert him. This man was his enemy. The greatest one he had known.

"Get ya' ass off my doorstep before I lay you down man," Ethic said. He went to close the door, but Ezekiel placed his hand to the wood, preventing it.

"Son."

The feeling of looking his father in the eye unnerved Ethic. Someone was pulling at the one loose string that was left undone in his life and it was causing him to unravel. In those coal eyes he saw every moment in his life where he had needed a father, every moment where fear had been pushed down and he had placed a street creed on top of it to overcompensate for the lack of mentorship that was supposed to come from his old man.

"Don't ever call me that," Ethic stated.

"I'd just like to talk. Man to man. You don't owe me anything, but I'd appreciate just a moment and then I'll be on my way," Ezekiel said.

Ethic stepped out onto his porch. Everybody wasn't welcome inside his home. He was particular when it came to the type of energy that crossed his threshold. He didn't know this man.

"Ezekiel is it?" Ethic asked. "Nice name."

"I changed it. Ezekiel Oakland."

"So, we couldn't find you," Ethic scoffed, completely exasperated. The effort and cruelty it had taken to pull off

273

such an elaborate disappearance was sickening. The lack of responsibility. The hatred. The desertion. Ethic felt like that little boy who hugged his knees while his mother extinguished cigarettes against his skin all over again. This visit had peeled back layers of brick he had built around the memory of his father long ago. The injury this was causing, this re-opening of wounds, was unbearable. Ethic had enough demons, enough pain. He would have been okay not ever seeing this man again. The re-emergence would surely kill him. It hurt all over again.

"I made a lot of bad decisions back then. Some selfish choices."

"You had a whole family. Gave them a good life while me and my mother fell apart."

Ethic was floored. The man whose name he bore, had erased all lineage to the son he had left behind. Only to raise a new son, Nyair, and a daughter, Zora. The revelation gutted him inside. Why a man would not want to be connected to his flesh and blood he could never understand. No reason justified this. Eazy and Bella were the best parts of him. They were the purest portions of his soul…the good parts that hadn't been tainted by the world. They were second chances to get things right. How could Ezekiel not want that? The name change explained why Ethic had never been able to find him. It explained how a man could disappear from the face of the earth without a trace. Ethic had always assumed his father had died over the years. It would have been the only forgivable explanation that would excuse a father's absence. Ezekiel was standing and breathing before him, however. Nothing he could say would excuse what he had done.

"Get the fuck off my property before I murder you, man," Ethic said in disgust.

"I want to make amends. Ezra, I know I've done a poor job, but you have children I hear. My grandchildren. I'd like to make up for what I didn't do with you through them. I'm a different man now," Ezekiel stated.

"That's never happening. You'll never breathe on my kids, nigga. Don't even mention them. The damage you did. You'll never even meet mine, Ezekiel. You killed her…"

Ethic's chin quivered as his mother ran through his mind. He had to stop speaking.

"She sucked crack pipes and dick after you left," Ethic stated coldly. "You broke her so bad she beat me to punish you. Then it all killed her. You killed her."

"I loved your mother," Ezekiel said. "I was just a coward. A man who got caught up in a lie. I didn't know how to do right by a woman. I got caught up in an affair and didn't know how to be a man and just face my wrongs. So, I ran. I was a coward. I thought you two would be okay eventually. I was a bad man for a long time. Even after I left, but I'd be a liar if I said I didn't love your mother. I loved her very much."

"Yeah well if that's what love does; I'd hate to find out what you do to people you hate. We're done here. You ever show up in any space I occupy again…"

"What have you become son?" Ezekiel interrupted.

"What all abandoned black boys become when they have bitch ass fathers who give up on them," Ethic said. His tone sent a chill down Ezekiel's spine. "A gangster." Ethic tapped his chest with the back of his hand. "That's on you."

"I'd like to fix it. Right my wrongs," Ezekiel answered, eyes brimming with emotion.

"I'm 35 years old, Ezekiel. I've starved out here on these streets, I watched my mama pay for crack with pussy, felt her punish me for your short comings. I've taken lives with these hands, sold dope to people who look like me, fucked women knowing I could never love them, because I'm fucked up inside. It's too late to play daddy now. Fuck you, man. Get off my porch."

Ethic slammed the door so hard that chandelier above his head swayed violently.

He lowered his head onto a balled fist as he leaned into the door. So much anguish filled him. He felt like his father had wrapped hands around his throat.

"Ezra?"

Ethic turned and looked up at Alani.

"Come."

The order she always followed.

Nimble feet came down the stairs until she stood in front of him.

The forlorn look on his face caused her to frown. Concerned. She held the look of a woman who wanted to protect. He stared in her eyes. Trying to find direction there. He was lost in the painful memories.

"Help me baby," he whispered.

Alani gasped before placing a hand to his face. He leaned into her palm, then grabbed her wrist, then kissed there as his eyes closed.

Alani was mesmerized by him. Ezra was beautiful. The boy in him was showing, was hurting and she closed the space between them, wrapping her arms around his neck as he locked both hands around her waist. A hug. Their first expression of love. It had been abandoned since they had ventured into a deeper physicality, but it hadn't been forgotten. It was their most intimate form of connection.

"I'm so sorry baby," she whispered. He squeezed her tighter. "I love you. I'm in love with you. Your darkest parts. Your sharpest edges. Your most dangerous depths, Ezra. Remember you told me that's what I had to love for it to be real? It is baby. It's real. I'm here. You're here. We have three kids."

"Four," he corrected.

"You're right. We have four," she whispered, her heart fluttering at his acknowledgement of Love. The son he never dismissed.

"Our parents failed us. They threw us away, didn't want us, didn't raise us. We can be better. We can be all we need for each other and for them. Fuck Ezekiel," Alani said. Ethic pulled her in again and kissed the top of her head, holding her tight. He was used to being the foundation; used to being the strong one. This time it was her holding him down and he was proud of the fact that she could handle the shift of energy. She was a real woman. A real partner, one he hoped to spend forever with. He didn't have a ring. He didn't even know if she would even consider saying yes, but he had an overwhelming urge to ask her the most important question in the world. He pulled back and looked her in the eyes.

Marry me, baby.

The sentiment echoed throughout his entire body, but he couldn't will the words from his lips. One day he would. Because he needed to bind them. Mind. Body. Soul. As one because if she wasn't it, he didn't want another. Alani Lenika Hill was the woman he was meant to spend every breath he had left with. He was now more certain than ever before. He just had to figure out how to convince her of it too.

CHAPTER 20

essiah had never felt pain like this. It wasn't one specific thing that tormented him. It wasn't like a wound that he could patch up. It was a leaking of life from his soul, like he was running on empty and every, single thing he did took great effort. He ached. The nausea felt like one, giant wave, rushing over him, like he was swimming and was suddenly being pulled under by a renegade swell that made it hard for him to breathe. There was only one image in his mind that helped him through the hard times. Morgan Atkins filled his brain. Pictures of her smile ran behind the lids of his eyes, because he spent a lot of time with them closed these days. He had been reduced to enjoying her presence on Instagram, but she hadn't been active at all since the dance video and he was craving her energy. He was craving any type of energy because his was leaving him. The radiation and chemotherapy treatments were torture. It sucked the life right out of him. He had felt better when he was ignoring his illness and just letting nature take its course. Trying to fight this disease, by poisoning everything else inside him, was a slow death. Most people were afraid to die. Messiah wasn't afraid of shit, not even that. The only thing he feared was what Morgan would do when she found out he was gone. That tore him up inside; and the weaker he became, the more he wanted to reach out to her. He hoped she would forgive him for deceiving her, for plotting, for being related to Mizan and disrespecting her space with his treasonous DNA, but he couldn't help himself. When she had said his name...the moment he heard it fall off her pretty lips, he had fallen in love. All bets had been off. He had just wanted to indulge in her essence...he wanted to know what it was like to love her, because whether she knew it or not, she was the fucking queen of the city. It was inherited. Raven had been before her, Justine before her, and Messiah felt chosen, like royalty had handpicked him while perched high upon her throne. Messiah just wanted to live in her light for a little while, and he had, and then it had ended. His lies had ended it. When she thought back on him, she would visualize an old image, not the nigga in a hospital bed, with tubes running everywhere, barely moving, barely breathing. She would picture her king. She would hate him for the lies he'd told, but she would still remember him at his best, not at his weakest. Not in these embarrassing times. She would recall the things he'd done to her body, the ways he had trembled her heart; and beneath all the hurt, somewhere deep in her soul, he was confident she would remember that it had been real. Their love had been real. He also knew that she would hurt. She would grieve him hard and he needed people in place to make sure she was okay. He would make sure she got the attention she would need.

"The fuck this nigga at?" Messiah asked.

The knock at the door caused him to look up. "I'm right here, bitch nigga, simmer down," Meek said, as he entered the room, leaning against the frame of the door. "Bruh, I ain't gon' lie to you. This shit...this hospital bed, and these tubes, and this..." Meek's voice cracked, and he brought a balled fist to his mouth, clearing his throat. He sniffed. "What is it, man?" he asked.

Messiah felt the burn in his eyes, as he stared into the red eyes of his friend.

"Lymphoma," Messiah said.

Meek turned away, lifting his hoodie and placing hands over his head.

"Nigga, you ain't my bitch, get cho ass in here," Messiah barked, sniffing away, or attempting to sniff away, but damn why couldn't he sniff away the fucking emotions? He pinched the bridge of his nose, as Meek nodded, gathering himself, before flipping down the hood and approaching the bed.

"Damn, G," he said. Meek sat in the chair beside the bed but there was only so much a man could take. Messiah was his friend, had been since they were young boys. He loved that nigga with his entire heart. Unspoken love had pulsed between them for years. Since before they had hair on their chins, or body counts, both kinds, corpses and bitches, they had been two, little, nappy-headed boys with a dream. His face twisted in pain and he locked his jaw, lifting his head to stop himself from bitching up. "How long?"

"Doctors said a few months a few months ago," Messiah said. "Bleu's waiting to see what the radiation does. The shit is everywhere, though, man. I went a long time without doctors. A nigga ain't afraid to meet his maker, though. I was cool with it when they first told me. I was getting money, fucking bitches, living fast until..."

"Shorty Doo-Wop," Ahmeek finished. "I saw her, bro. When I was picking up from the club, she was there. She didn't even look the same. She's fucked up over the whole thing. Kept asking questions about you. Kept telling me how much she loves you. You should let her come, nigga. Even if it ends, at least she'll be there."

Messiah went silent. "She gave a nigga a reason to be fucked up about the shit. I've been mad as hell at her little-ass ever since. She made me want to live, and now I'm dying and I'm mad as fuck about the shit. Do you know what it'll do to her to see me like this? To watch me go? Nah, she can't be here for this." Messiah pinched the corners of his eyes. Stubborn tears, persistent emotions, were leaking out of him, sneaking like a mu'fucka because he was trying his hardest not to release them. Meek nodded his head and bent over, elbows to knees, as he broke down, each man, fighting themselves, battling this unfamiliar feeling of weakness. "I remember days when I used to pray for food. A nigga stomach used to touch his back. You used to sneak them nasty-ass Vienna sausages Auntie used to buy to me. Brought a nigga a backpack full of Pop-Tarts, little sausages, and Capri Suns, so I wouldn't starve. You always looked out for me; and when we came up, we came up together. You my brother, nigga. No lie. You and Isa."

"Three ways, all day, bruh. You already know how it's laying," Meek answered. "It ain't a lot of niggas I would die for. Take a bullet for. Fucking Ethic put one through a nigga center."

"Word?" Messiah asked, chuckling. "You should consider yourself blessed, nigga. I've never seen homie take less than a head shot. We got pussy together. We would have gotten them wings together, bruh."

"And I would have been good with that," Ahmeek stated.

Messiah steeled...grew silent, as grief took over the room. "I know. You're a good fucking nigga, bro. The best I know. That's why I need you to do some shit for me," Messiah said.

"Whatever you need, man. Just say the word," Meek said, tucking his turmoil and restoring order.

"Morgan. She's going to be fucked up over this. She don't know I'm sick and she don't need to know. I don't want her to know. Just that I'm gone, but not how I went. Let her think a nigga got lit up, holding court or some shit, I don't care, but don't tell her I got weak. Don't put them images in her head. When the day comes, I need you to make sure she's straight. I need you to pull up on her. Don't let her fold. Don't let her give up, because shorty gonna want to give up after this. She gonna want to die right next to a nigga because she's loyal... she's more loyal than I've ever been. She's better than I even know how to be, and I wish I could have been better to her. Wish I could have been different, but all I know is how to take care of me. You know how, though. You know how to love women the right way. Take care of her, man. You got to show her shit will be straight without me. After me. You got to show her love after me. Tell her to live. Tell her that's all I ever wanted her to do… is live…live for me," he said.

"Why me?" Meek asked. "Why not Ethic? Why not Bleu?"

"Because I want to break your fucking jaw when you look at her," Messiah said. "Like, you see her. Like you looking at her through my eyes."

Meek's head raised, and his brow dipped. "Bruh, I would never…"

"I know," Messiah said. "Because you're the second most loyal person I know; but you want to, there's a part of you that wishes you pushed up on her first. That's the part she'll need. She'll need you to lean on, when I'm gone, because the shit is going to hurt her. Take care of my bitch, nigga."

Meek looked away, eyes glancing out the window, as he swiped hands over his head and then dragged them down his face as anxiety filled his body.

"If it got to be somebody, it might as well be you," Messiah said. "We ain't got to dwell on it. I know what it is, you know what it's going to be. I want you to get Isa up here. I'll let you know when. I'll tell him myself. You bring your joints like I asked?"

Meek stood and pulled the clippers out of his Louis Vuitton backpack.

Messiah climbed from the bed, bare feet touching tile so cold that it sent a shock up his spine. Messiah's legs were weak, and he stumbled. Meek caught him, holding him up, and then pulled Messiah in for an embrace. Messiah broke. Niggas had never touched him. After what his father had put him through, he had never allowed it. Ethic was the only other, and even their last embrace had made him uncomfortable. He clung to Meek, chin quivering.

"You a soldier, G. The roughest nigga I know out here. I don't know a lot about how this shit go, but I know niggas who suffer down here get to rest up there. You going home, bro, and my ol' lady say it's like paradise up there. Keep a seat for me, G," Ahmeek stated, holding Messiah by the back of his neck. He gave him one pat to the back of his neck, and Messiah gritted his teeth, as he sobbed. Damn, he didn't want to go but he could feel that it wouldn't be long. Ahmeek placed him in the chair and caped him.

"Cut 'em off," Messiah said, wiping the emotion from his face.

"You sure about this?" Meek asked, as he leaned down to plug up the clippers and liners.

Messiah reached up to his head, and with ease, he pulled one of his locs away from his scalp. "It's dead, man. Everything is dying. Every part of me, my nigga. Cut it off," Messiah said. He held his chin high, as Meek clicked on the clippers and the loud buzz drowned out the sound of Messiah's soul cries.

CHAPTER 21

Bella laid in bed, eyes glued to the ceiling, as the high winds caused the branches of the tree outside to tap against her windowpane. Her heart pounded. The storm outside was so bad that the wind screeched through the air and she heard the cadence of the raindrops marching as they beat the concrete. She laid on her side, holding the pink bear to her chest.

BOOM!

The thunder was so loud it startled her. She was on edge, worried because while she was safe and sound inside, she knew that Hendrix was not. It weighed on her so heavily that she couldn't quite breathe right. She reached for her cell phone and FaceTimed him. Her stomach turned when he didn't answer.

Bella
Are u good?

BOOM!

A streak of lightning cut across the sky and a deafening crack erupted. She came up on her knees, looking outside her window, as the large tree across the street was struck down. Bella's eyes zeroed in on her phone screen. He always responded. Even when he couldn't respond, he never left her guessing. He would send a short line to tell her he was busy, and he would hit her up later. This time, his silence was driving Bella mad. Bella felt her eyes prickle and she closed them, pulling in a deep breath to calm her nerves.

Knock! Knock!

Her bedroom door cracked, and she saw Alani poke her head inside.

"B? Are you asleep?" Alani called.

Bella sat up. "No, I can't sleep," she answered.

"Your dad wants everyone in the basement," Alani said. "Bring your covers and your pillow. We can make it a slumber party. Rent movies. Hopefully, we won't lose power."

"Is there a tornado? That's why he wants us in the basement?" Bella asked.

"There's a warning, but we'll be fine," Alani said. "Your dad is about to go over to Nannie's to get her. That whole side of town is flooding, so we want her to come here for the night. He wants us downstairs until he gets back."

Bella's legs went numb and she sat to avoid falling.

It's flooding. The tunnel will flood.

Bella's eyes misted, as her fingers danced across her phone screen.

Bella
Henny, where are u?

"B?" Alani frowned because Bella was shook. Alani saw it. She could feel the apprehension in the room.

"I have to tell you something," Bella whispered. "I need your help telling my daddy something."

Bella paused and wiped her nose, as she sniffled. She was about to expose herself…about to admit all the sneaking and lying she had been doing. She was terrified, but she knew Hendrix couldn't stay outside tonight.

"Little girl. You better start talking," Alani said, getting serious, when she saw Bella's chin quiver.

"I've been seeing Hendrix," she said.

"Little Hendrix? From Susan Street?" Alani asked. She shook her head, dumbfounded by this admission. "Seeing him where? How?"

"When I'm at Nannie's. I've been sneaking off with him."

"Sneaking off with Hendrix's little-ass where?" Alani asked.

"That's the thing. He doesn't have anywhere to go, Alani. He's homeless. We hang out at the park and he sleeps in a tent. I can't reach him and I'm worried because it's flooding where he is."

The bedroom door swung open, as Ethic entered, interrupting. He halted, when he saw Bella's face.

"What up? Why the look?" Ethic asked, gripping the doorknob, as his forehead knitted in concern.

Alani kept her eyes to Bella, frowning, angry as hell, and Bella could barely take the scrutiny. She kept staring at that inactive text. Where were the bubbles? Why wasn't Hendrix texting her back?

"Alani, please," Bella said, a tear slipping from her eyes.

"Bella..." Ethic wanted her to look at him. Bella couldn't.

Alani sighed. "There's a boy, Ethic," Alani whispered.

"Nah, there *was* a boy," Ethic corrected. He was already building assumptions in his head. "Because the little nigga is dead. Bella..."

Bella lifted her eyes to her father.

"What boy?" Ethic asked.

"His name is Hendrix," Alani informed. "He's a kid from the neighborhood."

"Talk, Bella," Ethic ordered. Ethic and his orders. People knew not to defy him, even his daughter. Her lips parted and secrets she vowed to keep for Hendrix spilled out.

"I've been with him when you think I'm with friends," she stammered.

"I'm about to put this little nigga face on a fucking white t-shirt," Ethic stated, swiping his hand down his face in overwhelm.

"He's my friend, Daddy! He's not like that. He's willing to wait for me."

Ethic's jaw locked. "Wait for you to do what?" Ethic felt fire flow through his veins. He was physically hot. He felt like he would combust, as he used all his restraint not to snatch Bella up and demand answers. He knew what Hendrix was waiting on. He was waiting on what every, little, young nigga from the block was waiting on, and Ethic was waiting too because he was gon' chop shit up over his baby girl. He already had the clip waiting.

"Bella, you're only thirteen," Alani whispered.

"I'm a teenager!" Bella shouted. She said it with pride, like it made a world of difference. Like being in her teens made her wiser, stronger, more capable of handling what Alani feared she could not.

"You can't go sneaking off. You can't tell us you're one place and be somewhere else. How are we supposed to trust you? What if something had happened to you?"

"Hendrix wouldn't let it. I'm safe with him, but he's out there and he doesn't have a place to stay. Daddy, he's living in that tunnel at the park where Raven died. It's bad outside and I've called him a thousand times!"

Ethic pinched the bridge of his nose. "I swear, between you and Mo…" He turned to Alani.

"Who is this little mu'fucka?" Ethic asked, unable to control the temper that was threatening to erupt. "How old is this nigga?"

Alani placed her hands to Ethic's chest. "He's a kid, baby. He's 13 or 14, I think."

"So, I got to put somebody's son in the dirt," Ethic said, pressing his forehead against Alani's.

"Daddy!" Bella protested. "He's not like that! He gets me! We talk, and we have plans."

"You might as well leave me, baby, because I'm killing this little boy. I'ma kill him. Messiah took all my restraint. He took it and I ain't got no more, and she talking about making plans and I'm about to kill her little-ass too," Ethic whispered. "Get your daughter."

Alani's eyes widened. He was so angry. He hadn't even meant to let it slip, but she was honored. She was floored that he thought of her as Bella's second parent...he thought of her as his partner, as the other person responsible for raising his children. This was something he couldn't handle, so he needed her to help...needed her to lift some of this off of him.

Ethic was like a bull, he was breathing so hard and Alani soothed him, rubbing his face, as she looked at him with sympathy. He was raising two, beautiful daughters and they were taking him through the worst. Teenage years were every father's worst nightmare. First Mo, now Bella. Ethic felt like he was having a heart attack.

"He can't sleep outside in this storm, babe," Alani whispered.

"No. The answer's no, before you even ask the shit," Ethic stated.

"Daddy, please," Bella shouted. Ethic knew his baby had transitioned into the next phase of her life right under his nose. She was a young girl who had let her very first boy into her heart and he hated it. Before, he had been the only occupant, but he could see his daughter, extending her care to another, and it was enough to make him want to cry. His eyes burned. He had never wanted to keep her closer than he did in this moment. "He hasn't called me, and he always calls me at 7:30, every night, except tonight," she pleaded. "I know I'm in trouble. I don't care. I'll take my punishment, but you

have to go find him. He doesn't have anybody but me!"
Ethic ached. He ached like he had never ached before. He
was fucking sick. These tears his daughter was crying and
this angst on her young soul was carving away at him. He
didn't want this for her. This dangerous rush that came with
the attraction of a boy like Hendrix. He could see it all over
her. Young love, and he just wanted to rewind the clock a bit.
He wanted a do-over. She was becoming a real teenager and
he had just been raked over hot coals by Morgan. She hadn't
cut him one break, and now he had to survive those delicate
years all over again.

"What park, B?" Ethic relented.

"Mott Park," Bella whispered. "I'll show you."

"You'll stay here," he said.

"But, Daddy, you're going to hurt him!" Bella protested.

"Bella, baby girl, the weather is only getting worse. Let him
go get Nannie and go get Hendrix. We'll figure everything
else out once everyone is safe, okay?"

Bella felt Ethic's disappointment, and when he walked out
of the room, she broke down.

"He's so maddd," Bella said, lip quivering.

"Ethic loves you, Bella. There isn't an amount of anger he
could feel that will make him un-love you. You could have
been eighteen and he would have still been this way. He has
had all your love until this very moment. Now, he has to
share, and it hurts because you're growing up, but I want you
to promise me something, B…"

"Anything," Bella answered. She sniffed and wiped her
nose with the back of her hand. Alani reached around her

neck and removed the small cross necklace she wore. She sat next to Bella. "Turn," she instructed. She placed it around Bella's neck.

"...That you will give yourself time to learn the young woman you're about to blossom into, before you let Hendrix, or any other boy, pick you from your stem. You need to stay rooted in the soil to grow."

"You're talking about sex?" Bella asked. "We don't talk about that."

"I believe you, but one day, you'll think you're ready and you'll be wrong. Your body will make you think you're ready, but your heart isn't ready, B. It won't be for a long time; and Hendrix is the boy right now, but he might not be in a year or two or three. If he's your real friend. If he's here for the right reasons, he won't ever try to pick you too early because it's selfish. He'll let you grow. Let you bloom. Become a woman first. I can see that you like him. I hear it in your voice. I want you to be able to talk to me and come to me about everything. So, if you get to a point where you think you're about to do something grown, you take this necklace off. You don't even have to use words. You take it off and I'll notice, and I'll be here to help you make a decision you can be proud of."

"What if you don't notice?" Bella asked, fingering the cross.

"I notice everything about you, beautiful," Alani answered. "I won't miss it. When you need to talk, I'll be here."

"Does that mean you and Daddy are good? Like, you'll be in our lives forever?" Bella asked.

"The way your father has robbed me of my soul, Bella..."

Alani paused and shook her head, as a ghost of a smile played at her lips. "No matter what happens between Ethic and I, I'll always be here for you."

"I love you so much. Life was hard before you. I'm really glad you're here. I'm sorry how we got you. I'm really sorry that you had to lose so much before you got here, but I really needed you," Bella whispered.

Alani's eyes betrayed her, and tears rolled down her cheeks. She laughed a little, as she wiped them away.

"Daddy's going to kill him, isn't he?" Bella whispered. She laid her head in Alani's lap.

"Yeah, B, Hendrix is probably gonna die," Alani snickered. "Come on. Eazy's waiting for us in the basement."

Ethic didn't know if he was racing through the rain to end or save a life. He was grateful for the escape. He had to get out of the house. He hated to raise his voice with Bella. She was sensitive, and her feelings bruised easily, and he felt himself losing it. He felt the strings around his heart unraveling. His baby girl. The light in his dark, the peace to his turmoil, had a boyfriend. She hadn't said it, but she hadn't needed to. He knew the game. Somebody's nappy-headed son had gotten inside his daughter's heart. He feared that everything he had put in her would be unlearned by love because love had a way of snatching logic right out of a situation. Ethic drove through the empty streets, tires swooshing through the water that was building up inch by inch, until he pulled up to the park.

He frowned, as he opened the door. The wind was so strong it felt like his door would be ripped off the frame of his truck. He dipped his head low and flipped up his hood, attempting to shield himself from the heavy downpour. His stomach tightened. This park was like a graveyard for him. He could still envision the blood stains on the concrete from all that had been spilled that day. The fact that Bella was hanging out here, in the middle of the hood, ignited him. The fact that this Hendrix was the one to bring her back here made the fire spread. Ethic took wheat Timberlands across submerged grass. There was at least a foot of water just sitting on top of the lawn and he groaned, as he sloshed across the field that led to the tunnel. He knew the park well. It was a staple in the city, and if someone was living in the tunnel beneath the bridge that led to the golf course, he knew they wouldn't make it through the night. It would fill within hours. He had to widen his legs, as he trudged through the muddy waters.

"This fucking kid, man," he complained. Those who didn't know the park well would never be able to locate the tunnel in the dark, but Ethic found it with ease. It was pitch black, except the glow from a lantern in the center.

The water inside the tunnel was even deeper because it was below the natural elevation of the rest of the park. It came to his knees, as Ethic stepped forward.

How the fuck is he living down here?

He made it to the tent, and when he pulled back the fabric, he was face to face with the barrel of a .9mm pistol.

One twist of Hendrix's wrist and Ethic disarmed him and then pointed the gun directly at him. Hendrix's entire body was soaking wet and he was shivering.

"You know who I am?" Ethic asked.

"You're a legend, bruh," Hendrix answered. He held his chin high, like he was ready to take whatever beating Ethic was there to deliver. He didn't flinch. He wasn't afraid. Ethic scoffed.

"That ain't who I am. That ain't why I'm here. Who am I?" Ethic asked.

"You're Bella's old man," Hendrix answered. "And a motherfucking legend."

"Carrying a fucking pistol," Ethic muttered. He couldn't believe Bella had gotten involved with a boy from the block. He paid big money for her to go to a fancy school outside of the city limits, just so she would never fall victim to some smooth-talking, money-flashing, young hustler, and here Hendrix was. He was Ethic's worse nightmare. Ethic had never been afraid of anyone, but this little nigga right here terrified him. The possibility of the ways he could ruin Bella gripped him. Ethic removed the clip from the gun, popped the bullet out the head, and put the gun on his hip.

"Let's go," Ethic chastised, as he stepped aside. As Hendrix walked by him, Ethic grabbed the back of his neck sternly. "Bring yo' li'l bad-ass."

He pushed Hendrix out of the tunnel and they walked in silence until they were seated safely inside his Range Rover.

"You fucking my daughter?" Ethic asked. There would be

no walking light with Hendrix. He was cutting straight to the chase.

"No, sir." Hendrix was no dummy. He came off with the respect, without Ethic having to demand it.

"You fuck my daughter and I'ma fuck you," Ethic stated. He didn't even look at Hendrix. He leaned against the driver's side door and finessed his beard, as he kept his eyes in the side mirror. They were in the middle of Flint. It was necessary to keep his bearings. The six-figure vehicle he was in was a jack boy's dream. He stayed on point, even now. "Do you hear what I'm saying?"

"Yes, sir," Hendrix answered, again. "Bella's the best part of my day. I don't want to do nothing out of bounds with her. Nothing, man. She keep my head in the clouds. I can talk to her without her laughing at me. She the only one think I can get off these blocks. I ain't on no foul shit with her."

"You're a fucking kid. Watch ya fucking mouth in my car," Ethic snapped. He gritted his teeth and held onto the top of his steering wheel with his right hand. He squeezed the leather so tight. Like a vise-grip. Like it was Hendrix's neck beneath that grip and he was choking life out of him. Ethic was thrown at how Hendrix was handling his own. He had made grown men fold with just the tone of his voice, but not Hendrix. Hendrix was owning what was his and denying the rest, making it clear to Ethic what was what. Ethic wanted to respect it, but he hated it. Hendrix had the makings of a young man that could steal his daughter's heart.

"No disrespect, O.G.," Hendrix answered.

"You talk to my daughter like that?" he asked.

"No, sir," Hendrix answered.

"Oh, so you finessing my daughter? You talking sweet? Fuck you talking sweet for, li'l mu'fucka?" Ethic asked.

Hendrix opened his mouth to answer but he was searching for words, trying to figure out how to explain what he and Bella shared, without setting off her father. There clearly was no right answer. Anything he said, Ethic would pick him apart.

"You better finesse the fuck out of me, homie, cuz your life is on the line," Ethic stated.

"I respect Bella," Hendrix said. "I couldn't talk sweet to her, if I wanted to, because she don't fall for it anyway. She means a lot to me, but I'll never cross those lines because I've hurt a few girls before. I get what I want and then they want something else and they end up hurt. I don't ever want to hurt Bella, so I'll never even take it there."

"Yeah, you talk real sweet," Ethic stated, as he started the truck. "Got me out here in this shit. Don't have my daughter in the middle of the hood in no fucking tent and don't have no gun around her. As a matter of fact, this sneaking shit is a wrap. You want to see Bella, you come to where she be at."

"Where's that?" Hendrix asked. Ethic could have choked life from Hendrix. The young kid was brazened, forthcoming, letting Ethic know that, shit, he had no problem hopping the fence to play on Bella's side.

"With me. My daughter be with me; so, if you want to see her, you gon' see me too. You gon' sit in my house, under my roof, where my guns at, where I can see your hands, where I can hear how you talk to her," Ethic barked. "You lucky I ain't popping your fucking melon."

He was in a rare way. He couldn't calm himself if he wanted to. He pulled away from the curb. "Where your people stay?"

"My mama live on Fleming Road, but she ain't fucking with me," Hendrix said.

"It's storming outside. I'm sure she would rather have you home, kid. Put the address in the GPS," Ethic stated.

Hendrix entered the information and fell into silence, as he nodded his head to the low-playing music knocking through Ethic's speakers.

Asked me if I do this every day, I said, "Often"
Asked how many times she rode the wave… "Not so often"
Bitches down to do it either way, often
Baby, I can make that pussy rain, often

Hendrix nodded to the music, singing the words, as he held his hand up, curling his ring finger while pointing, like he was singing to someone. In Ethic's mind, he was singing to Bella and his temper went through the roof. The corner of Hendrix's mouth pulled in a smirk and he bit his bottom lip, as he looked out the window. Ethic wanted to choke his little-ass. It bothered him more that Hendrix could actually sing. Ethic reached for the console and turned off the damn radio.

Yeah, I'ma have to kill this cool-ass, little nigga, Ethic thought.

They pulled up to a small, one-story home and Ethic turned off the engine. Ethic followed Hendrix to the door.

A heavy fist to the door and it was pulled open. "Look at what we have here."

Hendrix rolled his eyes and blew out a sharp breath, as he looked at the shirtless man.

"Who is this?" Ethic asked Hendrix.

"My mama's boyfriend," Hendrix stated, sneering, sniffing, as he pulled up his pants a bit and burned a hole through the man.

"Who the fuck are you? You on my porch, talking about who am I?" The man snickered.

Ethic was losing patience with this entire night. "I'm just dropping him off. He was under the bridge in Mott Park. He can't stay there."

"I don't know why you brought him here!"

A woman came up behind the man and Ethic could smell the crack cocaine coming from her pores. He had sold it too long not to remember what it smelled like. Her beady eyes and balmy skin told him she was high.

"Man, I told you she don't fuck with me like that," Hendrix stated. There was injury in his tone, like he had gotten his hopes up for a different reaction.

"Nigga, don't come over here talking that bullshit! You stabbed him, last time I let you up in here! Get yo' sorry-ass off my porch! Ain't no room in here for yo' ungrateful-ass! Can't even look out for your mama! Every time I ask you for something, you acting stingy," the woman screamed. She pulled a pack of cigarettes from her bra and lit one. She took a long pull and then balanced it between two fingers. She used those same, two fingers to point at Hendrix.

"You just want to smoke on me! No! I ain't paying for that shit! I pay everything in this bitch! The rent! The lights! But I say no about some dope and I ain't shit all of a sudden! I woke up and the nigga was going through my shit, like a fucking fiend. He hit my whole stash! I still owe niggas for that!" Hendrix barked. "He smacking you around and I'm the one you put out?!"

The man came out the house, lunging for Hendrix, but before he could touch a hair on his head, Ethic lifted his hoodie, revealing the gun that rested there.

"You don't wanna do that," Ethic said. His tone was calm. Sure. "Yo, Hendrix, go get in the car."

"Nigga, what you gon' do? I'll beat yo' muthafuckin'-ass. You better ask around about me."

Ethic drew on the man, without hesitation. He didn't play games. He wasn't like most men. He didn't carry a weapon for fun. His shit kept the silencer on it, for instances just like these. He was about action. Less talk. More action. He was already in a mood. Ethic put the gun to the man's head.

"What's that now?" he asked.

"He ain't mean nothing by it. I swear. Please," the woman said.

"Nah, he meant it. I just want him to repeat it. You gon' beat my ass, no? Like you do her? Is that why he stabbed you up? Cuz he owed you a couple? You took his stash, but he was ready to pop off because he laid under this roof for a while, listening to you beat on his mama?"

Ethic read the situation like a five-star book. The green bruise beneath the woman's eye and her willingness to put this man over her own child were clear signs of manipulation and abuse.

"Man, I don't want no trouble," the man said.

"Too late for that. Trouble came to your doorstep tonight, my man. You stole from him. That's one shot. A threat to me left your tongue. That's another. I'ma let you choose. You want to keep your knees or your dick?"

The man's lips quivered. He hesitated. He shouldn't have, because Ethic didn't. Ethic pulled the trigger twice.

The man dropped to the wooden porch, hollering in excruciation. Ethic had chosen for him.

"Get some help. I'll bring him by to check on you once a week. When you're ready to get clean, I know a place that can help. Get this nigga out your house. If he ain't gone by next week, I'ma blow his head off next time."

Ethic tucked his pistol and climbed back into his truck. Hendrix wasn't fazed one bit and that bothered Ethic even more. He put his car in reverse and pulled off into the night.

"We need more candles, B. Are there any more?" Alani asked.

"No, this is all we have, I think. Daddy might have some in the garage, but I don't know where," Bella said.

"My Minecraft flashlight is upstairs. Will that work?" Eazy asked.

"Yes, go grab that, Big Man, and be careful. Don't run. It's dark and I don't want you to hurt yourself, okay?" Alani instructed.

"I won't," Eazy said. He walked out of the kitchen, but Alani heard his steps quicken, as soon as he was out of eye sight. "Eazy! Walk!" They slowed, again, and she smiled, shaking her head, as she bent down to search more cabinets for a lighter.

The front door opened, and Bella looked up, hopefully. Nannie came through first, as Ethic held the door open for her. Disappointment filled her, when he let the door close behind him.

"Did you find him? Was he okay?" she asked. Her chest tightened when she saw him step inside alone.

Before Ethic could answer, the front door opened, and Hendrix came through, holding Nannie's overnight bag.

"You suck at keeping promises, Pretty Girl," Hendrix stated. He was soaking wet. Bella dropped every candle in her hand and ran across the room. Baby Bella didn't care that her father was standing right beside Hendrix, she threw her arms around him. Wet clothes and all, she hugged him tightly.

"I could kill you!" she shouted. Hendrix was afraid to close his arms around her, so he held them out in surrender. "Why didn't you answer my texts?"

"I forgot to charge my phone today while I was on the block. It died on me," he explained.

Ethic cut eyes of astonishment over to Alani and rubbed the top of his head.

"B, come help me search the garage for more candles," Alani said. Bella pulled back and then she rushed Ethic.

"Thank you, Daddy," she whispered in his ear, pecking his cheek, quickly, and with much less enthusiasm. "Hey, Nannie," Bella greeted, again, with another kiss to her cheek, before rushing out with Alani.

Ethic pointed a finger at Hendrix.

"I didn't even hug her back, O.G., so if somebody got to die, it got to be B," Hendrix stated.

"Pretty Girl? No sweet talk, huh?" Ethic shot back. "Finessing-ass little nigga. You sleeping in the basement. Far away from my fucking daughter. Come on. Let me see if I can find some dry clothes you can fit. Tomorrow, we'll spin by the mall and get you what you need while you're here."

"Here?" Hendrix asked, surprised.

"Better than the tent, no?" Ethic asked. "Just until I figure something else out. You're a smart kid. You know what happens if you disrespect me… under my roof."

"Say less, O.G., I got it," Hendrix answered.

"No, I'ma say more cuz you a slick mu'fucka. Don't touch my daughter. Don't even breathe on her, cuz I'm bringing grown man problems your way if you do. You in the streets. You're light years ahead of her. I don't want her to try to keep up. I don't want her nowhere near that shit. What you moving? Pills? Weed? Dope?"

"Whatever," Hendrix said, honestly. "I'd sell niggas air if I could bottle the shit up."

Ethic snickered. He eyed the young boy, curiously. He was a problem. He was the type of worker O.G.'s prayed to stumble upon. He reminded him of Messiah, but sharper, calmer. Messiah had rocked his world, however, and his trust was at an all-time low.

"That's over too. If you want a job, I'll put you to work at one of my businesses. I find out you still working, and you and I will have a different set of problems," Ethic stated. "Who you owe?"

"Herbo and 'em from Merrill Hood," he stated.

"Herbo. Messiah's lieutenant?" Ethic asked.

"Yeah," Hendrix confirmed.

"You don't owe him no more," Ethic stated. "You follow my rules and respect me and I'll respect you. That's how this works." Ethic held out his hand.

Hendrix gave him a lazy and weak shake.

"You shake my hand like a man. You look a nigga in his eyes when you come to an agreement," Ethic stated.

Hendrix stood up straight and shook Ethic's hand, firmer, stronger. Bella walked back into the room and saw her father and Hendrix shaking hands. She couldn't stop the smile from gracing the corners of her lips. Ethic didn't know it, she was pretty sure Hendrix didn't either, but her father and a young man she was beginning to love had just become acquainted, and it was a relief to her young heart.

CHAPTER 22

London, UK

W ow. This place is massive," Morgan whispered. Morgan stood in the middle of campus. Green lawns sprawled in front of her, as the castle-like buildings surrounded her. "I can't believe I'm here."

"I'm glad you decided to come. Nothing quite changes who you are like seeing a different part of the world. I took my first trip abroad at twelve years old and I've been addicted to traveling ever since," Bash said. "Come on. Let me introduce you to the dean of students, and then I'll show you to your apartment."

Morgan felt butterflies of excitement swarming inside her. She was so far away from home. An entire ocean separated her from the hurt that existed there, but still pieces of the person whom had destroyed her grew inside her. She placed hands on her belly.

"I can't believe I'm doing this. I'm so scared," she said, looking up at him, eyes misting.

"Scared of Cambridge or afraid of motherhood?" he asked.

"Both," she answered, honestly. A sharp kick took her

breath away and she grimaced, slightly, sucking in air, as she reached out for him, gripping his forearm. She was so terrified of losing her son. Every kick, every, little pain, every step of the evolution of pregnancy had Morgan on edge. She couldn't go through that again. It would kill her.

"You good?" he asked.

She sighed, in relief. "I'll just never get used to somebody kicking my ass from the inside," she said. "You want to feel?"

Bash stared at her, unsurely, and she took his hand and placed it on her stomach.

The baby was kicking like crazy and Bash's eyes widened in wonder.

"That's the craziest thing I've ever felt," he said. Morgan laughed, as he placed a second hand on her stomach and then met her eyes. "You're gorgeous, Morgan Atkins. Thank you for making my summer more interesting."

Morgan smiled and lowered her head, breaking eye contact, and then took a step back. "Dragging a pregnant girl around Europe for two months doesn't sound like much fun at all. I'm just going to slow you down," she said.

"It'll be the story we tell our kids one day. The story of how we fell in love over the summer in Europe," he said.

Boring, she thought. *Boring and corny.* Messiah flashed in her mind. The motorcycle ride he had given her when he had placed her hand in his and put a bawled fist to his heart. The sex backstage after her gigs. Her saying his name for the first time in his car. Him walking naked to the door to greet the pizza man because he had a point to prove. Fighting over him at the skating rink. Him sucking strawberries out of her center like she was edible. He had given her butterflies every step of the way. He had set her soul on fire with his every touch, his every interaction. She had thought those days would last until the end of time, but forever didn't last. As she stood in front of Bash, she felt none of those things. In his presence she was dulled. *But he's safe,* she thought.

She wiped a lone tear from her face, quickly swiping it, as she looked off into the distance at the massive campus in front of her. She had her entire life ahead of her. She didn't have to stay stuck in her mind with Messiah, with the Messiah she knew, not the one he had turned out to be. She didn't have to hold onto that hurt when there was someone in front of her who wanted to love her...who was willing to look past the fact that she was pregnant with another man's child and accept her package - girl plus baby. Maybe Bash wasn't the one, but she could try, she could try to live without Messiah...she could try to close her eyes at night without crying herself to sleep. She could live. He had always told her to live. She looked back up at Bash.

"Maybe," she whispered. There wasn't hope in her voice, but sadness. She didn't ever think she would feel love again. It didn't even seem possible. Morgan laced her arm through his elbow and leaned her head against his shoulder, as they headed inside.

Bella crept down the basement steps, her feet hitting the floor as quietly as possible, because she knew if she woke her father there would be hell to pay. The glow from the television was the only thing that illuminated the space. Hendrix laid on the couch, one leg propped up over the back of it and one hand behind his head, as he flicked through the channels.

"Hey," she whispered, as she crossed the empty space to him.

"What you doing up?" he asked.

It had been two days since he had come to stay with them and Bella had hardly seen him at all. Every morning, Ethic forced Hendrix out of bed and took him to one of his businesses. By the time he would return, they would sit at the table, eat dinner, and then Hendrix would be taken by Ethic into his study. A book. They were reading a book. The 48 Laws of Power had been the selection. They would read and talk all night, leaving no room for Bella. On the weekends, Ethic had arranged for Hendrix to spend time at his older brother's house. They were making plans to move Hendrix there permanently, and soon, Bella wouldn't see him much at all. Her stomach had been in knots for days.

"I can't sleep, I guess," she answered.

"Are you really leaving? To live with your brother?" she asked.

"Yeah, Ethic's going to put us up in a property, give my bro a job. He ain't got to hustle. I'ma stay with him and his girlfriend and their new baby. Nigga making me go to vocational school for the summer, though, but I'll have a roof over my head, so I guess it's worth it," Hendrix stated.

"You have a roof over your head here," she said.

"You know your pops ain't letting me stay here, Smart Girl," Hendrix said.

Bella smiled but it was halfhearted.

"I feel like now that he knows, I'm never going to see you," she whispered.

"Your pops is a good dude," Hendrix said. "He's cool. Right now, I kinda think I need him more than I need you. I ain't never had a nigga that can show me shit, you know? Like, give me game and show me shit that men know. Not like a daddy or nothing, but just to show me, you know? I've only been here for two days and I don' soaked up so much game it's crazy. He don't even be talking to me half the time, but I be listening and watching. You're lucky he's in your life, Bella. Niggas don't have that...I just don't want to fuck that up."

"So, we can't be friends because you want to stay in good with my dad," Bella whispered, heart aching. She scoffed. "Glad you got what you wanted, Henny." Bella couldn't understand the role that Ethic filled in Hendrix's life. Her feelings were shattered on the floor. She turned to leave, but Hendrix grabbed her hand.

"I'ma come back and make you my girl one day, Bella. That's on my mama, but I got to learn how to be a man. You love your pops. Let me learn from him, so one day you can love me," he said.

"I already do," she whispered.

Her heartbeat was out of control, and when Hendrix pulled her face to his, she died a little. He kissed her. A second kiss. A better kiss because this time Bella knew what to expect. Under her father's roof, she French kissed Hendrix and her eyes closed in bliss. If this wasn't love, she didn't know what was. Puppy love. Young love. Wet behind the ears love but love all the same. Bella felt like she was melting. Hendrix didn't go as hard as he could. He was fourteen and living fast. He was already popping cherries in the hood, but he didn't want that from Bella. Even though he was sure he could get it. He didn't want it at all. This kiss felt like a stolen gift. Something about her was different. He ended with two pecks to her lips, stealing Bella's air. She couldn't even think, let alone remember to inhale.

"You promise you're going to come back for me," she whispered.

"I promise you that. On my life; and when I do, we won't be kicking it in tunnels, or sneaking kisses in your daddy's house. I'ma go hard for you, Smart Girl. When I'm ready, I'ma step to you right. Until then, I'll see you around when you come to the hood."

"That door we talked about... Get to the door, Henny," Bella stated. "I'ma be there on the other side...waiting."

"I will. That's my word."

(Two days later)

Alani didn't even realize she had fallen asleep until she opened her eyes. The sun was setting. It glowed orange with flashes of red outside the bedroom window. Her entire body ached...it ached so good that she could still feel the aftermath of his love making. Ethic was the best lover she had ever had. He did things to her that she would never let another man think of trying. He had literally put her to bed, knocking all her insecurities out of her mind, and fucking her so good...into an exhaustion that had caused her to sleep all day. She knew his side of the bed was empty before she ever even glanced there. She didn't feel him. His energy. The security in her heart when he was close was gone. It was what had caused her to leave dreamland in the first place. She sat up and smiled, as he entered the room. It was like he felt her discontent and showed up to ease her mind.

"I ordered food," Ethic said, as he held up a brown paper bag.

"I would have cooked for you," she said.

"No time for that," he said. "I want to feed you, and then fuck you."

Alani lifted astonished eyes to Ethic. He licked those full lips and then leaned over her, his balled fists denting the space around her as he stole deep kisses. "Then, you can feed a nigga, cuz I got a taste for you, baby. I want to eat it real good for you."

Alani placed both hands on his face, lacing her fingers through his beard and holding on tightly, as she whispered, "You're so mannish, Ethic." She loved when he was this way, unapologetic about the need he had for her. It was so rare that he was so direct, it always made her wet. Then again, there wasn't a time that she was dry around him. He just aroused her. Mind, body, and soul ignited for him. His insatiable ways left her a victim to his love and Alani's body tingled at the thought of what he had planned for her.

He nudged her with his face, a challenge, and Alani charged him, bullying her tongue into his mouth with little effort because he was a willing victim.

He groaned and pulled back. "Eat first. Your food will get cold," he said. He moved to her neck and then to her breasts, indulging in her nipples.

"I can't," she whispered, letting a soft chuckle escape, and then a gasp, as she felt his tongue dip into her belly button. "If you're doing that."

Ethic was on his knees in front of her and he straightened his torso, as he reached for the greasy Chinese food.

He handed it to her. "You eat," he said…he lowered his face between her thighs and widened them, capturing her clit between his lips. "While I eat," he groaned.

Alani dropped the goddamn bag, as Ethic pulled her hips off the bed, eating her up like she hadn't fed him in days.

Alani came twice because she had been taught to always feed a man a second plate, and when he stood to his feet, he smirked. The knowing leer on his lips made her roll her eyes. He was cocky…proud at the ways he'd made her cum.

"Don't think you all that. You ain't all that," she teased.

He lifted hands in surrender and then clapped them together once, and then opened them again. "I ain't said shit," he answered. Alani gave her eyes the privilege of lingering. He was magnificent. Black on black, strong but lean, and his smile that he rarely gifted just did things to her soul. That smile, and those eyes, warmed her entire body every time. *I'm so lucky. God, thank you.* It felt sinful to love him so much because of the way he had come into her life. Alani struggled with that, but she would just have to deal with the guilt because she was too far gone to turn back...too deep in love to not sink...he was the love of her life. It felt so good that it ached. An overindulgence of Mr. Okafor had made her lovesick, but there was no cure. When she died, this plague would remain on her heart. His love was just with her. It always had been, ingrained in her. He reached down and picked up her food, and then kissed the top of her head. "I'll put it on a plate and warm it up. You get cleaned up. I'll meet you downstairs," he said.

"You aren't showering? You can join me," she suggested.

He licked his lips, again, sucking on the bottom one for a beat, and then his white teeth broke through in a smile. "Nah, I want you to live on my tongue for a minute, baby."

Alani blushed hard and shook her head. She loved that shit. That nasty shit. He was in rare form.

"I hardly have clothes here, Ethic. I really have to move the rest of my stuff here. I should have been the one going back with Nannie and the kids," she said, as she stood to her feet. "Did you get Henny settled in with his brother?" she asked.

"I did," Ethic answered.

"I guess we know why Bella likes to hang out at Nannie's now," she snickered. "Hood boys and their good girls." She shook her head and Ethic turned to look at her in disdain.

"She's not his girl. She's a girl. My little girl, and he's a dead man if the thought even forms in his head. I'm not going to make the same mistake I made with Messiah. He can come around on my terms. They can be friends. Do friendly shit. Movies, bowling, whatever the hell 13-year-old kids do, but I'ma be right there with them, cuz that little nigga too smooth. Fucking singing to my daughter, calling her pretty girl and shit. Singing to you around here like he Tevin Campbell or some shit."

Alani laughed. "Give little Henny a break. He's a cute kid. He's had a hard time, but I have a good feeling about him," Alani said.

"That's because he don' finessed you too," Ethic said, smirking. "Take your shower. I'll be downstairs. The clothes thing, I'll take care of for you. Just grab one of my shirts out the drawer. Preferably, not one of my thousand-dollar joints. I'll have my shopper bring you some options by in the morning," he said.

"Your shopper? You have a person that goes to the store to pick out your clothes?" she asked.

He turned to her, brows raised in confusion. "I don't have time to walk around a mall and all that. I pay for convenience. Now, I'm paying for your convenience. I'll have him pick up pieces for you to choose for your book reading too. He'll bring a whole rack by. You're what a ten? Twelve?"

"A twelve," she answered, still astonished.

"Consider it done," he said, before walking out the room.
Alani would have to get used to the luxuries that came with
a man like Ethic. His lifestyle was so heightened. Even having
Lily around felt awkward for her. Alani didn't need her. Alani
would bust her ass to make sure Ethic was covered, that his
children were covered, and that they all were loved on. As long
as she was doing the job, Lily wasn't necessary. Alani hadn't
wanted to come in making changes, however, or requesting
transitions that would make her seem ungrateful. She was
just an old-school, simple girl; maids, personal shoppers,
and such had never even been a possibility, but Ethic liked
to hire people to make his life simple. His time was precious,
and he wanted to spend it wisely, on her, on his children, so
Alani would just have to adjust. She was with a king and he
did king shit. It just was what it was. She showered and the
hunger pangs in her stomach reminded her that she hadn't
eaten all day. She was thankful for his consideration, because
suddenly, she was starving. Ethic had taken all her energy.
It always took every ounce she had, just to make sure he
was satisfied...just to ensure that she expressed how much
she appreciated him. Her sex, her willingness, her eagerness,
her freakiness, it knew no bounds, because his effort, his
attention, his loyalty, his security, knew no bounds. Their
love was limitless, and she was exhausted from trying to turn
what she felt inside into his physical pleasure. She needed a
good meal, and if she'd had to cook, it would have prolonged
the hunger. She wrapped a towel around her wet body and
went to his closet. She reached for a hanger and pulled a shirt

off the rack and boxes from the shelf above came tumbling to the floor.

Alani bent to pick up the contents, but her hands froze when she saw the old news clipping. She picked it up and the beautiful face of Raven Atkins smiled back at her. She was a splitting image of Morgan and Alani placed one hand over her mouth in stun. She looked through the pile on the floor, as her heart raced. This was a part of his life that he was so secretive about. He never shared that part with her and her hands shook, as she snooped through the things. She picked up a photo. Light, glowing skin, long hair that was parted down the middle, and a smile that made Alani's heart pang with jealousy. Raven was beautiful. She flipped the picture over and the loopy handwriting in red ink read:

To the love of my life.
Thank you for saving me from myself.
You mean everything to me.

-Forever Rae

Alani lifted the box and her heart stopped. A silver, silk sundress was bawled inside.

Is this blood?

The dark brown stains covered it and it was riddled with holes. Alani's heart seized in her chest because she knew what it was. She knew because she had done the same thing with the clothes Kenzie had died in. She was holding the bloodied dress of Ethic's lost love.

"What are you doing?"

Alani startled and began to scramble to put the belongings back inside the box.

"I'm sorry, the box fell and…"

Ethic snatched the dress from her hands.

"I've never thought of you as the intrusive type," Ethic stated. He gathered Raven's belongings and put them back in the box.

"I'm not…I wasn't trying…" She reached to help him pick up the mess.

"Just don't touch her shit!" The words came out harsher than he intended.

"I apologize. I didn't mean to…" Alani was flustered and embarrassed and so damn jealous that he was this upset at her over Raven. "I was grabbing a shirt and it fell."

"There are shirts in the drawer. There's certain shit you can't touch. Anything that you even think belongs to her is off limits. That's not your place."

Alani recoiled. He had never spoken to her with such regard. Such disdain. Her place? He had never assigned her to a place…to a section of his life where she was allowed. He had given her free reign…over his heart, over his kids, over this house, until now.

"Not my place," she repeated, stunned. He was so angry, so cold. She had never seen him like this. Not toward her. He had always made her exempt to every part of him that wasn't motivated by love. Except tonight. Tonight, she saw him boxing her out, drawing lines in the sand. He and Raven were on one side, she was on the other. It was clear to her that whatever part he had given to Raven wasn't a part of himself he was willing to share. Her heart cracked because she hadn't reserved any part of herself when dealing with him. She had given her all to him, even the parts that hated him, even the parts she wasn't proud of, she hadn't held back…but Ethic had…Ethic was holding out on her, holding back, saving a piece of himself for Raven and not allowing her to touch that part. She didn't know what she felt. Jealousy, sadness. A recipe of hurt swirled in her chest and began to rot there but she couldn't protest. You just couldn't protest over the limits a person set up over their dead loved ones. Out of respect, even if they were wrong, you had to play by their rules. She understood because she had so many. She had never assigned them to him, because he was elevated beyond any rule she could set…but not her…apparently, he had stipulations…limits. *His love has limits.* "You're right. I'm sorry. I shouldn't have touched them. You just never talk about her. Why is it so hard for you to open up to me about Raven?"

"Stop," he muttered, as he lifted the box and returned it back to its original place. Alani stood to her feet and grabbed his elbow, forcing him to face her.

"Raven is Eazy's mom, Morgan's sister and…"

"She wasn't shit to you," he barked. Alani's eyes misted at the tone of his voice. He was yelling, and yelling was something that Ethic didn't do. The volume alone would have cut her into pieces, but paired with the look of frustration and fury he gave her, Alani shrank. "So, just stop. Her name on your lips…" Ethic shook his head and swiped a hand down his face, before storming by her and out of the closet. "Nah," he finished.

Alani didn't know what to feel, as she stood there, floored. She understood that grief was personal and that everyone dealt with it differently, but when it came to Raven Atkins, Alani felt reduced. It was like, compared to her in Ethic's life, she was put right back on that sales rack, discounted, cheap, worthless...like the thing you picked up when you went to Target and put back before you got to the cash register. Unneeded. An option but not a necessity. Something you thought you wanted but could go without. Raven was in the cart, Alani was on the shelf and her feelings were disintegrated.

Ethic had gone so hard. He had put her in her place and Alani's eyes burned with emotion. He had crushed her. She walked out of the closet and gathered her clothes from the floor. Ethic sat on the end of the bed, leaned over, elbows to knees, the position he took when he was stressed. His head hung low, as he rubbed the back of his wavy, low cut.

She didn't speak. Neither did he. He just sat there, eyes to the floor, as she slipped on her clothes.

"I'm sorry for intruding," she relented, as she grabbed her car keys and her handbag. She couldn't get dressed quick enough, couldn't get away from him faster.

He reached for her, but she maneuvered out of his grasp. "You don't have to leave," he said.

"You know, I've always known that I didn't belong here. That it was wrong," she whispered, as she looked down and twiddled her fingers. Large tear drops clung to her lashes.

"But you made it feel okay. You made me feel welcomed. You convinced me that I could do this and that I belonged here with you and your children."

Your children.

Ethic's heart stopped beating. He felt it stall inside his chest and he knew he had fucked up because it was the first time she had ever separated herself from his kids. The blow behind those words, while he was sure was unintended, was mighty. The sting burned.

"Lenika…"

She scoffed, and then shook her head. "I wanted to believe you, I wanted to belong to you…to them, but I don't. You're absolutely right, Ethic. It's not my place…it's hers. I'm just standing in her place, just filling some void for you."

"Baby…" Ethic stood, and she backpedaled. As if a sudden revelation came over her, Alani fisted her curly hair and closed her eyes.

"I've got to get out of here," she said, as two tears fell, one from each eye. Walking out on him gutted her, but she couldn't stay. She needed to go home, so she could cry in peace; but even still, she wouldn't be able to escape him because at this very moment Bella and Eazy rested under her roof. She wondered if she had done the same thing as him. If she was guilty of the same emotional crime. Had she tried to supplement her loss with his children? It was obvious to her now that he was substituting her for Raven. She felt like a knockoff version of his first love. Was she just like him? Was she using Bella and Eazy to even out her emotional inequity. The thought alone injured her because it meant that what she shared with them couldn't be real. But it was. She felt it. She breathed it. She felt those babies in her spirit every moment of every day. She couldn't go to the grocery store without wondering if Eazy would try a new dish. She couldn't go shopping for feminine products without picking up something for Bella. Or shop for a new book without grabbing something interesting for them to indulge in. Even Morgan, the child who resisted her, lived in her daily prayers because Alani knew she was in a stage of transition and she was lost. Alani prayed on Morgan's behalf, daily, because she wanted her to come home. They belonged to her even without sharing her bloodline. They were simply her children. Why couldn't their father simply make her his woman? How could he make her feel so unworthy of placement in his life? Why wouldn't he just share his pain with her? His pain over Raven? She had shared every ounce of her pain with him. There was nothing personal that she kept from him, and this wall that he put up, barricading her outside of what he had experienced with Raven, was hurtful. Alani felt left out. She felt foolish, like she was all in and taking the risk of heartbreak by herself. *He's still in love with her and you can't be in love with two people at the same time.* Alani pulled away from Ethic's home, in distress. He called her phone and she sent him to voicemail. She didn't want to talk. She wanted to cry. He had to give her a little space because she didn't want to say the wrong thing or do the wrong thing because, once spoken, words couldn't be unheard. Alani was very aware that she was fighting a memory, that she was in competition with the ghosts of his heart, and she just didn't want to disrespect him or Raven, but she had to go…she had to cry, and she didn't want to do it in front of him.

Ethic heard the door slam on her way out and his heart lurched in protest. He could feel the distance. Every step that she took in the opposite direction pulled at him. He hadn't meant to lose his temper, but the sight of Raven's bloody dress in Alani's hands had done something to him. He hadn't opened that box in years, and it was like, as soon as she popped the lid, Raven's spirit had infiltrated his home. He had felt it, from the kitchen, like Raven had tapped him on the shoulder and said, "Baby, I'm home." He picked up his phone and tried Alani's line. A second attempt. A second denial of access. Voicemail. He stood and sauntered back to the closet, pulling down the box. He opened it and pulled the picture from inside. A heavy sigh escaped him, and he sat. *So damn beautiful,* he thought. His lip quivered, and he trapped it between his teeth, as his eyes took Raven in. Hours passed as he sat there, with Raven…with all he had left of her. He had so many regrets. He had failed her. His thumb traced her face and then he stood and traveled the short distance to Eazy's room. He affixed the picture to Eazy's mirror, in the top, right corner, and then went back to the box and put it back where it belonged. He showered, with haste, brushed his teeth, and then snatched up his keys. He had to go after her. He couldn't let his past stop his present and prevent his future. He had done that for too long. He had gone without for too long. He simply couldn't do it any longer. Not after experiencing *her.* It wasn't possible to experience her and then live without her. He had done that with YaYa. He had come out of the darkness, briefly, and then gone back to grief, back to seclusion. He was unable to retreat after Alani. He wanted her. He needed her; and if he wanted to keep her, he realized he had to give her access, he couldn't keep her out, he had to face his sins and present them in front of her, so she would know exactly who she was loving... he couldn't hide his past from her. He raced to her because letting discontent sit on her heart wasn't an option. Even the hours that had passed was too long to allow her to second-guess her position in his life. It was the middle of the night. He was sure she was asleep by now, but it couldn't wait. He owed her an apology and an explanation. He would deliver both, before sunrise.

CHAPTER 23

Baby, would you mind kissing me
All over my body
You missed a spot - there
Baby, would you mind tasting me
It's making me all juicy
Feeling your lips on mine

Ethic bricked, instantly, at the sight of Alani in her bed. She just had a pull on him, like he was designed to be inside her, like the balance of the world wasn't right unless he was soaked in her depths because she stayed wet for him. The silhouette of her body beneath the sheets was beautiful and Ethic took heavy steps toward her. The closer he got, the lighter his heart felt. He wasn't with the bullshit. The arguing and fighting unsettled him. They had done enough of that for a lifetime. He couldn't go to bed with that weight on his heart and he could tell from the tension in her forehead, the scowl on her pretty face, and her swollen eyes that she had fallen asleep with discontent in her soul. He could also tell that she'd gone to sleep with her fingers inside her panties. The sound of Janet Jackson playing softly out of the Beats Pill on her nightstand, told him she had been in need. He wondered if she'd filled it. He stepped out of his sweatpants and pulled off his jacket, undressing, as he watched her chest rise and fall gently. The summit of her left breast spilled out the top of her camisole and the darkness of her areola teased him. He grew harder. Alani was a hood nigga's dream. Flint-bred, home-grown, and FDA approved, with the slick mouth and pretty looks to match. She set him ablaze with need. Ethic wasn't a man who walked around hitting any and everything walking. He knew men like that. The ones who thought pussy had no face. He disagreed. He needed the aesthetic to be pleasing and Alani was a vision, but she hooked him because she had the soul to match. His affinity to her was hard to ignore. He didn't have that type of restraint.

I just wanna
Touch you, tease you, lick you, please you
Love you, hold you, make love to you

Ethic got on his knees near the head of the bed and watched her sleep, only able to restrain himself from touching her for a few seconds. There was something about her mouth that aroused him. The way her lips curved, the way she pouted, like now. When she wrapped them around his dick, it took great effort not to blow too soon because the visual looking down at her, with those lips on his strength, did something to him. He placed a thumb to her lips, and as she stirred from the dreams that arrested her, he kissed her. Alani was a flavor. She tasted so fucking good, as he captured her tongue, sliding into the bed, lifting the sheets to join her.

"Mmm," she moaned, as she frowned, eyes closed, slightly confused. She was so sleepy she couldn't process his presence. She was lethargic and a little drunk, a consequence of the bottle of wine she had drowned her sorrows in just hours before. It felt like a dream. Like the bad one she had just been trapped in had suddenly disappeared and was replaced with visions of the one she loved. She remembered those dreams, so erotic… she used to have them before she could have him… when it was unacceptable to have him…when she was mad at him…she would dream of him, every night, just like this.

"I'm sorry, baby," he whispered.

Her eyes popped open, as consciousness crashed into her. This wasn't a dream. He was traveling south, down the interstate of her body and pulling her panties down along the way. He looked up over his brow, making eye contact, and then he focused on the task at hand.

"Agh!" she cried out, as he pulled her clit into his mouth. It melted on his tongue like ice that had been left to linger. His mouth, that tongue, those lips were so warm.

"Hmm," he moaned. "I love this shit."

Alani fisted her wild hair with one hand and gripped the iron bars of her headboard with the other, as her stomach contracted. "Ethic, baby…"

"You told me to use the key…to pull up on you…when I

want to eat your pussy. You said to pull up," he whispered, stopping only for a second to kiss her inner thigh.

A lick to her center made Alani buck.

Baby, would you mind
come inside of me
Letting your juices free
Deep in my passion

"You been playing in it," he groaned. "I can tell, baby. I can taste it."

Alani's eyes widened, ever so slightly, a guilty tell, as Ethic licked his lips before diving back in.

He wrapped his tongue around her clit like he was trying to milk it, tugging, rolling, his flesh over her flesh, making Alani breathless, as she arched so far off the bed only her ass and head touched the mattress.

"You don't waste this shit on fingers, baby. I want it on my tongue, every time you nut, or we got problems," he grunted. Ethic's head moved between her legs like he was waltzing with her pussy. He was moaning like he got pleasure from her pleasure, enjoying it like she was made of confections. He was having a pie eating contest in that pussy, cleaning his plate. With one hand wrapped around his dick, he stroked himself, while he was nose deep in her wetness. The sight of his hand sliding up and down that black dick like he couldn't wait to enter her, like he had to relieve a little bit of pressure from it while he ate her… and the sounds of his tongue lapping at her, made Alani weak.

"Ethic ... God, Ethic...Godddd...Ethiccc..."

The more she called his name, the better he ate it and the faster his fist pumped his dick, his thumb circling the head because Alani knew from experience that it was his most sensitive spot. He was eating her pussy so good that he ate her ass while he was at it. She was a mess; one, big, wet mess. It felt so good that she couldn't take it anymore... it was so goddamn good that the sensitivity of her clit was overwhelming. She couldn't hang. She couldn't keep up. She needed him to slow down because he was showing no mercy. If this was make-up sex, she had to remember to fight with this nigga more often. She hadn't known it could get better than what he had already done to her body, but this shit here...this nigga here...he was good at all things seduction. No two times were the same. The only thing she could count on was that she would cum multiple times every time he laid her on her back.

"Ezra!" she cried out. Government name because this was serious business. She came and trembled, as he played with her knob with one finger, like he was admiring the work he had done with his tongue. She was so sensitive that waves of residual orgasm rippled through her and she jerked in response. He kissed it one last time and then climbed her body, wiping her from his beard. His smirk was cocky, like he knew he was the best she'd ever had.

He broke through her dam like a storm, filling her river, swimming deep in her flood, as she adjusted to accommodate his size. Ethic's fists balled and pressed into the bed around her head, as her thighs butterflied around his waist, and he hit her with relentless strokes. His body. *My God, his body*, she thought, as she put her hands against his toned abs to try to stop him from going so deep.

He arrested those hands, taking her wrists and pinning them backward above her head. "Don't stop me," he groaned. "Trust that I won't hurt you, Lenika." Their eyes met, and Alani's flickered with emotion. He wanted complete access. He wanted her to allow him full reign of her body, no hands to stop the depths of his stroke, no protests, no timid thighs trying to snap closed. He wanted her open for him and her heart thundered because he was just so big, his stroke was so powerful, his dick so long, if he hit it wrong…God, she just might fucking die. But she trusted him. She nodded, and he continued. The way he ran five fingers down her neck, starting at her jaw, gripping it like he wanted to choke life from her, and then letting them drag slowly over her skin. Alani's head fell back in pure ecstasy. Ethic was all man with his rough hands and expert touch. He helped himself to a mound of her breasts, wrapped his lips around her nipple, biting it slightly. Alani's pussy clenched.

"Mmm," he moaned, in appreciation. "Lift them legs, baby." Alani obeyed, because what else would she do? He was king. He was the warden of this sexual prison he had her trapped in. He was the creator of her world, like he sat up in the sky on a throne looking down over all the mortals. Ethic was god. Her god, because although he had the devil in him, she saw a lot of God's image too. She worshipped this man. It was a sin and a shame. His hands walked up the length of her legs and then he opened them, wide, almost into a full split, and the tension pulling in her hamstrings was a glorious pain, one she couldn't focus on because he was beating her up, knocking the back of her, pushing shit around inside her like he was moving furniture around, redecorating and shit. Making her house his home. "This shit so fucking wet, baby."

"I know."

She frowned. *Did I just say that shit?* Ethic had her on some cocky shit...on some my-nigga-is-the-shit-so-I-must-be-the-shit type shit, because Alani never gloated on her sex. Ever. The way this phenom of a man was moaning in it, she knew it had to be incredible. The way Ethic used his body, those lips, his hands, his dick to give pleasure was unlike anything she had ever known could exist.

He lifted, letting her legs hang over his shoulders. "Ezra fucking Okafor!" she shouted, reaching an orgasm for the third time in hours. One had been courtesy of her hands, two had been on him. That wasn't even counting the ones at his house. Alani was an addict. She needed rehab.

"I know, baby. Damn, I know."

She squeezed her eyes tightly and he picked up his pace, until she felt him throbbing, she felt her body milking him, as he found his nut.

KNOCK! KNOCK!

Ethic steeled and looked over his shoulder at the door, as Alani covered her face with both hands, trying to catch her breath.

"I'm trying to sleep, damn it! Yelling like these babies ain't in here!" Nannie fussed through the door. "Ethic, take her fake mad behind back to your house with all that noise. Might as well get a damn crib on the way because she pregnant after that!"

"Yes, ma'am," he called out, snickering. He turned back to her, kissing the inside of her knee and wearing a smirk. "Your ass got a nigga in trouble." They heard Nannie's footsteps, as she creaked back down the hallway and then heard the slam of her heavy, wooden door. Ethic shook his head, in embarrassment. He felt like a busted teenager.

Alani bound her wrists together with an invisible robe and placed them above her head. "I think I need some punishing then, sir," she said.

Amusement played in Ethic's eyes and she felt him react. The beautiful strength between his legs somehow finding its way back to her opening. How he hardened for her, again, always aroused by her, always filling her, blew Alani's mind. Most men couldn't even satisfy in round one, and here Ethic was bouncing back with ease. Going back to back like it was nothing for him to hit her with a dope verse and then come with more off the top...because he wrote his own lyrics. He stroked her slowly, gentler this time, making sure to keep his tongue in her mouth to stifle her moans, until she erupted all over again.

They laid in the aftermath of their lovemaking, spent, satisfied, as the sun snuck through the curtains.

"I love how pretty the sun is when it's rising," Alani whispered, as she ran her fingers through his thick beard. One thigh draped across his sheet-covered body and he held her securely under one arm, his other arm tucked behind his head. Ethic's eyes were on top of her. "I didn't notice. I don't notice shit but you when I'm with you."

Alani smiled, as she craned her neck up to look at him. From his lips, it didn't sound like game. He was the most honest man she had ever encountered. The things he said were pure fact. He filled her with so much confidence. To be prettier than the sun to a man like Ethic...she warmed at the thought. This nigga here.

"I don't like the beard," she whispered.

Ethic removed his hand from behind his head and finessed the hair on his face, as his brows lifted in surprise.

"No?" he asked.

She shook her head.

"Don't get me wrong. It's sexy. Aesthetically speaking, I love the beard. It makes me wet," she said, as she licked her dry lips and blushed. "But you grew it when I was gone. I don't like that it reminds me that we were apart for so long."

Ethic rolled up, forcing her to sit up too. She covered herself with the sheet, as he stood, reaching for his boxer briefs and stepping into them.

"Come."

That order that she always followed. Alani wrapped her body in the sheet, tucking the edge in the front so it didn't fall, before trailing him to her adjoining bathroom. He opened her medicine cabinet.

"You've got a razor? A good one, preferably, so I don't fuck my shit up," he said.

She frowned. "You don't have to cut it, Ethic, I just…"

He silenced her with a kiss, a quick one, and then bent to open the cabinet under the sink. "Razor, woman, and shaving cream."

Alani bent to retrieve the items.

"Almond and shea, huh?" he asked, as he read the bottle she handed him. "More like dope when it's on your skin."

She turned her head, blushing, and then rolled eyes of content back to him.

"Glad to know you like it."

She opened a new pack of razors and then slid in front of him, sitting on her sink's vanity, as she plugged it up to run water inside.

"Let me," she said.

He lifted his chin, curling those full lips up, as she covered his beard with shaving cream.

"I apologize about shutting you out," Ethic said, his eyes on the ceiling, as she started on his beard. "Raven is a touchy subject for me. I haven't talked about her with anyone in a long time."

Alani's breath caught in her throat, as her hands began to shake. Not wanting to cut him, she took in a deep breath to calm her nerves. He was about to do this. He was about to tell her about the history of his heart; and although she had initially thought she wanted to know, she now questioned that.

"I loved her. From the first time I saw her. Like you. That's how I knew I loved you. I got that same feeling. It's something I haven't felt in years."

"I killed her."

Alani nicked him.

"Shit," Ethic grimaced, as Alani pulled back. Her shaky hands reached for paper towel.

"Ethic, I'm sorry. My hands. I can't stop them from shaking," she whispered. She placed the towel to his face, as he looked down the bridge of his nose at her.

"I know you. You're not a killer. How did it happen?" she said, as she sniffed back emotion.

He's not a killer. He's not. He's killed, but he's not a killer.

"She was in an abusive relationship. I tried to save her. Knocking him off would free her. So, I ordered a hit. I put money on his head. Everyone knew the car he drove. A black Audi, black rims, black tint with the plates MIZ 5000. It should have been a clean kill. I was there, waiting for her. She was supposed to meet me, and I was going to take her somewhere safe, probably marry her, probably put another baby in her, because Raven was beautiful, and I just wanted to make a bunch of babies with her…"

Alani felt her stomach tighten and her eyes watered. Even the thought of a baby brought her to tears. If Eazy was the evidence of Raven and Ethic's chemistry, the rest of those babies he had planned would have been gorgeous.

Alani steadied her hand and lifted his chin, as she continued his shave. Even the fucking landscape of his neck and face intrigued her. Such a rugged, beautiful man, one that she now felt she only had by default…default of the death of a girl named Raven, because it was clear to her that if Raven had lived, Ethic would be with her…a married man with babies.

"She took his car to come to me that day and I watched the same men I hired pull alongside the car and wet it up. There were so many shots. The sound of those bullets piercing the steel frame of that car. I still hear them in my head. It's the alarm clock that wakes me up every morning. Eazy was in the back seat."

Alani's eyes widened, but she didn't interrupt.

"It's a miracle he even lived. Not one bullet touched him. Riddled the fucking car seat, but didn't hit him," Ethic whispered.

"That's God," Alani whispered. "Nothing but God."

"Raven and her best friend died that day. She died in my arms." He could barely manage those words. "I killed her."

She felt his chin quiver and heard the sniff. He was trying to stand tall, battling to keep this grief he had been carrying for years inside.

"Oh, Ethic," Alani whispered. "You can cry. It's okay for a man to grieve the woman he loves. Have you ever even done that? Allowed yourself to grieve her?"

"I couldn't. My kids were babies. Morgan had lost everything. I couldn't..."

"You can now. I'm here to cover them and I'm telling you, you can," she whispered, as she stared him in the eyes, her concern overwhelming.

As if he had waited for her specifically to give him permission, he folded. Alani released the razor, dropping it to the floor, and wrapped her arms around him. He broke down, burying his face in her shoulder, while securing strong arms around her waist. She didn't speak. She didn't want to say anything that would shame him for feeling. Instead, she just held him as he held her. He had so many ghosts. He was drowning in death. Melanie's. Raven's. His mother's. Her daughter's. Love's. It overwhelmed her, so she knew it had to overwhelm him. He pulled back and bent down to grab the razor, sniffing away his emotion and pinching the bridge of his nose. She could see him, rebuilding that wall.

Alani stared at him. His pain made her hurt because he didn't deserve any of it. He reached around her and dipped the razor in the water-filled sink. He lathered the remaining hair on his face and resumed the job, while staring in the mirror, hating the sight of the weakness he saw staring back at him.

"It's a sacrifice for you to fuck with me. I'm aware and I'm grateful," Ethic said. Alani felt the tear on her cheek, before she could stop it. She reached up and grabbed the razor and then continued to do the job for him.

She sniffed, as she kept her eyes on the task.

"It's a blessing to be with you and I want to be with you forever. I'm going to love on you for the rest of my life, if you let me. All this self-hate, all this blame you've carried with you, all this hurt. I'm going to love every, single piece of it away because you don't deserve it. You don't deserve anything less than love because that's what you give. We're done with everything except love, Ethic. I don't want to do anything but love you."

"You're a fucking blessing, Lenika…"

Alani shook her head. "I don't want to do that either. The Lenika thing. I don't like it. Why do you still call me that?"

"Because I haven't earned the right to call you Alani. I'ma earn it, though, baby. I'ma work to restore you the way you've restored me. You do things to the inside of me…to parts of me that I thought died with Raven." Alani put down the razor and grabbed a towel, then unplugged the sink. She rinsed it with warm water and then began to wipe away the mess on his face. A perfectly lined goatee and mustache was all that remained. He looked the way he had when she'd first met him.

"How do I compete with a ghost?" she whispered.

Ethic cupped her face… his sweet Alani. He could see the insecurity in her. "You don't compete. It isn't a competition. I'm a different man than I was all those years ago. She was young love, you're the love I'll grow old with. I'll always love her. I'll always acknowledge her because what we had was beautiful, what we could have had and the unknown of where that could have gone, how it could have grown, is what haunted me…still haunts me; but when I met you…I don't know. It was like I stopped being afraid of the ghost of love…of possibility. There's just something about *you*. You satisfy my soul, as a man, and somehow, I don't think she would mind me loving you. You're the love of my life, Lenika. You know how you go to church to be saved?"

Alani nodded.

"I come to you for that. You save me. You've rebirthed me. I'm laying all I've got down at your altar, Lenika."

"And I'll never turn you away. Not again. I'll die before I lose you again," she said. Her chest quaked and Ethic cleared her teary eyes with his thumbs.

"These tears do something else to me, baby. Why are you crying?" She lifted her head in surrender and he kissed her. Just a peck and Alani sighed.

"Because I'm in love."

Ethic hoisted her legs up and balanced them in his arms and Alani held on tightly, as he took her for round three.

By the time Ethic was done with Alani, she felt like she had run a marathon. Every part of her body was depleted of energy. They made love from sunrise to sunset, breaking to sleep for a few hours and waking up to soft kisses, sometimes his on her body, sometimes hers on his thighs, as she made her way to his dick, and then they sexed all over again. They didn't even answer the knocks at the door from the kids. They were in another world, a world where only the two of them existed. By the time they were done, Alani's entire body hurt so good she felt injured, like she had been the starring wide receiver in a Friday night football game, like she had brought home the win for her team. He had sucked on her pussy so long he'd given her lips a hickey and she had left scratches all over his back from the way her nails dug into his skin while he stroked her. Never had they made love like that. Sex between them was amazing, and by the time they were done, they both had been pumped dry. Alani couldn't take another inch of penis if her life depended on it. As they lay in the afterglow of their lovemaking, Ethic pulled her face close, his thumbs caressed her cheeks so softly.

"I want you to have my baby," he whispered.

Alani stiffened, and just like that, their bubble was popped. She sat up and backed up against the headboard. She pulled the sheet up to cover her breasts. "I can't," she whispered.

"I know Love's death is hard..."

"It's impossible. Thinking about Love is impossible, but even if it wasn't...even if I wanted to have a baby too..." Alani felt a lump form in her throat and it trapped her words. Her heart went haywire, sinking into her stomach and aching so badly she felt like she would be sick. This was the moment she had dreaded. This was the moment she would admit that she was defective. He would leave.

"What aren't you saying?" he asked.

"I can't give you babies, Ethic."

The words landed callously, confusing him, marring him with pain because babies with Alani was something he desperately wished for.

"I don't even know how Love was made. I have endometriosis, Ethic. Two babies were a miracle for me. My body just doesn't cooperate. I don't know if I can give you another one."

He could hear the injury in her voice. This new revelation made him understand her so much more...it made him respect the bullet she had put in him that much more... He had really taken her all from her the day he'd killed her daughter. He knew that. He had always known that, but learning this...her infertility issues, it put weight behind his chest. It put understanding in his soul.

"I had a miscarriage, Ethic," she whispered.

"I'm sorry you had to go through that." His voice was low, sad.

"After Love, Ezra. The day I said I was sick. The day of Bella's tryouts. I was pregnant. I had a miscarriage on your bathroom floor, after you left," she admitted.

The entire room blurred, and Ethic swiped a hand down his mouth and chin. He, instantly, identified the day. He had felt it. It was like someone had been digging a hole in him the entire day. The day she had been sick.

"I didn't tell you because I don't want you to leave. I don't want you to throw me away," she sniffled.

"That's why I couldn't touch you," he whispered, the revelation hitting him hard.

He turned to her, placing a hand on her cheek and feathering her tears with his thumb. "Come here," he whispered. He kissed her forehead and then pulled her into him, tucking her beneath his arm.

"You don't keep shit like that from me. You don't hurt by yourself. That's not how this is supposed to go. Not when I'm here. You don't conceal pain from me. If I can't take it away, I'ma feel it with you. I want to know every detail when it comes to you and when it comes to children that belong to me. Everything of and a part of you is mine and I want to know that shit."

He wanted to be mad with her, but he couldn't. The shit she had endured in silence, not even just with him, but over her lifetime. During both childhood and adulthood…it tore him apart.

"How many times has this happened to you?"

"Four," she barely said it. The utterance was a ghost on her lips. "I have a whole graveyard of skeletons."

For the first time since meeting her, he didn't know what to say so he didn't use words at all. He pressed his forehead to hers and wrapped four fingers around her neck, his thumb swiping at her tears.

"I watch the type of father you are, and I know what you'll want with me. I wish I could have that with you, but I can't give you another baby, so if that's a deal breaker..."

"It's not," Ethic said. "There are no deal breakers with you." He placed a hand on her stomach.

"There's a reason why God gave you miracles. If we're meant to have another one, we will; if we're not, we won't. This between us is enough. It's a gift, Lenika. Besides my kids, it's the best I've ever received. You chose me, baby. I know you have to keep choosing me every day because of what I did. The type of forgiveness that takes..." he stopped, shaking his head. "You're made of love, Lenika, and I'm just lucky to be in attendance. You're more than enough. You're overflow; and when you're hurting, I want to be here. You've got to let me. Come."

The order she always followed. She tucked herself beneath one arm and he kissed the top of her head. "I've always felt like half of a woman because of that." The admission was a ghost on her lips. He barely heard it.

"Any nigga that ever made you feel like that is half of a man, baby. They don't matter because I'm all man, all yours. You're more of a woman than I deserve, more than I could ask for. You're fucking perfection."

"Daddy! Alani! Open up! We know you're in there!" Eazy shouted, through the door. Alani lifted.

"Yo, where you going?" Ethic asked.

"My kids are summoning me. Duty calls," she said, with a shrug. "Get dressed and come down for breakfast."

Her fucking kids.

Ethic's entire heart opened. All the ghosts and demons that were trapped inside cleared right out because Alani had moved in.

He watched her slip into clothes and put on a robe before opening the door.

"About time!"

He chuckled, as she pulled the door closed.

"I'm sorry, I'm sorry," he heard her say, as her voice moved down the hall with his kids' voices following.

So much excitement, so much love, so much family in the air and Ethic lifted eyes to the sky and said, "Thank you." Because, finally, God had answered his prayers.

CHAPTER 24

The smell of old books filled the air and the yellow lights illuminated the library, as Morgan sat at the wooden table. Books were spread out in front of her and she held a bawled fist to one forehead, as she wrote furiously with her other hand. Cambridge University was nothing like Michigan State. She had kept up well enough at home...halfway around the world, all her classes seemed so much harder. The earbuds plugged her ears as Keyshia Cole sang about losing love...about remembering love. It was background music...something to make it feel like she wasn't stuck inside doing chemistry equations.

The music pulsed through her body and she nodded her head to the beat...a little off beat, always a little off beat, but she felt that shit. It stirred her soul because she could relate. She remembered the exact day, time, and second that her heart had broken, each time that hit had broken. First, with her father's death, then, her mother's imprisonment, then, Raven's death, then, Messiah's betrayal. This song was vibrating through her soul. She felt her baby kick and she placed a hand to her round belly. There was no hiding it now. What barely showed before, now bulged in front of her. Messiah's seed, manifesting inside of her, made her crave his presence. She felt him. Wherever he was. Messiah's energy was tugging at her and Morgan missed him…she missed Mizan's brother and that guilt made her cry…every day and every night because love shouldn't be what she still felt for him.

She felt hands on her shoulders and she jumped in startle. "Bash!" she shouted in the library.

A room full of eyes turned toward her and she exhaled, marking him with an irritated gaze. "You can't sneak up on me like that," she protested.

"Hey. I'm sorry," he said, taking a seat beside her. He placed a hand to the side of her face and another to her stomach. "He's going crazy in there, huh?"

"Because somebody just scared his incubator shitless," she snapped.

"You're moody. What hurts?" he asked.

"My back is killing me, and my feet are swollen, and I can't remember any of this," she griped.

Bash reached down and took her feet into his lap. He removed the Ugg boots on her feet.

"Bash, we're in the library," she said, half whispering, as she looked around.

"There's no rule against rubbing feet in the library," he said. He lifted one of her feet to his nose and sniffed, his face frowning. "Yo' feet stink, Mo. Your pretty, pink-painted toes smell like corn chips."

She pulled her foot back, laughing. "You're fucking lying," she snickered. He grabbed her foot, again, and sniffed it.

She smiled. "They don't stink too bad, you got 'em all in your face," she said.

He began to rub, masterfully, and Morgan sighed.

"You seem overwhelmed. Let me see what you're dealing with," Bash said. Morgan slid the homework into his line of sight and Bash nodded. "You got this, Mo. What's the first thing you've got to do when balancing chemical equations?" he grilled.

"Identify the most complex substance," she fired back, without hesitation.

He pointed to one of the problems on the table and Morgan squinted, as she looked at her work. "Oh!" she said, picking up her pencil to erase her errors. "Why couldn't I see that before? How do you make it seem so easy?"

"You've got a lot on your plate. I'm not creating life right now. Don't be so hard on yourself. Look at all this," Bash said, as he nodded toward the table. "You've got Chem, you've got AP Calc, Bio." Bash reached over to close the book in front of Morgan. "You can't do everything at the same time."

"I can't fail this baby," she said. "I'm all he has."

"You won't," Bash said. He moved her foot out his lap and helped her put her shoes back on. He lifted her chin. "You won't, Mo. You're extraordinary. If you listen to me and follow my lead, I can put you on top of the world, Morgan."

She scoffed because at seven months pregnant, she felt like a mess. Her life was in shambles, but somehow Bash saw a masterpiece. He never judged. He was by her side, proudly parading her around the prestigious university, as if he was the father of the baby that grew inside her.

Morgan still couldn't bring herself to love him. She liked
him. She enjoyed his company, but the stars she saw in his
eyes weren't reflective because they didn't live in her. She
didn't feel.

"Come on. Time for a break, Mommy," he said.

"I can't believe someone is going to be calling me that
soon," she whispered, as she stood. He gathered her things
and carried her tote, and then guided her out of the building.

"Where are we going?" she asked, noticing the black SUV
sitting outside.

"I know you're worried about your future and about
if you're strong enough to raise this baby. I want to
put you in position, Mo. My family is very powerful. I
come from old money and older connections. I want to
introduce you to my parents...to my world. I know what
you're used to. The hood is cool and all. Being a hood
princess comes with its perks, I suppose. I want to show
you something else."

The back window of the SUV rolled down.

"Sebastian, you don't have to prep the girl, I'm not going
to bite her."

"Bash, no. I'm not ready for this. I don't even know what
this is. We're not together, we haven't even defined what
we are to one another. I don't even have closure from my
last relationship. I'm carrying another man's baby." She was
rambling, nervous, intimidated by what this introduction
meant. She was listing all the reasons she had to pull out
on him because Mo knew she wasn't ready to move on. She
wasn't ready by a long shot.

"And where is he, Mo? He's not here. Let me be here," Bash said. He was putting her on the spot, applying pressure and Morgan hated it.

Morgan blew out breath of angst, as her heart galloped out of her chest. He placed his hand on the small of her back and guided her toward the car.

"You must be Morgan Atkins."

"Yes, ma'am," Morgan replied.

"Christiana Fredrick. It's very nice to meet you. I've heard a lot about you," she said, glancing at Bash. "He called me months ago, talking about the undergrad student who made him look like an idiot while teaching his first class. Something about love not being something you could teach..."

Morgan turned to Bash. "That was your first day?" she chuckled, and he pinched the bridge of his nose.

He nodded, in embarrassment, and opened the car door. "Yeah, and a not so good one, might I add. No one listened. Including you."

She laughed, and he helped her into the back seat. "I'll see you ladies later for dinner."

He stood in the doorway, looking into the car. "You aren't coming?" she asked.

"I've got some things to take care of here. You're in capable hands," he said. "Have fun today. Don't worry about anything but having a good time. Who knows? I might even finish your Calc for you."

"You would be the absolute best boyfriend in the entire world if you did."

"Boyfriend?" Bash nodded, as a smirk lived on his lips. He

gripped the top of the car and leaned in slightly, staring her in the eyes. "That's progress. If I do the Chem stuff, to what will that get me?"

"A whole wife, boy," Morgan replied.

He laughed. Christiana did too.

"I'll see you later. Have a good time."

Chanel No. 5 filled the interior of the car, as Morgan lifted the window. A white man with gray hair sat in the driver's seat. "Martin, back to the house please."

Morgan felt her nerves chewing away at her, as she clung to her side of the car.

"Relax, Morgan. You never let another woman see you sweat, dear," Christiana said.

Morgan lifted shocked eyes to Bash's mother, who sat staring out the window, as the city passed her by.

"Have you seen the city yet? London is a beautiful place," Christiana said.

"No, ma'am. Not very much of it. Classes have kept me busy, and well, the baby...by the end of the day, I'm too tired to do anything," Morgan said.

"When you refer to your child, you shouldn't do so like you're apologizing for something," Christiana said.

Morgan lowered her head to her lap, as she twiddled her fingers. "I just know what people see when they look at me."

"Screw people, Morgan. If I let what people thought about me dictate who I became and what I accomplished, I would be trash right now. I would be absolute filth," Christiana countered. "What do you see when you see yourself? That's what you rely on."

The words weighed on Morgan the entire ride. She didn't know who she was. She had never known. She always viewed herself through the perceptions of others. When she was with Messiah, she felt strong because he handled her like she wouldn't break. He had handled her like he knew she would be able to take all he dished out. When she was with Bash, she felt fragile and priceless, like she was one of the world's most rare exhibits...something you had to place behind a glass case and a velvet rope to keep people from ruining it. He made her feel like she was one of a kind, like he was lucky to even be laying eyes on her at all. But when she looked at herself, without either of them around, she saw nothing...Morgan saw no worth at all. Her heart panged at the realization.

The car came to a stop in front of black, steel gates and Morgan looked up in awe as they opened. A beautiful, castle-style home sat in the distance.

"This is where you live?"

"It is," Christiana said.

Morgan looked at the uniformed men that stood like statues in front of the gate.

"Ignore them. Every royal family is required to have guards at the gate," Christiana said.

The words jarred Morgan's attention. "Did you say royal?"

"Yes, dear. Pick up your lip. Bash's father is in succession with the queen. A million people would have to die before we ever stepped foot inside Buckingham Palace, but the last name carries weight. My husband is a Duke."

"So, Bash is..."

"Royal, yes, love," Christiana answered. "Which is why you and I need to get to know one another. Royals don't just date to date. They date to marry. He wants you. So, I must know you." The car stopped moving and a man stood, waiting on the home's steps. The driver, Martin, exited to open Morgan's door and help her from the car. Her mouth hung open, in disbelief, as she looked up at the opulence in front of her. *Date to marry...are we even dating? Are we even anything? We're nothing. We're hanging out.*

"Come, love," Christiana said, as she waited at the top of the staircase.

Morgan hustled hurried feet up the concrete stairs and followed Christiana inside. Stepping inside was like being inside a museum.

"You live here?" Morgan asked. She wasn't new to luxury. Ethic had an estate of his own and Benjamin had provided the very best before that, but this...this...was...well...it was royal. It was history...it was legacy...and Morgan felt intimidation creeping up her spine. She placed delicate hands on her belly. It was what she did when she felt insecure; touched the only thing left that she had of him... his seed...Messiah was inside of her, and when she needed to feel strong, she pulled it from inside. This baby, his baby, was keeping her strong; and even still, she felt weak.

"Bash grew up here," Christiana said. "You can imagine my disdain when he told me you were a freshman. Then, to learn that you were pregnant. Leave it to Bash to choose the most difficult path, but he's always thought with his heart and not his head."

"Bash and I are…I don't know what we are. We're friends. I'm not ready for more. I don't know if I can handle more than that…" Morgan said, honestly.

"Bash will love you until you love him back. It's just the type of man he is. He'll wait, and he'll do everything right. He'll earn you. He's his father's child," Christiana said. "And inevitably, you will realize that his love is exactly what you require. It's the type of love that families are built on. So, if you're going to be around, you need to be put in position. You and your child."

Morgan stood, baffled. "I'm not sure I know what that means," she said. She was almost afraid to express her confusion.

"It means you've hit the lottery of life," Christiana said. "We'll get to business, but Bash tells me that you and that baby need some relaxation."

Christiana opened two, French doors that led to a covered terrace. Two women stood dressed in white linen. Middle-parted, blonde ponytails, and friendly smiles seemed to be a part of their uniform.

"A deep tissue for me. A pre-natal massage for her. Manicures, pedicures, and I'll take a sugar scrub," Christiana ordered. She looked to Morgan. "Anything else you'd like?"

"Oh, um…" Morgan looked at the two massage therapists and shook her head. "No, thank you. This is more than enough. More than expected, actually."

"They're on staff here. Whenever you feel like making an appointment, feel free. I'll leave you with their information."

Christiana handed Morgan a white robe and pointed to a door. "You can change there."

Morgan was dumbfounded. Bash's mother was assertive, straightforward, not mean, but not quite nice, yet oddly accepting. Morgan was lost.

She changed quickly and folded her things up neatly before emerging.

Christiana stood, sipping a mimosa, with her back turned to Morgan. When she turned to Morgan, she took pause. Morgan stood, belly bulging below the belt line of the robe, hands fidgeting nervously in front of her, and eyes wide with uncertainty.

"You certainly are a beautiful girl. I can see what he sees." Morgan blushed, and Christiana handed her a champagne flute.

"Virgin mimosa for you," she said. "What do you say we get to know one another?"

Morgan gave a tight-lipped smile and sipped from the flute.

She climbed up on the massage table and closed her eyes. She felt the tears seal them shut. Bash could give her the world, he was giving her the world, or at least showing her how people lived on the other side; and still, Messiah filled her thoughts. She took a deep breath and pulled her trembling bottom lip into her mouth.

He doesn't want you. He left. It's okay to let him go. He isn't coming back for you.

"Messiah, you have to eat," Bleu said, as she held the spoon up to his mouth.

"Get that shit out my face, B. Shit tastes like fucking Ramen noodle water," he stated.

Bleu stuffed the spoon in his mouth anyway. "Boy, this ain't hospital food! I cooked this!"

Messiah grimaced, as he swallowed it down. "I know, and your ass can't cook."

She laughed, shaking her head, as tears filled her eyes.

"Come on, B. Don't do that. You my soldier. You fighting this shit with me. You can't fold on me now," Messiah said, his voice low, barely above a whisper.

Bleu's face contorted, as she battled with her emotions. She lowered her head and mourned for a few seconds, wiping the tears from her face, and then lifting dry eyes back up to him.

"I'm your soldier, Messiah," she stated.

"Don't it seem backwards to you that the only way to live is to kill myself? This radiation is killing me, B. This chemo. It's eating me alive," Messiah whispered.

"It's going to help, Messiah. I believe that," Bleu said. She had said it a hundred times, but Messiah could see the hope dwindling in her eyes.

"Yeah, whatever you say, Bleu," he said. "I feel like she needs me. I feel like shorty crying out for me, B. I just want to smell her. She used to leave this scent in my sheets, Bleu. I just want to smell that right now. A fucking whiff of Mo right now would put a little fight in me."

"Please, let me call her, Messiah."

He shook his head. "I'm a shell out here. I'm skinny as fuck. My locs are gone. Skin dry as fuck. Eyes sunk in like I'm on that shit. That's not what I want her to remember," Messiah said. "I don't want her feeding me soup through straws. I got you for that," He tried to joke, but it wasn't funny. He was disappearing before her eyes. He was like a mirage, and the closer Bleu got, the more he vanished into thin air. Her entire soul ached. She cried for him, daily. She prayed for him, hourly. She was injured. Her entire chakra was unbalanced. Watching death slowly take her best friend brought love to her in a different form...grief. Love was the brother of grief and Bleu was grieving so heavily that she couldn't breathe. She tried not to show it, but Messiah saw the pain in her eyes. At least one person would miss him. At least one would remember him without hate accompanying the thought of his name. Bleu would mourn him without dilution. She wouldn't taint him because she had no bad memory of him that would allow her to have mixed emotions.

Messiah was grateful for the knock at the door that interrupted them. A black woman in a white lab coat entered the room.

"Dr. Nash," Messiah greeted.

"My most stubborn patient. How are you feeling?" the woman asked.

She wore a smile, white teeth broke through chocolate skin, long, blonde-dipped locs hung over her shoulder.

"Like I'm dying," he answered.

"Well, I'd like to speak with you for a moment. Bleu, can you give us the room for a moment, please?" the doctor asked.

Bleu froze. There was sympathy in the doctor's eyes. This was it. Bleu knew that look. She had seen that look before. Death filled the room and a pit devoured her stomach. She reached for Messiah's hand and then stood and leaned over his bed, until her lips were at his ear. "I love you. I'm right outside."

He nodded, and Bleu headed for the door, sniffling the entire way. She pulled it open.

"Yo, B," Messiah called. She swiped at her tears, before turning to face him.

"I love you too, Shorty Doo-Wop. The original Shorty Doo-Wop," he stated, with a wink. The dark circles around his eyes made Bleu's chin quiver. He was reaching the end. She knew it. He was so frail. His body was weak, but Messiah's spirit was strong. He was a warrior. He was lovely. He would be a G until he took his last breath. "You know I'ma be fine. Noah's there. He'll show a real nigga the ropes."

She smiled, for his sake, but his words cracked her heart wide open. She turned to leave.

"B?" he called, again.

She held her cries, as she faced him once more. "It's time to get bro up here. Go get Isa," he said.

Bleu nodded. If Messiah was ready to let Isa come, then Bleu knew it wouldn't be long. She rushed out, so that Messiah wouldn't witness her fall apart. She had lost so many people before, so she knew the grief would be unstoppable and she didn't want to fold...not in front of Messiah, because if he could be strong...if he could stand tall, so could she.

CHAPTER 25

Who are all these people here for?" Alani asked, as she entered the bookstore.

"You," Alex said. "They're all here for you."

Alani blew out a sharp breath. She was intimidated. She was struggle, dressed up in designer clothes that Ethic had gifted. Pink, Chanel, wide-leg pants, with a blue, ruffle neck and bell sleeve top that she tucked it, with a skinny tie to match. Subtle, diamond jewelry... real diamonds, reluctantly accepted because she was bad at keeping up with the fake stuff, let alone these. Her hair had finally grown out to shoulder-length and was pressed bone straight with a center part. Black, So Kate's graced her feet, and damn if she didn't want to kick them off because her toes felt like they were dying inside those pointed heels, but she shined like new money. She was an author today. The Ethic of Love by Alani Lenika Hill was being soft launched, and she was expected to speak and sign copies for a few, select elites in the publishing industry.

"This is a lot of people. I thought you said only a few people. I was expecting something small," Alani whispered. She couldn't breathe. She unbuttoned the jacket she wore, in an attempt to access more air.

"This is a few. All editors, press, media, and elites in publishing," Alex said. A look of fret crossed her face and he turned to her, gripping both shoulders. "You can do this."

She nodded.

Alani's eyes searched the crowd for Ethic. They fell on Morgan. She had come back, especially, for the reading - to Alani's surprise. It was progress. It was effort on Mo's part and Alani was grateful. Even though she came with a shitty attitude, Alani was still happy to see her. Eazy, Bella, and Hendrix, sat next to Morgan, and Bash was next to her. The five of them gave her a bit of relief. They were in the front row, in their reserved seats, and Alani wanted to run to them.

But where's Ethic?

"I just want to speak to my family first before we begin," she said.

"No time," Alex said. "You're the woman of the hour. I just need you for the next two hours. He can have you back after that."

Alex gripped her elbow and pulled her toward the small stage that had been assembled in the middle of the store.

Alex walked up to the microphone, as Alani stood at the bottom of the stairs on the side of the stage. She was twiddling her fingers, shifting from foot to foot, as she searched the crowd.

"Ladies and gentlemen, I would like to introduce a beautiful and talented young woman to the stage. The author of The Ethic of Love, Alani Hill."

She took the stairs, carefully, and a round of applause erupted in the store.

"Woo! Go, Alani!"

"Yay! Alani! Yay! Alani!"

Bella and Eazy were on their feet, the most enthusiastic in the crowd, and eliciting laughs from the rest of the adults in the room.

Alani smiled, as she stood in front of the microphone. "As you can see, I have my very own fan club right there. My babies. They have saved me in ways they could never possibly understand. I love them…all three of them," she said, making eye contact with Morgan, who gave her a small smile, a stubborn smile, as she looked down into her lap, and then placed hands on her bulging belly. "But I guess you're not here to hear about that."

She ran her hands down the front of her tie and then placed them onto the podium. She was grateful for the wooden object in front of her. It gave her something to hide behind, a barrier between the crowd and herself. Alani felt hot, like the lights shining down on her were melting her and the makeup on her face was too heavy, and the clothes too tight. Nerves were eating her alive, as the group stared at her. She hated this…being the center of attention. It had never been her thing. She was ready to run off the stage, until she heard the sturdy rumble of the clearing of a throat from the back of the room. She could pick that baritone out of a crowd of screaming kids, even without words, with just the cadence of the sound he'd just made. Her eyes lifted to him. He stood off to the side, leaning against one of the bookshelves. A navy suit so dark that it almost looked black graced his body, and he held a bouquet of blood red roses at his side. She stared at him for so long that everyone in the room went silent and turned toward the back to see what had caught her eye.

"I love you."

Her voice carried over the microphone. He nodded, a small smirk playing at the corner of his mouth, a half smile, and then a hand to the top of his head, rubbing his waves… too many eyes on him for his taste.

"I'm sorry, guys. I'm so nervous. Just…I need one second," she said. She stepped away from the microphone and ran down the steps and up the center aisle to Ethic, throwing her arms around him. He wrapped her in his embrace, fisting her hair with one hand and pulling her waist to him with the other.

"I'm so nervous. God, I can't do this in front of all these people," she whispered over his shoulder, as he held her tightly.

"Yes, you can. You can, baby," he whispered. Cameras flickered all around them, the media, the press, capturing this intimate moment. She pulled back, looking him in the eyes. "Just focus on me. I'm here. You can do this. All these people are here to see what I've seen in you from the day I met you. There's no way for you to mess this up. It's love at first sight, when it comes to you."

Alani nodded, lowering her head, as she pressed her forehead to his. He held both her hands.

"God, please let her see herself through my eyes. She would never doubt herself, if she could see what I see. Give her strength. In Your name I pray. Amen."

Alani lifted teary eyes to him. A man who hadn't believed in God a few months ago was praying for her, with her. She kissed him, like she would never kiss him again, and more cameras flashed. Then, she turned on those So Kate's and walked back to the stage.

"Sometimes, a girl just needs to stop everything and go kiss her man," she said, as she stood in front of the mic. He winked at her and the crowd chuckled. The nerves were gone.

"I've been through so much this past year. I lost my daughter and then I delivered a stillborn baby. I felt empty and so lost, so abandoned. Then, I let love heal me and I poured everything into this book. I was supposed to birth a baby a few months ago; instead, I'm standing here holding this," she said, holding up a copy of her novel. "My baby. My book, about Love. I don't know if you'll love it or hate it. I don't know if it's good or bad. It got me here, on this stage, in front of all of you." She shrugged. "But I hope you feel it. I hope you feel every word, I hope you feel every tear that I cried while writing these pages. Thank you for allowing me to touch your soul."

Alani opened to her favorite passage and read it, becoming emotional and choking up so badly on the stage that Eazy rushed up to her side, wrapping his arms around her, as she read. He stood up there with her for fifteen minutes, as she managed to finish a few chapters, and then she kneeled and wrapped him in her arms. There wasn't a dry eye in the house, as the crowd clapped in appreciation.

"Oh, you are your father's child. You're such a blessing, Big Man. God, I'm so lucky," she said, gripping his shoulders and shaking him, slightly, before pulling him in for another hug. She held his hand, as she stood to her feet and faced the crowd, blushing and wiping tears.

Alex joined her on stage. "Alani will be signing copies of her book. We'll do one row at a time," he orchestrated. He escorted her to the signing table and Alani never let go of Eazy's hand, bringing him along.

"I'm going to need another chair," she said.

"It's really important that we keep this professional. People will be taking pictures. We don't want a little kid in every shot…"

Alani turned to Alex, with stern eyes. "I wasn't asking permission. I need a chair for my son," she said.

Alex conceded, and within seconds, she and Eazy were seated at the signing table. She looked for Ethic, Morgan, and Bella through the thick crowd and spotted them in the long line. She smiled, took pictures, and signed books, until Ethic stood in front of her, a copy of her book in hand.

He handed it to her and she opened the first page. "And who should I make this out to?" she asked, jokingly, as her pen lingered over the page.

"To My Husband," he said.

Alani's heart locked inside her chest, as she saw Nannie and Mr. Larry part through the crowd. Where had they come from? She looked at Bella, who smiled brightly, while nudging Hendrix, and then to Eazy who spun in the chair next to her, grinning. She looked at Morgan, who even had a look of awe on her face. Finally, she looked at Ethic. Surely, he would have the answers. This had to be a joke. "This isn't funny, Ezra," she whispered. Alani could barely breathe, and her eyes prickled. Why did her heart feel like this? She could barely process what was happening, as Ethic rounded the table and took a bended knee.

Alani looked up as she heard her favorite song begin to play.

Her eyes betrayed her. *Jagged Edge*. She placed both hands to her heart and closed her eyes, as she began to sway.

Don't wanna make a scennneee
I really don't careee if people stare at ussss

"Ethic..." she gasped, as he turned her swivel chair so that she was facing him.

"Old-school R&B, right?" he asked, smiling coyly up at her. "Shit you can relate to?" He hoped she could relate to this. It wasn't how he would have done it, but Bella was so proactive in helping him plan, even down to scouring Alani's playlists for days to see which song Alani would love most.

She nodded in excitement, as she snapped her fingers...

The entire room buzzed with excitement. "Daddy's doing it! He's going to bring Alani home for good!" Eazy shouted.

I gotta be the one you touch
I gotta be the one you loveee

Ethic shook his head, licked his lips and then looked up at Alani. She was beautiful. With tears sparkling in her eyes as she looked down at him in disbelief. She didn't even glance at the ring. He could have put a counterfeit on her finger and it would still be the most authentic symbolization of love she'd ever seen. She stared into his eyes and he knew she was in her head, debating with herself. Was it okay to love him? Did it dishonor her daughter? Could they weather the hard days?

The music was throwing him off and he finessed his beard, as Alani grooved in her seat.

"Yo, can we turn it down a little, B?" he asked.

"Noooo," Alani protested, laughing. "This is my favorite part."

You make me whole. You make me rightt
Don't ever wanna think about you leaving my lifeee

Ethic snickered, shaking his head and rubbing the back of his head, but this is how she wanted it, so this is how she would get it.

"You have put me back together, Lenika," he began. Her eyes soaked.

"Boy, don't play with me," she cried, putting a hand over her mouth, as she shook her head. "Ethic, nooooo. Nobody wants me. You don't want me. Me?"

Ethic lowered his head, that one corner of his mouth lifting. So charming. So fucking handsome and in control. Even in a position of submission, he looked powerful. A whole king. A king was choosing her, and Alani couldn't believe it. Alani melted. "Yeah, baby…" He smirked, and wiped one hand down his head, shyly. The crowd was throwing him. He would have much rather done this in private, but Bella had insisted. It had to happen in a bookstore. "I want you," he whispered.

"Ethic," she gasped.

"You've forgiven me, you've loved me, even when I wasn't worthy of you. You love my kids..." Ethic looked down to compose himself. Alani got down on her knees with him, lifting his chin. It was symbolic of their entire relationship. She pulled him out of the darkness and back into the light every time. She admired him. Her eyes hooded, as she cocked her head to the side, as if she was seeing him for the first time. This man loved her. She knew that. He loved her in every way, unconditionally, even through the restrictions she had placed on her heart. He still loved her when she couldn't love him back...he didn't fold. She could see the worry in him. The uncertainty. The fear that she would reject him.

"I can't say yes, if you don't ask. Hurry up," she urged. Everyone in the room laughed. Ethic licked his lips, sucked in a deep breath, and shook his head, marveling at her resilience, at her charm, at her incredible beauty. The outside was obvious, but the inside was a gift.

"Marry me, Alani," he said. "Will you, Alani Lenika Hill, do me an honor I don't deserve and be my wife?"

Alani went to answer him, but she had lost her voice. She trembled. She was so overwhelmed, as she stared into his eyes. Her chest leapt in emotion, as cries left her lips. She had never believed in a happily ever after. Could they have this? Could it end here? Could they really be man and wife? She had always expected to love him for a little while and then lose him. Like she was borrowing him and would one day have to give him back. It was why she had tried to love him so potently. The experience of him was like a dream, like she was a character that existed on pages that would never come true. Like they were an epic love created in the mind of Ashley Antoinette or something. Certainly, one day the story would have to end, so Alani never anticipated a ring. She never thought he would even think to propose.

"You've got to answer him, Nika."

The voice pulled her eyes to the crowd and Alani lost control. Her mother and father stepped through the sea of people. She hadn't seen them in years. Since she was Bella's age, and they had so much bad history to dissect, but somehow none of it mattered right now. She was a little girl in this moment, waiting by the door for them to come home and they had finally arrived. Her eyes scanned her mother's. *She's clean? She's better? How did he do this?*

Seeing them now ripped the beat from her heart. She could see the flood rising in her vision. The water rose and rose until it drowned her sight. She looked to Ethic for an explanation, because, suddenly, her defenses were up, and he was the only person she trusted to supply her with truth. Her mother was a liar. Her father too. Deserters. They had given up on her. Ethic had not. Even when she was difficult to love, he had stayed. She needed him to fill in the blanks.

"I want a family, baby. A healthy, functional, forgiving family. They made you. They created the person that saved me. You fill in my missing pieces and I'm so grateful. They are your missing pieces. I owe you them. I needed to tell them how beautiful you are…how fucking lucky I am… how appreciative of them I am for making you. I told them what they were missing. They didn't want to miss anymore, baby. So now, your pieces aren't missing. My pieces either…"

Alani looked up and saw Zora and Nyair walk up behind her parents. His brother and sister. She sobbed. When Ezekiel came into view, her chest heaved.

"Ezra," she cried.

"I called him; not because I wanted to, but because I want a whole family with you, baby. I want you to be the queen to my kingdom. To our kingdom. This is it. This is everyone we have. We aren't perfect, but it's worth fixing for you. I want to break the generational curses with you, I want to forgive and repair with you, Lenika. I want to build family with you and love you for the rest of my life. If you'll have me. Will you? Marry me?"

"Yes."

Her answer was certain, her voice confident, her eyes sincere. It took no time to manufacture. He took it as truth. The stun in his eyes made her laugh.

"Yeah?" he asked, with a humble half smile. His bottom lip trembled, as he lowered his head and brought a closed fist to his mouth, biting his knuckle. He sprang to his feet, scooping her into his arms, startling her, as she let out a yelp of surprise. "Yes?" he asked, again. "You sure?" He brought his lips to her ear. "You can say no. These people don't matter to me, Lenika. Only you. Are you sure?" Their guests looked on, as she wrapped her hands around the back of his neck, as she brought her face to his. She rubbed her nose against his… intimacy…the Alani way…the simple way. She made him feel like a whole man.

"I'm sure."

He kissed her, and the sound of applause erupted around them. Never would he have expected her to share a lifetime with him, after what he had done. He had always expected to live in the depths of her heart, the parts she was too embarrassed to expose to the world, and he had been satisfied with that. This was better.

Ethic turned to his children who were beaming, and he focused on Morgan who had tears in her eyes. She stood next to Bash and Ethic took him in. The way he held Morgan, the way the young man's eyes glistened when he looked at her. The way he was standing by Morgan's side, while she was pregnant with another man's child. Ethic pulled Morgan into his embrace.

"Congratulations, Ethic," she whispered. "I guess you have your family now."

Ethic pulled back, noticing the hurt in her eyes. "I've always had my family, Mo. You're my daughter. My oldest daughter, and I love you. Nothing and no one will ever alter the amount of love I have for you because it's infinite. It knows no end," he said, as he placed a hand on her belly. "It's just growing. That's what family should do. Grow, so that it lives on… forever." Ethic kissed her cheek and swiped a tear off her face and then turned to Bash and extended his hand.

"Nice to see you again, sir," Bash greeted. "Congrats."

"Likewise," Ethic said. He turned to Alani who was being showered with love from Eazy and Bella, but the tight hand that gripped his arm forced his attention away from her.

"Ethic?" Morgan's face crumbled in pain, as she folded.

"Mo!"

Morgan reached one hand between her legs and pulled back bloody fingers.

Her legs weakened, and she staggered, as Bash caught her.

Alani stood in concern and Ethic scooped Morgan into his arms.

"Ethic, my water broke. It's too soon. I think something's wrong..."

"Nothing's wrong, Mo. I'm going to take care of you. Nothing's wrong, baby girl. Don't say that," he said, voice tender because he wasn't sure.

Bash and Alani trailed them with the kids and Nannie close behind them.

Alani kicked off those So Kate's and rushed to Ethic's side.

"Alani! It's too soon. He's not ready!" Morgan cried, as soon as she saw her.

Tears filled Alani's eyes. "Shh, he's going to be fine. He is, Morgan. We're going to get you help." *God, please, let him be okay. Cover them.*

Bash opened the back door to the car and Ethic climbed inside, cradling Morgan in his arms like she was still the six-year-old girl he had met years ago.

"Take the kids home, baby," Ethic said.

"No! She has to come. She has to be there," Morgan shouted. "She knows what to do. Plea-as-se," Morgan cried.

Ethic stared Alani in the eyes and she turned to Nannie. "Take the kids with you. I'll call as soon as I can." She turned to her parents. "We'll talk. I want to talk, but I can't right now. I have to go!"

Nannie and Mr. Larry corralled Eazy and Bella.

"No! I want to come," Bella protested. Alani turned with fire in her eyes.

"Bella, get your little behind in that car with Nannie. Now," she said.

Bella silenced and stopped resisting.

Ethic climbed in the front seat with Bash, as Alani climbed in the back with Morgan.

"Okay, Mo. I'm right here and you're right. I've done this before, so we're a team, right? The vet and the rookie. We've got this. Morgan was panting and crying and panicked. Her hands gripped the headrest, as she braced herself for the waves of pain that kept sweeping over her. "Morgan..."

Mo met her eyes. "I've got you, sweetheart," Alani whispered. "Just breathe." Alani parted Morgan's thighs and her eyes widened in alarm when she saw the amount of blood that had soaked through Morgan's underwear. "Drive this car faster, Bash. Run every light." Alani moved the seat of Morgan's panties to the side and her heart sank.

She turned worried eyes to Ethic. "I see feet, Ethic. He's turned the wrong way," she whispered into his ear.

"What's wrong?!" Morgan shouted. "Alani! What's wrong? Owww!"

"Nothing's wrong, Mo," Ethic whispered. "Nothing's wrong, baby girl. I swear on my life, I'm not going to let anything be wrong, Mo. Just hold on."

They made it to the hospital and Ethic carried her inside, running, screaming for help, as Morgan howled in agony. He was desperate for help, for a doctor, because he just couldn't lose any more babies.

She was rushed off and Ethic was at her side for every minute. "No, I need a mother for this. I don't know what I'm doing. Please, Ethic, please, just bring Alani!"

He doubled back for Alani and took her hand, pulling her into the back, leaving Bash standing in the reception area, waiting alone.

"Oh my god, Ethic," Alani whispered. Tears filled her eyes, as she looked down at the 7lb 7oz bundle of joy in her arms. He was a cinnamon-tinted piece of her heart. As soon as she saw him, he stole her heart. "He's beautiful. I want one. I really, really want one," she said. "He's giving me baby fever." She laughed.

"Hi, Messari," she cooed. "I'm going to love on you so good."

She looked to Ethic who held another sleeping infant in his arms. "I swear you look so good with a baby in your arms," she said, chuckling. "Okay, let's switch. I want to hold her now."

"I can't believe there were two of them in there," Ethic said.

"Three," Alani whispered. "We can't forget the one she lost. It may not be here, but there is an angel in this room. Morgan was pregnant with three babies, and this little girl was keeping safe behind her brother." She took the baby girl from Ethic's hands.

"Hiii, Yara," Alani cooed.

Morgan had delivered twins, and by the grace of God, they were perfectly healthy. Messari Benji Atkins and Yara Rae Atkins. Her babies. Messiah's babies, but they may as well have been Ethic and Alani's because they had been doting over them for hours.

"I want you to have my baby, Alani. Whatever we got to do. The best doctors, pray, all that. Let's start working on that," he said, as he stared at her with a whimsical look, while holding Messari in his arms. "I can't believe Mo is a mother."

He glanced at Morgan who was sleeping, peacefully, and then at Bash who was sleeping in the chair beside her.

"He never left her side," Alani whispered. "He loves her. He lights up when Morgan smiles."

Ethic cut his eyes to Alani. "I know somebody else who loves her too. He dropped off the fucking planet. My people can't find him. He needs to be here for this. He's already missed too much."

"Morgan seems happy with Bash," Alani said. "She has the twins to think about and Bash is safe. He is here with this girl and her two babies. He held them and shed tears over them, like they were his. Let her be happy."

"If she was happy, I would, but she's not. She's settling," Ethic said, as he kissed Alani on the cheek. "That's different than happiness. This is happiness."

He found her lips, as they stood in front of one another, each holding new life in their arms. He kissed her.

"So, the engagement kind of got overshadowed," he chuckled.

"It was perfect. This is perfect," Alani said. She looked down at the newborns. "They are perfect. I don't want to wait. I want to marry you right away."

"Then, let's get married, baby..."

CHAPTER 26

BANG! BANG! BANG!

"Isa!" Bleu shouted, as she knocked on his door. The urgency in her causing her to ring the bell at the same time.

She didn't want to walk into his house unannounced. She had the key but there was just no telling what you would find running up on him without an invitation, but this was an emergency. She found his key on her ring and entered.

"Isa!" she called out. His bachelor pad was spotless, hardly lived in because he was always in and out of town. Bleu stormed to his bedroom and pushed open the door.

He was laid out, fully clothed, and arms wide, as Aria slept beneath him. Bleu was stunned at the sight. She almost didn't want to interrupt.

She knocked on the doorframe, rousing Aria first. She looked at Bleu, in confusion.

"I'm sorry, I need to borrow him. It's an emergency," Bleu said.

Aria frowned but she could tell by the tears building in Bleu's eyes that it was important. Aria shook Isa out of his sleep.

"Hey! Bleu's here," she whispered, feathering his face with her hand. He wouldn't wake-up. He groaned but kept his eyes closed and Aria ran her tongue down the length of his face, starting at his chin and ending at his hairline. Isa groaned.

"I swear you get on my fucking nerves, yo. Withcho stank-ass breath," he groaned.

"Should have got up the first time," Aria snickered. "I'm gonna go."

There were no clothes to gather because she had never gotten undressed. No matter how hard he tried, she wouldn't give it up. She made her way to the bedroom door, as Bleu stood there stunned.

"Yo, you gon' call me, Ali?"

"Probably not!" she shouted, as she walked down the hallway. Isa waited until the front door slammed shut before he spoke.

"What up, Bleu?" he asked.

"It's Messiah. You need to get dressed - now."

Isa's eyes darkened. "Where the fuck bro been at, man?" Isa asked.

"He's sick, Isa. He's been sick. Hurry up," Bleu whispered.

Thirty minutes later, Isa rode down the highway at a hundred miles an hour, as Bleu held on tightly. She heard Ahmeek's bike on the side of her. The crew was on the way. She felt the tension in Isa, as he rode. She wasn't even afraid. She knew that he had her covered. He wouldn't let her fall.

They rode so fast that they cut the three-hour drive in half.

"Where the fuck he at, man?" Isa asked, as they climbed off the bikes.

"This way," Bleu said, urgently.

"How the fuck both of y'all knew this shit and ain't tell me!" he shouted.

"He didn't want you to know, Isa. Meek either. He asked for you when he thought it was necessary," Bleu said.

"Excuse me, sir, you can't park your bike..."

Isa spun on the valet guy so quickly, the man never saw the gun coming.

"Nigga, shut up! I'ma park my shit wherever the fuck I want!"

"Isa!" Bleu shouted. "He can't wait."

Isa holstered his pistol and rushed into the hospital behind Bleu and Meek. He was devastated. They were all wound so tightly that tension filled the air between them.

"How bad is it? He got more time, right? This can't be it, right? What the fucking doctors doing in this bitch, B?" Meek asked, jaw tensing in emotion, as they took the elevator to the cancer ward.

"They're doing all they can," Bleu whispered.

They burst out the elevator, like they were about to shoot up the entire floor. Two aggressive niggas with screw faces following Bleu all the way to his room. When they entered, and Bleu saw the empty bed and the stripped space, her stomach hollowed.

"Where he at?" Isa asked.

She stepped inside.

"Did they take him for tests?" Bleu asked.

The old woman shook her head, as tears fell down her cheeks. "He coded and then they wheeled him out of here. They came back clearing out his stuff a little while after, put his stuff in plastic trash bags and started cleaning the room. He's gone, baby."

Bleu stood there, as seconds ate away at time and space. She heard their screams. Heard shit being knocked over, heard the roar of Isa screaming. Heard Meek calling for a nurse or a doctor, demanding answers, and she felt sick. She felt… she felt…hot…nauseous…absent…like life was leaving her…her legs…why wouldn't they work? Why wouldn't her mouth? It felt like she was swallowing her tongue. Choking. Bleu was choking.

The ground opened and swallowed her whole, and then she felt the descent. Her stomach was snatched from her body, like she was on a roller coaster, like this was the biggest drop of them all, and then she felt the crack of her head hitting the tile floor. Then, nothing…then, Bleu felt nothing. Like Messiah. Felt Nothing. Felt. No. Thing. No.

Haunted. Aggressive. Protective. Loyal. Messiah. The chosen one. Ethic's chosen one. Morgan's chosen one. Was gone. They had lost a real one and the love of his life, Morgan Atkins, had no idea.

THE FINAL CHAPTER

I knowwww
That when you look at meeeee
There's so muchhh, that you just don't seeee
But ifff you would only take theee timeeeee
I know in my heart youuu'ddddd findddd
Ohh, a girl who's scared sometimes, who isn't always strong
Can't you see the hurt in meee, I feel so all alone
I wanna runnn to you, ooooo-oooo

Alani stood in the full-length mirror, as Whitney Houston played softly in her bridal room. The reflection was beautiful, too beautiful to be her. The music played so softly that it whispered the lyrics to her heart. It was exactly how she felt. She craved him. Ezra. Ethic. Finally accepting both parts because they both belonged to her. He had taught her that people weren't good or bad. They were a myriad of both, a mixture of choices, and that everyone was just trying to do the best they could every day. Ethic was a man of character, a man of morals, of love, of unbelievable loyalty... and today, he was becoming hers. She still couldn't believe it. Girls like her didn't end up with the king. Then again, he had taught her that she was a queen; so, perhaps they did. Girls like her sat next to men like him because kings chose queens, even when they weren't born royal. If a man loved a woman enough, he would crown her. Alani was honored. She had gone all out for him. Her gown was exquisite, made of lace and Swarovski crystals, the tight bodice rode her curves until flowing at her thighs in a mermaid style. Alani was perfect. Her messy chiffon made her beauty look effortless, despite the hours it took to get it done. Her nails were painted a pretty nude and her makeup was done to simple perfection. She had thought she would be nervous on this day, but her heart was still. She was certain the man she had promised herself to was worthy of her companionship, worthy of her loyalty, and she vowed to be the same. She couldn't wait to be the same, in fact. A knock at the door lifted Alani's eyes. She didn't turn. Bella's face could be seen through the reflection.

"You look so pretty," Bella said, almost breathless, as she hung out near the door.

"Why are you all the way over there? Get over here, little girl," Alani said, waving her in. She carried a beautifully-wrapped package in her hands.

Bella entered, and Alani extended both hands. Bella sat the gift down and then grabbed a hold of Alani, clinging to her hands tightly. Alani pulled in a deep breath.

"You've always felt like family to me, Bella. Now, we'll really be family and I want you to know that I love you so much. I'm going to try really hard to be the best stepmother I can be."

"You're not a stepmother," Bella said. "You're my mom. You're the only mom I've ever had. I was afraid Daddy would lose you and then I would lose you, but you stayed. You stayed because that's what moms are supposed to do. They don't leave their kids. So even when you wanted to run, you never left me and Eazy. You always came back for us."

"And I always will," Alani whispered, her eyes glistening with emotion. "My beautiful girl. You're mine and I'm yours. The greatest love story God ever told." Alani knew that she and Ethic had constructed their love, but she and Bella were fated. They were made in pairs, and she was so grateful for the timing of which she had found her match in this young girl. Bella had saved Alani in so many ways that she would never be able to repay her. "I'm going to love you down for the rest of my life, Bella."

Bella kissed Alani's cheek. "See you out there," Bella said. She pointed to the box. "Daddy said it's your something old."

Alani smiled and picked up the package. She peeled back the paper and smiled at the stunning raindrop diamond earrings that shined from the box. She frowned when she saw the old, black and white photo inside.

"Why would he..." She gasped.

A picture of Martin and Coretta Scott King trembled in her hand and the earrings...the beautiful diamond earrings...her something old...were hanging from Coretta's ears, on what was clearly her wedding day. She flipped the picture over.

Dear Alani Lenika Hill,

You are the Coretta to my Martin
I will love you well

-Forever Ezra

The tear that slid down her cheek settled in the crease between her lips and Alani had to close her eyes to stop more from coming. "God, thank you for this man, for love, for mercy after loss. I'm so grateful," she whispered. She felt her legs weaken and she had to sit, as she placed praying hands to her lips. "God, please guide us."

"He will, my stubborn girl. All you've got to do is keep Him first in your marriage. You let Him lead and the rest will fall in place." Alani looked up to see Nannie there. She broke down. "There's a good man waiting on you out there."

"What did I do to deserve him?" Alani cried. "He dug a hole in my soul and then filled it. How did he do both?"

"Great men usually are both, our greatest loves and greatest hurts. You're safe with him, Alani. That much I'm sure of. I've known since I was laid up in that hospital. He sat in that chair by my bed one day and he told me that he loves you so much that your hate felt like affection, baby. That man told me that he thought you were brought into his life to ease his suffering…to end his life, Lenika. He wanted you to be the one to do it because he said he knew it would be done with love because your hate for him felt better than anything he had ever considered love before. He's crazy over you, Alani. You don't have to doubt his word, second-guess his intentions or his character. He's honest and kind and fair. You can allow him to love you without feeling guilty about reciprocating. Kenzie's fine. Kenzie's chasing butterflies in that big field in the sky she used to dream about. The back and forth, the constant running and sabotaging because you think it's wrong. You can stop now. You can be happy." Nannie reached for the earrings and placed them in Alani's ears.

"I'm marrying him," Alani whispered, laughing in amazement, as her lip quivered. "After all the hell I took him through, he still stayed. He always comes back for me. Someone finally stayed, Nannie. He's all mine." Alani tipped her head back and her lips flattened, as she cried. "That man is mine. He's mine. God, he's mine." She laughed, again. Alani felt like she had hit the lottery. Ethic was an emotional jackpot. She stood, grabbed a Kleenex and dabbed at her wet face. "I'm ready."

Alani lifted the bottom of her dress and followed Nannie out of the room. Their party was small. A bride, a groom, a maid of honor in Bella, and a best man in Eazy. Morgan hadn't wanted to stand beside them. She had blamed it on the twins...on needing to sit with them because they were only six months old and Alani hoped that much was true. It hurt a bit that she had declined, but Alani hoped a real union would make them feel like family.

"This is as far as I can walk you, baby," Nannie said.

Alani nodded, extending a cheek to Nannie who planted a kiss, before entering through the sanctuary doors. It was time. The day had come for Ethic and Alani to become man and wife. They had prepared for months. Ethic had spared no expense. Alani wanted to play H.E.R through speakers, so Ethic hired her to sing live. Alani wanted to have soul food made by the church mothers to keep costs low, so Ethic hired a five-star chef who specialized in African American cuisines. He opened up the vault, without limit, and she cringed with every extra penny he spent to make this day feel like a dream. She didn't require any of it. Only him.

Alani held her bouquet in her hands and peered through the glass slits in the door. He stood at the front of the church. She felt so close yet so far away. Bella had already taken her walk down the aisle. The fellas were already in position, all she had to do was make it to him...that's it...all she had to do was not run...simple enough, no?

The soft keys of the piano began to play, and Ethic's chest tightened.

Iiii wanna run away, with youuuuuu
Just take me to places I'veee never knownnnn
When no one else seems to be getting throughhh
Only you can tellll what's going onnnnn

The sight of her, as H.E.R. sang so beautifully, was overwhelming to him. Alani was perfection in a blush-colored dress because Alani was nobody's virgin. Her words, not his, but with the amount of spins Ethic had taken her on in the bedroom, he understood. The way he was hitting that, she should have worn black. Still, her blush wedding gown was stunning. It was timeless, and she was flawless. A veil covered his bride. Only an aisle's length of pews separated them. She was breathtaking, and he was spellbound. She was walking toward him. For so long, she had run from him, but on this day, under this cross, in God's house, Alani was walking toward him. It broke him down. Ethic lowered his head and trapped his left wrist in his right hand. He pulled in air and then exhaled deeply, to steady his rampant heart.

When I hear your name, put a smile up on my faceee
It don't matter the timeeee or the placeee
You make it all better nowwww
I could love you forever nowwww

Ethic's bottom lip quivered, in overwhelm, and he sniffed back emotion, trying his hardest to control how much of himself he let show. There was a room full of eyes watching and he had never exposed his insides to this many people, but someone had taken his reserve. Perhaps, Eazy had stolen it out of the room where they had dressed and had hidden it, because Ethic was searching high and low to no avail. He pulled his bottom lip into his mouth and looked up at her.

Let me sing my sonnnggg, don't wanna be alonneeee
I know that when I listennn, I'll find what I've been
misssinnnng
Right here in my heartttt

Alani was too pretty to take in. She shined. Something this magnificent wasn't supposed to be possessed by man. It grew in the wild, like a flower, it flew with the gusts of the wind, like a butterfly. How he had caught her for himself...how he had plucked a flower to keep, one that wouldn't die, he had no clue. He didn't feel worthy, but here she was, walking *toward* him. Ethic lost the war of wills he was fighting, and a sob escaped him. He tightened his jaw. Damn, why was he so weak? Why was the bottom of his stomach gone? Had Eazy stolen that too? The little crumb snatcher had left him unarmed. Ethic couldn't defend his emotions, as his eyes watered against his will. Alani was like the harmony to his favorite song. She was the crescendo before the bridge hit. The oooh-ahh to his R&B; the part that made you close your eyes and feel the rifts of every croon. The melody of her love for him was brilliant. God, how had he managed to keep her? Ethic felt Nyair's hand on his shoulder, giving him a brotherly squeeze of encouragement, and Ethic nodded. She was his. Finally. They had worked for this moment. They had won, and Ethic was falling apart. Just withering, as if the storms of his life were all mounting on him at once, blowing down all the hardness he had built over the years. Why did his wedding feel the same as Raven's funeral? Damn, how did he feel just as vulnerable as he did then? It was like her spirit was there, giving him away to Alani, giving him permission to move on, to live on without her. Through the veil that covered Alani's face, Ethic saw a ghost. Raven Atkins coming down that aisle, in the folds of the sheer fabric, and he calmed.

"I will always love you, Ethic. I love how she loves you. She loves my son and I love her for that. I'm loving her babies too. They're fine. We're all family and we'll all be just fine, as long as we stick together. Be happy, Ethic." He heard her words…the ones he had dreamt the night before. They echoed in his mind and he closed his eyes. He could hear Raven, as clear as day, like she was standing beside him.

I'm so sorry, Rae.

"Sorry? Ethic, I knew love. I felt love. That's all life is. Love and love never dies. I live through you. In you. You're solemn has been killing me. I only die if you don't love. Love her, Ethic. She is life. She's breathing life back into you. Live with her. I choose her for you. She's got it from here."

Ethic felt the burning behind his closed lids.

Live in me, Rae. Always with me. Show me how to love her better…protect her better. Watch over us.

"I will. I will live inside you forever, baby, and I'll be right here waiting for you when you get here. Me, Love, and Kenzie will be waiting for you all, but you have to live first. You have to love first. Until then, I'll be watching. Now, go. She's waiting for you."

When Ethic opened his eyes, Raven's face was gone, and Alani's was there. She was almost to him, paces from him, but he couldn't wait.

He came down from the altar with urgency, lifting her veil and gripping her face.

"What are you doing?" she asked, with a smile. He stared at her with such conviction, with such sadness, that it scared her. "Ethic?"

"There's some people missing, baby. We can't do it here. Do you trust me?" Ethic asked.

She nodded, and he pressed his forehead to hers, gripping her face. "I know you do. After everything, you still do."

She nodded. "I always have."

Ethic took her hand. "Come on."

Alani's mouth fell open, in confusion, but she didn't question him, as she was whisked off.

"Bella, Eazy!" she called. They sprang from the front of the church, breaking the positions she had bribed them not to squirm in. "Morgan, Bash, get Nannie and the twins!" Morgan picked up Messari and Bash grabbed Yara, before helping the old woman out of the front pew. They all followed behind the lovely couple.

Ethic rushed Alani out of the church, as the guests whispered in suspense...in alarm.

"Ny, come on!" Alani shouted. She wasn't sure where they were going but she was marrying this man today, no matter what.

It wasn't a runaway bride. It was a runaway family, as Ethic led the way out of the church in haste.

Ethic ushered Alani into the white Rolls Royce that sat waiting outside. He held the door open and turned to his children.

"Mo, you guys take the second car with the kids," Ethic said.

Mo paused. "Where are we going, Ethic?"

Ethic's eyes teared and Morgan's accumulated emotion as well, because somehow, she knew.

"To Rae? You're getting married in front of Raven?" she asked.

Alani's eyes lifted to him and then rolled to Morgan, who looked hopefully at Ethic. Alani stepped high-heeled feet onto the pavement and lifted from the back seat of the car.

"She can't miss this, Mo. She's family. We have family that can't come to us, so we have to go to them. If that's okay with you?" Ethic said, turning his attention to Alani.

Alani never caught his eyes because she was too busy looking at Morgan. Morgan with her shitty attitude, her walls for defenses, and her snide remarks. Morgan was her daughter to be. Morgan was her family and Alani suddenly realized that Morgan had fears of no longer having a place now that Alani had secured one.

"I wouldn't have it any other way," Alani spoke. Morgan looked at her in shock and Alani took determined steps, closing the space between them. Alani curved her finger tips, placing the back of her hand on Morgan's face. Morgan's tears fell between the creases of her fingers and Alani's brows dipped in empathy. Morgan Atkins, the angry, volatile, rude, mean, young woman who had always been unpleasant to Alani, just looked like a little girl. *I'm the evil stepmother in her story.*

"You are his daughter, Morgan. She is your sister. He loved her." Alani shook her head because that wasn't completely accurate. She moved her hand underneath Morgan's chin; a flat palm lifted her head. Their eyes met. "He still loves her. He will always love your sister and I will always love who he loves. His love is my love, Morgan. His love for her, is my love for her. His love for you is my love. You are mine too. I will never ever push you out. I *could* never push you out. I would never want to erase her. I'd just really love to be a part of your lives too. I love him." Alani closed her eyes and shook her head, as she sucked in a soul-stirring breath. *I love him.* "I'm so, so in love with your father. I just want to be here." Alani's voice was soft and weighted in an emotion that was much different than what she felt for the rest of Ethic's clan. What was rising in her heart was unlike what she felt for Eazy and Bella. They were younger. They were easier, in a sense. They were seeking her, whereas Morgan was fighting her. "I can't marry him without your blessing, Morgan… without Raven's blessing. You're her sister. She took care of you. She protected you, as best she could. Let me do that now. I know I'm not your mother or your sister, but I'd like to be something for you…something other than the sister of the man who hurt you. You decide, but just let me in," Alani whispered.

Morgan gave a stubborn nod, as silent emotion ran down her face. Then, she gave another nod, as she looked at her feet. Then, devastation spilled from stubborn lips and she nodded some more.

"It's okay," Alani whispered. "You can cry. It's okay."

Morgan was resistant and angry at herself for closing the space between she and Alani, but something drew her right into her arms.

Ethic had to look away. Alani and her beguiling. She had drawn another moth to her flame. Alani held Morgan tightly and Morgan wept without fear. It was the first time since her sister had died that she had felt like she could trust another woman.

"I know you don't care for me. I know you have your doubts about me," Alani whispered into Morgan's ear, so that only the two of them could hear. "I'm going to love every, single one of them away, if you let me."

"So, what you say, Mo? We having a wedding or we going home? This is a family. We all got to be on one page. We all got to want this, if it's ever going to work," Ethic said. Ethic looked at Alani and Morgan. He wanted Alani more than anything, but Morgan was his child...Morgan may not have been his blood, but she was his soul. He had loved her since meeting her at her birthday party all those years ago. She had hustled him out of a hundred dollars to compensate for the fact that he hadn't shown up with a gift. She had done it to all Benny Atkins' lieutenants and had come out two thousand dollars richer. She had been hustling Ethic ever since. She was his daughter, and if she didn't want Alani in their lives, Ethic would make the sacrifice. He prayed to God Morgan would be self-less in this moment. She was spoiled. First, by Benny Atkins, and then Ethic had taken the reigns. He had never let up. He had given her everything. He had done things her way. He had bent to her will her entire life because he was totally invested in her happiness; but somewhere along the way, she had forgot he deserved a bit too. He hoped he had taught her a bit of compassion for others. He desperately needed her to have some for him, in this moment, because he wanted Alani. Damn, he wanted

Alani. An awkward silence filled the air and Ethic gave Alani apologetic eyes, as those damn emotional levees failed him, again. His eyes flooded. Then…

Morgan nodded. "We're having a wedding," she said.

"Yay!" Eazy shouted.

"Praise God!" Nannie yelled. "Now, get your narrow tail in here, Ms. Morgan. I got a few words for you."

Ethic winked at her and Alani laughed, as she rushed into the car with Ethic.

"I can't believe this is finally happening and it's happening perfectly. So perfectly," Alani swooned, as she raised her eyes to the sky, exhaling the last of her doubts into the air. She looked over at Ethic and caught his intense stare.

"What?" Alani asked.

"I love you, Alani" he said. Alani smiled. She beamed from the inside out. He hadn't called her Lenika. It was Alani.

"Say it again," she said.

"I love you, Alani Lenika…"

Alani shook her head. "Mmm, mmm, no. I don't ever want to hear my middle name ever again from your lips," she stated, with a laugh. "Say it again, and say it right."

"I love you, baby. A man named Ezra loves you, Alani Okafor," he finished.

Alani's nude-painted lips spread so wide he saw every, single one of her teeth. It was a fucking vision, that smile, so broad, so genuine, so foreign because he had learned to love her through grief and smiles had been rare.

"Say it again," she ordered, laughing.

"Alani Okafor."

She placed both hands over her heart and her head fell back. Nothing felt better than this. Alani pressed her manicured fingertips to the button that lifted the partition and then she rolled her dress up above her hips.

"I wouldn't even be able to find it under all that fabric," Ethic chuckled.

She fumbled with his belt buckle and released him.

"You're starting something you won't have time to finish, baby," Ethic said, as he leaned his head against the plush, leather seats. "This got to be bad luck or something."

"We'll make our own luck," she whispered, as she straddled him. The lingerie she wore was crotch-less and she slid onto him effortlessly. He was drowned in her, pussy and tulle, as she rode him passionately, kissing him, indulging, over-indulging... a glutton for a man she never thought she could have.

"Hmmm," he groaned.

She rolled down onto him. "I love you," she panted, with her eyes snapped shut and forehead tense from pleasure. He submerged himself into the crook of her neck, the softest part of her. He had discovered it long ago, dreamt of it often when she wasn't around, but she was here now, and he planted kisses there. His favorite spot. His tongue against her caramel, sucking, like he wished he could swallow her whole. Alani's hips rolled so deeply that he felt her walls closing in on him, squeezing him, pulling on his manhood, as she chased release.

"Oh, shit, baby, slow the fuck down," he whispered,

"I can't," she moaned. "God, Ethic, agh!"

The back seat was as spacious as a car could be, but still limited their movements. Ethic gripped her dress. There were so many crystals; so much beading and chiffon. He wanted to rip that shit off, but he didn't. He knew how much it meant. He had watched her stress over every detail of this day for three months, so he would give her the dream. He matched her movements, rising into her as she rode him, but he craved skin to skin. The clothing that separated them was even too much distance. He wanted to connect with her, with no people around, no fabric in the way, just his skin, her skin, his tongue to her womanhood, capturing her soul in the form of an orgasm. Souls tied. Rings infinitely wrapped in a circle around their fingers. Unending. Forever. Or at least until he left this side of the dirt and the way he felt; the way she had him believing in God, he was sure he would love her still…after…wherever he ended up. Ethic absorbed her features through hooded lids and his pleasure heightened. She worked hard to bring him there, where she was, in heaven. Her eyes were closed, and her bottom lip was trapped between her teeth. He saw the ecstasy in her tense face. It reflected what he felt in his heart. In his black, dead, decrepit center…she had revived him, pumping fresh blood, fresh love, new life into him. She was his redemption. The way he loved her from this day forward would be the legacy he left behind.

"Shit, boy, I love you!" Alani cried. He felt her flood him and then felt her tighten around him. He followed her there… to that place they knew so well. They could lead themselves there without any directions at all. The pair cleaned up, as best as possible, and she leaned on his shoulder, silent, whole…no longer two halves, but one, as they pulled into the cemetery.

"You ready?" he asked. She gazed up at him; at her dark, mysterious, damaged, but perfectly imperfect husband-to-be. She nodded. He reached for the door and helped her from the car.

Nannie, Nyair, Morgan, Bash, and the kids were already in front of the second car.

"We couldn't find the gravestone, Ethic!" Morgan said, panicked.

"Follow me," he said. He held Alani's hand so tightly, as he led the way through the green grass, taking care not to disturb any of the souls resting there. Alani held her breath, as she followed him. She knew where he was going. He was leading the way to Love and Kenzie's resting places. When they arrived, she froze.

"What is this?" she asked, as her eyes filled with emotion. "When did you do this?"

There were flowers everywhere, planted between two, large trees that was draped with flowers as well. Butterflies and moths clung to the petals and branches around them.

"Ethic?" Morgan called, as she stood in front of Raven's grave. "You moved her," she whispered. She looked to the two graves beside her sisters. "And my parents."

Bella touched one of the stones. "And my mom?"

"We're together. They should be together," Ethic whispered, with a nod. "They are our angels. They'll watch over us, walk with us in spirit, as we love one another and live for them…to

make them proud. The butterflies represent resurrection...
rebirth... and they transcend heaven and earth. They'll carry
our love from earth to heaven every time we visit here."

Alani was in tears. "A butterfly garden," she whispered, in
disbelief. "Everyone we love in one place. All the hurt and
the loss in one place." She was breathless, as she stared up
at him. "This is perfect. You are perfect and there's no better
place to say I do because I really, really do, Ethic."

"And on that note. Shall we?" Nyair asked.

Alani took Ethic's hands, as they stood across from one
another. Alani couldn't stop the tears that wrecked her. Her
feet were planted firmly on Kenzie's grave and his shiny
shoes stood atop of Love's. Their children. The most painful
parts of their history were present on this day. Ethic looked
around, as Morgan stood underneath Nannie's protective
shoulder. Bella and Eazy stood next to Mo, holding hands.
The smile on his children's faces were undeniable and he
winked at them.

"This is an unconventional place to have a wedding, but
this is an unconventional love story. You've been through
the fire, but your love never burned. It was like steel, as
the heat intensified. You came out sharpened and now
you're armed. You're blessed to fight every battle to come
as one. Do you, Alani Lenika Hill, take this imperfect man,
to make a perfect love? Do you accept God into your
marriage to add a third chord of strength in the center
of this union? Do you take them both to love, honor, and
obey, in faithfulness, seeking only him for as long as you
both shall live?"

Alani didn't pause, she didn't think, she didn't blink. "I do."

Something inside Ethic exploded and he broke. He blubbered, like he had never done before. He lost all composure and Alani reached up, cupping his face. She didn't speak, she just watched him, appreciated him. He loved her so much. She could feel it. There wasn't a day she hadn't felt it. She deserved him, and she was going to have him, without apologizing for it.

"That's all right, baby," Nannie whispered. "Let it out."

Ethic pinched the bridge of his nose.

"Do you, my brother, Ezra Okafor, take this imperfect woman, to make a perfect love? Do you accept God into your marriage to add a third chord of strength in the center of this union? Do you take them both to love, honor, and obey, in faithfulness, seeking only her for as long as you both shall live?"

Ethic sucked in a stabilizing breath, as she cleared his emotion from his face with gentle strokes of her thumb. She was so fucking maternal, so caring, so accepting of the things that made him a good man and the ones that made him not so good of one. She was willing to take them all, help him fill in the gaps. Where he lacked, she supplemented.

"I do," he said.

"We made it," she whispered. She sighed, in relief. She hadn't thought they could ever endure the pain it took to get here, but they had done it and it felt like graduation...like they had made it, despite the failing of tests and such.

"By the power vested in me..."

It was all Nyair got out before Ethic broke the rules and kissed his wife. He didn't care who was looking, he kissed her deeply, taking her entire tongue into his mouth...stealing her air, along with the strength from her legs, as he swept her backward...right off her feet.

"Yes!" Eazy shouted, as he ran into them, full force, all boy, just the way Alani loved, wrapping his hands around Ethic's waist. "You did it, Daddy! You brought her home! She's ours! I told you! You owe me a hundred bucks!"

Alani laughed and widened surprised eyes. "Oh, really? It was a bet, huh?"

Ethic winked, and Bella entered the huddle, beelining straight for Alani.

"I love you," Bella whispered.

"I love you with all of me, little girl. Thank you for always being by my side. You are my very best friend, Bella." Alani scrunched her face to stop her emotions, but she pulled Bella Okafor into her arms. She couldn't believe that they shared the same last name...that for all those nights she had wished Bella was really her family...and now, she was. Nannie hobbled up next and Ethic embraced her. He knew that she had been his saving grace. If it had not been for her understanding, Alani would have never forgiven him. Nannie was a blessing. His blessing.

"Hey, beautiful," he greeted. "Thank you."

"Thank you, young man," she said, giving him a loving pat on the cheek. "Thank you. Now, I can go on yonder and not worry about what's going to happen to her. I know as long as she has you, she will be okay. So, no...thank you." She turned to Alani and Alani couldn't contain her glee. She smiled, with laughter breaking through her lips, as she grabbed both of

Nannie's wrinkled hands. "Happiness isn't like the picture that comes in the frame at the store. You make it look like whatever you need to make it look like to keep it. I'm proud of you, baby. I'm real proud." Alani hugged her.

"I love you, Nannie."

Morgan stepped up, reluctantly, holding Messari in her arms and Ethic released the brood and rushed her, pulling her into his arms, and then kissing the top of his grandson's head. "I don't care how old you get, you're my baby girl, forever and always," he said.

Ethic and Morgan rocked from side to side,

"Thank you for giving me a family and a father," Morgan whispered, choking up. "You're the best father a girl with no father could ask for. You took his place and I never missed a beat. I never missed out on anything because of you. I love you, Ethic, and I like her for you. She's good for you…"

"For us," Ethic responded.

Morgan nodded. "For us."

Alani stepped up, with hopeful eyes and full hands because she'd taken baby Yara from Bash. She took Ethic's free hand. Morgan smiled.

"Take care of him. He takes care of everybody. It's about time somebody took care of him," Morgan said.

Alani nodded. "I will."

Nyair interrupted. "Congrats," he said. He extended a firm hand to Ethic and then kissed Alani's cheek. "I'll manage the chaos at the church. Enjoy your bride, man. Love and forgiveness is a beautiful thing. They're the same thing. You deserve it, G."

Ethic nodded, grateful for his counsel...for his friendship... for brotherhood.

"Hey, Daddy! Can we stay here? And read to them?" Eazy asked.

Ethic looked to Alani and he saw such a peace in her eyes that he couldn't believe how lucky he was. She held no animosity. Not one grudge. She had found serenity, in spite of the storm. She nodded.

"Of course, we can," she whispered.

She took Eazy's hand. "Morgan, do you have your phone? I can pull up the kindle app," Alani instructed.

His children followed, and they sat on the grass, in their suits and pretty dresses. Ethic loved the image, and normally his children were his focus, but Alani stole all his attention on this day. She was an image, in her non-virgin white. When Alani leaned her back against Raven's headstone, Ethic felt his soul stir. Such a lovely woman. Such an understanding woman. Such a confident woman, unbothered by the woman he had loved before her, accepting of his past, because she knew she was his future. Such a godly woman. His. Assigned to him by a God he now believed in - thanks to her. She made him better. She was a gift.

He placed Messari in his car seat and placed him on the ground. He sat across from his bride, wrapping his arms around his knees and locking his left hand around his right wrist, as he dug his heels into the dirt. Mo sat beside him and Alani handed Yara to Bash. She pulled Eazy into her lap. Bella rested her head on Nannie's shoulder. They were a family. After so long they were finally whole. It was a destiny hard-earned and it felt incredible.

"The Autobiography of Malcolm X by Alex Haley," Alani began.

"Yo, Mrs. Okafor?" Ethic called out.

She rolled her eyes up from Morgan's phone and he saw a bit of irritation at the disruption. It was the Lenika in her. Ethic chuckled, as he licked his lips.

"I LOVE YOU," he said. Her face melted into a smile because it was an interruption she appreciated.

"I love you more," she returned. "I love every, single one of you."

Thank you, God, Ethic thought. *Thank you for her...*

They were proof that you could forgive...that you could love past a person's worst mistakes...that you could grow through pain. They were human, and life was hard...it was impossible, sometimes, but love and faith conquered all. Love had won. Still, through it all.

Morgan entered her old apartment carrying a hand full of mail that had piled up in her box and a sleeping baby in her arms. She hadn't been back in so long, but after witnessing the purest love she had ever seen, she felt the overwhelming need to come here. She felt him inside these walls. Inside this cocoon of love they had built. His memory lived here. Morgan could almost smell him. Messiah. Her Messiah. Her Saviour. Only he hadn't saved her at all.

"You sure you don't want company?" Bash asked.

"I'm sure," she answered. "Thank you for helping with them."

She walked through the place, setting down the mail and turning on every light, and then took Yara and laid the sleeping infant in the center of the bed. Bash followed, and Morgan took Messari, placing him next to his sister.

"Can you rebook the flights to London? I'd like to head back soon. Maybe day after tomorrow? The twins are old enough to fly now."

"We'll fly private. I'll have my mom send the jet, so that you're comfortable," he said.

Morgan nodded. "Thanks, Bash."

"You were beautiful today, Mo," he said.

She scoffed. For some reason, his compliments did nothing for her. No racing heart, no blushing.

She gave him a halfhearted smile. An awkward silence fell over them and Bash cleared his throat. "I'll call you tomorrow."

"Okay."

When she was alone, she turned to face the space that she had called home. Her first piece of independence. She could practically hear his voice bouncing off the walls.

"Shorty Doo-Wop."

She heard him. So loud. So brazen. So...

Morgan's heart locked. In London, it was easy to contain the emotions. He felt like he was a world away when she was at Cambridge, but here, this felt like his den...like the lair of love he had trapped her in. Morgan had grown here. Into a woman. From a girl to his lover. God, she missed him. Morgan couldn't believe that after all this time, after he had missed the birth of their babies, after he had shunned her, turning his back on her without explanation, she loved him…still.

He had hurt her. Incredibly. Overwhelmingly. In totality. Morgan had been decimated by him, but it was only because she had loved him in totality had he been able to destroy her. She hated him, as equally as she loved him. He was the love of her life; and as she stood in the middle of the living room, she felt like crying. She was living a life she had never imagined, doing incredible things, immersing herself in a culture so different than her own, but if she could rewind time and come right back to this apartment…if he was waiting here for her…if he would just come back…she would give it all up in a heartbeat. She would love him, again. She wanted him home, but she had a feeling he was never coming back to her and she was learning to accept that. Morgan pulled out her phone and pulled the clip from her hair, sending it falling down her shoulders. She removed her dress, leaving it in a heap on the floor, as she rushed to her room to pull out leggings and a sports bra. Then, the living room became her solace.

She grabbed her phone, connecting it to the Bluetooth speaker.

PLAY.

> *All of the good things. Good things…*
> *Only the good, the good, the good…*
> *Only the good, the good, the good…*

Morgan danced. She danced so hard that she cried, because under this roof, it felt like he was watching, and she just wanted to feel like his eyes were on her. She just wanted a little bit of his attention. Morgan made art out of every second of the song, until it faded. She leaned over the kitchen bar top, breathing heavily, as she swept her hair out of her face. The tears in her eyes didn't stop her from zeroing in on the envelope in the pile.

It was addressed to her. *Morgan Jacqueline Atkins.* Morgan frowned and picked up the envelope. She was hesitant to tear it open. Whatever was inside that manila envelope made her insides twist and her stomach hollow. She picked it up and ran her fingers under the seam. Before she could even reach inside, something hard fell out, dinging against the countertop. Morgan's entire body malfunctioned. Her hearing, her heart, her eyes, her stomach. Everything shutdown, like someone had cut off her engine. Her ring. His ring. The one he had given her stared at her, as it shined against her granite countertops. Trembling fingers reached for it. There was no return name on the envelope. Just hers. Just her name. Tears burned her eyes, as she opened her balled fists and slid the ring on her finger. She hadn't worn it in so long, it felt heavy. The stunning diamond was brilliant, but she could barely see it. She saw a piece of paper inside the envelope and Morgan tore it open. As soon as she read the words, she lost strength.

"Nooooooo!" she cried. Her legs left her. Morgan's hands tried to catch her, gripping the lip of the counter, as gravity and grief pulled her to the floor.

"Ssiah, nooooo!"

She bawled that piece of paper in her hands, not caring about it's worth.

She had a million reason to care. He had made sure of it. That his life had been worth something in the end to her. He had no idea it was priceless. Not even the check she held in her hand could compensate.

A million dollars. From him to her.

Her heart cracked in as many pieces.

Morgan bent over, sobbing. He couldn't be gone. She had always assumed, always hoped, secretly prayed, that one day they would reconnect. If she just gave him some time…if they just grew a little, matured into who they were as individuals, that one day he would think of her…one day he would come back home. This money. This check told her he was never coming home, and she would never be okay living in a world where he didn't exist. Her cries awoke Messari. She heard his tiny cries and Morgan could barely pull herself from the floor. She couldn't find her legs. She was sick. Someone would have to pull her from the ground. Help her stand because she couldn't.

But I can still feel him. I can still feel his heart. God, please let this be a mistake. Please, don't do this to me. Why can I still feel him?

If it weren't for the crying babies in her bed, Morgan knew she would end it all. She would follow Messiah to the grave because she couldn't imagine life without him; but as she listened to her babies crying, she realized she couldn't. He had made sure he left her with something. With him. With the ultimate gift a man could give. With the ultimate reminder of love that a man could extend. His children. Morgan had his legacy. As she sat on the floor with a broken heart and shattered soul, she felt a little strength. She heard him in her ear. "Live, shorty." She felt him in her gut. "Live, shorty." She felt him in her legs, lifting her from the floor. "Live, shorty." Morgan made her way to the room and picked up her son... his son. Her breasts swelled at the sight of him. Yara was still lying, peacefully, beside him. She was oblivious to the pain and Mo wished she could be. She wished she could go deaf to it all. She grabbed a receiving blanket and picked up her son, lifting her shirt to give him her breast. Sustenance. Life. Strength, and as she fed Messiah's child, she closed her eyes. Tears melted down Morgan's face. "I love you, Messiah." Those SS's for ZZ's. His name. Her lips. It would forever live there. His face in her mind. She would always see it. His beat in her heart where he would always live.

But why can I still feel him?

EPILOGUE

The magnitude in which this story has touched me is significant. I have lived in this world for thirteen months and wrote all six books in that time because I couldn't bring myself to stop. I have cried, smiled, laughed, and felt every single word of this journey. God put something different on my soul, when I began writing this one. I was tapped to tell this story and I thank each of you for receiving it. My pen will be forever transformed because of Ethic and Alani. I am a better writer because of them. So, as I start a new series with Morgan …a series about transformation…a series about growth, I can only hope to be as attached to her journey as I have been to E&A. Thank you, all, for living in this world with me, for immersing yourself so deeply into the universe that I painted. It was full of pain, full of grief, but we made it through…we made it to love and I'm happy for these characters, as if I know them in real life. May they live happily ever after. I can finally let them go. I can let Ethic and his children go because Alani Lenika Hill has it covered from here.

Stay tuned…

BUTTERFLY
The Morgan Atkins Story

COMING JANUARY 7ᵀᴴ, 2020
(EVERY WHERE BOOKS ARE SOLD)

Until then...I hope you revisit Ethic's series, as often as you need to, in order to believe in love after pain.

-xoxo-
Ashley Antoinette

As you guys know, I love these people like they are real, and I just really want to write about them forever.
Flip the page for a bonus scene ;)

AFTER THE WEDDING

Wait, Ezra. I'm not ready to leave," Alani whispered, as she grabbed his hand, halting his steps, as she turned back toward the main floor.

"Everyone's gone, baby," he said. "We've got an early flight in the morning."

"And a 22-hour flight to sleep. I want to stay up all night with my husband," she said, pulling him back into the historic library.

It was the perfect place for their reception. Ethic had rented the entire building, using the main floor for their celebration. It was elaborately decorated in blush tones and white. The ceiling was covered in lights and Swarovski crystals, and chiffon covered the walls from floor to ceiling. They were surrounded by books. Thousands and thousands of shelves of books, and the smell alone made Alani smile. She pulled him right back to the center of the dance floor that had been installed – specifically, for them.

"Don't move," she said, rushing on tip-toes up to the abandoned DJ booth. She pulled out her phone and hooked it up to his system.

Music filled the empty space and Alani hurried down the

stairs, her pretty dress following her, as her heels clicked across the floor.

Her face. Ethic appreciated the glow in her eyes, the tint of rose to her cheeks, because she had been flushed all night, just blushing with happiness. He held out his hand for his bride and she placed delicate fingertips in his, as he lifted his arm, spinning her into him. A gentleman, in a classic, black suit. A black man with a family, a wife and kids, intelligent and strong, kind and saved, a millionaire with manners, disproving the stereotype...Ethic had grown into a king and the sight was beautiful. He still kept that pistol on his hip, however, because his gangster didn't slip, not even on his wedding day.

Mmmmmmmmmmmmmmmm, mmmmmm, mmmmm, yeahhhhh
Ohhhhhhhh, ohhh, ohhhhhhhh

KeKe Wyatt's voice had Alani mesmerized, as she fell into his arms.

I must have rehearsed my linessss, a thousand timesss
Until I had them memoriiiiiized

They swayed under the crystal chandelier. Alani's heart was so full that she didn't even want to drown in him. This wasn't like the last time they had danced. She wasn't clinging on for dear life. She wasn't dying in his arms. She was living. She wasn't suffocating. She was breathing. He had asked her once to let him breathe her, and she hadn't known what that meant until now. She was breathing Ethic, taking him in, being one with this moment, as she enjoyed this dance with her husband. She couldn't even contain her joy. She pulled back and opened her arms, as he held the tips of her fingers as they danced. The look in his eyes mesmerized her. It was like he had climbed to the highest peak of a mountain…one that had taken him days, one that had come with some falls, some sharp cliffs, broken ladders, sweat, blood, and tears. He had almost given up on that climb, had wanted to turn back halfway through, because making it to the summit of that mountain was almost impossible. The expedition alone would surely kill him, but today, this dance, her in this fifty-thousand-dollar dress, was the view from the top. He had made it to the summit and the way the sun hit the valley below, was a once-in-a-lifetime picture. Alani was worth the climb. She was worth the effort.

"Ohhhh ifffff only you kneewwww how much I doooooo, dooooo loveeeee youuuuuu."

Alani sang to him, badly, but loudly because she couldn't keep this song in her heart. She had fought what she felt for him for a long time. She was singing her heart out to him and Ethic glowed because he had a woman and a home and three, healthy, happy kids to call his own. Her palms were open to him.

"Ohhhhh iffffff, only you kneewww, how much I doooo. Doooo neeeeed youuuu, babe," she sang.

Ethic received every word, every bad note, as he spun her and pulled her back to his body. Chest to chest. Every beat of her heart he wanted to feel. This girl had resuscitated him.

She was CPR. Alani kicked off her shoes, shortening herself, allowing him to dwarf her, and Ethic wrapped his arms around her back, picking her up. Hugging her so tightly, dancing so close that her feet didn't even touch the floor. He stopped dancing. The beat didn't even exist. He just stood there, swaying her slightly, hugging her, absorbing her.

"I'm going to love you, Alani. Fucking, Alani."

Her face was over his shoulder and his hand to the back of her head kept her in place. She was so damn happy. So overjoyed. So blessed. He was holding her off the ground, but if she was honest, even when she had planted heels to the floor, he made her feel like she was floating. Her feet never touched the ground, in his presence. His adoration. His love. His longing for her kept her in the clouds. It elevated her. Exalted her. Ethic had built her a castle of love and the throne sat so damn high nobody else could touch it, let alone sit in it. They didn't even know how to get to it. No man could even attempt to give her the feeling he provided. They simply weren't equipped. Ethic didn't slip. She would see only him, until the day she died. The greatest love, from the greatest man.

Ohhhhh—iffffffff
iiiiffffffffff
Ohhhhh youuuuuuuu
Donnnnnn'ttttt
Knowwwwww
Howwwwww muchhhhhhhhh
I saiddddd, you donnnn'tttt knowwww howwwww muchhhhh I
neeeeed youuu

Alani let her head fall back, as he held her and belted the last word. "Suggaaaaa!" He chuckled, and Alani laughed in absolute glee, as she brought her chin down, rubbing the back of his head and kissed her groom.

Onnnlyyyyy if you knewwww

The song began to fade, and they stayed there in the center of the dance floor, just staring, just swaying. His hands on her waist and his face cupped between her pretty fingertips. The beard was back because Alani loved it. She just wanted to be there as it grew. She wanted to witness his evolution, because missing it, not being a part of it, had been heartbreaking. She ran her fingers through it and reigned him in. Nose to nose.

"Let me breathe you for a minute, baby," she whispered. His words. Her oxygen. Their bond. Fucking beautiful. A world wonder, because most wouldn't have survived the test of elements that it took to carve out something so damn exquisite and enduring.

She closed her eyes. He watched her take a deep breath and blow it out so slowly until he stole it. Ethic stole her air, as his lips covered hers. They were so in love. Dripping in it. Covered in it. It was all over them.

The lights went out. A sign that the night was over, whether they wanted it to be or not, and Alani, regretfully, pulled back, a bit dizzy from the flood of emotions.

"You ready to close this book, baby? Last chapter. Last scene. Very last line... because when we step out of here, we're starting a whole new journey. A whole new story. What's it going to be?"

She beamed, smiling, as she mulled it over. "Ethic and Alani loved one another for the rest of their days and lived happily ever after."

"The End," Ethic finished.

See!!!!! The hood has fairy tales too. Ashley Antoinette novels have happy endings too...not often...rarely, in fact...but for the most beautiful characters, like Ethic and Alani, nothing less would do.

We made itttt! Together!!! We made it to the end!!! It has been an absolute honor to pen this love story. Thank you for experiencing this with me. I know. Messiah hurts. Trust me, I know. I feel it too, but Messiah was Morgan's cocoon and now Morgan is ready to fly out into the world on her own. She still feels him though. Why? Butterfly is available for pre-order NOW at amazon.com and everywhere books are sold. Please, hop on this new wave with me and place your order today. Morgan isn't finished yet. Trust me. You do not want to give up on Morgan Atkins. You might miss something really special if you do.

-xoxo-
Ashley Antoinette

ETHIC SERIES DISCUSSION

ASPIRE-CON

Saturday October 26, 2019
Hyatt Regency Atlanta Perimeter Villa Christina
Hosted by Angela Yee
Tickets available at www.aspirecon.info
Follow me on IG @ashleyantoinette @theaspiringwoman

Join the Ashley and JaQuavis Reading Club on Facebook!

BOOK CLUB QUESTIONS

1. Who was the most pivotal character in this series?

2. Why was there no chapter 6 in the final book?

3. What did the Ethic series teach you about love and forgiveness?

4. Why can Morgan still feel Messiah?

5. Will Morgan Atkins ever be able to heal from her relationship with Messiah without closure?

6. Did Ethic & Alani deserve their ending? Or do you think they should have gone their separate ways?

7. What were the running themes in the entire series?

8. Why did you connect so personally to this series?

9. What characters do you relate to most? In what ways?

10. What characters do you not identify with and why?

11. How has the Ethic series changed you as a person?

12. How has your experience as a reader transformed after reading Ethic series? Has it remained the same? Or has it done more for you? Elaborate.

Thank you so much once again for helping me transform ink to love.

s/o to Bianca

Until next time my loves
-xoxo-

CPSIA information can be obtained
at www.ICGtesting.com
Printed in the USA
LVHW111406230919
631940LV00002B/144/P